DOUBLE ILLUSION

By Barbara Nadel

The Inspector İkmen Series
Belshazzar's Daughter
A Chemical Prison
Arabesk
Deep Waters
Harem
Petrified
Deadly Web
Dance with Death
A Passion for Killing
Pretty Dead Things
River of the Dead
Death by Design
A Noble Killing
Dead of Night
Deadline
Body Count
Land of the Blind
On the Bone
The House of Four
Incorruptible
A Knife to the Heart
Blood Business
Forfeit
Bride Price
Double Illusion

The Hancock Series
Last Rights
After the Mourning
Ashes to Ashes
Sure and Certain Death

BARBARA NADEL

DOUBLE ILLUSION

HEADLINE

First published in Great Britain in 2023 by
HEADLINE PUBLISHING GROUP

1

Cataloguing in Publication Data is available from the British Library

ISBN 978 1 4722 9374 9

Typeset in 13/16pt Times New Roman by Jouve (UK), Milton Keynes

Printed and bound in Great Britain by Clays Ltd, Elcograf S.p.A.

Headline's policy is to use papers that are natural, renewable and recyclable
products and made from wood grown in well-managed forests and other
controlled sources. The logging and manufacturing processes are expected
to conform to the environmental regulations of the country of origin.

HEADLINE PUBLISHING GROUP
An Hachette UK Company
Carmelite House
50 Victoria Embankment
London EC4Y 0DZ

www.headline.co.uk
www.hachette.co.uk

To Alex, Lia, Senan, Malcolm, my mum
and all my wonderful friends.
I am lucky to have so much.

Cast List

Çetin İkmen – retired İstanbul detective
Inspector Mehmet Süleyman – İstanbul detective
Inspector Kerim Gürsel – İstanbul detective
Sergeant Ömer Mungun – Süleyman's deputy
Sergeant Eylul Yavaş – Gürsel's deputy
Çiçek İkmen – Çetin's daughter
Sedat Bey – Çiçek's boyfriend
Gonca Süleyman – Mehmet's wife
Nur Süleyman – Mehmet's mother
Samsun Bajraktar – Çetin's cousin
Rambo Şekeroğlu senior – Gonca's brother
Rambo Şekeroğlu junior – Gonca's son
Didim Şekeroğlu – Gonca's sister
Şeftali Şekeroğlu – Gonca's cousin
Sinem Gürsel – Kerim's wife
Melda Gürsel – Kerim's daughter
Peri Mungun – Ömer's sister
Yeşili Mungun – Ömer's wife
Dr Arto Sarkissian – police pathologist
Dr Emir Doksanaltı – police psychiatrist
Dr İlker Koca – police psychiatrist
Dr Sebnam Altan – police medic
Sergeant Fatıh Asmalı – custody officer
Constable Altay – custody officer
Officer Kenan Sağlam – technical officer

Technical Officer Türgüt Zana – IT specialist
İsmail Toksoy – retired OKK Special Forces marksman
Sergeant Hikmet Yıldız – scene-of-crime officer
Superintendent Cihat Şen – incident commander
Commissioner Selahattin Ozer – commissioner of police
Kemal Gurkan – public prosecutor
Eyüp Çelik – lawyer
Havva Sarı – lawyer
Bishop Juan-Maria Montoya – Catholic Bishop of İstanbul
Juan, Tomas and Lola Cortes – Spanish Romany flamenco
  dancers
Şevket Sesler – Romany crime lord
Selami Sesler – Şevket's son, a thug
Munir Can – Sesler's henchman
Filiz and Ayda – lap dancers at Sesler's club
Ceviz Elibol – Romany lap dancer and victim
Hüseyin Elibol – Ceviz's father
Beren Elibol – Ceviz's sister
Esat Böcek – religious crime lord
Ateş Böcek – Esat's son
İlhan Böcek – Esat's son
Neşe Böcek – Esat's mother
Feride – Ateş's psychiatrist
Hakki Bürkev – Böcek family guard
Kasım – tenant of the Böcek family
Murad Ayhan – gangster
Irmak Ayhan – Murad's wife
Aylın Ayhan – Murad's daughter
Yıldırım Ayhan – Murad's son
Dr Gibrail Sezer – Murad's doctor
Serdar İpek – Ayhan's thug
Esma Nebatı – Aylın's best friend
Faruk Nebatı – Esma's father

Numan Bey – pickle-juice seller
Madam Edith – drag queen
Belisarius Doukas – coffee shop owner
Rahul Bey – haberdasher
Mete Bülbül – victim
Aaron Kamhi – academic
Bayza Akyılmaz – quilt maker
Sibel – Romany madam
Kurdish Madonna, Nikki and Fındık – prostitutes

Pronunciation Guide

There are 29 letters in the Turkish alphabet:

A, a – usually short as in 'hah!'

B, b – as pronounced in English

C, c – not like the c in 'cat' but like the 'j' in 'jar', or 'Taj'

Ç, ç – 'ch' as in 'chunk'

D, d – as pronounced in English

E, e – always short as in 'venerable'

F, f – as pronounced in English

G, g – always hard as in 'slug'

Ğ, ğ – 'yumuşak ge' is used to lengthen the vowel that it follows. It is not usually voiced. As in the name 'Farsakoğlu', pronounced 'Far-sak-orlu'

H, h – as pronounced in English, never silent

I, ı – without a dot, the sound of the 'a' in 'probable'

İ i – with a dot, as the 'i' in 'thin'

J, j – as the French pronounce the 'j' in 'bonjour'

K, k – as pronounced in English, never silent

L, l – as pronounced in English

M, m – as pronounced in English

N, n – as pronounced in English

O, o – always short as in 'hot'

Ö, ö – like the 'ur' sound in 'further'

P, p – as pronounced in English

R, r – as pronounced in English

S, s – as pronounced in English

Ş, ş – like the 'sh' in 'ship'

T, t – as pronounced in English

U, u – always medium length, as in 'push'

Ü, ü – as the French pronounced the 'u' in 'tu'

V, v – as pronounced in English but sometimes with a slight 'w'
     sound

Y, y – as pronounced in English

Z, z – as pronounced in English

Later, when he attempted to describe what had confronted him when he had arrived at the Şehzade Rafık Palace, Inspector Mehmet Süleyman found himself referencing two famous artists.

'The suspect, armed with a sword, pinwheeled between two cohorts of uniformed men, his face twisted and bloodied like a figure from a painting by Goya,' he said. 'Embedded in a background of shiny cars, sculpted gardens and a palace resembling a wedding cake, it was also pure Salvador Dalí.'

What it had been too was a nightmare . . .

Chapter 1

There weren't many İstanbul palaces Mehmet Süleyman didn't know. The scion of an Ottoman family related to the sultans, he was one of those who, prior to the foundation of the Republic of Turkey, would have lived in a palace. But the Şehzade Rafık, located just off the high-end shopping street of Baghdat Caddesi, wasn't familiar to him.

As he approached it, through huge electric gates via a manicured garden just lightly dusted with snow, he snapped on a pair of plastic gloves and asked the uniformed officer walking beside him, 'What do we know?'

'First report came in at 19.55,' said the officer, a Sergeant Taşdemir. 'Fifth-floor apartment in the Deniz building.' He pointed to his left. 'Complaint basically about noise from the palace, screaming.'

Although extensive, the palace was hemmed in on three sides by expensive apartment blocks. This meant that a large number of homes overlooked the old building.

'And then?'

'Then less than five minutes later, we had multiple calls,' Taşdemir said. 'A man was running about outside the palace attacking cars. He was covered in blood . . .'

Two marble staircases led up to the palace entrance, separated by a marble platform. Süleyman could see that a man holding a sword, his shirt and trousers soaked in what looked like blood, was running between two groups of police officers who had him effectively trapped between them.

'Has he attacked any of our men?'

'No, sir,' Taşdemir said. 'He just runs. He's covered in blood, as you can see, but whether it's his or not . . .' He shrugged. 'I've got officers guarding all the entrances into the palace, but I wanted to wait for you before I ordered them inside.'

'Quite right.' Süleyman looked down at his sergeant, a dark young man called Ömer Mungun. 'I'll attempt to talk to this man first. You, Ömer Bey, go with Sergeant Taşdemir and prepare to enter the premises with his officers if I can't get anywhere with our agitated friend.'

And the man was agitated. Much of the time he screamed, bending over double as if in pain; then every so often he would look at one of the police officers, point his sword at him and say, 'You!'

But he didn't follow these momentary recognitions with any sort of action. He would pin someone down with his gaze and then, as if a spell had been broken, he'd quickly look away and scream again.

Before Sergeant Taşdemir left with Ömer Mungun, Süleyman asked him whether he knew the man's name.

Taşdemir frowned. 'Not definitively,' he said. 'But the owner of the palace is Ateş Böcek.'

Süleyman felt his face pale.

'And yes,' Taşdemir confirmed, 'I do mean the son of Esat Böcek.'

'İkmen!'

Why the woman felt the need to wave her arms in the air when she was both unusually tall and dressed up for a Spanish fiesta, ex-inspector of police Çetin İkmen didn't know. One could probably see Gonca Süleyman from space. Not that he was particularly focused on his friend Mehmet's wife. He was rather more concerned about how he was going to continue walking, because it hurt.

It had been his daughter Çiçek's idea, the walking thing. They'd arranged to meet Mehmet, Gonca and the latter's Spanish guests at 8.30 outside the Church of Saint-Antoine on İstiklal Caddesi. The biggest Catholic church in İstanbul, Saint-Antoine was famous for holding a multilingual Mass every 24 December to usher in Christmas in the Western church. Orthodox Christians, like Çetin's oldest friend, the Armenian pathologist Arto Sarkissian, celebrated on 6 January. And while Çetin, Çiçek, Gonca and Mehmet were nominally Muslims, they had agreed to take these Spaniards to Mass because they didn't know the city, and Çetin and Gonca, at least, rather enjoyed the theatricality of Christmas Eve Mass.

However, Mehmet, it seemed, was not with them.

Gasping for breath, İkmen dragged himself over to Gonca and said, 'Where's the boy?'

Çetin and Mehmet had worked together in the İstanbul City Police Force for decades. At the beginning of his career, Mehmet Süleyman had been İkmen's deputy, and although he was now in his mid fifties, İkmen still referred to him as 'the boy', especially when speaking to Gonca. Like İkmen, Gonca was over a decade older than her husband – she was also a woman with a sharp sense of humour.

'Working,' she said. Then, looking at İkmen properly, she added, 'You look like shit.'

İkmen pulled his daughter towards him. 'Blame her.'

Çiçek İkmen was an attractive woman in her forties. It was never easy for her to make conversation with Gonca. The striking Roma woman had effectively stolen her boyfriend and gone on to marry him. But Çiçek smiled and said, 'Dad's doctor says he needs to get fit.'

Gonca grinned at İkmen. 'Since when did you listen to your doctor?'

'Since he told him that if he doesn't get some exercise he will end up housebound,' Çiçek said.

5

İkmen muttered, 'Bastard.'

'And so,' Çiçek continued, 'we have just walked from Sultanahmet and across the Galata Bridge. We did ride the Tünel to get up here to İstiklal . . .'

'Thank God!'

'. . . and now here we are.' Çiçek looked up at the New Year lights strung across İstiklal Caddesi, twinkling red, ice blue and white, and added, 'So beautiful.'

Then, suddenly realising that the three people Gonca had been with were huddling at the entrance to the church, waiting for something to happen, Çetin and Çiçek went over to introduce themselves. It was snowing again, and the two men and one woman looked up into the dark sky with dread.

The Böcek family had been associated with organised crime in İstanbul since the late 1970s. This was when Ateş Böcek's grandfather, Nedim, had come with his family from the eastern city of Antakya and settled in İstanbul's Üsküdar district on the Asian side of the Bosphorus.

Family legend had it that Nedim Böcek had been a famous wrestler back in Antakya who had come to the big city to seek his fortune. The reality was that he occasionally rented his 'muscle' out to a couple of the İstanbul godfathers, but basically lived off his wife's earnings. Renowned for the skills of its falcıs, or fortune-tellers, Antakya imbued these – mainly women – with a mystical quality second only to the Roma. Neşe, Nedim's wife, was one such Antakya falcı, and it was she who funded the property speculations of her eldest son, Esat. Neşe had always been, and remained, the power behind the Böcek family's brutal throne on the Asian side of the Bosphorus.

Mehmet Süleyman approached Neşe's grandson with his hands held out to his sides. Ateş was, he had learned, just twenty-one.

And like a child, he giggled when he saw the older man make this peculiar gesture.

'I'm unarmed and want only to talk to you,' Süleyman said as he reached the top step of the left-hand staircase.

Ateş Böcek, if this ragged, blood-soaked entity was he, laughed again for a few seconds and then became still. Looking past the four officers who stood between him and Süleyman, he said, 'I know who you are. I see you.'

'Are you hurt?' Süleyman asked.

'Hurt?'

'Yes, you have a lot of blood on your clothing and your face.'

Ateş looked down at himself. He wobbled a little, and Süleyman wondered whether he was drunk or under the influence of drugs. The sword in his hand, a traditional Turkish weapon called a yataghan, clattered to the ground, quickly followed by the young man's unconscious body.

Gonca pointed to the younger of the two men and said, 'He is Señor Tomas.'

The Spaniard, unsure about what to do, bowed slightly when İkmen bowed to him.

'The young lady is Señora Lola, and this . . .' she took the arm of the elderly man standing between Lola and Tomas, 'this is Señor Juan. He is the most famous Roma in Spain!'

And, İkmen mused to himself, he was once your lover. But he didn't say anything. Just before she'd seduced Mehmet Süleyman and then been his on-and-off mistress for the next twenty years, Gonca had taken a Spanish Roma lover called Juan. And while Çetin İkmen had never known him, he recognised that this old man was one and the same person. Juan Cortes had, it was said, bewitched her with his flamenco singing, his dancing and his sexual technique for one hot, crazy month back in the dying days of

7

the twentieth century. Juan had clearly continued to attract beautiful, young women, judging by his nubile wife.

Gonca pushed Çiçek towards the small group and said, 'Well? Do it then . . .'

Çiçek İkmen, an ex-Turkish Airlines flight attendant, could speak Spanish. It was in reality the only reason she had agreed to come to the church. It was cold and dark and she really hadn't wanted to see Mehmet so soon after his marriage. She had loved him, but he had always been unfaithful to her, mainly with Gonca, something she still found hard to forgive. But she'd come along anyway, as a favour to her father.

Addressing the younger man she said, 'Good evening. My name is Çiçek.'

Tomas was small and slim, with a dazzling smile. He said, 'You are the friend who speaks Spanish!'

'Yes.' She smiled back.

The older man introduced himself and the woman. 'I am Juan, and this is my wife, Lola.'

'Pleased to meet you.'

İkmen, watching this exchange, wondered whether Çiçek would find out any more about these people. Gonca had told him that they had come to perform flamenco as part of a huge entertainment designed to celebrate the birthday of local Roma godfather Şevket Sesler on 26 December. A bully, a crook and possibly even a murderer, Sesler 'ran' the Roma section of the nearby district of Tarlabaşı. Gonca, though an artist by profession, made sure that he left her and her family alone by regularly reading his cards. Her policeman husband was aware of this connection, even though İkmen knew he didn't like it. Sesler was a fact of life for İstanbul's Roma, and keeping him happy whilst distancing oneself from his activities was a dangerous balancing act.

One of the priests from the church opened the huge front doors,

8

and Gonca and her party, together with a large group of other worshippers, piled inside.

The palace's great central staircase was a mirror image of the one leading up to the main entrance. Two great curving marble structures rose to the first floor and what looked from the ground like a vast door-encrusted landing. Ateş Böcek, or whoever the man was, was now receiving treatment from a doctor who had been called after his collapse. Bloody footprints descending the right-hand staircase seemed to suggest that he had been upstairs at some point. And because there were no ascending footprints on either staircase, it would appear that he had hurt either himself or someone else, or found someone in distress on the first floor.

Süleyman and Ömer Mungun slipped plastic covers over their shoes and walked up the left-hand staircase. When they arrived at the landing, it was easy to see from which of the many doors arranged around the four sides the man downstairs had come. Straight in front of them, it was the second door to the right, and it was open. The two men approached. There was a large pool of blood at the threshold, and the air smelt sharp and metallic.

Ömer looked at his boss and said, 'There's a lot . . .' His voice trailed away.

The room was unlit and so it was impossible to see what lay beyond the blood pool. Süleyman took his phone out of his pocket and switched on the torch function. He shone it inside, and both men regarded what they thought at first might be a storage room of some sort, maybe for bedding. Because bedding, it seemed, was flung around everywhere. Sheets and duvet covers were on the floor, stacked up against cupboards and even on the huge bed in the middle of the room.

It was Ömer who noticed something else, although later on he wouldn't be able to say exactly what. Maybe it was a movement.

As the beam from Süleyman's torch began to travel away from the bed, the younger man said, 'Sir! Back a bit!'

Süleyman obliged, and it was then, amid the white sheets, the satin, the lace and the overwhelming, dripping blood, that Ömer Mungun managed to make out a hand.

Saint-Antoine's high, vaulted interior was awash with light, and not just from its considerable number of electric lamps. Candles burned everywhere, in wall niches, at the base of statues and in the hands of choristers and worshippers. Çetin İkmen stood in front of the statue of St Anthony and wondered whether the saint, known for his ability to help people find lost things, could help him recover his fitness. He knew it was his own fault. Fifty years of heavy smoking, drinking and ignoring the benefits of a good diet had finally rendered him the type of person doctors bothered. And Dr Eyüboğlu was a constant thorn in his side. According to him, İkmen had to give up drinking and smoking immediately and follow the diet sheet he had thrust into his hands. Now Çiçek, who did most of the cooking in the İkmen apartment, was presenting him, and his horrified cousin Samsun, with 'low-carbohydrate' meals. This meant no rice, pasta or potatoes, which were his favourite things. Not that weight was his issue, at least not a surfeit of it. İkmen had always been, and remained, underweight. No, this was all about getting healthier, and he hated it. He'd already cut down to a mere twenty cigarettes a day; what more did the damn doctor want?

'Çetin Bey.' A hand landed on his shoulder, and he looked around to see his friend Bishop Montoya at his elbow.

'Your Excellency.'

The two men embraced. Bishop Juan-Maria Montoya was the Catholic Bishop of Turkey and a friend of both İkmen and Süleyman. He had assisted them considerably during the course of İkmen's last criminal case before he retired. Mexican by birth, he

10

was a tall, slim and striking man in his sixties. He was also, İkmen knew, very knowledgeable, with a wide range of interests. Oddly, given where they were, he was not wearing his ecclesiastical robes.

'Like you, I am a congregant this evening,' he said, as though he had read İkmen's mind. 'Father da Mosto will say Mass tonight. But what are you doing here? I suppose a moment of religious enlightenment . . .'

İkmen laughed. 'I fear not.'

'My door is always open, Çetin Bey.'

'I know, and I appreciate it,' İkmen said. 'No, I'm here with Mehmet Bey's wife, who is entertaining some friends from Spain. She thought it would be nice to bring them to Mass. Çiçek has come to act as translator, as they speak no Turkish.'

The bishop spotted Çiçek with Gonca and the Spanish Roma. He waved, and she smiled and waved back.

'I didn't know that Çiçek Hanım could speak Spanish,' he said.

'Oh yes.'

'And Gonca Hanım's guests, I take it they are Roma?'

'They are.' İkmen nodded.

'Well, why don't you all come to my apartment after Mass for a glass or two of the excellent mezcal my brother sent me for Christmas,' the bishop said. 'Spaniards and Mexicans have many Christmas customs in common, and I have a piñata waiting up there too.'

'A piñata?'

'It's a custom of Christmas Eve. All the children of the household must hit a papier-mâché model in the shape of a donkey or a star or something, until it bursts open and sweets fall out on the floor. I should love to share my piñata with you and your daughter and friends.' He smiled. 'It will also save me from the sin of gluttony.'

*

Normally Mehmet Süleyman would take a dim view of fellow police officers who were unable to control either their emotions or their physical responses to stressful situations. But in the case of what was found on the bed in the Şehzade Rafık Palace, he made an exception. When Ömer Mungun had put the light on in that room, he had almost thrown up himself. Ömer had, plus the two uniformed officers who had followed them in. To his credit, the sergeant had quickly regained his composure, but he was still shaking. Süleyman could see his hands trembling as one of the uniforms brought him some tea in a paper cup.

Nobody had been left with that ghastly mess. Just one uniform stationed outside the open door. All the other officers were in the garden, waiting. Süleyman himself had put the call through to police pathologist Dr Arto Sarkissian. Due to increasing nervousness amid İstanbul's burgeoning traffic nightmare, the doctor had a driver when he was on duty these days. A vaguely unhinged man in his forties, the driver, Devlet, tended to handle the pathologist's huge black Mercedes like a Formula 1 car. They would not, Süleyman thought, be very long. In the meantime, he had to try to concentrate on anything other than what was in that room. He also had to focus on not being sick.

Mezcal was an interesting drink. Pale yellow in colour, it was served neat save for some orange and lime slices arranged on a large plate and, the bishop told him, sprinkled with salt and chilli. Dr Eyüboğlu would no doubt have something to say about this combination, but İkmen found he didn't care. It was quickly making him feel more optimistic about life.

'The Aztecs believed that mezcal was an elixir of the gods,' the bishop said as he refilled İkmen's glass. 'It's made from the agave plant, of which we have millions in my country. But the Aztecs were very against drunkenness and so the form in which it is served today is one that was synthesised by the Spanish

12

conquistadors. Europeans will always drink.' He smiled. 'Gonca Hanım tells me that Mehmet Bey was meant to be with you tonight.'

'He's working,' İkmen said. 'The nature of the job is uncertainty.' He shrugged.

The bishop put a hand on his shoulder. 'You know the older Spanish man is famous in Mexico?'

'I knew he was famous in Spain,' İkmen said.

'Ah, flamenco is very big in Mexico too. Juan Cortes has played sell-out concerts in Mexico City.' The bishop lowered his voice. 'It is said that some years ago, he performed for Joaquín Guzmán, known as El Chapo, at his mansion in Sinaloa. Apparently it was on the occasion of Guzmán's birthday.'

İkmen had heard the name. 'You mean the leader of the Sinaloa drug cartel?'

'The same.' The bishop shook his head. 'The most destructive narco syndicate in Mexico. When El Chapo was arrested in 2014, he was supplying more cocaine into the USA than anybody else. Can you imagine the quantities?'

This was a story İkmen knew. When El Chapo had finally been arrested, there had been some in the Turkish police who had comforted themselves that such things couldn't happen in their country. But İkmen knew they were wrong. There were currently three big crime families, all heavily involved in drugs, in İstanbul. And Juan Cortes, his wife and the boy Gonca had told him was Cortes's son were going to play for one of them on his birthday.

'Well, you just never know, do you?' Dr Arto Sarkissian said as he entered that awful, reeking, blood-soaked bedroom. 'One moment you're drinking a very fine Merlot and the next you're transported back to nineteenth-century London.'

Süleyman, who was using his necktie as a makeshift face covering, said, 'Meaning?'

13

'I mean, Inspector,' said the pathologist, 'that this scene reminds me of a photograph of one of Jack the Ripper's victims. He absolutely terrorised London in the 1880s, but was never caught. His last victim was a prostitute called Mary Jane Kelly. He cut her to shreds.'

'At the risk of sounding ignorant, where will you start?'

He looked at his watch. 'My assistant, Dr Mardin, is on her way. We will decide together how best to approach this.'

'Then I will leave you with it,' Süleyman said.

As he descended the stairs and made his way back to the front entrance, the inspector yet again found himself marvelling at the way in which Dr Sarkissian always approached his work with such calm professionalism. If asked how he could do his job day after day, year after year, he always joked that 'someone has to do it'. But that wasn't of course the whole truth of the matter. He was always very respectful of those who came into his hands, and although he wasn't responsible for apprehending those who had killed them, he was passionate about doing everything he could to obtain justice for them. Süleyman knew he paid a price for his diligence. Whereas his friend Çetin İkmen had always smoked his way around his feelings, Arto Sarkissian ate his way out, and Süleyman was horrified to see how much weight he had put on since they had last met.

The blood-soaked man was still lying across the entrance to the palace, but now he was awake and cuffed. Ömer Mungun was talking to him, but from the blank expression on the man's face, it appeared that the sergeant wasn't having much success. The doctor who had attended him stood to one side.

As Süleyman approached, Ömer stood up and walked over to meet him.

'And?' Süleyman asked.

'He can't or won't talk,' Ömer said. 'But I've been looking Ateş Böcek up online and this man, it seems, is him. Not that there's a lot about him, mainly pictures with his daddy and grandma.'

Süleyman sighed. Ateş Böcek's father Esat ran the biggest crime family on the Asian side of the city. Assisted by his formidable mother, Neşe, he controlled the supply of drugs, female flesh and slum property from Üsküdar to Gebze. Ateş was his elder son and therefore his heir. But Süleyman, for whom the crime families of İstanbul were of particular interest, knew there were dark, if infrequent, rumours about the boy. He was, it was said, hot tempered and at times out of control. But then that was a fairly standard description of most spoilt children of crime lords.

Dr Mardin, a short woman in her forties, arrived, and after greeting her, Süleyman instructed one of the uniformed men to take her up to Dr Sarkissian.

Then he turned to Ömer, 'Where's the yataghan?'

'Bagged up,' the sergeant said. 'Scene of crime are on their way.' He looked back at the man who could be Ateş Böcek and added, 'What do we do with him now, sir?'

'I'll arrest him on suspicion of having unlawfully killed a person or persons unknown,' Süleyman said. 'I think it's going to take Sarkissian and Mardin a long time to work out just who it is on that bed upstairs. When forensics arrive, we'll have to get Böcek transported to headquarters.' He scrolled through his phone. 'I'll need an initial psychiatric consult on this one.'

Unlike Gonca and her people, Juan Cortes and his family were travelling Roma. They were based for much of the time in the southern Spanish city of Seville, but spent nine months of the year elsewhere in Spain and abroad. While they flew to engagements outside Europe, within the continent they used an elderly campervan.

When Gonca had told her husband that these performers she was providing with shelter as a favour to Roma godfather Şevket Sesler were going to sleep in their garden, he had been horrified.

15

'We have four empty bedrooms,' he'd told her. 'Why do they want to sleep in the garden? It's winter!'

Although he had been married to Gonca for only a matter of weeks, Mehmet Süleyman had been her on-and-off lover for twenty years. In that time he had learned much about the Roma population of İstanbul, but he was very aware that he knew only what they wanted him to. The exact nature of the relationship between Gonca and Sesler was a case in point. He knew she read the gangster's cards, but what else she might do for him, he didn't know – apart from the fact that it was most definitely not sexual. It had taken Gonca Şekeroğlu a long time to capture the exclusive affections of a man who was not only younger than her but also one of the handsomest men in the city. In addition, he was a scion of an old Ottoman family and so had class as well as good looks and fine manners.

She'd said, 'They're Roma, my pampered prince, they are tough. We must respect their need for freedom. They will live alongside us, that is their choice.'

He hadn't understood, but that was OK. As she helped them light their fire and brought water for their kettle, Gonca smiled. Doing these things reminded her of her childhood in the old Roma quarter of Sulukule – now long since demolished. Back when the community had been all together in their five-hundred-year-old home, everyone had helped everyone else and she had frequently lit fires and carried water for visiting Roma.

Before they had bade farewell to İkmen and Çiçek outside Saint-Antoine, she had asked the latter to tell Lola Cortes to come and get her if she needed her, no matter what the time. The pretty eighteen-year-old was pregnant, and Gonca, the mother of twelve children herself, was very experienced in the art of childbirth. Lola had kissed her hand in thanks. Her husband and his son by a previous marriage had turned away. Roma men always left that sort of thing to women.

Once her guests had settled in for what remained of the night, Gonca went into the house and up to her bedroom. As she showered prior to getting into bed, she thought about how old Juan Cortes had become since last she saw him, when they had been lovers. He'd been ugly even then, but what had attracted her had been his artistry, the way he held himself as he danced, the songs he sang, which wrenched the heart even if one could not understand the words. Flamenco was the most passionate magic and, in spite of his age, Juan still had it.

In bed, though, her mind began to turn towards her husband. She'd missed him at the church and afterwards in the bishop's apartment, but she'd resisted the urge to call him. Policing was his life, and although she feared for him all the time, she would never seek to stop him doing it. In lieu of his body, she hugged one of his pillows and waited for the sound of the front door opening.

Chapter 2

It wasn't the first time Filiz and Ayda had covered for Ceviz. Ever since she'd started seeing this mysterious new boyfriend of hers, she'd missed several late sessions. Rammed into close proximity with two other girls, who were new, they tried to talk in whispers to each other in the tiny area outside the toilets that served as their dressing room.

As well as the women, this cramped space was heaving with tattered skimpy dance costumes, feather boas, empty rakı bottles and overflowing ashtrays. One of the new girls, a seventeen-year-old from Edirne, coughed on the clouds of smoke that filled the air.

'Do you know how many she had booked tonight?' Ayda asked.

'Only three,' Filiz replied. 'Although one of those is Muharrem Bey.'

'Oh God, he's disgusting!' Ayda said. 'Just the thought of those sausage fingers down his trousers . . .'

Filiz put a hand on her arm. 'Don't worry, I'll do him,' she said. 'If you do the others.'

Ayda kissed her. 'You are an angel!'

Filiz wondered what Ayda would think when she saw Ceviz's other two punters. But now it was done. Lap dancers couldn't just change their minds; it wasn't in the job description. Unless apparently you were called Ceviz and had the ear of your employer.

Şevket Bey had always favoured Ceviz over the other girls. In part it was that, like him, she was Roma, but also he genuinely seemed to like her. Whether she'd ever slept with him wasn't known, but he did protect her father's apartment building, and the two men had been seen talking. But Ayda and Filiz both knew that three absences in one week was going to infuriate Şevket Sesler and would put Ceviz in a precarious position with regard to her employment.

Like Filiz, Ceviz had been working at the Kızlar lap dancing and strip club just off the noisy Tarlabaşı Bulvarı for the last two years. It was a rough place, where fights frequently broke out and a lot of the punters were on crack cocaine. But Sesler always made sure his girls were safe. Any man caught touching one of them had his fingers broken. And that happened whether the boss was on site or not. His men were well trained.

Slipping into a tight schoolgirl outfit, Filiz said, 'Do you know whether Şevket Bey is in tonight?'

'I don't,' Ayda said. 'But if Ceviz doesn't turn up soon, I'm not going to lie for her like I did last time. I'll cover, but I won't lie to Şevket Bey again. That's too dangerous.'

Dr Emir Doksanaltı was already at police headquarters when he answered Süleyman's call. He was taking a break from the assessment he was doing on a man who had tried to set his own apartment on fire.

'He's broke,' he told the inspector. 'Rent arrears, multiple credit card debt, child maintenance. On one level his response is perfectly rational, but . . . I've no idea when I'll be finished here. I'm inclined to suggest I see your suspect in the morning. Is he agitated? Do you want me to call a colleague?'

'He was, but he seems to have calmed down now,' Süleyman said. 'When we bring him in, who knows?'

'Well, I'm about if you need help,' the doctor said. 'What's he charged with?'

'Murder.'

'Of?'

'We're not sure yet,' Süleyman replied. 'Dr Sarkissian is attempting to identify whatever is lying on a bed in this man's house. Person or persons unknown.'

He heard the psychiatrist take a sharp intake of breath.

'Well, just make sure he's seen by a medic.'

'He already has been.' Süleyman said this a little stiffly. Did the psychiatrist think he didn't know what he was doing?

'Let's say ten a.m.,' Doksanaltı said after a pause during which, maybe, he registered that he might have caused some offence.

'Yes, let's,' Süleyman said. He ended the call, then turned to Ömer Mungun. 'I'll see you at headquarters.'

'Yes, sir.'

'Get him booked in, and then I think we should both go home and get some sleep. Dr Sarkissian has a long night ahead of him, and by the morning I should like to have a notion about how many people this man may have either killed or witnessed being killed.'

They got into their respective cars. Ömer Mungun had returned to work only the previous day. He'd taken leave to go back to his home city of Mardin in order to get married. Like his bride, Ömer's family belonged to an ancient sect that worshipped a Mesopotamian snake goddess called the Şahmeran. The girl, who Süleyman knew was eighteen, had been carefully chosen for him by his parents. Not that Ömer behaved as if he were a new husband. He had told his colleagues nothing about the wedding or his wife, who had come back to İstanbul to live with him and his sister Peri. Maybe he had discovered he didn't really like the girl.

Süleyman's first marriage had been arranged for him by his mother, and that had been a disaster. As he drove away from the Şehzade Rafık Palace, he couldn't shake the conviction that Ömer was rather more keen on staying at work than he was. For his part, he was aching to get home to his new wife. He was also, once again, having flashbacks to what he had seen in that blood-soaked bedroom, and it was making his nauseous.

Aylın was getting drunk. Her father put a hand on her shoulder and whispered, 'You're becoming loud, darling.'

She looked up at him and said, 'I'm perfectly in control of myself.'

Her father sat down beside her. 'I just don't want you to feel ill tomorrow, my soul.'

Murad Ayhan organised a Christmas party for his business associates every year on 24 December. A fast-fashion clothing exporter, Ayhan had factories all over Anatolia, but those who bought his products were mainly western Europeans, principally from Spain and the UK. These people were almost exclusively Christian, and so it made sense for Murad to put on a Christmas party for them at one of İstanbul's most prestigious hotels. It was good PR, and it also made him happy that everybody who attended the party would go away thinking what a generous man Murad Ayhan was. The only fly in the ointment was his daughter, who, when drunk, liked to behave like a whore around all the men. Fortunately, because she was still sitting at the dinner table, he should be able to head off too much bad behaviour before the dancing began.

Aylın took a packet of cigarettes and a lighter out of her hand-bag and lit up.

This was an old red flag she'd used since she was a teenager, smoking indoors just to piss him off. She knew that smoking was no longer allowed in enclosed indoor spaces, and Murad saw several people look at her, and not in an approving fashion.

He put his hand in the pocket of his tuxedo and removed something that he then pressed against her ribs.

'I think it's time for bed now, my little pigeon,' he whispered as he pulled her to her feet, the small pistol in his hand just grazing the bare flesh on her back. She looked at him with such venom in her eyes it almost took his breath away. Almost. In reality, Murad was used to this from his daughter. He it had been who had made her like this, always giving her everything she wanted, and he accepted that. But there were limits.

Slipping the gun back into his pocket, he replaced it with two of his thick peasant's fingers and began to walk her out of the dining room. Only once did he catch his wife's eye. Irmak Ayhan only cared about her son, Yıldırım, who sat by her side like an acolyte. A hugely fat woman in her fifties, she turned her jewel-encrusted head away when her husband and daughter passed. Even when Aylın hissed bitterly at her, 'Hello, Mother', Irmak did not respond.

It was only when her father had managed to half pull, half drag her to the exit that the girl screamed out, 'Look, he's got a gun! My daddy has a gun and he's going to kill me!'

But although everyone looked, no one actually said anything, and even amongst the western Europeans, conversation resumed almost immediately once Aylın and her father had gone. Most people were aware that, sadly, Murad Bey's beautiful daughter was also deeply troubled. Why, no one knew.

Once alone with her father in her room, Aylın sat on the edge of her bed, waiting to see what he might do. In the past, he had hit her, but this time he just stroked her hair and said, 'You know, Aylın, I would give you everything if only you would learn to behave.'

Cringing away from him, she said, 'Why should I?'

'Because I am your father and I love you,' he replied. He stroked her shoulder.

Aylın froze; then, suddenly springing off the bed, she turned on him and shouted into his face, 'You pretend you're this normal businessman, but you're not! You're lying to all those people in there and it makes me sick! I'm not allowed a few drinks and yet my father sells cocaine, he has people killed—'

He punched her in the face so hard that she tumbled backwards and hit the floor. Then she began to cry.

Murad stood up and adjusted his jacket. Once he'd made eye contact with her again, he said, 'You will have your breakfast here tomorrow morning. Disobey me and you will never see our guests again. Instead you will see Serdar Bey.'

Varicose veins. Çetin İkmen had always had them, and yet looking at them now, with his trousers rolled up to his knees, they seemed to be bigger than in the past. As soon as he'd arrived home after his visit to Bishop Montoya, his cousin Samsun had got to work making some sort of potion to ease his aching feet. Like İkmen's mother, Samsun Bajraktar was a witch; unlike his mother, she was a transsexual woman. What she was brewing up in the kitchen was anyone's guess. All İkmen really wanted was a bowl of hot water in which to put his feet, but Samsun was doing all sorts – eye of toad, neck of bat . . .

'Oh fuck off!' he heard her yell, and then he knew that she was also being watched by that bloody djinn.

Shortly before İkmen's wife Fatma had been killed in a car accident back in 2016, the djinn had appeared in the kitchen of the İkmen apartment. Creatures of smokeless fire, djinns were common across the Islamic world, and this one was particularly ugly and troublesome. It seemed to like the corner by the cooker, and would from time to time rear up to frighten anyone trying to cook, or in fact do anything, in peace. It was only seen by those members of the family who had inherited the 'magical' gene from İkmen's mother; he himself could see it, as could Samsun, Çiçek and one of his sons, Bülent. A less troublesome presence was the ghost of Fatma herself, who sat quietly out on the balcony, where İkmen went to share his thoughts and troubles with her on a daily basis. The couple had been deeply in love, and İkmen still needed her in his life, on whatever level, in order to function.

Samsun entered the living room carrying a large bowl of hot water that smelt of, amongst other things, tarragon.

'I nearly dropped this because of that bastard,' she said as she placed the bowl down by İkmen's feet and then gave him a towel. 'I know I should be used to it after all this time, but I'm not.'

İkmen lifted his feet up and then plunged them into the bowl.

'God!' he squeaked.

'Well, if it's not hot, it won't do any good,' Samsun said.

'My feet are the colour of tomatoes!'

'And your veins are like whipcords.' Samsun lit a cigarette. 'I could go down to the Yeni Valide Cami tomorrow . . .'

'No!' İkmen, lighting a cigarette of his own, held up a hand. 'I am not applying leeches gathered by itinerant Anatolians and imprisoned in jars. I don't hold with it.'

'Your wife did.'

'Fatma did a lot of things I don't and won't do,' he said.

Religion had been the biggest bone of contention between them. Fatma had been pious, while İkmen remained a lifelong atheist, albeit one with an apparent direct line to the unseen.

As he gingerly wiggled his toes in the hot, pungent liquid, Samsun said, 'Çiçek told me Prince Mehmet didn't show up. The Queen of the Gypsies must have been disappointed.'

'He had to work,' İkmen said. 'And Gonca had her hands full with her guests from Spain.'

'Roma?'

He nodded.

'Going to be part of the entertainment at Şevket Bey's birthday party,' Samsun said.

'You know about it?'

'Not much.'

Samsun worked in a gay and trans bar in Şevket Sesler's territory, Tarlabaşı, colloquially called the Sailor's Bar. Her role was officially bartender, but she was also an agony aunt to many of the younger girls, as well as, occasionally, a bouncer.

'Only,' she continued, 'that it's going to take place on Emin Cami Sokak.'

'Whereabouts on Emin Cami Sokak?'

'The whole street. Just like the old days, back when the Roma were in Sulukule, it will be one big party street.'

'It's winter!' İkmen said.

'Oh, that means nothing to the Roma!' Samsun said. 'Emin Cami will be a drunken, feasting, dancing asylum for the whole day and night of the twenty-sixth. But much as I love a party, I will be keeping away. You know what the Roma lads are like for firing their guns in the air. And it only takes one stray bullet . . .'

'Do the police know?' İkmen asked.

'I don't know. Ask Mehmet Bey,' she said.

Headquarters was a nightmare. As well as the usual individuals and groups lurking outside in the hope of seeing their incarcerated relatives, the main entrance was rammed with petitioners, lawyers, uniformed cops and a smattering of what appeared to be very smartly dressed men and women. As Mehmet Süleyman looked at the latter, he realised that the smallest man in that group was crime lord Esat Böcek. The covered woman to his left was probably his mother, while the man at his right hand was celebrity lawyer Eyüp Çelik. Süleyman knew Çelik well and didn't like him. The feeling was mutual. The presence of Esat Böcek meant that the man they had brought into custody was definitely his son. Clearly the İstanbul rumour mill was in good order.

When he saw Süleyman, Çelik smiled. 'Ah, Mehmet Efendi,' he said, choosing as he always did to use the old Ottoman form of address.

Süleyman, who hated such anachronisms but knew that Çelik

25

was only using it to rile him, said, 'Eyüp Bey. What brings you to our door on this freezing cold night?'

'I was called by my client Esat Bey,' the lawyer said as he gestured towards the diminutive crime lord. 'He is of the opinion that you have his son in custody.'

Ateş Böcek had been brought around the back of the building and was being booked into the cells by Ömer Mungun.

Süleyman said, 'A man has been arrested at an address we believe belongs to Mr Böcek, yes.'

'In connection with . . .?' the lawyer asked.

'A serious offence,' Süleyman replied. 'As yet we are not in a position to go into detail, but I am sure that if and when the individual involved requires legal representation, he will ask for it.'

'Yes, but—'

He held up his hand. 'That is all for the moment. In the meantime, I would suggest that you and your client's family return to your respective homes and get some rest.' He turned and walked away.

Süleyman had little experience with the Böcek family. Of course he recognised Esat Böcek; as well as being a gangster, the man was also influential in certain charitable organisations in the city. So far he had managed, in spite of his criminal activities being widely acknowledged, to keep away from the long arm of the law. But now that his son was in custody, how would he react?

Down in the cells, Süleyman supervised the incarceration of Ateş Böcek, who seemed to have descended into some sort of catatonic state. A preliminary examination by the on-site doctor confirmed that he was physically fit, with the exception of a high pulse rate. On the basis that this could be a sign of amphetamine use, a blood sample was taken for analysis and a sedative administered. Süleyman gave instructions to the custody team to check on the prisoner every thirty minutes and call him if he started to become agitated.

It was three o'clock in the morning by the time he and Ömer Mungun left to return home.

'Ayda!'

Filiz had already left, and because neither of them had seen Şevket Sesler that evening, both the girls thought they had got away with covering for Ceviz. But now here he was, large and sweaty as life, blocking Ayda's way out of the club.

'Ah, Şevket Bey . . .'

It had been a difficult evening. Ayda had taken part in the main strip show of the evening with the other girls, which had been OK, but her two lap dances plus the two that had been assigned to Ceviz had been hard work. One of her own bookings had tried to touch her, and Ceviz's men had both been annoyed that she wasn't there. As a consequence, they had been nasty to Ayda. One of them had told her she needed to lose weight – the fat pig! – while the other had masturbated copiously and loudly and then called her an ugly whore.

But she'd not once seen or heard anything about Şevket Bey being in attendance. Nevertheless, here he was. 'Where's Ceviz?' he asked.

Well known for getting to the point when he wanted something, Şevket Sesler evoked the kind of fear Ayda knew would not permit her to lie effectively in any way.

'I don't know,' she said.

'Because I got two complaints about her not being available for our clients tonight. Where is she?' he repeated.

'I don't know, Şevket Bey.'

'You covered for her,' he said. 'You and your friend . . .'

'Filiz,' she said. 'Yeah, we've no idea—'

One of his thick, hairy hands shot out, gripped her throat and pinned her to the wall. Then he moved his face in close to hers.

His breath smelt of rakı and tobacco. She tried to move her head away, but he wouldn't let her.

'If you know where she is, you will tell me!' he said. 'Because I know that this is not the first time you and Filiz have covered for her. And do you know how I know that?'

Shaking she said, 'No, Şevket Bey.'

He increased the pressure on her throat. 'Because,' he said, 'I know everything that goes on in my businesses. I know every trick you whores try to play on me.'

'I know—'

'Think before you speak, whore,' he said. 'Because if you disobey me, I will not hesitate to make sure you never work again. No man wants to look at a woman whose face is cut to shreds.'

Ayda had not been born to this kind of life. Her family were pious middle-class people who knew little of – and indeed actively avoided – minorities like the Roma. Ayda, always rebellious, had been different, more curious about people unlike her own, and when her father had told her he was going to arrange her marriage, she had run away. That had been horrible too.

'Şevket—'

'Think, girl, and tell me the truth!' He shook her.

Squealing in pain, Ayda knew she'd have to give in. 'There's a boy she's seeing.'

'Who?'

'I don't know, I swear on the Holy Koran! I don't know a name. All I know is that she's in love and this boy has told her he'll make her rich . . .'

Mehmet Süleyman closed his bedroom door behind him, took his clothes off in the dark and got into bed beside his wife.

As soon as he lay down, she turned over and regarded him with wide, alert eyes.

'You're awake,' he said.

She placed one of her large, tattooed hands on his naked shoulder. 'You know I can't sleep without you.' She kissed his lips. 'I am always afraid in case something has happened to you.'

'Oh Gonca! I'm a big boy now.'

'I know that,' she said. She wound one of her long legs around his hips. 'That's why I married you.'

He laughed. 'You're a terrible woman!'

'And that is why *you* married me,' she said. 'I'm terrible, I'm crazy and I'm always hot for you, baby.'

He'd responded as soon as she'd kissed him. He always wanted her too, but his need for sex became particularly acute when he'd seen or heard of horrors in the line of duty. Gonca was a generous woman, curvy and fleshy, and when he needed to hide from the grim realities of man's inhumanity to man, there was no better place for him to hide than in her arms.

Was he using her? Did that even matter? He'd been with her on and off for twenty years and he loved her. That she was besotted with him was deeply erotic, and there was nothing he enjoyed more than making love to her. He leaned down and took one of her nipples in his mouth. Gonca gasped appreciatively. 'Baby . . .'

The very distinctive taste of her flesh – a mixture of anise, rose, nicotine and frankincense – aroused him still further and, in spite of his tiredness, he knew he wouldn't be able to sleep until they'd had sex.

Afterwards, as she lay in his arms, he suddenly remembered about their Spanish guests.

'Do you know whether they're warm enough?' he asked. 'I mean, it's freezing tonight.'

'They're fine,' she said. 'We made a fire and they've got water. They will have gone to sleep hours ago. Oh, and Lola – that's Juan's wife – is pregnant. I am so happy for them!'

He sighed. 'Pregnant and sleeping outdoors on the ground.'

'Darling, I had my first baby on the floor of my father's kitchen.'

'Yes, but you weren't thousands of kilometres from home.'

She kissed him. 'She's a strong eighteen-year-old . . .'

'This gets worse!'

'. . . and if she's in any difficulty, I will help her.'

'Gonca . . .'

She kissed him again. 'You worry too much, Şehzade Mehmet,' she said. 'Anyway, you must get to sleep now. I don't know what has happened and I know better than to ask you, but what I do know is that you will need your strength tomorrow. Sleep, angel.'

But he didn't. For a short time he had managed to lose himself in her body and her love, but now that it was over, whatever had been on the bed in that old palace was manifesting in his brain again, and he had to fight not to let the nausea overwhelm him.

Chapter 3

Numan Bey was the last traditional turşu suyu man to still wander the Eminönü docks. Back in the day, almost all the vendors like him had been mobile, plying their trade in cucumber- and cabbage-infused pickle juice up and down the dockside, selling small glasses of the well-known hangover cure to those either boarding or leaving the ubiquitous Bosphorus ferries. Pushing a large juice container on a handcart, the small glasses rattling against each other as he moved, Numan Bey knew he couldn't compete with the places where fez-wearing, fancy-waistcoat-sporting competitors sold the stuff mainly to curious tourists. But he liked his job even if it made him very little money. And in recent weeks it had also allowed him to meet up with an old friend every morning.

Ex-inspector of police Çetin İkmen had been put on a strict regime by his doctor. Apparently if he didn't get more exercise, eat more fruit and vegetables and give up smoking and drinking, he was at risk of developing major health problems. His daughter Çiçek enforced all the doctor's recommendations, with the exception of the not drinking and smoking, which İkmen flatly refused to accept. Consequently İkmen now walked down from Sultanahmet to Eminönü every morning and then, after a short rest, walked back up the hill again. He hated it, especially on this particular morning after a whole night of wandering about with Çiçek, Gonca and her Spanish Roma friends.

As was his custom, Numan Bey took a small plastic stool off

his cart and put it down by the dockside when he saw İkmen approach.

'Çetin Bey,' he said as he poured him a glass of turşu suyu, 'come sit, drink. You look exhausted!'

İkmen took the small glass from the old man and sat down on the stool. Although it was only 7 a.m., ferries were already filling up with people commuting to work, going to school or heading to the shops. Men, women and children threw themselves onto departing ferries at the last minute, many holding large bundles, children and sometimes pets. Even now, with three bridges across the Bosphorus, which separated Europe and Asia, thousands still preferred to travel by ferry, avoiding as it did the huge traffic jams on the roads.

Once he had recovered his breath, İkmen told Numan Bey about his visit to Saint-Antoine the previous night.

'My daughter has turned into a fanatic,' he said. 'I mean, it was late, we could have driven to Beyoğlu. I would have done it myself! But Çiçek Hanım would have her way. And in the snow! I mean, where's the sense?'

Numan Bey, who at eighty-five was over twenty years İkmen's senior, shook his head. The snow had stopped in the early hours of the morning, but it was still iron cold and there was a thick layer of slush on the pavements. İkmen had been lucky he hadn't slipped on his way down to the docks. Walking through Sirkeci, where the trams sometimes forced people to press themselves against the buildings to avoid being splashed, was particularly hazardous.

'But she loves you, Çetin Bey,' the old man said. 'It is a wonderful thing for a man to have a daughter who really cares for him.'

İkmen shrugged. He knew that Çiçek was doing the right thing by him, but he still resented her for it. He drank his turşu suyu down in one, and Numan Bey refilled his glass.

'And what of the Queen of the Gypsies and her friends?' the vendor asked. 'Did they enjoy Saint-Antoine?'

'I don't know whether Gonca knew what was going on any more than I did,' İkmen said. 'But the Spaniards seemed to cross themselves and get down on their knees in all the right places. It was also nice that Bishop Montoya was present.'

'Oh?'

'He's Mexican, so he could speak to them in their own language.'

'But Mehmet Efendi wasn't with you,' the old man said as a statement of fact.

'No, he wasn't,' İkmen said. 'How do you know?'

Numan Bey shook his head. 'A terrible incident in an old palace, I heard,' he said. 'Word is that Mehmet Efendi was called over the Bosphorus last night to a scene some say was like something from a horror film.'

'Good morning, Dr Sarkissian,' Mehmet Süleyman said, answering his mobile phone as he climbed into his car and started the engine.

'I apologise for calling you so early, Inspector,' the doctor said, 'but I thought you'd appreciate my preliminary findings with regard to the Şehzade Rafık Palace affair.'

'Indeed. Also, you must be exhausted.' Süleyman knew the doctor and his assistant had worked through the small hours, while he had been lying sleeplessly beside Gonca.

'I was, but I think I may have woken up again now,' the Armenian said. 'Though that is immaterial. Inspector, it is the opinion of both Dr Mardin and myself that what lay on that bed was the remains of one person. I can fully appreciate that it might have looked like more – we even found pieces under the bed, plus an internal organ on a light fitting. I will not trouble you with further details at this stage.'

Süleyman breathed in deeply in order to calm himself. 'Thank you.'

The doctor continued. 'And the subject is female.'

'Ah. So maybe a lovers' . . .'

'I think not, Inspector. This was a frenzied attack that may have been mounted against this woman while she slept. If the suspect you have in custody did do this, then his sanity must be called into question.'

'I see. Thank you, Doctor,' Süleyman said.

'Pleasure.'

The Armenian ended the call, leaving Süleyman to ponder what he had told him on his way to headquarters.

First she heard the front door slam shut, and then the sound of the girl crying again. Peri Mungun got out of bed and went to the door of the bedroom her brother shared with his new wife. She knocked.

'Yeşili?' she said. 'What's the matter?'

But the girl just carried on weeping, and so Peri pushed the door open and walked in.

Ömer had bought a new bed and lots of cushions and fancy covers just before he'd gone back to their home city of Mardin to get married. He'd told his sister that his bride would probably like such things. The 'probably', to Peri's way of thinking, simply demonstrated how little he knew about his intended. But then that wasn't completely his fault. Peri and Ömer's parents had arranged this marriage. Yeşili and her family, like Ömer and his, were adherents of a fast-disappearing faith devoted to a Mesopotamian snake goddess called the Şahmeran. If the community wanted to live on, there were limited choices when it came to marriage.

Peri went over to the bed and put her arms around her new sister-in-law. Speaking in their native Aramaic, she said, 'Oh Yeşili, what's wrong?'

The girl didn't answer. She turned her head away. But then Peri knew full well what was wrong. It was what had been wrong ever since the couple had returned to İstanbul.

'Has my brother spoken harshly to you?' she asked.

Yeşili was small for eighteen, with long dark brown hair, big grey eyes and a body that possessed hardly any curves. Peri was not dissimilar herself, except that she was also tall – and opinionated. The latter, however, had more to do with her age and experience. At forty, she had worked as a nurse in İstanbul for fifteen years. She was also unmarried, and while she liked men, she also enjoyed being her own boss.

Yeşili wiped her eyes. 'No. No, he's always kind and polite to me. It's me that is wrong, not him.'

'You?'

Clinging to Peri's arm until her knuckles went white, she said, 'I cannot please him. Whatever I do, he always looks sad. And he wants to get away all the time.'

'No . . .'

'Yes, Peri! He wants to be at work all the time. I don't know what to do. What if he divorces me?'

Peri hugged her. 'Shh. Shh.'

Yeşili began to cry again. But what could Peri say? Her thirty-three-year-old brother had given up girls some years ago. As far as she knew, all his more recent affairs had been with women in their forties and fifties – women who knew what they were doing, in other words. And while Peri was certain her brother had performed his conjugal duties on the night of his wedding, she wasn't sure that anything had happened since. It didn't take a genius to work out that when Yeşili alluded to not pleasing her husband, she meant in the bedroom.

In addition, Peri knew that her brother was unhappy too. Whenever he was miserable, he threw himself into his work, barely bothering to come home to sleep.

*

Dr Emir Doksanaltı watched through a one-way mirror as Süleyman and Ömer Mungun attempted to interview Ateş Böcek. The suspect appeared to be in a state of fugue.

Süleyman said, 'The body of a woman was found in a bedroom in your house last night, Ateş Bey. I don't know as yet whether you had a hand in her death. At the moment I am merely trying to establish her identity. Can you tell me her name?'

Böcek said nothing. The clothes he had been arrested in had been taken away for analysis and he was wearing a grey coverall. Whether it was grey because that was its colour or because it was dirty, the doctor didn't know.

'The dead woman,' Süleyman continued, 'in all probability has a family who will be concerned for her. If you know who she is, I would urge you to tell me so that I may inform them.'

Nothing.

'We're not saying you killed her,' Ömer Mungun said. 'At the moment, we don't know what happened. But if you talk to us, perhaps we can work towards finding that out. As the inspector says, the name of the woman would be a start. And if you don't know who she is, that would help us too.'

Emir Doksanaltı could see that Ateş Böcek was very far away from what was happening in that interview room. He sat slumped in a chair, his wrists cuffed, head down, staring fixedly at the floor. The doctor would lay money it would be hard to get so much as a reflex out of the kid. He'd shut down. But whether that was because of what he'd done, what he'd seen or as a result of his arrest, Doksanaltı didn't know. And although he knew that Süleyman couldn't see him in the viewing room, he saw the inspector look towards the one-way mirror and shrug.

The youngest of Gonca Süleyman's twelve children was a twenty-one-year-old boy called Rambo. Like his many brothers and sisters, he was a smart kid. However, unlike his sister Asana, who was a lawyer, or his brother Erdem, who worked in IT, Rambo had decided to take what many considered to be a traditional mode of employment and made his living hustling on the streets of Beyoğlu. Part tour guide, part barman/mixologist, part muscle for hire, Rambo Şekeroğlu was the type of handsome, confident Roma many gaco – non-gypsy – young men both resented and feared. He was also the apple of his mother's eye.

When Rambo sauntered into his mother's kitchen and saw her hurriedly serving tea to her Spanish guests, he said, 'What's up?'

Looking flustered, she ran over to him and kissed him. 'Thank God you're here, baby boy! Do you have your car?'

'Yeah.'

Although he often slept elsewhere in the city – mainly at the homes of his various siblings – Rambo still officially lived with his mother, even if she rarely knew when he would make his next appearance.

'I need you to take me over to Tarlabaşı,' she said.

'Why?' He sat down and looked at her guests with grave, unmoving eyes.

'Because Şevket Bey wants me to read his cards,' Gonca said. 'Wants to know that his birthday will be a happy one. He sounded as if he was in a foul temper, so I had to agree to it. What I'm supposed to do with Juan and his family while I'm out, I don't know.'

'They don't speak any Turkish?' Rambo asked.

'No, of course not! And whatever Roma dialect they speak is beyond me.'

'What about English?' Rambo asked.

'What about it?'

'They come from Spain, Mum. Tourists from England have been going there for years.' He turned to the younger man, Tomas, and said, in English, 'Do you speak English?'

Tomas's face lit up. 'Yes,' he said. 'You can . . .?'

'Some,' Rambo said.

His mother butted in. 'Tell him I have to go out. They can help themselves to food and put on the television. This is their home while they are in the city.'

It was cold, he'd finished his third glass of turşu suyu and İkmen was looking out at the Bosphorus before the long, arduous climb back up to Sultanahmet and his apartment. The great waterway was a forbidding grey underneath the heavy, snow-filled sky. Ferries still ploughed their routes from Europe to Asia and vice versa, while enormous tankers brought coal and gas from the Black Sea, headed for the Sea of Marmara and beyond.

As he turned his back on the water, he thought about the information Numan Bey had given him about Mehmet Süleyman. Yes, the inspector had been unable to accompany them to Saint-Antoine the previous night, but was it true that he had been attending a murder scene in an old palace on the Asian side of the city? If so, which one? İkmen could think of only a couple off the top of his head. But then he remembered what the day was. It was Western Christmas, and Bishop Montoya had invited him to a traditional Mexican Christmas lunch at his apartment. This made going home up the hated hill a waste of time. Except that it was only 8 a.m., and the lunch didn't start until 1 p.m.

Theoretically he could go home, rest his legs, read for a few hours and then catch the tram to Karaköy and jump the Tünel up to Beyoğlu, but his whole being rebelled against it. So he didn't celebrate Christmas? So what? He knew a couple of Western Christians who lived in trendy Cihangir, as well as the nominally Muslim family of his one-time colleague Inspector Kerim Gürsel, who lived in nearby Tarlabaşı. And although Kerim would be at work, his wife Sinem, their baby daughter and who knew what other examples of İstanbul's waif-and-stray population would be in their apartment.

Between all of those, at least one of them would know what Mehmet Süleyman might be up to.

'Do you think we ought to go out to the family, boss?' Ömer Mungun said to Süleyman as they settled themselves in the viewing room and waited for Ateş Böcek and Dr Doksanaltı to arrive.

'Absolutely not,' Süleyman replied. 'Anyway, we've nothing to tell them, or their lawyer, not while Ateş refuses to communicate.'

In the interview room, two constables led Ateş Böcek in and sat him down. When the doctor arrived, he asked the officers to uncuff the suspect, which they did.

Süleyman said to Ömer Mungun, 'Not sure that's wise.'

'Why not? He's got two men in there with him.'

Süleyman shrugged.

Dr Doksanaltı began by introducing himself and explaining why he was there.

'Unlike the police officers who spoke to you, I don't want to talk about what happened last night,' he said. 'Rather, I'd like to talk about you. Now, I know that your name is Ateş, and you're twenty-one years old, but I don't know anything else about you, and I'd like to.'

Ömer Mungun rolled his eyes.

'He's trying to build some kind of connection with him,' Süleyman said. 'Pierce the armour that surrounds this catatonia he's slipped into. He's attempting to find a route in that hopefully we can take advantage of.'

Prior to his marriage to Gonca, Süleyman had been married to a Turko-Irish psychiatrist called Zelfa Halman, with whom he had a son. During his time with her, he had learned a lot about how psychiatrists dealt with offenders.

The doctor continued, 'I've seen pictures of your house, or rather, palace. Very grand. I may be wrong, but I assume your family paid for it? You're very young. Unless of course you're something like a digital influencer. I understand they can make millions of dollars. What do you do, Ateş?'

Still the suspect failed to even look up from the floor. Doksanaltı brought one hand down hard on the table in front of him. Ateş merely twitched.

Süleyman said, 'Looks as if Ateş Böcek is deep inside himself. Unless he's faking. That's not without precedent. But if he is faking, then he's good.'

'I'm a psychiatrist,' Dr Doksanaltı said. 'I think I always wanted to be a doctor. My father was a family doctor. My decision to be a psychiatrist happened later, when I went to university. Higher education opens one's mind to possibilities one hadn't thought about before. I began to appreciate that although a healthy body is a wonderful thing, a healthy mind is just as important.'

Süleyman watched a look pass between the two men guarding the doctor. Like Ömer, they thought he was wasting his time.

Şevket Sesler was sweating. This was because he was agitated, not because the weather had suddenly become warm.

'Come on! Come on!' he shouted at Gonca Süleyman as she laid out three cards in front of him.

They were sitting in his office at the back of his lap dancing and strip club, the Kızlar club in Tarlabaşı. He'd changed nothing since the death of his father, Harun, and so his lair was still dominated by dark panelled walls and fat leather chairs. Sitting at his father's old desk, he looked like a hoodlum from a US cop drama of the 1970s.

Gonca, resplendent in multiple brightly coloured scarves, sat back while she contemplated the three cards. Sesler had told her to be quick, and so she'd opted for a simple layout, representing his immediate past, present and future.

40

'Well, that doesn't look good!' He pointed one fat finger at the first card, the past.

'As you know, Şevket Bey, Death doesn't always mean physical death,' Gonca said.

Something occurred to him. 'Maybe that represents my father's death? You know about that, don't you, Gonca Hanım?'

Harun Sesler had been murdered by the mother of the underage girl he had been due to marry back in the autumn.

Gonca looked at him with stony eyes. Afife Purcu, the girl's mother, had pleaded guilty to the death of Harun Sesler and not once had she mentioned Gonca's involvement. There was no proof that Gonca had put that idea in her head. Not as far as the police were concerned. But Sesler and some sections of the Roma community believed otherwise. Gonca, after all, had owed Harun Bey a considerable sum of money.

'Elmas's mother didn't want her daughter to marry an old man,' Gonca said. 'Would you want one of your daughters to marry a man of over seventy?'

'Afife Purcu didn't give a shit until you poisoned her mind!' Sesler yelled. 'She's a junkie! She only cares about her next fix!'

Gonca went to pick up the cards and leave. But Sesler stopped her.

'Do your reading, witch, and let me know what I have to do to make my birthday a good day,' he said.

She shrugged and then looked at the layout again.

'The second card, the Devil, represents your present,' she said. 'It tells me that whatever is wrong now, you must act quickly and without fear in order to put it right.'

'Hah!'

She looked at him and frowned. 'Şevket Bey?'

It wasn't easy being the personal falcı to a paranoid crime lord, even if your husband was a senior policeman. Gonca's Roma life was in many ways quite separate from her life as a professional artist and wife effectively living in the gaco world.

'One of my girls has gone missing,' Sesler said.

Girls who worked for Sesler were always coming and going. Gonca said, 'So?'

'So? So she's one of us,' Sesler said. 'Ceviz Elibol. You know her?'

He knew she knew everyone.

'I know Hüseyin Elibol,' she said. 'He was a bear man, like my Şükrü.'

Now dead, Şükrü Şekeroğlu, Gonca's older brother, had in his youth been a street performer and trainer of dancing bears. A traditional Roma profession, it had been outlawed in the 1990s, and Şükrü had spent the rest of his life living by his wits at the edge of organised crime.

'Have you spoken to Hüseyin Bey?' Gonca asked.

'I sent the boy round this morning. The old man said he knows nothing.'

'The boy', Sesler's only son, Selami, was an unpleasant, spoilt little thug of twenty-three. Gonca could imagine how he'd threatened and possibly even attacked the girl's father. A tough veteran of the Cyprus war of 1974, Hüseyin Elibol was not the sort of man who responded to force.

'Let me speak to him,' she said.

'Why?'

'Because Hüseyin Bey is a proud man who appreciates the respect I will give him.'

Their eyes locked for a moment, and then Sesler said, 'What about my future card?'

She looked back down at the layout again. 'The Wheel of Fortune.'

'What does it mean?'

'I'm thinking,' she said. 'A layout has to be interpreted. Cards affect each other.'

'And so?'

'Let me think, Şevket Bey! Either you want my expertise or you don't. Be quiet.'

The doctor was effectively talking to himself. Süleyman could see what he was doing. Going through as many subject areas as he could, trying to find one that might unlock Ateş Böcek's frozen mind.

'Which football team do you support?' he asked.

Süleyman heard Ömer Mungun sigh and then mutter, 'God!'

Dr Doksanaltı went on, 'I never really had a choice, because of my school. Galatasaray Lisesi. So of course my team is Galatasaray. I believe you went to the Lisesi yourself . . .'

Süleyman too had attended İstanbul's most prestigious school, a few years after Emir Doksanaltı. But he hadn't known that Ateş Böcek had been there too. How had the doctor discovered this? Was he one of those people who always looked up where those he came across had gone to school?

Of course, the school itself didn't actually matter. What Süleyman imagined the doctor was doing was trying to use Ateş's childhood as a lever into his mind. Whether whatever was there was negative or positive was almost irrelevant.

'I loved my time at the Lisesi,' Doksanaltı continued. 'The educational benefits go without saying, but I also made friends for life. Boys with whom I first discovered the delights of Anatolian rock. We explored the city together, looking at the European youngsters through the windows of the Pudding Shop in Sultanahmet. We didn't dare go in. They were so strange. Long-haired youths on their way to India. Our parents told us they were all on drugs. We were both fascinated and appalled. Not of course that we were boringly good all the time.'

Ömer said, 'Where is this going, boss?'

He was impatient these days! Süleyman put a finger to his lips.

'We had a game whereby one of us would distract one of the kokoreç vendors in the Balık Pazar while the rest of us attempted to steal the succulent lamb's intestines from the grill,' the doctor said. 'We all burnt our fingers, vile little thieves . . .'

Was Süleyman seeing things, or did Ateş Böcek's face move?

Doksanaltı continued, 'And if any of us got any money, we'd go straight over to Sulukule. The gypsies sold cheap beer, and of course the Roma girls would dance—'

It happened so quickly, it was as if Ateş Böcek had a spring underneath his backside. He threw himself across the table, reducing it to matchwood, and clamped his fingers around the psychiatrist's neck. The two constables in the interview room, entirely caught off guard, stood frozen, while Süleyman and Ömer Mungun ran out of the viewing room and hammered on the door. Süleyman yelled down the corridor, 'Medic! Now!'

When the door opened, both men barged into the room. The doctor was on the floor, with Böcek seemingly gnawing on his neck and making alarming growling noises. The other constable was attempting to pull him away, but without success.

Süleyman pushed the officer aside and tried to unclamp Böcek's jaws. Blood was everywhere, and Doksanaltı's face was white with shock and pain.

'Let go!' he yelled.

And Ateş Böcek did – only to clamp his jaws around Süleyman's wrist. Using his weaker left arm, Süleyman punched him in the face. He heard the man's nose break before he let go of Süleyman's wrist and slumped to the floor.

While Ömer Mungun cuffed the unconscious Böcek, one of headquarters' resident doctors ran in and held Süleyman's bleeding wrist above his head. Then she hunkered down to inspect the condition of the wounded psychiatrist.

Chapter 4

'Çetin Bey!'

He recognised the voice coming out of the Gürsels' intercom immediately.

'Edith,' he said. 'Good morning. Is it all right to come up?'

'Of course!'

Four flights of stairs and a lot of breathlessness later, he met Edith – or Madam Edith, as she chose to be known – on the threshold of the Gürsels' apartment. Famous amongst İstanbul's LGBT community for her impersonations of French chanteuse Edith Piaf, Madam Edith was an elderly drag queen and part-time carer of Sinem Gürsel and her baby, Melda.

'You look as if you're about to die,' she said as she let him in. 'Do you want a glass of water?'

He nodded, and she went into the kitchen and got him one. Once he'd recovered enough to be able to speak, she asked, 'What are you doing here? Kerim Bey's at work.'

'Yes, I know.' He flopped down in one of the living-room chairs. 'It's Christmas. Here's a present.' He held out a box of sweets he'd bought from Hacı Bekir on İstiklal Caddesi.

'Western Christmas, yes,' Edith said. 'But we're all Muslims here, as are you.'

'Then it's an early New Year gift. But I went to Mass at Saint-Antoine last night with Gonca and some guests of hers from Spain, and now I've been invited to Christmas dinner by the bishop. It was on my mind.'

She laughed. 'What do you want, İkmen?'

Edith had known İkmen for years and was aware of the fact that he very rarely did anything that didn't have an ulterior motive. But just at that moment, a small, tired-looking woman carrying a baby came into the room. Sinem Gürsel.

'Oh, Çetin Bey,' she said. 'I'm afraid you've missed Kerim . . .'

'I came to see you,' İkmen said. 'And Edith and Melda.' He smiled in the direction of the child.

'Do you want to hold her?' Sinem asked.

'I'd love to.'

She put the sleeping baby into his arms and he rocked her gently.

'She looks like you, Sinem Hanım,' he said.

She sat down beside him.

'How many grandchildren do you have now, Çetin Bey?' she asked.

'Seven,' he said. 'The latest one, my daughter Hande's little boy Ara, was born just two weeks ago.'

'Oh, how lovely. Does she live in the city?'

'No, İskender. Her husband manages a tyre factory out there. So far I've only seen pictures of little Ara.'

İskender, a city in the far-eastern province of Hatay, was a long way from İstanbul.

İkmen nodded his head at the box of sweets, 'I brought those for you.'

Sinem Gürsel had a sweet tooth, and she opened the box immediately. 'Thank you!'

'Early New Year present apparently,' Madam Edith said.

'Oh Çetin Bey, that's so kind.'

Edith snorted. 'Sinem, honey, while this silly old man is holding the precious girl for you, would you like a glass of tea?'

'Oh yes, thank you,' Sinem said. She popped a large piece of

Turkish delight from the box into her mouth and closed her eyes. 'Wonderful lokum, Çetin Bey.'

The Elibol family were poor. Hüseyin Elibol had lost a leg in the Turko-Greek war in Cyprus in 1974. After that, he'd made his living first as a bear man, then playing the accordion in and around the drinking dens of the old gypsy quarter of Sulukule. When that had been demolished in 2008, he'd plied his trade in the meyhanes of Beyoğlu. The mother of his daughter Ceviz and her little sister Beren had died just after the family had left Sulukule, and now they lived in the basement of one of Tarlabaşı's many half-derelict houses.

Gonca Şekeroğlu didn't know Hüseyin Elibol well, but she knew that her late brother had liked him. She found him sitting on an old chair outside his basement, covered in a heap of blankets. As she drew near, he raised his hand and called out to her. 'Gonca Hanım!'

She smiled. 'Hüseyin Bey.'

She walked down the outside stairs that led to the basement and kissed Hüseyin's hand. He motioned for her to sit in another battered chair next to his own, then called out, 'Beren! We have a guest! Tea, please!'

He shifted uncomfortably in his seat. Unlike back in his youth, now his prosthetic leg caused him pain. 'So, Gonca Hanım, to what do I owe the pleasure of your company?' When she didn't answer straight away, he said, 'I hear you are married now. To a gaco.'

'Yes, Hüseyin Bey,' she said.

'At the Çırağan Palace Hotel, no less.'

'We will marry in the Roma tradition at Hıdırellez,' she said. 'Everyone will be invited.'

'That's good. Your Şükrü would have liked that. Although—'

'Hüseyin Bey, I've not come here to talk about my marriage or

47

my husband,' she said. 'This morning I visited Şevket Bey. He wanted me to read his cards before his birthday tomorrow.'

The outlook for the godfather had been bleak. Gonca had tried to soften what she saw for his consumption, but the fact remained that some sort of loss would soon cause Şevket Sesler to act decisively in some way. But even if he did that, the reversed Wheel of Fortune pointed towards possibly unwanted new beginnings. Things were about to change.

'During my reading,' she continued, 'Şevket Bey told me that your daughter Ceviz is missing.'

A small girl of about twelve came out of the apartment carrying glasses of tea. This was Ceviz's younger sister, Beren. Thin and barefoot, she wore what looked like an old military coat and observed Gonca with black, suspicious eyes. Once she'd given the adults their tea, she left without a word.

When she'd gone, Gonca said, 'He told me that he sent Selami round here.'

Hüseyin laughed without mirth. 'That vicious little bastard.'

'Did he threaten you?'

'Of course, he's a thug. Grabbed me by my collar, threatened to stab me in the arse. I laughed at him. I said, "My daughter does not work for your father with my blessing." I said, "Ceviz sacrifices herself for me and her sister. She says what else can she do with no education?"' He looked at Gonca. 'I never wanted her to work at that disgusting club, Gonca Hanım. But she makes good money, which means we can eat.'

Gonca reached out a hand to him, 'Hüseyin Bey . . .'

'Is that beast assaulting my daughter? I don't know,' he said. 'Sometimes she comes home and sometimes she doesn't. I told the boy I don't know where she might be. I told him he could cut me to pieces if he wanted to, it would change nothing. I don't know where my daughter is if she's not with Sesler, and that is the truth.'

*

48

'Go home.'

Dr Sebnam Altan had been working as a police medic for almost thirty years. A smart single woman in her late fifties, she'd seen a lot of macho posturing during that time and was completely contemptuous of it. She knew Inspector Mehmet Süleyman well enough to recognise that he was a serial offender.

'Doctor,' he said as he rolled down his bloodied shirtsleeve and attempted to cover the bandage she had wrapped around his wounded wrist, 'you may have noticed that I am in the middle of a murder investigation . . .'

She turned on him. 'Don't take that tone with me, Inspector. And respect my professionalism as your physician. God, isn't it enough that even educated men like you refuse a local anaesthetic when I have to stitch you up? It's ridiculous!'

'In my defence,' he said as he stood up and put on his jacket, 'the last thing I need when at work is a fuzzy mind.'

She turned to face him. 'That's nonsense. Local anaesthesia doesn't make the mind fuzzy.'

'Yes, well . . .'

'Go home,' she reiterated. 'I'm not asking you. You're not fit for duty. Come back tomorrow with my blessing, but give your body a chance to heal.'

He left the clinic and went back to his office. Ömer Mungun was waiting for him.

'You all right, boss?' he asked as Süleyman took his seat behind his desk.

'I'll live,' Süleyman said. 'How is Dr Doksanaltı?'

'Transferred to the Cerrahpaşa. I reckon he'll have to have plastic surgery. Böcek ripped into his neck like he was trying to eat him.'

'And Böcek himself?'

'He's got a broken nose, which you know about . . .'

'Getting him off me was no easy feat. He's young and strong.'

49

'Yes, but now he's sedated,' Ömer said. 'Sleeping like a baby. Won't be able to do a thing with him for the rest of the day.'

'Well, I have to go home,' Süleyman said. 'Doctor's orders.'

'Probably a good idea, boss,' Ömer said.

'Yes, but what about Böcek's family? They're still in the building, I understand. I've not had anything to do with them professionally, but I imagine they're here to give him a clean character reference.'

Ömer laughed. 'No guilty men in our cells, boss.'

'God.'

'But seriously, I've spoken to Kerim Bey. He doesn't know them well, but he did have cause to interview the father back when he worked for Çetin Bey. The old man walked free, but I gather that as an organisation they're up there with the Seslers and the Ayhans, although a bit rougher round the edges than the latter.'

'Meaning?'

'Meaning that they don't do all the society stuff the Ayhans do. Murad Ayhan had his annual Christmas party at the Çırağan Palace Hotel last night. All his Christian associates from Europe, wined and dined at his expense. The Böceks don't do that. If they like you, they let you live; if they don't, they kill you. Not subtle, but they make it work for them.'

Süleyman stood. 'Well, if Kerim Bey is agreeable, I'll leave it in his hands – and yours. Call me if anything breaks, and remember we're still awaiting results from forensics, not least on the bloodied clothing Böcek was wearing when we arrested him.'

She hadn't meant to go back and see him. But Gonca had to pass Kızlar on her way up to Taksim Square to get a taxi home. The famous yellow İstanbul cabs were few and far between in Tarlabaşı.

Sesler was standing in the basement area outside his club, and their eyes locked. Gonca walked down the stairs. 'I've just been to see Hüseyin Elibol. He doesn't know where Ceviz is – and by the way, next time you send Selami round to do your dirty work, make sure the little shit knows his place. He threatened Hüseyin Bey, a war veteran. Shame on you, and your son!'

He grabbed her by the throat and pulled her towards him.

'Luckily for you, witch,' he said, 'I've had some good news, or a comment like that would result in my giving you a black eye!'

'If you did that, Mehmet Bey would break your face,' she said.

He smiled, and she felt one of his hands touch her breast.

'And if I do this? What will he do to me then?' he said.

Gonca's face drained and she began to feel sick. As the crime lord continued to paw at her breast, she felt him press his erection against her belly.

'You are disgusting!' she hissed.

'Mmm. That's what you said to me all those years ago when I tried to seduce you,' he said. 'Before you met *him*.'

It was something Gonca had put out of her mind. When her second husband had left her, just after Rambo had been born, a twenty-something Şevket Sesler had visited her house in Balat. She had sent him away. Then she'd met Mehmet, and Sesler had never returned.

She spat in his face as she broke away from him. Weirdly, he laughed.

'What's this good news?' she asked. 'You've found Ceviz? You know she has a boyfriend? Hüseyin Bey didn't know that, but her little sister followed me. She told me there's a boy, but she doesn't know who.'

'Oh, Ceviz be damned,' Sesler said. 'I've just been told that the eldest spawn of Esat Böcek was arrested last night for murder – by your husband.'

Gonca knew that the Böcek family controlled much of the illegal business on the Asian side of the Bosphorus, but she'd had no idea that Mehmet had arrested one of them.

'News to me,' she said.

51

'Not covered by pillow talk?'

'Mehmet Efendi is a professional,' she said. 'He tells me nothing.' Nervously she moved closer to him again, 'And remember, Şevket Bey, it will only take one word from my old friend Çetin İkmen to get that vile thing you harbour taken away from you.'

Sesler said nothing. She was referring to one of his most trusted henchmen, a man called Munir Can. Earlier in the year, İkmen had discovered that this man was planning to marry an underage girl. If Can went ahead, İkmen would report him; ditto if his boss ever tried to use Gonca to get to her husband.

'So no, I know nothing,' Gonca continued. She began to make her way back up the stairs. 'Anyway, who has the Böcek boy murdered?'

Sesler shrugged. 'Don't know and I don't care,' he said.

Sinem Gürsel talked to İkmen for only a short time before her pain medication overtook her and she had to go back to bed. Melda, who was still asleep, went with her, leaving İkmen and Edith alone.

As soon as they had gone, Edith said, 'So I reiterate, what do you want, İkmen?'

He sighed. 'Mehmet Bey was called out last night, something on the Asian side? I thought Kerim Bey . . .'

'I imagine he knows now,' Edith said. 'He's gone to work. But Tarlabaşı knew all this a couple of hours ago.'

'Knew what?' İkmen asked.

'That Mehmet Efendi had arrested Esat Böcek's son Ateş at the boy's palace just off Baghdat Caddesi. It's said that Şevket Bey has been laughing about it all morning. Not that he's immune from similar incidents when it comes to his own son,' Edith added. 'His Selami is a little bastard. But of course he's very happy that one of his rivals should fall from grace like this. And Ateş Böcek is like all these gangsters' kids, a complete waste of space.'

İkmen frowned. 'Mehmet arrested him for what?'

'Murder,' Edith said. 'Apparently whoever they found in Ateş's palace was barely recognisable as a human being.'

After İkmen left the Gürsel apartment, he wandered back into Beyoğlu and settled himself down at the open-air tea garden and café on Hazzopulo Pasaj. It wasn't really the weather to be outside, and he had to scrape snow off the table and chair he chose to use. But he wasn't prepared not to smoke, because he needed to think. A waiter in a greatcoat ventured across the slippery cobbles and took his order for coffee – Turkish, very sweet.

A few years back, when he'd still been in the police, İkmen and his then sergeant, Kerim Gürsel, had arrested Esat Böcek on suspicion of a domestic violence offence against his wife. The poor woman had presented at the Memorial Hospital in Ataşehir with horrific injuries, including a ruptured spleen that had subsequently caused her death. Böcek had denied he'd ever raised a hand to her and no solid evidence to support her case had been recovered. But both İkmen and Gürsel had been convinced of his guilt. One chilling memory of Böcek's elderly covered mother smirking at them had stayed with İkmen ever since. A crime family was a crime family however they signalled to people about their supposed morality.

His coffee had just arrived when his phone rang. The call was from a number he didn't recognise.

'Hello?' he said through a lungful of smoke.

'Oh, Çetin Bey, I am sorry to disturb you. It's Peri Mungun,' a deep female voice said.

Ömer Mungun's sister.

'Peri Hanım. How lovely to hear from you.'

They hadn't seen each other since Süleyman's wedding back in October.

'As I say, I am sorry to disturb you, but I need to speak to someone I trust.'

İkmen looked at his watch. It was 12.30 and he had to be at Saint-Antoine by one.

'I have an appointment soon, Peri Hanım,' he said, 'but if later . . .'

'I'm on night shift,' she said. 'Çetin Bey, it's not urgent. But maybe tomorrow on my way home I could meet you in Sultanahmet?'

'Is Sultanahmet on your way home?'

'It can be,' she said.

'What time do you finish work?'

'Six a.m., but by the time I've done my handover, I usually don't get away until seven. I can be in Sultanahmet by seven thirty, if that's not too early . . .'

'Not at all,' he said. 'Why don't we meet at Çiğdem? My treat.'

'No!'

'Yes,' he said. 'Those are my terms, Peri Hanım.'

She laughed. Çiğdem was a pastane, or pastry shop, on Divan Yolu, which was only a short walk from the İkmen apartment. Everyone who knew him was aware of how much İkmen enjoyed their chocolate eclairs.

She said, 'OK, I give in, and thank you.'

'See you tomorrow,' he said, and ended the call.

Quite what Nurse Peri could want to talk to him about, İkmen couldn't imagine.

Gonca had got out of the shower and wrapped a towel around her body. When she went into the bedroom, she found her husband there.

'Mehmet? I thought you'd be at work,' she said.

'I was sent home.' He showed her his bandaged wrist.

'Baby, what happened?' she asked as she walked up to him and kissed his lips.

'I was bitten,' he said, 'by a suspect.'

'Oh . . .'

'Don't worry, it's not bad and the doctor gave me all the requisite shots. What are you doing? Have you only just got up?'

'No,' she said. 'I had to go over to Tarlabaşı to see Şevket Bey about the celebrations tomorrow. I got covered in snow waiting for a taxi home and needed a shower to warm myself up.'

'I see our guests are practising for Sesler's birthday.' He'd heard flamenco music even before he'd opened the front door, and then he'd seen them playing and dancing in his salon. They hadn't seen him, so he'd just left them to get on and walked up to his bedroom.

'It's too cold outside,' Gonca said.

He sat on the bed. 'It's OK.'

She made to sit down beside him, but he pulled her onto his lap and kissed one of her naked shoulders. 'You look beautiful.'

She stroked his hair. 'Mehmet,' she said, 'is it true that you arrested Ateş Böcek last night?'

He pulled away from her a little and frowned. 'Where did you hear that?' he asked.

'Tarlabaşı is buzzing with it,' she said. 'Of course Şevket Bey is delighted that one of his rivals is having trouble – if he is. Is it true?'

He put his arms around her. 'I have to trust you not to confirm—'

'I won't!'

He kissed her again. 'Yes, I did arrest Ateş Böcek last night.'

'For murder?'

'Oh the Roma teyzes know that too, do they?' he said. A teyze, or auntie, was shorthand for a neighbourhood gossip.

'You know what they're like.' She kissed him back.

'And what are they saying about the victim?' he asked.

'Nothing. Just that whoever it was had been cut to pieces.'

'Mmm.'

'Well, Mehmet?' she said. 'Is it true?'

He shrugged. 'It wasn't pleasant,' he said. 'Between me and you.'

She cradled his face. 'I knew something had upset you last night.'

'Your love always makes me better,' he replied.

Gonca pulled her towel off and dropped it on the floor. He took her breasts in his hands and kissed them. She felt instantly aroused, unlike the revulsion she'd experienced when Sesler had touched her. That was why she'd had to shower as soon as she'd got home, to get the stench of that pig off her body. But then in spite of her husband's caresses, a thought occurred to her, and she said, 'Mehmet, do you know whether the victim is male or female?'

He sighed, a little shakily. He was aroused too and didn't want too much more talking.

'Er, female,' he said as he licked the side of her face. 'According to Dr Sarkissian.'

Now that was interesting, and worrying. But Gonca was nothing if not a pragmatic woman, so she decided to leave any further musing on this subject until after they'd made love.

Kerim Gürsel looked down into the car park behind his office and watched Esat Böcek and his mother get into a brand-new Range Rover. A weirdly uniformed flunky opened one of the back doors for the old woman and then helped his boss climb into the passenger seat.

He said, 'When I see sights like that, I wonder how I will be able to look my daughter in the eye as she grows up and tell her honestly that crime doesn't pay. When I live in Tarlabaşı while people like that have palaces and high-end apartments.'

Ömer Mungun, who together with Kerim's sergeant, Eylul Yavaş, was also looking out of the window, said, 'I don't know. Maybe tell her that shit always rises to the top.'

They all laughed, then went and sat back down, Kerim behind

56

his desk, Ömer and Eylul in front of him. After a moment of silence, Kerim opened the window behind him and lit a cigarette. Eylul, who was accustomed to his habits, locked his office door. It was illegal to smoke in enclosed spaces, but Kerim and Mehmet Süleyman frequently flouted this rule – as had İkmen.

'So what did you think of the Böcek family?' Kerim asked his colleagues.

Esat Böcek, his nineteen-year-old son İlhan, and his elderly mother Neşe, had come to headquarters not only to provide a character reference for Esat's older boy, but also with the real expectation that they would be able to get him out. The old woman had been the worst, shouting her mouth off about her rights.

Ömer said, 'The old falcı was a bit of a challenge.'

Kerim shook his head. 'Neşe Hanım,' he said. 'Part tiger, part witch. I remember when Çetin Bey and I arrested Esat for assaulting his wife, old Neşe came flying down the staircase of the couple's yalı, cursing us, her hands raised to claw out our eyes.'

'And they're supposed to be pious?' Eylul asked. One of a relatively recent intake of graduate police officers, Eylul Yavaş was a pious Muslim who covered her head and prayed five times a day.

'Yes, Sergeant,' Kerim said, 'they are pious gangsters, as opposed to Şevket Sesler and his Roma and Murad Ayhan and his secular gang. All criminal tastes catered for in this city.'

'No one, as far as we can tell, was in the Şehzade Rafık Palace with Ateş Böcek last night, except the victim,' Eylul said. 'So the family's contention that he is innocent . . .'

'Is rubbish,' Kerim said. 'But then this is standard stuff when dealing with family members. The accused is always a "good boy" or "misunderstood" or even the victim of some conspiracy so Byzantine it makes your head hurt.'

'He's got a record, Ateş Böcek,' Ömer said. 'Nothing much – speeding, bit of possession . . .'

'Possession of what?' Kerim asked.

'Cannabis. Hardly crime of the century, Kerim Bey.'

'Look, I'm not excusing his behaviour, especially after his attack on Dr Doksanaltı and Mehmet Bey, but while Ateş may not be "misunderstood", he has to be a troubled young man,' Eylul said. 'Whether or not he killed our victim, he inflicted some serious damage on the doctor particularly. I mean, what sane person bites like that?'

'I accept your thesis,' Kerim said. 'But difficult though it may be to accept, clinically sane people can do some dreadful things. It's hard to rationalise sometimes, as we all prefer to think it's only the mad who do this stuff. But it isn't.'

His phone rang and he excused himself so he could take the call. Eylul and Ömer heard him say, 'All right, send him up to my office.'

After he ended the call, Kerim said, 'Apparently Ateş Böcek's brother wants to talk to us.'

'But he's only just been in, with his father and grandmother,' Eylul said.

'Seems he now wants to speak to us without them,' Kerim replied.

Chapter 5

'Darling, if the dead woman is Ceviz . . .'

'We don't know that, Gonca,' Mehmet Süleyman told his wife. 'And I must impress upon you that you mustn't say anything to anyone about this.'

'I won't!'

'Because the last thing we need is for Sesler to find out and start some sort of vendetta with the Böcek family.'

'Yes, but—'

He put a finger to his lips just as Gonca's son Rambo entered the kitchen.

Sitting himself down at the breakfast table next to his step-father, the boy addressed his mother.

'What time are we going over to Tarlabaşı?'

'Not until three,' she said. 'Will you go outside and tell Tomas that I've made breakfast?'

'OK.' The boy left.

Gonca put a large slice of menemen, a scrambled egg dish with tomato, garlic, onion and peppers, in front of her husband. 'I'll have to stay with the Cortes troupe, so I don't know what time I'll be home tonight. You know what Şevket Bey's like. If the men aren't all fighting drunk, he'll consider his birthday a failure.'

'Will Rambo bring you home?'

'Yes,' she said. 'Provided he's not out of his mind too.'

Mehmet sipped his coffee and then forked some menemen into his mouth. Gonca had told him that the Roma lap dancer

59

Ceviz Elibol was missing. He was concerned, but didn't tell her that.

'I'll come and get you,' he said.

'You won't!'

'Why not? I'll ring you first and we'll agree to meet somewhere well away from the festivities.'

'If Şevket Bey sees you, he'll laugh at you, call you a hen-pecked husband. You know what he's like,' she said.

'And I don't care.' Mehmet pushed his breakfast to one side and lit a cigarette.

Gonca sat down beside him. 'Baby, don't you like my menemen?' she asked as she stroked his face.

He took her hand and kissed it. 'I love it,' he said. 'But there's too much and I can't afford to put on weight, you know that.'

'But you're perfect!'

He laughed. 'I'm not . . .'

'You are!'

'Well, anyway,' he said, 'I mustn't put on weight or it will affect my ability to do my job. Besides, you don't want to be married to some fat old man who almost collapses when he tries to please you in bed.'

She smiled. There was no way he was fat but, like Çetin İkmen, he was inclined to substitute cigarettes for food, and even though she smoked herself, Gonca knew that wasn't good.

Rambo came in from the garden with the Spaniards in tow. Amazingly, considering that they'd slept outside in a tent, they all looked rested and fresh, even the pregnant Lola. Süleyman nodded to them in greeting, then addressed Tomas in English. 'You are Tomas, I am told. I am Mehmet, Gonca Hanım's husband.'

The young man smiled. 'Yes, sir,' he said. 'You are a police officer.'

'I am.'

The doorbell rang and Gonca sent Rambo to answer it. She

served their guests their breakfast while Mehmet explained the food to Tomas.

Rambo returned with Kerim Gürsel in tow. He said to Mehmet, 'He wants to talk to you on your own.'

Mehmet stood. 'Let's go through to the salon, Kerim Bey.'

'I don't know what to do,' Peri Mungun said.

She was sitting opposite Çetin İkmen at a small table outside the Çiğdem pastane, eating a chocolate eclair and drinking sahlep, a hot, milky drink made with orchid root. İkmen had the same, but he was also smoking.

'I've known arranged marriages like your brother's to work,' İkmen said. 'But I have to say it was never for me, and luckily, my father concurred.'

'And your children?' Peri asked.

'Oh no,' he said. 'My wife did go through a phase when she thought it might be a good idea to arrange our daughters' marriages, but that never went anywhere. I objected, and my girls were always too headstrong to agree to anything like that. Both Çiçek and Hülya married Jews, Hande's husband is Kurdish, and Selim, my oldest boy, is married to an Englishwoman. All very happy except for Çiçek, who is divorced, but these things happen. Peri Hanım, I know that people who worship as you do are few now . . .'

'We are in the hundreds only,' she said.

'. . . so I understand that your parents and Yeşili's parents made this match for very good reasons.'

'Ömer is not religious,' Peri said. 'It's not easy being away from the Tür Abdin. Of course, the goddess lives in our hearts, but . . .'

The Tür Abdin, or Slaves of God region – so called on account of all the Christian monasteries that existed there – was in Turkey's far south-east, on the border with Syria. It was where the last worshippers of the Şahmeran lived.

'I will be honest, I don't know what to advise,' İkmen said. 'Ömer Bey is married now.'

'But he's so unhappy, and so is Yeşili,' Peri said. 'She cries every day. She told me she doesn't please my brother.'

'How is he with her when you are all together?'

'Indifferent,' she said. 'They don't sit together in the evening, even on the few occasions he comes home before midnight.'

'Is he working all that time?'

'I imagine so.' She leaned towards him. 'Before his marriage, Ömer had a lot of affairs, mainly with older women. I sometimes wonder whether he's still doing that. At the wedding, he was moaning to me about "marrying a kid". She's eighteen and I thought that was what most men wanted, a young bride. Am I wrong?'

'Yes and no,' İkmen said. 'The young, beautiful virgin bride is the acceptable trope, but the older, wilder, experienced woman is also a fantasy too. Look at Gonca Hanım.'

'I think that may be part of the problem,' Peri said. 'You know that my brother both admires and resents Mehmet Bey. He calls him the "perfect detective" because he is so relentless and passionate about the job. But then his success with women makes Ömer angry. I think he feels that if Mehmet Bey is in a room with him, he just sort of disappears. And when Mehmet Bey married Gonca Hanım, he was genuinely pleased for him, but jealous too.'

'Of Gonca Hanım?'

'She is his type of woman,' Peri said. 'Generous and bold, mysterious. From the way he speaks about her and the way I've caught him looking at her, I know he desires her.' She took one of İkmen's hands. 'Çetin Bey, I have told no one else about this. I'm sorry I had to speak to you, but I honestly don't know what to do! Yeşili is so unhappy, and so is my brother!'

*

Gonca Süleyman's salon was as colourful and ornate as her clothes. Decorated by the artist herself, it was in no way a reflection of her husband's more restrained tastes. But then as he was always the first to admit, the old Greek house in Balat that they shared was owned by his wife.

'So what did İlhan Böcek say about this woman?' Süleyman asked Kerim Gürsel after he had lit his guest's cigarette and provided him with an ashtray.

'He said his brother went with a lot of women,' Kerim said. 'Apparently Esat Böcek was aware of Ateş's promiscuity, even though he himself made the boy sound like a saint. But according to İlhan, his father didn't know about this Roma girl. Had he done so, he would have lost his mind.'

'But İlhan didn't name this girl?' Süleyman asked.

'Said he didn't know what she was called.'

'Mmm.' Süleyman leaned back in his over-stuffed sofa.

'I thought you needed to know before we go any further,' Kerim added.

'You're right,' Süleyman said. Then he sat forward again and lowered his voice. 'Gonca has told me that a Roma girl called Ceviz Elibol has been missing for at least two days. She's a lap dancer at Şevket Sesler's Kızlar club.'

'God! Does Gonca Hanım know that you're involved with the Böcek case?'

'Yes,' he said, 'but she has sworn to me she will say nothing. I told her that if our victim does turn out to be this gypsy girl, we will have to handle both Esat Böcek and Şevket Sesler with firm yet delicate hands.'

'I dread to think!' Kerim said. 'The gypsies on the one hand, the puritans on the other . . .'

'How did you leave things with Esat Böcek last night?' Süleyman asked.

'I'd spoken to Dr Sarkissian by that time and he'd told me that you and Ömer Bey are attending today's post-mortem. I'm due at Esat Böcek's penthouse at ten,' Kerim said. 'Ateş apparently kept a room there.'

'They will have removed anything incriminating.'

'I know, but Esat Bey and his mother don't strike me as technical types. Ateş is the exact opposite, it seems. Scene of crime have removed multiple machines from the Şehzade Rafık Palace. I wonder whether he also had some back at home. On the basis that a good place to hide incriminating material might be at his technophobe father's place. Not that the boy is exactly exhibiting much in the way of critical thinking at the moment.'

'Still silent?'

'Completely. I should also tell you that the psychiatrist is staying in hospital, at least for today.'

'Yes, I received an email about it,' Süleyman said. 'I've to meet with a Dr Koca at one o'clock to discuss how we might take the psych assessment forward.'

'It's probably for the best, Mehmet Bey. I mean, I know I wasn't there, but talking to Ömer Bey about it last night, it does seem possible that Böcek took against the doctor.'

'No,' Süleyman said. 'At least I don't think that's the whole story. I woke early and replayed it over in my mind. Hopefully not projecting what Gonca told me about this missing Roma girl, I seem to recall that Ateş Böcek lost control when Doksanaltı alluded to visiting gypsy girls in his youth.'

'Really?'

'I'll need to play the recording back to be sure. However . . .'

'If that's the case and if indeed Ateş Böcek has killed one of Şevket Sesler's girls, then we could be in what Çetin Bey always called a world of shit.' Kerim lowered his voice. 'I take it Gonca Hanım is attending the festivities this evening?'

Kerim and his family lived in Tarlabaşı, on the same street where Sesler's party was due to take place. This was also where

Gonca's brother had his meyhane. The Gürsels, like many of the families in the area, were bracing for a night of little sleep.

'What choice does she have?' Süleyman asked. 'When we married, it was on condition that we live our own lives. We're adults. She's Roma, and I love that about her. I love everything about her and I will not deny her her own culture; it means too much. But I don't like or trust Sesler, and Gonca knows it.'

'The price we pay for love, eh, Mehmet Bey?'

Süleyman smiled. It had in part been Kerim Gürsel who had given him the courage to finally propose marriage to Gonca Şekeroğlu. Although married to Sinem and the father of her child, Kerim was in reality homosexual. It had been in the wake of his lover Pembe's death that he had urged his colleague to cling fast to those he loved.

Süleyman said, 'Is three p.m. convenient for you and Sergeant Yavaş to go over scene-of-crime evidence so far?'

'Yes. Mehmet Bey, what about CCTV?'

He sighed. 'Inoperative in and around the palace. I really don't know why so many of the rich and famous have it; they almost always never use it. But apparently we do have some recordings from one of the apartment blocks over the back.' He stood. 'Anyway, I must prepare myself and Ömer Bey for this post-mortem. Dr Sarkissian, who as we know has the strongest stomach in this city, has warned me that today's event may be "challenging".'

There had been a lot to think about trudging down the sometimes icy, sometimes slushy road to Eminönü. Pressing his back hard against warm bakery shop windows while trams clanged past, almost plucking the buttons off his coat, Çetin İkmen wondered whether Gonca Süleyman was aware of how Ömer Mungun felt about her. She was usually very sensitive to such developments – men had desired her almost all her life. But she was newly married and ragingly in love with her husband, and so it would make sense if Ömer's attentions had passed her by.

As he crossed the road bridge over Kennedy Caddesi, stopping only to catch his breath and give a beggar boy two lira for a packet of tissues, he wondered whether he should tell her. On the one hand, were she warned, she would be prepared for any potentially awkward moments. On the other, if her husband found out, he would go berserk. On balance, İkmen thought, it was best not to mention any of this to the Süleymans. Rather, he would probably need to speak to Ömer Mungun, and that did not fill him with joy.

Wearily he approached Numan Bey, who took what had become İkmen's stool off his cart and put it down on the ground.

'Come! Sit, Çetin Bey!' the old man said as İkmen slumped onto the low stool and lit a cigarette. Numan Bey gave him a glass of pickle juice, which he downed in one.

Once he was able to speak again, he said, 'Thank you, Numan Bey. Were it not for you, I would have given up this mad pursuit a long time ago.'

The old man gave him another glass of juice. 'You had Christmas dinner at Saint-Antoine yesterday. Was it good?'

'It was,' İkmen said. 'You know, Numan Bey, the Mexicans have a very interesting cuisine. Very hot, a little bit Spanish, a lot of it very unusual to me, native South American dishes. At Christmas, they put alcohol, tequila I think, in their hot chocolate. And loving both chocolate and alcohol as I do, I had rather a lot.'

Numan Bey refreshed İkmen's pickle-juice glass. 'Two more glasses and the headache will go.'

İkmen smiled and drank on.

'So are you going to Şevket the gypsy's birthday party this evening, Çetin Bey?' the old man asked. 'Dancing in the street, I hear, and that meyhane Gonca Hanım's brother runs open all night. All drinks, it is said, on the great man himself.'

'I know the Roma have a bad reputation in some quarters, but I

66

like them,' İkmen said. 'I grew up with them and so I know they have to struggle just to survive. I admire that, even if I have no time for Şevket Bey. He does his people no favours with his protection rackets and his thinly disguised whorehouses. It will be cold, which I don't enjoy, but I'll go for Gonca Hanım's sake, and I'd like to see her Spanish friends dance.'

'Not Mehmet Efendi, though?'

'No,' he said.

Numan Bey shook his head. 'You know, Çetin Bey, how this city shifts?'

İkmen knew that the old man wasn't alluding to the occasional earthquake that shook İstanbul from time to time. Like him, Numan Bey was a keen observer of the subtle everyday variations in the underlying ancient power that coursed through the city. Some called it magic, others the whims of a place where time was mobile and thin, where things could and did break through the fabric of the modern city, turning corners of it on its head.

'What is troubling you, Numan Bey?' İkmen asked.

The old man sighed and gave İkmen yet another glass of pickle juice.

'Mehmet Efendi has arrested the Böcek boy, Ateş,' he said. He pulled another small plastic stool off his cart and sat down next to İkmen. 'I know I can talk to you about these things, and only you, Çetin Bey. Esat Böcek is as powerful as the gypsy, Sesler – probably more so. Then there is Murad Ayhan and his nationalist mob. I go to see a falcı, a woman who works out of her apartment near my home. She's Roma, I trust her.'

İkmen narrowed his eyes. Now he was in the world of his mother, the Albanian witch Ayşe, and it made him feel elated. He had known that Mehmet had been called out to what everyone was saying was a hideous incident in Kadıköy. He also knew that Ateş Böcek was implicated. But those were only the bare facts.

67

Now it seemed that someone possibly in touch with the unseen webs of the city was on the case too. If they were genuine . . .

'And so . . .'

'And so it's not real,' Numan Bey said.

'What isn't?'

'Çetin Bey, this death will cause terrible suffering.'

'How?'

'I don't know! But what my falcı told me is that it's not real.'

'You mean the death of whomever has been killed isn't real?' İkmen asked.

The old man shrugged. 'I don't know,' he repeated. 'Maybe. It's difficult to question her sometimes. She's goes into a sort of trance. But she's worried, and that doesn't happen. Also, it's the first time she's ever talked to me about things that don't just involve me. This death in Kadıköy will affect us all, Çetin Bey!'

Even though he knew that Çetin İkmen believed, on some level, in this sort of thing, Kerim Gürsel couldn't get away from the idea that old Neşe Böcek's use of a scrying bowl in his presence was part of a mind game designed to unsettle him. As it happened, it didn't. Let the old woman mumble away to herself in her son's vast atrium above Baghdat Caddesi; he was only really interested in what had been Ateş's room.

A little servant girl watched as he and his sergeant, Eylul Yavaş, opened drawers and looked in cupboards. This, apparently one of the minor bedrooms, was almost as large as Kerim's whole apartment, and so it wasn't a job that was going to take five minutes.

When they had arrived and been led into the apartment's central atrium, Kerim had noticed how Neşe Hanım had treated them differently. He she had ignored, while she'd given a great beaming smile to Eylul. Probably because his sergeant was another woman and, no less, one who chose to cover. He wondered how shocked the old woman would be to learn how thoroughly Eylul was not taken in by any notion of 'sisterhood' amongst those she was investigating.

He opened a drawer in a 'distressed' old filing cabinet – very chic, very now – and was confronted by many packets of condoms and boxes of Viagra tablets.

He turned to his colleague. 'Come and look at this, Sergeant.'

Eylul walked over and looked in the drawer. 'Do you think he was dealing, sir?'

'In Viagra? You can buy that from the pharmacist,' Kerim said. 'Ateş Böcek's only in his twenties. I can't see he would have a problem . . .'

'Maybe they actually belong to his father,' Eylul said. 'Maybe Esat hid them in here so we wouldn't find them in his room. Not that we can ask him. Wasn't Esat Bey meant to be here during the search, sir?'

'Yes, he was.' Kerim looked at the tablets again. 'Maybe Ateş likes the rush I hear one can get off Viagra,' he said.

Although a lot of men were rather nervous about talking about sex and death around a covered woman, in the case of Eylul Yavaş frank conversations were part of her reality. And she was happy about that. Although by choice she covered her head, she had never wanted the men she worked with to treat her differently. It had taken some time to school them, but she'd now reached the stage where they spoke about anything with and in front of her.

Eylul returned to the wardrobe she had been going through. Kerim bagged up the Viagra and the condoms. She could be right about them belonging to Esat Böcek. When his son had been arrested, there had been no sign of Viagra in his system. Just industrial quantities of coke.

'Sir,' Eylul said, 'come and look at this.'

She was holding up a rather old, slightly worn-looking tablet computer.

*

'However I choose to talk about this, I always come back to the jigsaw puzzle analogy,' Dr Sarkissian said.

He was standing behind a mortuary table upon which, covered by a sheet, was the body of the unknown woman who had been found in the Şehzade Rafık Palace. In front of him, at the end of the table, Mehmet Süleyman and Ömer Mungun wore protective suits and face masks.

'I don't know whether that makes it better or worse . . .'

'Doctor, let's just get on with it, shall we?' Süleyman said.

One of the mortuary assistants, a man, pulled the sheet off the body, and Süleyman heard Ömer Mungun gag. Süleyman himself was grateful he'd had the presence of mind to eat as little breakfast as he could get away with that morning. What there was, clearly, wanted out, together with the coffee he had drunk.

What the two men found themselves looking at was a roughly human-shaped patchwork of skin, tendons, fat and blood. Whether the flayed and butchered body was actually underneath this patchwork seemed unlikely, as the whole assemblage appeared to be flat.

'Doctor . . .'

'I've laid out essentially the skin, in a manner experience tells me is probably correct,' the Armenian said. 'As you can see, gentlemen, the subject was essentially flayed – as well as savaged internally. You have probably worked out that the rest of this unfortunate woman is currently in the anteroom. We will come to her shortly. However, while I know that viewing a corpse under these circumstances does make identification well-nigh impossible, I should like to draw your attention to the face, just here.'

He pointed to something at his end of the table and the two men walked over to look at what he was indicating. Provided Süleyman kept in mind that it was simply meat, he could manage. Ömer too was holding up, although what could be seen of his face had noticeably paled.

70

The section the doctor was pointing at consisted of holes where the eyes should have been, nostrils again consisting only of holes, and then, very strangely, a plump, full pair of lips. It was probably the most shocking thing either of the officers had ever seen.

'As you can see, gentlemen, the lips alone have been removed intact. I am loath to speculate about the motive for this, and so I will leave any conjecture to you and your psychiatric consultants,' the doctor said. 'I believe the subject was killed by exsanguination prior to the removal of the skin, but the mutilation of a corpse on this scale is unprecedented in my practice of almost forty years. I also have to tell you that while the yataghan recovered at the scene may well have killed the subject, it was not used to skin her. I know it may seem like a terrible mess to you gentlemen, but I can tell you that what has been done here was done with a lot of skill.'

Chapter 6

Aylın's right eye was blood-shot, plus the entire area around it was black, purple and swollen. Not even her mother alluded to it, because everyone knew that her father Murad was still angry with her. Not that Aylın thought her mother would give her any sympathy even if she *had* alluded to it. Her mother only had eyes for her younger brother Yıldırım, a silly little nineteen-year-old gay boy – although no one, least of all Yıldırım, ever said it.

Aylın sat down next to her mother Irmak who, with Yıldırım, was watching some dizi soap opera on TV. 'I want to go out. Esma has asked me over.'

'You can't. Your father has forbidden it. If he won't let you attend the party tonight, what makes you think he'll let you out now?'

'I can go to Esma's house through the back gate,' Aylın said. 'Anyway, Daddy's out.'

'And he pays for everything, so he gets to say who comes and who goes,' her mother said, without once taking her eyes away from the television.

'Don't you at least think I should see Dr Sezer?' she asked. 'I mean, my eye really hurts.'

'Dr Sezer is on holiday,' her mother said. 'He's a Christian.'

Yıldırım, who had been silent up until then, said, 'Can you both be quiet, please? I'm trying to find out whether Defne has eloped with that simit boy.'

It was hopeless. Aylın left her parents' enormous, over-stuffed salon and went up to her bedroom. She could, if she wanted to, just creep out into the back garden and open the gate that led to Esma's house, and soon she'd be watching her friend's sexy big brothers swimming in their indoor pool. Her mother and brother wouldn't notice! But what if her father came home suddenly? If he found she'd gone out, he'd lose his mind.

Where her father had gone, Aylın didn't know. All her mother would say was 'out'. Logically, he'd probably left the house to go and pick up his costume for the party later on in the evening. But Aylın didn't trust him. In spite of his supposed love for Ataturk and the Republic and modernity, she had a notion that he was quietly arranging her marriage. Hypocrite! That was what all the crazy Islamist families did, and she knew he hated them. But just lately, he had started alluding to her single status as something of an embarrassment. *All* his friends' daughters were getting married, so he said.

Well, Aylın wasn't going to do that, no way. If her father thought he could palm her off on some rich, ugly type, he could think again. She watched the dizis with her mother and brother; she knew what happened. But where, she thought, was the handsome prince disguised as a humble simit seller who would come to save her?

The tablet had been stuffed behind a load of battered shoes at the back of the wardrobe. However, unlike the footwear, the tablet, though old, wasn't dusty.

Eylul switched it on. Of course, it was password protected, and while she suspected that if the machine did belong to Ateş, that password was simple, she took Kerim Gürsel's advice and just bagged it up ready for the technical team to play with.

Unlike Ateş's ornate palace, Esat Böcek's apartment was cool and understated. And while his mother's room was somewhat more colourful, adorned as it was with boncuk beads, horse's tails and other more rural artefacts, the master of the house seemed to prefer cleaner lines – as did the son who lived here, Ateş's younger brother İlhan.

When Esat Böcek had been interviewed at headquarters, he had alluded to the fact that the mother of his boys had died over a decade ago. He and his mother had laid it on thick about how they had struggled to bring the boys up to be decent, clean-living Muslims. This seemed to be true of İlhan, but not of Ateş. But that was according to İlhan, and was he telling the truth, or was his father? From the evidence gathered from Ateş's home so far, it appeared that the father was the one who was lying.

'Where is he?' Gonca asked.

'Why?'

Her youngest brother, confusingly, had the same name as her youngest son. The tenant landlord of a meyhane on Tarlabaşı's Emin Cami Sokak, Rambo Şekeroğlu senior had been given the task of providing free beer for all of Şevket Sesler's many guests, and so he was busy filling up his bar. The idea was that Sesler would pay for whatever was consumed later – if Rambo was lucky.

'Why?' she echoed. 'Because I want to introduce him to the Cortes flamenco dancers. The best Roma flamenco dancers in the world! They've come all the way from Seville to perform for that pig, and he hasn't even got the good manners to be here!'

She smiled at the Spaniards. Tomas was in conversation with Rambo junior, who was apologising profusely.

'Everything is happening as it should whether he's here or not,' her brother said. 'Selma Hanım and our Didim are cooking the soup over at the Kızlar . . .' Selma Hanım was Şevket Sesler's wife, and Didim was Rambo senior and Gonca's older sister.

'And meanwhile I bring my dancers to a cold meyhane peopled by confused magicians, fire eaters and stilt walkers!' Gonca said.

Rambo senior shrugged. 'Up to them if they decide to turn up early.'

And she knew that in a sense he was right. But it was freezing out, and at least half of them had arrived in the expectation of getting some of the free food that was to be on offer. Most of them were Roma and so were probably in need of a decent meal.

'Anyway,' Gonca continued, 'I don't trust Sesler when he's away from Tarlabaşı. What's he up to?'

'I don't know,' her brother said. 'Why would I?'

Gonca lit a cigarette. 'Rambo, darling, do you think I could at least trouble you for drinks for my guests?'

'You paying?'

'No, put it on Sesler's bill. Señor Juan likes his brandy. I'll ask the boy to enquire about Tomas and Lola.'

She told her son to ask what they wanted to drink, and received the reply, 'Red wine.'

Once the Spaniards had been given their drinks, Gonca leaned across the bar and helped herself to a large measure of brandy, then downed it in one gulp.

'And you can put that on Sesler's bill too, my brother. That bastard is so rude!'

While Dr Sarkissian spoke into the voice recorder held by the mortuary assistant, Süleyman and Ömer Mungun stared at the body partly exposed on the table in front of them. A meat-covered skeleton, its vast exposed eyes bulging out of a face that was butchered and lipless. For Ömer, trying not to vomit took up every gram of his concentration, while Süleyman's mind engaged and then disengaged with the doctor's commentary in line with how light headed he felt.

The first time he'd seen this corpse, *in situ*, it had embossed itself onto his mind. Whatever he did, he couldn't get rid of it. Even when he was with Gonca, it wouldn't leave him.

The doctor said, 'I am awaiting toxicology results, but you might like to know, Inspector, that your suspect has tested positive for cocaine.'

'Mmm.' He had heard that. Scene of crime had also found cocaine powder on the bedcovers underneath the body.

'She's young,' Dr Sarkissian continued. 'I would say late teens, early twenties.'

This was consistent with what Süleyman knew about the missing Roma girl, Ceviz Elibol. He said, 'Ethnicity?'

'Not yet,' the doctor said. 'DNA evidence takes its own sweet time. Why?'

'Anecdotally, a young Roma girl is missing,' Süleyman said.

Ömer Mungun looked up at him. 'Boss, no one—'

'No one connected to Gonca Hanım, no,' he said.

The doctor turned to a large kidney bowl on his right. 'Internal organs collected from around the bed on which the subject lay include the right lobe of the liver, the gall bladder, the left kidney, plus approximately a metre of intestinal tissue, to wit, a section of the ileum.'

Why had whoever had killed her done such catastrophic damage to her body? Why remove seemingly random pieces of internal organs? Her death had been caused by exsanguination. Had her killer done this to her as she lay dying? When had he flayed her skin?

'What killed her was the severing of both left and right carotid arteries,' the pathologist continued. 'This I believe was performed with the yataghan blade discovered on the person of the principal suspect. Death would have occurred in four minutes or less. It is my contention that mutilation of the corpse – internal organ removal, flaying of the skin – occurred post-mortem. This was achieved in my opinion not by using the yataghan but by employing the services of a fine scalpel blade. That said, the removal of the organs was roughly and poorly executed,

76

apparently targeting random structures. The flaying, however, was most expertly performed, demonstrating a steady and unhurried cutting technique. It would have taken whoever did it many hours.'

Süleyman said, 'So how long do you think this woman had been dead when we discovered her?'

'My estimate is between eight and ten hours.'

'So she was killed in the morning?'

'Yes.' The doctor frowned. 'Which I imagine may complicate things still further with regard to your investigation, Inspector.'

'There's shit all over the floor, Sergeant.'

Custody Sergeant Fatıh Asmalı narrowed his eyes. Some of the kids being put on the guard duty roster these days were off the planet. Or rather not in the real world, in Fatıh's opinion.

He looked down at the thin young constable in front of him. 'All over the floor?'

Constable Altay, whose choice of profession as a high school student had included artist and fashion designer, had come to policing not from a place of desire, but from one of poverty. It was a job, one that now appeared to include cleaning up after a madman suspected of murder.

'He just squatted down and did it on the floor in front of me,' Altay said.

'So we're talking one turd?'

'Yeah, but . . . God!'

'Böcek is on half-hour observations.'

'Exactly! What am I going to find next time?'

'Maybe more shit, maybe not; maybe piss, who knows? The only thing that is certain in your life right now, Constable, is that at some point you will have to clean it up.'

'Sergeant, he bit Dr Doksanaltı on the neck!'

'Which means that me and a couple of the other lads'll hold him

77

down while you get the mop and bucket out and clear it up,' the sergeant said.

'Yes, but—'

Asmalı grabbed the boy by his collar. 'Böcek's got another head doctor coming to see him today. With Inspector Süleyman. Now if you want to deal with Mehmet Efendi when he's got shit all over his shiny pointed shoes, then you can leave that turd there, Constable. But it won't end well.'

It was like magic. No sooner had Eylul Yavaş handed Ateş Böcek's password-protected tablet computer over to technical officer Kenan Sağlam – who looked about thirteen – than the whole thing was demystified and she could get in.

Together with Sağlam, she took it back to the office she shared with Kerim Gürsel. When they arrived, Kerim made space on his desk and they all gathered around the small screen.

'Even quite savvy users sometimes employ ridiculously easy passcodes on their systems,' the young man said as he brought up the menu screen. 'What do you want to look at?'

'Is that Twitter?' Kerim asked, pointing at an icon of a blue bird.

'Yes.' Kenan went into Twitter and clicked on Böcek's personal feed. It seemed he tweeted under the name Enver Hoxha.

'Wasn't that the name of the communist dictator of Albania?' Kerim asked.

'Yes,' Eylul said.

'He had two other Twitter accounts,' Kenan said. 'One in the name of Sultan Abdülhamid and the other under Dr Jekyll.'

'Why?' asked Kerim.

'Don't know. Do you have a Twitter account, Inspector Gürsel?'

'No,' he said. 'I'm too old for all that.'

Kenan laughed. 'Where'd you get that idea? Everyone has one. Even the Pope, and he's really old.'

'I hate the subterfuge,' Kerim said. 'People being other people. Hiding.'

'In some cases, yes,' Kenan said. 'But mostly it's about connecting.'

As he scrolled through Böcek's Twitter feed, Eylul said, 'He doesn't add much to the stories he puts up, does he?'

'No. Maybe he thinks they speak for themselves.'

And in a way, they did. Amid many pictures of orchids, Ateş Böcek had retweeted articles from conspiracy sites ranging from theories about the death of JFK to outright racist rants about how the Jewish 'Illuminati' were taking over the world.

'We know he's not exactly stable,' Kerim said.

'Sadly you don't need to be delusional to take this rubbish seriously these days,' the technical officer said. 'Nonsense though it is, this is almost mainstream. So I can't see he would have hidden this machine away because of that. Let's have a look and see whether he's taken any photographs.'

He came out of Twitter and clicked on the icon leading to Böcek's photo gallery. The very first image had all three officers squinting to try to work out what on earth was going on. When Kerim finally realised what it was, he had to squash down an urge to tell Eylul to look away.

There were a lot of cafés on Vodina Caddesi in Balat. In recent years, the old Jewish quarter had been discovered by tourists. But in the winter, there weren't a great many of those in evidence and so not all the cafés were open. An exception was the Byzantium. Not much more than a hole in a wall with some chairs on the pavement, the Byzantium was Mehmet Süleyman's local café now that he lived in Balat.

When the owner, an İstanbul Greek called Belisarius Doukas, saw Süleyman approaching his establishment with Ömer Mungun in tow, he rushed out into the street and yelled, 'Mehmet Efendi!'

Süleyman smiled. 'Belisarius Efendi,' he replied. Then, indicating Ömer, 'This is my colleague, Sergeant Mungun.'

'Ah, you come to introduce your friend to the best Greek coffee in the world.' Belisarius bowed. 'I am flattered, bey efendi!'

Süleyman laughed. What was called by turns both Greek and Turkish coffee was a good-natured bone of contention between them.

Belisarius pulled chairs out for the two men. 'Your usual coffee, Mehmet Efendi?'

'Thank you, yes,' Süleyman said. 'Ömer?'

'Oh, er . . .'

'Turkish coffee,' Süleyman said. 'How do you take it?'

'Greek,' Belisarius put in. 'Greek coffee, efendi.'

Süleyman smiled. 'Ignore my friend, Ömer.'

'Oh, er, very sweet,' Ömer said. 'I think I need . . .' He ran out of words.

Belisarius disappeared into his café.

Süleyman had decided to stop in Balat for coffee in order to give Ömer Mungun a chance to calm down before they returned to headquarters. The post-mortem they had just witnessed had been hard on both of them, but Ömer had struggled with nausea. A tiny cup of strong, sweet Turkish coffee should make him feel better – so said Mehmet's old Armenian nanny when he'd been a child.

'Your friend's a bit . . .' Ömer didn't know what to say. Unlike his superior, he hadn't grown up knowing any Greeks. There weren't any in Mardin as far as he knew.

'Belisarius is more Turkish than he is Greek,' Süleyman said. 'His father I think was the last full Greek in his family. His mother is Turkish. But his father's family are true native Byzantine Greeks, and so Belisarius's ancestors were here long before we were.'

'How d'you know him, boss?'

'Through Gonca Hanım,' he said. 'When she came to live in Balat, Belisarius had just moved into the area too. She reads cards for his mother, I believe.'

'Oh.'

Belisarius arrived with the coffee, which he put down in front of the men with a flourish.

Süleyman said, 'Thank you, my friend.'

He waited until the Greek had gone before he spoke again. 'I've brought you here so we may talk in private for a while, Ömer.'

It was cold, and Ömer pulled his coat tight around his body. There was no way they could go inside, because as he knew only too well, Süleyman had to be able to smoke. But the coffee was very good and it did warm him.

'This morning was tough,' Süleyman said. 'I know I expect a lot from you, Ömer, but that was over and above, and I want to say that I really appreciated your support.'

Süleyman had only been married for just under two months, and already the gossip was that Gonca had softened him. Of course some people thought this was because she had put a spell on him, but Ömer always wondered about their sex life. What did she do to and with him that made him so contented all of a sudden?

He said, 'Thank you, boss. Never seen anything like that before.'

'I hope you never have to again,' Süleyman said. 'Would you like more coffee?'

'Yes please.'

The tiny cups took just seconds to drink, and so Süleyman ordered for them both again. Then he said, 'The other thing I wanted to talk to you about is the amount of work you are doing at the moment, Ömer Bey. I have noticed that you are often still working as I am heading home.'

'Paperwork, boss,' Ömer said.

'Which we all have, but if you are struggling, I should know.

Feel free to ask for help. I am aware of the fact that you, like me, are newly married, and so if I can help you to get your workload under control, I am happy to do so.'

'Thank you, sir.'

'And how is Mrs Mungun settling in to city life? It must be quite different to how her life was in the Tür Abdin.' Yeşili Mungun had not, like Ömer, come from the eastern city of Mardin, but from a village down on the Mesopotamian Plain.

'It is,' Ömer said. 'Her Turkish not being too good doesn't make it easy. But Peri helps her when she can, when she's not working. We don't know many others who speak Aramaic here.'

There was a small Syrian Christian population, who spoke Aramaic, based around the Church of the Virgin Mary in Tarlabaşı, but Ömer wasn't Christian and so he didn't know them well.

'I will ask my wife to invite you both and Peri Hanım to dinner,' Süleyman said. 'I will also invite Inspector Gürsel and Sinem Hanım. Gonca Hanım loves entertaining, and it will give Mrs Mungun a chance to meet the wives of those with whom you work.'

It was a nice idea, born out of genuine concern, Ömer was sure. But the thought of Yeşili coming face to face with Gonca made him feel cold again. A lot of gypsies roamed the Mesopotamian Plain – they always had done – but they only mixed with settled people when they had to, and settled folk, like Yeşili's family, were deeply suspicious of them. They also, in some cases, feared them. Ömer was anxious that with her minimal language skills coupled with her superstitious nature, his wife would embarrass him. Also he would hate to upset Gonca Hanım. He feared her a little bit himself, if he was honest, but he also admired her, probably sometimes too much. But how did he say those things to Süleyman? He didn't.

Instead he smiled and said, 'Thank you, boss, that would be very nice.'

*

82

'I think it's the same woman,' Eylul Yavaş said.

'In all the photos?' Kerim Gürsel asked.

'Well, we can't really see her face in all the photographs,' Eylul said. 'But it strikes me that the skin tone is the same or similar across all of them. In a considerable number of these images we do appear to be looking at the same face, albeit in different stages of . . . emotion.'

The photographs Eylul, Kerim and technical officer Kenan Sağlam had found on Ateş Böcek's tablet computer featured Böcek performing a variety of sex acts with an unknown woman. The woman's face was variously contorted in what could have been pain or orgasm, and in one case she was almost smiling. She was dark, heavy breasted and sensual, and the acts she was performing upon and with Ateş Böcek were athletic and, some would say, dirty.

'I thought young people mainly took video of themselves these days,' Kerim said. 'Seems strange he took pictures.'

'There's probably video elsewhere,' Kenan said. 'He had multiple machines and phones. What we took from the Şehzade Rafık is going to take a while to thoroughly investigate. I don't know of anything else like this at the moment, though.'

'So why did he leave this tablet at his father's apartment?' Eylul asked.

Kerim had witnessed Eylul being exposed to much more extreme material than this, and yet somehow he couldn't bring himself to say the word.

But she did.

'Maybe,' she said, 'he used these images to masturbate when he was at his father's place.'

Kenan Sağlam looked away and Kerim said, 'Mmm,' while Eylul smiled.

Kerim turned to the technical officer. 'Thank you for your help, Kenan Bey. I think Sergeant Yavaş and I now need to talk about how we might proceed.'

The younger man left them with the tablet and went back to his department. When he'd gone, Kerim said, 'You know this missing Roma girl . . .'

'I am way ahead of you, sir,' Eylul said. She scrolled through the images on the screen and stopped at the one where the girl was almost smiling. 'What do you think of this one?'

He peered at it. 'I'll show it to Mehmet Bey first.'

He hadn't expected to meet the locum psychiatrist actually in an interview room facing suspect Ateş Böcek, but that was what Mehmet Süleyman was confronted with when he arrived back at police headquarters. What also came as a surprise was the age of the man, who looked as if he might be in his late seventies or even eighties.

Small and thin, Dr İlker Koca was what Süleyman imagined İkmen might look like in old age. And also like İkmen, he smelt strongly of cigarettes and coffee.

'Inspector Süleyman,' he said, without looking round. 'So glad you could join us.'

Was this some kind of rebuke? Süleyman looked at his watch and found that he wasn't late.

'Doctor.' He sat.

Ateş Böcek was clearly still sedated, but was at least sitting up straight and looking at them. A guard stood each side of him and his hands were manacled together.

The psychiatrist looked first at Böcek and then at Süleyman. 'I've been explaining to Ateş Bey why I am here, but so far he has not deigned to respond. I suppose strictly, because you are here, Inspector, he is entitled to legal representation.'

'My understanding, Doctor, was that what was happening today was a clinical interview where my presence was not required,' Süleyman said.

'Oh, well we can do that if you like,' the elderly doctor replied.

84

'I just like to get as much done as I can all in one hit, as it were.'

Clearly this peculiar situation was one that Dr Koca had planned. Süleyman's marriage to a psychiatrist had given him some idea about just how unpredictable, not to mention inscrutable, they could be.

The doctor looked back at Ateş but continued speaking to Süleyman as if they were alone.

'So,' he said, 'I understand you found a heavily mutilated body in Ateş Böcek's palace, Inspector.'

'Yes.'

What was happening and where this was going Süleyman couldn't imagine. But he had no choice but to run with it. For better or worse he felt it would be unwise to undermine the doctor's authority. He was, from the look of him, possibly the last one available at this time.

'Distressing, I imagine,' Koca said.

'Yes.'

'And the post-mortem this morning . . . how was that?'

It was truly disconcerting being talked to by someone with whom you had no eye contact.

'It was . . .'

'Gruesome,' Koca said. He looked at a pile of papers in front of him. 'Mmm.'

Süleyman watched Ateş Böcek, who leaned very slightly forward in order to see what the doctor was perusing.

'Pathologist Dr Sarkissian sent me a brief overview of his findings at my request,' Koca said. 'And even this short summary makes for distressing reading. I mean, organs ripped out and flung to the ceiling . . .'

'They do that.'

It was said softly, but it definitely came from Ateş Böcek.

The doctor broke into a massive smile. 'Ah, there he is!'

85

Chapter 7

'What does one wear to a gangster's birthday party, do you think?'
Çetin İkmen asked his cousin Samsun.

'Glitter,' she said as she sat down opposite and lit a cigarette.
'Assuming you're talking about Şevket Sesler.'

'I'm going to meet Gonca at her brother's bar,' he said.

'Well, I'm glad the Sailor's Bar is a long way from the Şekeroğlu
meyhane.'

'It all apparently starts at around three, or more realistically
five,' İkmen said, 'which is when I've to meet Gonca and her flamenco dancers.'

'I'd quite like to see them,' Samsun said. 'I love all that. But I
don't want to be around Sesler and his men, they're just thugs. All
"we're Roma, we're real men" and then they come to the girls at
the Sailor's for a bit of hard core.'

'Turks do that,' İkmen said.

'Men do that, darling,' she replied.

'Samsun, there's a Roma trans girl comes to the Sailor's, doesn't
she?'

'Yes, Bardot,' she said. 'Poor little bitch has to turn tricks and
quite often read cards after they've buggered her raw. As soon as
men find out a girl's Roma, it's almost expected. She just makes
stuff up.'

İkmen shook his head. Then, remembering what Numan Bey's
fortune teller had said about the murder in the Böcek palace, he
asked, 'You heard anything about this killing over in Kadıköy?'

'What, Mehmet Efendi's case? Yes, that Ateş Böcek's off his head on drugs.'

'What drugs?'

'Coke,' she said. 'They're all on coke, all those gangsters' kids.'

'So it's said.'

'Yes, but Ateş Böcek has a massive habit. Running about in Kadıköy screaming at people, so I've heard. Esat Bey's been trying to keep it quiet.'

'And women?' İkmen asked.

'Oh, you mean that little Roma he's been seeing? That why you were asking about them?'

'Possibly . . .'

'Yes,' she said. 'There was a Roma girl. Don't know a name.'

'Who'd you hear that from?'

'A customer.'

'Roma?'

She smiled. 'A girl doesn't tell.'

'Well, if it's true, I can't imagine Şevket Sesler was very amused,' İkmen said.

'Only if she was one of his girls,' Samsun said. 'And that I don't know. Mind you, Şevket Bey's all about money, so if the price was right . . .'

'Yes, but it's one of his rivals' sons,' İkmen said.

Samsun shrugged. 'Surely you don't believe there's any honour amongst thieves, Çetin?'

Mehmet Süleyman knew that his colleagues wanted to know whether his wife recognised the picture on Ateş Böcek's tablet. But he chose to call her when he was alone. He'd also asked her to be as alone as she could be when she viewed the photograph and then called him back.

Now waiting for her call, he obsessively rearranged items on his desk and thought about why Dr Koca had succeeded in getting words out of Ateş Böcek, albeit minimal, where Dr Doksanaltı had failed. He had thought Ateş's reaction to Doksanaltı was possibly due to the mention of Roma girls, but could it just be because of that? Koca had alluded to the gruesome pathology of the case, which surely would agitate anyone, but it had been that detail that had apparently opened Böcek's mouth. Why? And what had the young man meant when he'd said, 'They do that.' They? Who?

His phone rang. It was Gonca. Usually she started talking immediately, but this time he just heard her sigh.

'Gonca?'

'It's her,' she said. 'Ceviz Elibol.'

'The missing girl?'

'Yes. Where did you get this, Mehmet?'

'Can't say,' he said. 'And you are to say nothing to anyone. But thank you.'

'I always keep my promises to you,' she said. 'This is bad, though, isn't it?'

'Not necessarily.'

But it probably was. So far the technical team had found only commercial porn on Ateş's other machines. These were the only images featuring the suspect and a woman. But then maybe the victim had been a casual pick-up?

He changed the subject. 'How are you getting on?' he asked.

'Well, it's cold and Şevket Bey is in a foul mood, but apart from that, the soup is cooked and the beer has arrived. Seriously, darling, some of our best entertainers are here. I wish you could come, you would love it.'

'Mmm.' He could go, provided work didn't intervene, and if it didn't, did he really want to go home to an empty house? And she did sound subdued.

Eventually he said, 'If I'm not needed here, I will come. Sesler can call me names if he likes. Small price to pay to be with my wife.'

Gonca, in typical Gonca fashion, said, 'I predict that in the early hours of tomorrow, you will have the best sex you've ever had.'

He laughed. 'Oh, and before I forget, I should like Ömer Bey and his new wife to come to dinner one evening. I thought we might invite the Gürsels too. The young woman is new to the city and knows no one except for Ömer's sister.'

'Of course!' Gonca said. She loved entertaining. She loved people and she adored dressing up and getting her daughters to cook to impress her guests.

'Thank you.'

'And I will invite Peri Hanım too,' she said.

'You are an angel.'

'I'm a dirty one,' she said, and cut the connection.

Süleyman laughed at her shameless audacity, which had always made him love her so much.

Şevket Sesler rolled up a fifty-lira banknote and snorted a line of cocaine from the table in front of him. As he sniffed hard, he leaned back into his chair and growled, 'That bastard will pay!'

The only other person in his office, one of his most faithful henchmen, Munir Can, said, 'You want we should go and give him a slap, Şevket Bey?'

'He fucking needs something!' Şevket said. 'But not today. He's not going to ruin my birthday. I want you and the others here. Why should you miss all the fun because of him?'

'We would . . . I mean, anything for you, Şevket Bey.'

The gangster looked at him with distaste. 'Don't be such a snivelling arsehole, Munir.'

'No, Şevket Bey.' Munir Can lowered his head as if in shame. Like his boss, he was a large, flabby man with a short temper and a liking for young girls. Unlike Şevket, however, he was a poor Roma, entirely dependent upon the gangster for his meagre living.

Şevket stood up and shook his shoulders, distributing the cocaine around his large, greasy body. 'Today I'm going to get drunk, get high, observe how much my people love me and do a lot of fucking.'

But Munir knew, even if no one else did, that he wasn't doing any of that to celebrate his birthday. He was doing it to forget how badly he had been disrespected.

The scene-of-crime team met Süleyman, Kerim Gürsel and Ömer Mungun in one of the squad rooms on the first floor. In charge of the team was a forty-something officer called Sergeant Hikmet Yıldız. Süleyman had known him when he'd been a young constable. Back then, he'd been an easily distracted kid with heavy family responsibilities. But he'd matured, put his back into the job and was now married to a very stylish and independent woman who had just recently given birth to their first child, a son.

Yıldız described the scene of chaos he and his officers had been confronted with when they had entered the Şehzade Rafık Palace. Both Süleyman and Gürsel were surprised by the scale of the mansion.

'It's a three-storey building,' he told them. 'On the ground floor there are reception rooms to the right of the central staircase and two to the left. Those on the left include a large salon. This layout conforms to the Ottoman custom of dividing palaces and yalıs into two sections – the harem, and the selamlık for the men. The basement is given over to kitchens and a marble-dressed hamam. On the first floor are seven bedrooms and two modern bathrooms.'

He pressed some keys on the computer in front of him and brought up a PowerPoint logo on the screen behind his head.

'I'm now going to run through a series of photographs that members of the team took upon first entering the property,' he said.

He pressed another key, and an image of a room in total chaos appeared.

'I know it's difficult to make out, but this is actually a photograph of the main selamlık salon,' he continued. 'As you can see, there is no order whatsoever. Furniture, much of it broken, appears to have been thrown around randomly; the curtains are ripped and lie abandoned on the floor. We found tables covered with cigarette ash, an as-yet-uncountable number of cigarette ends, plus a spectacle case filled with cocaine and a carrier bag containing skunk weed cannabis. These were not the only drugs found on the premises. The bed where the body was discovered was covered in a thin layer of coke, and more was found on top of the toilet cistern in the bathroom. There were many packets of prescription drugs all over the premises, most of them unopened. In addition, every room, with the exception of the entrance hall and the landings, featured faeces and urine on the floor and smeared on the walls.'

Süleyman wondered whether he'd somehow missed this feature when he'd entered that bedroom. Reflexively he looked at the soles of his shoes.

Yıldız brought up a photograph of a dark room where plastic bags appeared to march across the floor, items of food and culinary equipment spilling, sometimes oozing, out of them.

'This is the kitchen,' he explained. 'Again, chaotic, insanitary, stinking.'

Some other members of the team shook their heads.

Süleyman said, 'How far have you progressed in terms of specifically crime-scene analysis?'

'Apart from the obvious bloodstains on the bedclothes, mattress, floor and bed frame, visible blood spatter was surprisingly minimal, sir,' Yıldız said. 'However, the team subjected the area around the bed – principally the walls – to luminol spray, which lit up like a firework display.'

A ripple of nervous laughter unfolded across the room, and then Kerim Gürsel said, 'Sergeant, do you think the paucity of visible blood spatter means that an attempt was made to clean the scene up? I mean, can't bleach also react positively to luminol?'

Yıldız sighed. 'It can,' he said. 'And forensics made that point, which is why further tests are being performed upon samples taken from the wallpaper behind the bed. However, if that is the case, I have to ask why. Blood was all over that bed and all over the floor. Why clean the walls?'

'Unless one were irrational,' Süleyman said. 'So far our suspect is not behaving in ways that could be called rational. At the scene he was agitated and unresponsive. When interviewed by Dr Doksanaltı, he lost control and bit both the psychiatrist and myself. Sergeant, do you know the names of any of the prescription drugs you found on the premises?'

Yıldız consulted a stack of papers beside his computer. 'Something called zopiclone, which I've been told is a sleeping tablet. These have been taken at some point. Unopened boxes include olanzapine and aripiprazole, so far eight of the former and twelve of the latter. Both are antipsychotics. But no physician's prescribing details anywhere, nor on any of the meds.'

'So he could have bought them on the street,' Kerim said.

Süleyman shrugged. 'We know there is a street trade in both sleeping pills and antipsychotics, so maybe. People get high in all sorts of ways. But assuming these drugs belong to Ateş Böcek, we have to bear in mind that he may have received treatment from a psychiatrist. His behaviour so far appears to support the notion of a mental illness component.'

'But who?' Kerim asked.

'Did his brother mention that Ateş suffered from any psychiatric disorder?'

'No. Just said he was wild, out of control.'

'We'll need to get him in again,' Süleyman said. 'And the father.

If Ateş was under treatment and they withheld that, we need to know why.'

'You should also know that Ateş Böcek apparently used the floor of his cell as a toilet just this morning,' Yıldız said. 'It would seem that shitting on the floor is simply something he does.'

Was that his Çiçek with a man? And did that man have his arms around her?

Çetin İkmen's eldest daughter had experienced a rough few years. As well as having to divorce her unfaithful husband, she'd lost her job as a flight attendant over a misunderstanding about a mobile phone app. In the wake of the attempted coup in 2016, a lot of people with this application, supposedly the same one the coup plotters had used, had been dismissed from their jobs. Then more recently she'd had her heart broken by Mehmet Süleyman, who had chosen his mistress over his girlfriend of more than a year. After that, and especially in the wake of Mehmet's wedding, Çiçek had told her father that she was finished with men. She was, she said, going to live with her father and Samsun until she died. It wasn't a prospect Çetin İkmen relished. Not because he didn't want her to stay at home with him, but because he wanted her to love and be loved.

This man – or rather young man, from what he could see of him – was another matter. Çiçek had said nothing about going on a date or meeting someone, and yet she was clearly quite comfortable being held and kissed by this character while she looked in the window of the İpek silk shop on İstiklal Caddesi, which was famed for its scarves and ties. When his wife had been alive, İkmen had always tried to get her at least one beautiful piece from this shop on her birthday.

'Çiçek.'

She looked around and saw him, then blushed.

'Oh, Dad,' she said. 'I didn't know you were coming up here today.'

'I'm going to meet Gonca,' he said. 'One of the Roma dignitaries is throwing a party and she asked me to come along. You know what colourful events they have.'

'Er, yes,' she said. 'How nice.'

The man, who was probably at most in his thirties, was slim and tall and wore a neat beard. As soon as İkmen had approached, he'd let go of Çiçek and shoved his hands in his pockets.

After a moment of silence, İkmen said, 'So, Çiçek, are you going to introduce me to your friend?'

'Ah, yes. Dad,' she said, 'this is Sedat Bey. Sedat Bey, this is my father, Çetin Bey.'

İkmen put his hand out to the young man, who shook it slightly reluctantly. His grip, İkmen observed, was not the firmest.

'So, Sedat Bey,' he said, 'have you been friends with my daughter for long?'

Much as he believed passionately in leaving his children to pick their own partners and sometimes make their own mistakes, he was protective of Çiçek because of what she had been through. He wanted to know how this situation had arisen.

'I met Sedat Bey at work,' Çiçek said.

'I've been going to the Yemeni for my morning coffee ever since I began working here,' the young man said. His voice was light and cultured and he seemed shy.

'What do you do?' İkmen asked.

Çiçek's face told him that she disapproved of this line of questioning.

Sedat Bey said, 'I work for Ziraat Bank, Çetin Bey.'

'Ah, good,' İkmen said.

Çiçek said, 'My dad was a police officer before—'

'I became a miserable old bastard,' İkmen cut in. He hated it when people described him as 'retired'.

Çiçek, accustomed as she was to her father's behaviour, wasn't amused. 'Well, Dad, we're going into İpek now.'

94

'I said I'd buy Çiçek a shawl,' Sedat Bey said with a smile.

'Ah.'

After one venomous look back at her father, she guided Sedat Bey into the shop.

İkmen walked on towards Tarlabaşı, smiling to himself. Although he knew that appearances could be deceptive, he thought the young man seemed harmless enough. He certainly wasn't all ambition, as Çiçek's first husband had been, or arrogant like Mehmet Süleyman. So maybe he'd treat her nicely.

That said, he couldn't help wondering whether someone so innocuous could possibly stand their ground amid the massive personalities that made up the İkmen family.

İlhan Böcek agreed to speak to Kerim Gürsel on the phone. His father, he said, was unavailable. Kerim put his phone on speaker so that Süleyman and Ömer Mungun could hear too.

'İlhan Bey,' he said, 'are you aware of any . . . emotional problems your brother may have experienced?'

It wasn't easy talking to people about mental illness. A lot of stigma had always existed around the subject. In particular, people didn't like the idea that it was in their family somehow. Kerim consequently always approached this topic gently. But İlhan Böcek, for all his youth, knew the code.

'My brother's not mad, if that's what you're implying.'

'No, no . . .'

'He's a hedonist, yeah, and my father disapproves of that,' İlhan continued.

'Have you been to the Şehzade Rafık Palace lately?' Kerim asked.

İlhan paused for a moment, and then said, 'No.'

'Because I have to tell you that it is in a very poor state,' Kerim said. 'Very dirty and disorganised.'

'My brother does use drugs. I don't think it's . . . I think it's a social thing with him.'

Süleyman raised his eyebrows.

'Do you know whether your father visits?'

'Yeah, he does, I think.'

'We will need to speak to him at some point,' Kerim said. 'Can you please ask him to contact me when he is available.'

'If you like.'

Kerim gave the young man his mobile number and then ended the call.

Ömer Mungun said, 'How can anyone think the state of that place is normal?'

'Well,' Süleyman said, 'playing devil's advocate here, it is possible to be normal and live in that kind of environment.'

'You think?'

'As you know, gentlemen, my ex-wife was a psychiatrist, and she was of the opinion that people find the notion of a so-called sane person living a life of apparent disorder or committing criminal acts hard to deal with. The idea of the crazed killer is something we can all relate to. The crazed killer is not us. But sane people do commit terrible crimes – statistically many more than the mad.'

'How can Ateş Böcek be sane when he shits on the floor?' Ömer asked.

'He may be play-acting,' Süleyman said. 'He's a young man who takes drugs. Unlike his brother, I am inclined to think that Ateş Böcek does more than just smoke the occasional social joint. We know he uses cocaine.'

'Well, I've met a lot of addicts in my time, and I've never seen one deliberately shit on the floor,' Ömer said. 'And anyway, boss, he has to be mad! The way that body was sliced up, skinned . . .'

'We don't know beyond reasonable doubt that Ateş did that,' Süleyman said.

'You can't—'

'You heard Dr Sarkissian, Ömer,' Süleyman said. 'Flaying like that would take hours. That wasn't just some coke-head hacking away; it took skill.'

'Maybe Böcek has that skill.'

'Maybe he does, but maybe someone else was involved. We're still waiting on CCTV analysis from the area.'

'It's patchy,' Kerim said. 'None from inside the palace.'

'And we're still waiting for the new psychiatrist to furnish us with his findings.' Süleyman sighed.

'So we wait, boss?' Ömer said.

'Yes.' He stood. 'And given that we can't do a huge amount right now, I am going to go to Şevket Sesler's birthday celebrations.'

'Really?'

'My wife helped organise some of the entertainment, so why not?'

'That's not a conflict . . .'

'Ömer, half the city will be there, plus who knows how many curious tourists,' Süleyman said. He looked at Kerim, 'Why don't you join us, Kerim Bey? The festivities are going to be very loud, so it's not as if you'll get any sleep.'

Kerim said, 'Kasımpaşa officers are policing it, and to be honest with you, I'm hoping that because they're all conservative there, they'll limit some of the wilder behaviour. I know Sesler has assured them there'll be no guns.'

'Well, the Roma didn't come tooled up to my wedding,' Süleyman said.

'Yes, but that was for Gonca Hanım's sake. Will they do it again for a load of uniforms from Kasımpaşa? Anyway, I can't leave Sinem and Melda on their own.'

Süleyman looked at Ömer Mungun. 'Ömer Bey?'

'Oh, I need to get home too, boss,' he said. But he didn't look happy about it.

Süleyman put on his overcoat. 'Well then, I will see you in the morning, gentlemen.'

All his friends had died a long time ago, but Dr İlker Koca remembered one in particular most clearly now. A clinical psychologist called Dr Faysal Akkurt, he'd always maintained that conducting interviews with clients in 'repressive' environments like police headquarters was counter-productive. People were naturally nervous in those places. They would either babble, he'd said, as they desperately tried to talk their way out, or they would fold in on themselves, liquefying into silence.

With the exception of that one phrase, 'They do that', Ateş Böcek had liquefied. When Dr Koca had looked at him after that single statement, he hadn't even noticed whether he was breathing. The young man was shutting down. But then Koca felt that had he himself seen what Dr Sarkissian had outlined in his pathology report, he might well have shut down too. The pathologist had given it as his opinion that the young woman had been flayed by someone who had studied how the human body was constructed. According to Inspector Süleyman, that information did not fit with Ateş Böcek's profile as the spoilt scion of a crime family with a penchant for cocaine. And yet Ateş and only Ateş had been discovered at the scene, and he'd been carrying a yataghan dripping with the woman's blood. Further, Dr Sarkissian had cited the yataghan as the murder weapon, and so it seemed that Böcek had committed murder. But to whom did 'they' refer? Was it possible Ateş Böcek had had assistance? Moreover, assistance that had lasted many hours?

Dr Koca knew very little about contemporary crime families. In his youth, there had been gangsters active in the city, but in comparison with their modern counterparts, they were, whilst still lethal, generally unsophisticated. People like Kurt İdris and Nuri Ergin in the 1960s and 70s had made crude overtures to political factions and paraded any celebrities they had power over like recently stolen jewels. In the twenty-first century, while some mobsters made inroads into the political life of the country, any alliances they formed were often, although not exclusively, hard to substantiate. Modern gangsters were businessmen, groomed and smoothed, married to models, whose children went to school in the United States and listened to classical music.

That said, Inspector Süleyman had told him that the Böcek family were considered to be both politically and religiously conservative. Esat Böcek, the family patriarch, was a supporter of both the ruling elite and more extreme right-wing figures outside the mainstream. And if Ateş had indeed taken a Roma girl as his mistress, his father might very well have intervened. Against that thesis, however, was Süleyman's contention that the manner of the woman's death was far too eye-catching to be a parental hit. Why create such a lurid spectacle just to make a point to your own son? Why risk the involvement of law enforcement, who might well unmask you?

Dr Koca lay back on his chaise below his office window and began to wonder what kind of madman, if any, Ateş Böcek might be. And why, if he was, he didn't have any apparent history of mental illness.

Chapter 8

'How old is he?' Çetin İkmen asked Gonca Süleyman.

The freezing rain that had been falling for most of the day had stopped, but it was still cold and dark, and although they were standing beside a patio heater outside Gonca's brother's meyhane, the two of them were still cold.

As she huddled against İkmen for warmth, Gonca said, 'I've no idea. He's always looked like a slug; how can you tell?'

Şevket Sesler was sitting on a couch on the balcony above the meyhane, wrapped up in furs, waiting for his birthday celebrations to begin in the street below. Surrounded by his heavies, he looked as miserable as death.

'Yesterday he reminded me of something I had chosen to forget,' Gonca said as she lit a cigarette.

'What was that?'

'Years ago, when he was in his early twenties, he presented himself at my house with a view to seducing me,' she said. 'I must've been over thirty – Erdem was already at college. Apparently I sent him packing.'

'As you would. Where was your husband?' İkmen asked.

'Who knows? Probably getting drunk or high, or sleeping with another woman. Maybe all three.'

He put an arm around her shoulders. 'Bullies,' he said. 'I hate them. People like Sesler should be dragged through the streets in chains.'

'And yet who else stands up for us?' she asked. 'I know the

100

deputy for Izmir is Roma, but what can he do on his own?' Özcan Purcu, an opposition politician and ethnic Roma, had been admitted to parliament in 2015. It had been a huge leap forward for Turkey's Roma, but it remained an uphill struggle. 'Sesler knows which palms to grease,' she continued. 'Like it or not, he helps people on a day-to-day basis.'

'For a price,' İkmen said.

'Of course. Don't think I'm defending him,' Gonca went on. 'I still believe that with knowledge comes power. It's why, when I became successful, I put every kurus into my children's education. I told them they'd have to battle prejudice if they wanted to compete with the gaco, but they took it on, all of them. I am incredibly proud. I agree with you that Sesler should not exist. But while we fight to catch up with your people, how can he not?'

İkmen sighed. 'Where are your dancers?' he asked.

'Back in the meyhane.'

'Getting ready?'

'Yes. You know the girl, Lola, is going to dance barefoot? She has said she always dances barefoot because it allows her to make contact with the magic of the earth.'

İkmen said, 'God!'

Gonca smiled. 'Roma women,' she said. 'Tough.'

Süleyman parked around the back of Kerim Gürsel's apartment block. Kerim was one of the few tenants who had a car, so Süleyman knew he could usually get a space when he visited. As he got out, he wound a scarf around his neck and put on a pair of gloves. It was bone-chillingly cold, and he thought how typical it was of Şevket Sesler to hold his birthday celebrations in the street, rather than allowing his own people – who he probably considered beneath him – to experience his largesse in the warmth of one of his considerable properties. All gangsters, in Süleyman's experience, treated those they claimed to protect with contempt. It was about money; that was it, the only thing that mattered.

He began walking across the rutted, wet and litter-strewn street in the direction of the sound of many people talking and recorded Roma music, and eventually the sight of his wife wearing one of her thick, dark velvet coats. It was her favourite fabric, and in the winter months she wore it almost all the time.

'Mehmet!'

He looked up and saw Kerim Gürsel standing on the corner of the street.

'Kerim Bey?'

He walked towards his colleague and the two men embraced.

'Sinem was insistent I join you when I told her you were coming to be with Gonca Hanım,' Kerim said.

Süleyman smiled. 'Excellent.'

Dear Juan was still doing that thing he'd done all those years back when he'd briefly stolen Gonca's heart. Twenty-two years ago, he'd been performing with a Spanish dance troupe called Sevilla, who had come to İstanbul to play for two nights at the Ataturk Cultural Centre. Gonca had attended with her late brother, Şükrü, and fallen in love.

Unlike all the other dancers in the troupe, Juan had come on stage, then, as now, in an ill-fitting suit and scuffed shoes. He had looked so dowdy amid so much male and female glamour, but then he had begun to sing. While not understanding a word of Spanish, she was reduced to tears by his scarred, guttural, pain-threaded voice. And when he had started to dance, every eye in that vast concert hall had been pinned to him. There and then Gonca had decided she had to have this man in her life.

And she had. Juan had left Sevilla to be with her, and they'd spent almost an entire month in her bed making love, singing and dancing. She was still not entirely sure that he wasn't the father of her youngest son, Rambo. Not that it mattered.

When the Cortes troupe pushed their way out of the meyhane and into the street, Gonca followed the old man with her eyes. He winked at her and she grabbed hold of İkmen's arm to stop her legs giving way beneath her. Even though he was aware she was happily married, Juan Cortes still wanted to know he could elicit a response in her.

The huge crowds on either side of the meyhane began to simmer down as Tomas strummed his guitar and Lola pirouetted on one bare foot, throwing off the huge tasselled shawl she had worn over her red and black flamenco dress. As she snaked one long, slim arm into position over her head, only the most religiously conservative averted their eyes. Most people were bewitched.

Gonca gasped, and then, as she felt arms encircle her, she gasped again. Her husband, behind her, kissed the side of her face and said, 'Hello, my darling.'

Still unable to take her eyes off the dancers, she leaned her head back on his shoulder.

The musical tempo increased and Juan Cortes began to sing.

The elderly drag artist known as Madam Edith had been helping Sinem Gürsel look after baby Melda ever since the little girl had been born. Edith had come to İstanbul back in the 1960s and earned her keep as a rent boy until the lure of drag – plus her devotion to Edith Piaf – had overtaken her in the early eighties. She'd met Kerim Gürsel, then a furtive drag club attendee, in the early 2000s, which was when she'd also met the love of Kerim's life, the trans woman Pembe. Edith knew all about the Gürsels' marriage of convenience, Kerim's broken heart in the wake of Pembe's death, and how Sinem's obsessive love for her husband and old school friend had finally led to the birth of this baby.

Looking down into the street from four storeys up, she had a fine view of the Romany party down below. When Kerim had arrived home, he'd gone straight to this window to watch what was going on outside. That was why Sinem had told him to go. He'd always loved parties, dances and celebrations of all kinds. Sinem, probably because she'd had rheumatoid arthritis since she was a child, shied away from such things. The dear boy would have stayed with her had she asked, but Sinem loved him too much to deny him anything he wanted. She'd even let him have his Pembe back in the day.

'What's happening?' Sinem asked as she put Melda into her carrycot and joined Edith at the window.

'Flamenco dancing,' Edith said.

Floodlights strung high up from the roof of the meyhane picked out three stamping, apparently wailing figures down in the street, flanked on all sides by crowds.

'Can you see Kerim?'

'No,' Edith said.

'Oh.'

Sinem sat down on the sofa beside Melda's cot. 'You know, Edith, you can go home now if you want. Kerim is just across the road, and he has his phone with him.'

'Thought I might watch some of Sesler's birthday celebrations first,' Edith said.

'Of course.'

'I know he's an evil bastard, but these flamenco dancers he's got are marvellous. Come and have a look.'

Sinem returned to the window and Edith put her arms around her.

'And we can watch all nice and snuggled up and warm in here!'

Sinem smiled. But then she heard a noise that seemed to come from above their heads.

'What's that?'

'What?'

'Sounded like something happening on the roof.'

'Oh, that'll be the Roma,' Edith said. 'Probably putting more lights up or draping a banner or something. Poor sods spend half their time trying to please that miserable old bastard. In a just world, he'd disappear and leave all his wealth to them. But as we know, this world is shit.'

Süleyman had been taken over by it too – and Kerim Bey.

'The Spaniards call it *duende*,' Çetin İkmen told Gonca when he caught her staring at the faces of her husband and his colleague.

'What?'

'*Duende*,' İkmen repeated. 'It's when the spirit of the dance, the song, the art rises up inside a person, creating a moment of enlightenment and ecstasy. I can see you feel it.' He drew closer to her. 'It's sexual.'

Gonca felt her husband increase his hold on her, then she felt him kiss her neck. Kerim Gürsel had his eyes closed, blue, white and red lights pulsing across his strong features, making him appear slightly demonic.

Juan Cortes sang of Andalusian drought, about the death of a man's horse, his lover's skirts lying in the dust, her body returning to the earth, about passion that transcended death, revenge that never ended . . .

Only İkmen really saw what happened next. There was no sound save for the Spaniard's song. Maybe had he been closer to Sesler he would have heard a grunt, a cry of surprise and pain. But Sesler and his men were on the balcony three floors above their heads, and so whether the scream came before or after the body landed inside the area where the dancers were performing, he would never know.

But then the shooting started, and he had other matters with which to contend.

*

105

Süleyman dragged Gonca down to the ground with him and pushed her behind him. People ran, screaming; some of the Roma men produced guns. As he drew his own weapon, he shouted to Kerim Gürsel, 'Call it in!'

There had been fewer officers from Kasımpaşa station than either of them had envisaged. Mainly young men, they were scared, and some looked as if they were firing indiscriminately into the crowd.

Who the dead man in front of the meyhane was, Süleyman didn't know. Maybe it was Sesler himself? Behind him he could feel Gonca begin to rise to her feet.

'Get down!' he yelled.

She said, 'My son and my brother! Where are they?'

The last time he'd seen her brother, he'd been behind the bar in his meyhane. The kid could be anywhere.

'Get down and stay down, Gonca!'

Kerim Gürsel crawled towards him. 'Reinforcements are on their way. What the fuck is this?'

He too had his pistol drawn. He shouted at a young uniform who was firing into the air, then he said, 'Sinem! I must call Sinem!'

A woman dropped to the ground. Even amid the screaming there would have been some sound. Blood pooled around her as the pregnant dancer ran to her and began pulling her out of the road and onto the pavement, her ruffled skirts snaking across the ground like black and red fire. There was a smell on the air of smoke, of metal, of thick meat soup and the aniseed tang of rakı. People swore, fell, ran and screamed, and yet in the middle of all that, one cool head remained.

Çetin İkmen had never felt as if he actively wanted to die. Quite the reverse. Most of his life had been spent making sure he lived, because he loved his family, his city and his job. But when his wife died, very soon after his retirement, he began to develop the

106

kind of fatalistic attitude towards life that a lot of pious Muslims held. Not that his own lack of religion made what could be dubbed a careless attitude bleak. İkmen of all people did not believe that death was the end – the frequent appearances of his wife's ghost were proof of that contention; he just didn't believe in paradise or hell or the notion that being a good person changed one's ultimate disposal in some way.

He didn't want to die now, in the thick of whatever horror had come to Tarlabaşı. But he didn't care too much if his life ended there, which enabled him to do something that none of his colleagues had been able to, which was to really look at what was happening.

While Süleyman and Kerim Gürsel protected themselves and those around them and tried to discourage hysteria, while the Kasımpaşa cops panicked or threatened the terrified Roma, İkmen looked dispassionately at those who had been hit and, walking out into the melee, he worked out the possible direction from which those shots had been fired.

Süleyman screamed at him, 'Çetin! What the fuck are you doing!'

İkmen pointed to a building behind him. 'Up there,' he said. 'Sniper.'

Kerim Gürsel, standing beside Süleyman, also followed the direction of İkmen's pointed finger. 'That's my building,' he said.

'They were told not to bring guns!' Sinem said. 'They were told!'

In spite of being cradled by her mother, baby Melda was crying, probably because the street below was full of noise.

Edith, who had been almost as relieved as Sinem when Kerim had called to tell them he was all right, had locked the front door of the apartment and moved Sinem and her baby into the kitchen, which was on the other side of the building. She put cushions

107

down on the floor for them to sit on, on the basis that stray bullets could find their way almost anywhere. She'd lived in Tarlabaşı since the 1960s and so was a veteran of numerous gun battles between local people and immigrants, the artistic set and the Roma and trans girls at odds with their vicious pimps.

As she lowered herself down onto a cushion, Sinem said, 'Why did they have to go and ruin everything?'

'Who?' Edith asked.

'The Roma,' she said. 'All that firing is them, isn't it?'

'I don't know,' Edith said. 'Not necessarily, my soul. I mean, a lot of people have guns now. I don't know why . . .'

Her phone beeped to tell her she had a text. It was from Kerim, and it read:

Don't tell Sinem. We think there might be a sniper on the roof of our block. Lock the front door and keep away from the windows. Don't let anyone in except me.

'What is it?' Sinem asked. 'Is it Kerim?'

Edith replied with a heart emoji and then put the phone back in her pocket.

'No, honey,' she said. 'Kurdish Madonna wanting to know what's going on.' Kurdish Madonna was the madam of a local trans brothel.

'Oh.'

Edith put a hand on Sinem's shoulder. 'Darling, don't worry,' she said. 'This too will pass.'

'Yes, but Kerim is down there!'

'He is, but he's not alone. He's got Mehmet Bey and Çetin Bey with him. And if all else fails, Gonca the witch will curse anyone who messes with her husband and his friends. And she is not someone I would like to be on the wrong side of.'

'You can't go,' Süleyman said.

An ominous silence had descended on Tarlabaşı. People who

remembered the huge earthquake of 1999 recognised this as the lull that preceded the realisation of the scale of the horror.

Kerim Gürsel wanted to get to his wife and child. Süleyman and İkmen were fighting to hold him on the ground.

'Sinem and Melda are in there!' he screamed.

'You're a police officer!' İkmen said.

'You told them to lock the door. It's all you can do!' Süleyman added.

Sirens wailed across the city and car horns blared.

'They're on their way,' Süleyman said. 'We have to stay where we are until they get here, and then it's in the hands of the incident commander.'

Kerim, his breathing ragged, attempted to gain control.

Gonca, who had been watching what was happening in the street, made to rise to her feet, but Süleyman pulled her back down.

'I can see Rahul Bey!' she said. 'He's been shot!'

Rahul Bey was an elderly local haberdasher. All the Roma bought their linen from him.

'I'll go to him,' Süleyman said. 'Stay here!'

Keeping low, his pistol grasped in both hands to one side of his body, he ran to where the old man lay groaning in the middle of the road. When he reached him, he said, 'Rahul Bey, can you hear me?'

From what Süleyman could see, he'd been hit in the shoulder. The old man looked at him and said something in Romani. Süleyman removed his overcoat, bundled it up and pressed it against the wound. Then he took the old man's hand and told him to press down as hard as he could.

People were moving now, running, walking, limping away. He yelled, 'Stay where you are!'

It was going to be difficult enough for the officers assigned to this incident to get into the small streets of Tarlabaşı without hundreds, maybe thousands of people trying to get out. But only some listened. Even when the cops from Kasımpaşa tried to push them back, there were just too many of them.

The apartment block was silent. They couldn't even hear old Esma Hanım's television across the hall. Usually it was howling away day and night. But not now.

Sinem, although she'd been frightened at first, was now in full policeman's wife mode, whispering about how her husband's colleagues were on their way and it was everyone's duty to stay calm. And although it had been she who had originally called attention to the sound of footsteps on the roof, she either couldn't hear them any more or she was choosing to ignore them. Not so Madam Edith. She could hear them and she knew that in light of what Kerim had told her, she needed to contact him.

She took her phone out of her pocket and found his text.

When she began replying, Sinem said, 'Who are you texting?'

'Kurdish Madonna,' she said. 'You know how she worries about everything in the world. Telling her we're still all right.'

Melda shifted in her mother's arms, opened her eyes briefly and then went back to sleep.

Sinem said, 'Oh. Send her my love, won't you.'

Edith smiled.

The incident commander was a Superintendent Cihat Şen. Like the men and women under his command, he looked like just another heavily armed and armoured cop, his face partially obscured by a helmet, chin guard and microphone. Ignoring the sergeant from Kasımpaşa, he went straight to Süleyman, whom he recognised.

'Mehmet Bey.'

Süleyman looked up from his position on the ground, where he was still pressing down on Rahul Bey's shoulder wound. 'Are you the incident commander?'

'Yes. Superintendent Şen. I'm setting up incident command in the meyhane. Can you bring me up to speed? When did the Roma start firing?'

One of Süleyman's first thoughts after his shock had passed had been how he was going to convince his colleagues that the Roma hadn't started shooting first. Even if they didn't say it, many of his colleagues would believe he was simply in thrall to his wife.

'They didn't start firing,' he said. 'We were all fired upon from that rooftop.' He pointed to Kerim Gürsel's building.

Şen looked up as Gürsel approached holding his phone. He said, 'Text from Edith, who reckons she can still hear footsteps on the roof.'

Şen didn't know who Edith was and he didn't care. 'You know that building?'

'I live there,' Kerim said. 'My wife—'

Şen put a hand on his arm. 'How many entrances?'

'Three, including the fire escape.'

Şen said, 'Come with me.'

They headed back towards the meyhane, leaving Süleyman looking down at the old man, who said, 'You should go back to your wife now, Mehmet Bey. I will be all right.'

And Süleyman did want to go back to Gonca. But he also knew that if he did and let this old man wait on his own for an ambulance, she would be as angry with him as he would be disappointed in himself.

Chapter 9

The boy just appeared.

'Mum!'

Gonca, together with what felt like hundreds of other people, including police officers, was inside her brother's meyhane. When she saw her son, she first hugged and kissed him and then slapped him around the head.

'Where have you been, you little shit?' she asked. 'I've been losing my mind, thinking you're dead!'

'I'm not—'

'Where have you been?' she reiterated. 'Have you been with a woman?'

Rambo coloured. Of course he'd been with a woman! Women, especially those considerably older than Gonca's son, found him irresistible.

'Little bastard!' Gonca said.

'Be quiet, woman!'

The voice was male and aggressive. Everyone packed into the meyhane stopped talking, even the Spaniards, who didn't know what was going on.

Kerim Gürsel, who had been standing beside Şen when he yelled out, said, 'Superintendent, that is Gonca Hanım, Inspector Süleyman's wife.'

Şen looked at her and she looked at him. He was the first to look away.

'I apologise, madam,' he said. 'I realise that the situation is . . . tense.'

Rambo could see that his mother was about to say something back and put a hand on her arm. 'Don't,' he said. And she didn't.

Şen turned to Kerim Gürsel. 'Right, I've got men covering both doors and the fire escape, but we'll need your help when we're in the building.' He handed him a Kevlar vest and a helmet. 'Put these on and let's do it.'

'Superintendent, my wife and child are in that building, not to mention neighbours I've known for years. If a firefight can be avoided . . .'

'I can't give you any assurances, Inspector,' Şen said. 'You know that. If there is a sniper in that building, it's my job to take him down. That's all.'

Ambulances arrived. Held up by the monstrous İstanbul traffic, their crews got to work quickly. As far as Süleyman could tell, actual fatalities were few, but a lot of people were injured. He called out to a woman dressed in hospital scrubs and put Rahul Bey into her care. He left his overcoat with the old man.

Şen's officers had taken over from the Kasımpaşa uniforms and had cordoned off the northern streets of Tarlabaşı. He saw Gonca's sister, Didim, come out of the Kızlar club, a ladle dripping with uneaten soup in her hands. He went up to her and took her arm.

'Are you all right, Didim Hanım?' he asked.

'I'm not hurt,' she said. 'What's going on?'

'We don't know yet.'

'Can I go home now?'

'No. Officers will want to speak to you about what you might have seen.'

'I saw nothing,' she said.

'You think you saw nothing, but you may have,' he told her. 'Gonca is inside your brother's meyhane. Let me take you to her.'

Didim went with him and he deposited her at the door just as Şen, four of his men and Kerim Gürsel were leaving.

Süleyman and Kerim shared a tense glance, then the former said, 'You're going into the building.'

'Yes.'

Kerim was scared, not for himself, but because Sinem and the baby were in there. Süleyman wanted to go with him, but he was also aware of the fact that his presence added nothing to the operation.

'Superintendent Şen,' he said to the incident commander, 'I should like to begin witness interviews, starting with the man whose birthday celebration this was.'

'Sesler?'

'Yes,' he said. 'I know him – somewhat – and I believe one of the men who works for him has died. I should offer my condolences.'

Someone had finally thrown a blanket over the body of the gangster who had fallen from the balcony.

'Maybe you should,' Şen said, and then he and his men left, taking Kerim Gürsel with them.

Çetin İkmen watched. Alone, sitting beside the bar of the meyhane, he sipped the large brandy Gonca's brother had given him and observed. Although now organised, this major incident scene was still humming with tension and anxiety. People had died and those who had known them were weeping; others had been taken to hospital, where their wounds would be treated and they might, or might not, survive.

The police were already starting to interview witnesses, Rambo Şekeroğlu senior had thrown his premises open to them and was supervising his teenage son as he handed out tea to the

114

officers and those they were interviewing. Gonca was still, in spite of Superintendent Şen's harsh words, berating her son, Rambo junior. She was, İkmen had observed over the years, often to be found yelling at her youngest child. It was like a reflex; as soon as she saw him, she accused him of something. And yet she loved him, fanatically. İkmen recalled that his late wife Fatma had been exactly the same with their son Bülent when he'd been a youngster. And Bülent had grown up to be a fine young man.

He scanned the large bar area and, just for a second, he imagined he saw Fatma's face in the crowd. He missed her so much. The balcony outside his apartment was haunted by her ghost, which he talked to every day. And yet was it right to keep his wife's spirit earthbound in order to assuage his grief? It wasn't, and he knew it.

The Spanish flamenco dancers sat in a corner with their tea and looked bewildered. They couldn't understand what was going on and yet they must have been scared like everyone else. The Roma were usually stoic; they'd had to be. He saw Superintendent Şen and his men leave with Kerim Gürsel. He couldn't help thinking that if a sniper had been positioned somewhere on the Gürsels' roof, he was now long gone. Then he saw Süleyman make his way to the back of the room and head upstairs. Şevket Sesler was up there, and İkmen knew, just as he was certain Süleyman did, that the Roma godfather knew something about what had happened this evening. Getting him to reveal it, however, was going to be another matter.

Unlike the rest of the squad, Kerim Gürsel wasn't in contact with his fellows by radio. While Şen and four of his men plus Gürsel were to enter through the open front door of the building, another group would come in by the back door, while a third group of three would climb the fire escape.

The building, known locally as the Poisoned Princess apartments, had been constructed in the mid 1980s and was supposed to have heralded a vast new construction programme in Tarlabaşı. In 1984, former İstanbul mayor Bedrettin Dalan had described the district as 'İstanbul's poisoned princess' and had set about a programme of road building and gentrification. The apartments had been a project realised on the back of Dalan's dream, but rather than being sold to rich people, they had been rented out in the usual way to immigrants, Kurds, Roma and anyone else who couldn't afford anything better. Consequently the owner had done nothing in the intervening years to make life in his building bearable. Shoddy and dirty, the Poisoned Princess had only one staircase and no lift.

The officers, apart from those taking the fire escape, assembled in front of what was supposed to be the kapıcı's apartment but was in fact a ramshackle store for old tins of paint, bicycles and discarded scaffolding. The team assigned to the back door did a quick-and-dirty search of the place, and then both teams, some ten officers, proceeded to mount the stairs. The plan was to leave one officer on each floor while the rest proceeded to the roof. The shooter could be anywhere in the building, including in one of the apartments rented by Kerim's neighbours.

'I wondered when you'd turn up,' Şevket Sesler said.

He was seated on the same ornate bench, covered in carpets, that he'd been using out on the balcony. Now in Rambo Şekeroğlu's storage room, he sat between two large stacks of Efes Pilsen beer surrounded by his depleted crew of henchmen.

'Live long,' Süleyman responded. It was the traditional way in which one expressed one's condolences, even if the thought of Sesler living for a long time made him cringe.

'My cousin, Alaadin,' Sesler said. 'Good shot, though, straight in the chest.'

116

Süleyman found an old wooden chair and sat down. 'So, Şevket Bey. Who have you annoyed lately?'

The godfather said nothing.

'It's a fair question,' Süleyman said. 'I won't insult your intelligence by pretending I don't know what you are; that would be foolish. And I know you are not the only person who makes his living providing services frequently outside the law in this city. I know you jostle for position and I also know that there are some nascent operators who may well bear you ill will.'

Sesler said, 'Your wife's safe. I heard her shouting at that boy of hers downstairs.'

The three men behind him smirked.

Süleyman ignored them. 'Let's stick to the point, shall we? Who do you know who could make a hit like this?'

'I don't.'

'Oh come on, Şevket Bey! I was straight with you. Why insult my intelligence now? Peace between you and your fellow businessmen is never a given, is it?'

Suddenly and volcanically, Sesler roared, 'I'm the fucking injured party here! Fuck off and do your job, Mehmet Bey!'

'Oh, I will, Şevket Bey,' Süleyman said. 'Of that you can be certain. Nothing will escape the scrutiny of myself and my officers. This is why I am giving you an opportunity to tell me what you know now, rather than down the line, when the withholding of information will be considered a crime.'

Süleyman didn't know all the other men arrayed around Şevket Bey. He knew the short, greasy one, Munir Can, street brawler and lover of little girls; Elvis Bora, convicted of murder back in the 1970s; and Levent Kalafat, alleged torturer, but not the other two, and he hadn't known Sesler's cousin Alaadin. Not that it mattered much. Heavies came and went in criminal organisations like Sesler's.

Eventually Sesler said, 'We know nothing. And as I said,

Mehmet Bey, I am the injured party here. We get fired on by some cunt—'

'I made a point of impressing upon the incident commander, Superintendent Şen, that it was not the Roma who fired first,' Süleyman said.

'No, it fucking wasn't!'

'And yet the fact that some amongst the Roma were armed after having been ordered not to be as a condition of this event taking place . . .'

'Yeah, well I can't be held responsible for Turkish stupidity,' Sesler said. 'Did you really think our men would be here unarmed? A Roma's gun is an extension of his soul.'

'Don't give me excuses, Sesler. Had your people not been armed, there would have been no question about who fired first. However, at the moment, I don't give a damn about that. What I care about is who attacked you and why. Not because I like you – I don't. But my job is to protect your people and all the other innocent people in this city. Wars between businessmen benefit so few and, with respect, Şevket Bey, they tend not to be those I care about.'

'People like me?'

'I was too polite to say.' Süleyman smiled.

The gangster sighed. 'Feeling's mutual.'

'I don't doubt it,' Süleyman said. 'Not that our feelings for each other are relevant. I want to apprehend whoever killed people here tonight, and I will do that with or without your help.' He stood up. 'However, with your help would be better, because it would be quicker. Think about it.'

He'd started to walk back to the stairs when he heard Sesler say, 'Don't hold your breath. And don't imagine that you'll pick up anything from your wife during pillow talk, because until this is over, she is not welcome in my vicinity.'

*

On the first floor, on the left of the stairs, was old Safiye Hanım's apartment, which she shared with her dog Marilyn. Next to that was where the refugees from the Cameroon lived – two adults and four children. To the right of the stairs were a very young Roma couple, and next to them an unknowable number of students.

By recalling who lived where, Kerim Gürsel was able to prevent his anxiety overwhelming his mind. It was also a way of reminding himself who his neighbours were if and when Superintendent Şen needed to enter their properties.

Floor two – on the left a trans girl called Lale; next to her two ancient men who might or might not be gay. On the right, a Roma snake-dancer and her Romanian husband, who had adopted the name Dracula – one didn't forget such a thing in a hurry. Next to them, a family of Kurds from Diyarbakir who spoke to no one and eyed everyone with suspicion.

Would Kerim ask Şen whether he could go in and speak to Sinem when they reached the top floor? Of course he wouldn't! That was mad! But he wanted to. He wanted to hold his daughter in his arms and never let her go. Why had they ever come to live in Tarlabaşı when he knew how dangerous it could be? He knew the answer to that, and it was all about him. For a gay man, Tarlabaşı was an accepting place. It was also the place where his lover had lived. But now that Pembe was dead and he was leading a straight life for his wife and child, how could he justify living somewhere like this? They would have to move! When this was over, they would have to!

The third and fourth floors were occupied by Turkish families, including his own, with the exception of the smart middle-aged man next door to Kerim who was almost certainly a pimp. The main thing that connected all these people, with the exception of the pimp and Kerim, was poverty. Everyone knew the Gürsels and appreciated that Kerim tried to listen to their problems even if he could do little to solve them. He couldn't imagine that any of

119

his neighbours would willingly harbour someone who had come to disrupt life in Tarlabaşı, but then again, they were poor and therefore vulnerable to financial bribery.

When they reached the fourth floor and began moving towards the stairs leading up to the roof, Kerim held his breath.

Gonca Süleyman reached out and grabbed the young girl's arm.

'Beren,' she said. 'Are you all right?'

The girl was still insufficiently dressed for the cold, but at least this time she was wearing shoes.

'Yes, Gonca Hanım,' she said. 'Do you know what's happening?'

'No. Where is your father?'

'At home. He wouldn't come.'

Gonca offered the girl a seat, which she took.

'Any news of your sister?' she asked, knowing that in all probability Ceviz was dead.

'No,' Beren said. 'Do you know anything?'

She'd promised Mehmet she'd say nothing about the photographs found on Ateş Böcek's computer, and so once again she said, 'No.'

'Dad thinks she's dead.'

Gonca leaned across the table and took the girl's hands. 'Why does he think that, darling?'

'Because of rumours.'

'What rumours?'

'About that boy she was seeing.'

'What about him? Has anyone said who he is?'

'No one says any names,' Beren said. 'Just that he's an enemy of Şevket Bey. Didim Hanım says that Şevket Bey wants to avenge Ceviz's death.'

Gonca narrowed her eyes. 'Didim Hanım? My sister Didim Hanım?'

'Yes, hanım. It's said she overheard Şevket Bey screaming and shouting about it.'

There was nothing on the roof except empty washing lines. Nowhere to hide, no movement. Superintendent Şen and his men explored every corner; they looked down the sides of the building. Nothing.

There had always been a chance that the shooter had gone. In fact, given the time between the last shots and this operation, it was highly likely that whoever had been on the roof had now left the building, mingled with the crowds outside and disappeared.

But Superintendent Şen was not finished. He'd placed guards at the exits from the block, and now he instructed his men to search every apartment. Not wanting his wife and child to be subjected to what would be a loud and disruptive intrusion, Kerim asked if he could check his apartment alone. Şen, while not happy about this, gave his consent and the men descended into the building again.

In spite of his Kevlar vest and helmet, Kerim felt as cold as death as he began to walk along the corridor towards his apartment. Previously, the heat of the exercise had kept him warm, but now he was freezing, anxious to get to his family and to hold his daughter in his arms. But before he could reach his front door, he noticed something. Coming up, he hadn't seen it, but now he couldn't miss it. He tapped Şen on the shoulder and indicated the pimp's door, which was very slightly open. Şen nodded, and moved Kerim to one side while his men covered him. Then, after preparing his sub-machine gun for firing, he kicked the door wide with his foot.

The apartment was in darkness save for the flashing lights from the Şekeroğlu meyhane, but Kerim knew that the smell that confronted them did not bode well. Heavy and metallic, it was the familiar sharp tang of blood, and he saw one of Şen's men dry-heave.

121

They found the body of the pimp in the kitchen. There was a bloodied hole in his chest and a footprint on the windowsill that could be indicative of how his assailant had escaped. But when Kerim looked out of the window, he could see no sign of ropes, ladders or anything else that might have assisted the attacker's exit.

Şen told his men to search the rest of the apartment, then said to Kerim, 'Know him?'

'Not really,' he said. 'Single man, worked at night as far as I could tell.'

'You know where?'

'No. I always had him down as someone labouring in the black economy.'

'Meaning?'

'He came across to me as a pimp,' Kerim said. 'Simply based on seeing him with some of the local working girls. I may be quite wrong.'

And as they both knew, there was no guarantee that whoever had shot and killed the pimp was the same person who had fired on the Roma in the street.

Once the apartment had been checked and Şen had put a guard on the door, the search of the building resumed. Kerim knocked on his own front door and called out, 'It's me, Kerim.'

Edith opened the door as Şen's squad passed along the corridor. Inside, he found Sinem and Melda in their bedroom. The baby was miraculously asleep beside her mother, who held her arms out to her husband.

'I was so worried!' she said after he had kissed her. 'What's going on, Kerim?'

He told her what he knew, including the fact that their neighbour was dead, then said, 'Our people are going to be all over Tarlabaşı for days, and with Sesler and his men clearly on someone's hit list, I want you and Melda away from here until all this is over.'

'But where can we go? I can't go and stay with Derviş, because Mum lives there and we're not talking!'

Sinem's mother, Pınar Hanım, had fallen out with her daughter over her marriage to Kerim, whom she described as 'a pervert'. Her brother, Derviş, had taken the old woman in when Kerim had thrown her out of the apartment after Melda had been born.

'I don't know,' Kerim said. 'But I'll sort it out somehow. Put what you need for you and Melda into bags, and I'll be back to get you as soon as I can.'

As he left the apartment, Edith said, 'You have any idea about where they can go?'

He shrugged. After the latest economic hiccup, his sister, Merve, together with her husband and three children, had moved back in with Kerim's parents, so that wasn't an option. His other siblings lived away from İstanbul.

Eventually he said, 'I'll ask my colleagues.'

Edith smiled. 'Ask İkmen,' she said. 'He's got that great big apartment in Sultanahmet.'

'He lives with his daughter and his cousin,' Kerim said.

'Oh, you know him! He's got the biggest heart in this city! Go and talk to him, Kerim Bey. You know he won't say no, especially not to you.'

'By the book,' Süleyman said.

Gonca took his arm. 'But she'll only talk to you, Mehmet Bey Efendi,' she said.

'Didim Hanım is my sister-in-law,' her husband said.

'Yes, exactly. So she'll tell you what she won't tell anyone else.' She lowered her voice. 'Şevket Bey said he is going to avenge Ceviz's death! This is important! But it must be handled well, my love. If the police just go striding in demanding to know whom he intends to kill and why, he will realise that someone has betrayed him. Eventually he will arrive at the name of my sister.'

'Gonca—'

'Baby, please,' she said.

As yet, nobody had been allowed to leave the meyhane. Süleyman could see his sister-in-law sitting on her own over by one of the windows. However, Sesler's men were everywhere, so how could he get to speak to her without attracting attention?

Eventually he said to his wife, 'Phone her and I'll talk to her.'

For a moment Gonca frowned, until she worked out what he was doing. She dialled her sister's number.

Süleyman heard her begin to speak in Romani, and said to her, 'Tell her to tell me everything.'

When he took Gonca's phone from her, Didim started to speak.

'I don't know any names and that's the truth,' she said. 'Just him . . .' she didn't dare use Şevket's name, in case anyone was listening, 'losing his mind over the death of that girl.'

'Ceviz?'

'Yeah.'

'Whom was he talking to?' Süleyman asked.

'On the phone,' she said.

'You don't know?'

'No, but Munir was in the room with him. It was him as got screamed at when he put the phone down. That was how I knew what was going on, because of what he said to him.'

'What did he say?' Süleyman asked.

'He never mentioned no names,' Didim said.

'I gathered that, but what did he say?'

'Yelling about how someone owed him for destroying his property,' Didim said. 'He said if he didn't pay up, there'd be consequences.'

He knew what they were doing. Staring at him through that hatch in the door, laughing, pretending to be police officers. They were trying to get him to tell them the truth, but how could he? He didn't know what that was. When everything was a game, how could he?

They kept telling him that the girl was dead, and yet they didn't know her name. How could that be right? If someone had died, you had to know their name. If you didn't, you could be talking about anyone. What girl? He didn't understand, but then how could he if he didn't know whom they were talking about? He was surrounded by this fucking shit. Even this cell could be anywhere . . .

He heard someone outside laugh, and then a male voice said, 'Sniper, I heard.'

'Where'd you hear that?' another voice replied.

'Sergeant Asmali,' the first voice said.

There was more laughter, and then another voice said, 'You know he believes in aliens, don't you?'

And there it was. A glimmer of the truth, the reality, the man behind the curtain . . .

Chapter 10

Not going to bed was always a good way of getting up early. By the time Çetin İkmen had arrived home from Tarlabaşı, it had been just gone five in the morning. And after he'd settled Sinem Gürsel and her baby in Bülent's old room, it had been six.

Poor Kerim had looked really nervous when he'd asked whether his wife and child could come to stay. İkmen, of course, had told him that they could stay for as long they liked. Over the past forty-something years, the İkmen apartment had welcomed nine babies, an uncountable number of feral cats, all named Marlboro, and any number of waifs, strays and distant family members. As long as Sinem didn't mind sharing space with İkmen, his daughter and his cousin, it was fine by him.

As had now become his custom, he prepared for his seven o'clock walk down to Eminönü by taking tea out on his balcony where the ghost of his dead wife resided, and smoking heavily.

Fatma İkmen smiled gently as he recounted the tale of his adventures in Tarlabaşı.

'Mehmet is of the opinion that this is part of an inter-gang war,' he said as he lit his second cigarette of the day. 'Sesler's Roma and one or more of his rivals. Doesn't know who exactly, but he seems to think it might be the Böceks. The elder son, Ateş, is in custody for murdering a girl who might be one of Sesler's strippers. But I don't know. On the face of it . . .' He shrugged, at which signal the cat jumped up onto his lap.

'Oh, hello, boy!' İkmen ruffled the creature's filthy fur. 'Finished with all your girlfriends, have you?'

Marlboro lay down and promptly went to sleep. A massive dirty ginger and white beast with a heavily scarred face and very prominent testicles, he was, like all his predecessors, feral, sexually voracious and totally in love with İkmen.

'And yet,' İkmen continued, 'I have to remind myself that these are mobsters we're dealing with. Hardly subtle beings, but then unlike the ankle-snapping heroin peddlers of my youth, the modern gangster is somewhat more sophisticated. For a start, most of them wear suits now, and they all seem to be enormously tech-savvy. Gone are the days of laundering your dirty money by buying multiple bakkals across the city. No, it's all done via banks and governments these days, and by investing in the odd yalı on the Bosphorus. And it's international. I told Mehmet not to forget our Russian friends when it comes to looking at people moving in on Sesler. I mean, I know that a lot of lovely new apartment blocks . . .' he pulled a face, 'have been constructed in Tarlabaşı in recent years, but the quarter is still semi-derelict, still full of Roma, drag queens and refugees. The odious Sesler does look after these to some extent. They scratch his back, he scratches theirs. But the land he operates on is valuable, and so there will be players who will want him out of there.'

The cat purred in his sleep and İkmen stroked his back.

'But at least none of us got shot last night,' he continued. 'Once Samsun wakes up and finds out, of course, she will make a big drama out of it. We'll all have to slurp down enough yogurt to feed the military as she attempts to boost our immune systems after such a shock. And then there's Çiçek—'

'What about me?'

Both man and cat looked up at her as she stood in the doorway to the living room.

127

'Çiçek,' her father said. 'Come and sit with your old dad.'

Still in her dressing gown and clutching a cup of coffee, Çiçek, who could see her mother too, sat down in a chair beside her father and ignored the cat's growls. This particular Marlboro had taken against her for some reason.

'So,' İkmen said, 'did you have a nice date with your young man yesterday evening?'

She lit a cigarette. 'When I wasn't trying to contact you, yes.'

'Contact me?'

'Look at your phone,' she said. 'Sirens going off all over the city, reports of a shooting in Tarlabaşı. I tried to phone you at least five times!'

'Oh . . .' İkmen didn't really like using his mobile phone and often chose to ignore it.

'Eventually I was forced to call Gonca Hanım,' she said. 'Which was . . .' She paused. 'But she told me what was happening and that you were safe, and for that I owe her.'

Marlboro growled again and Çiçek said, 'Oh be quiet!'

'Seems local godfather Şevket Sesler has some enemies,' İkmen said. 'Five dead, including one of his henchmen.'

'God!'

'But we're all safe. I did bring Sinem Gürsel and her baby back with me, though,' he added. 'The shooter, we think, operated from the roof of Kerim Bey's building. He wanted his girls as far away from the scene as possible.'

Çiçek blew smoke out into the freezing morning air. 'I should think so,' she said.

'I put them in Bülent's room.'

'Good.'

'And so,' İkmen said, 'your young man?'

She sighed. 'Oh, he's nice enough.'

'Young . . .'

She threw him an acid look.

128

'I am simply observing.'

'He's thirty-seven,' she said. 'So I'm not quite ten years older, but . . .'

'But what?' her father asked.

She sighed again, and İkmen felt he knew what was coming.

She said, 'He's a banker.'

'Yes. Won't be poor.'

'I know, but . . .' She drank some coffee, then said, 'There's nothing there, Dad. I like a bit of a spark.'

Her ex-husband had been an attractive, interesting and fun Turkish Airlines pilot. Unfortunately, he'd had a penchant for extramarital affairs, which was why he was an ex. The next big love of her life had been Mehmet Süleyman, who had been handsome, dangerous and charming. He had also been having sex with Gonca at the same time as Çiçek. Now, so it seemed, she was dissatisfied with dull banker Sedat Bey.

İkmen patted her knee. 'There is no law that states you have to stay with this young man.'

'Except the law of my biological clock.' She looked at her mother, who, as usual, smiled.

In spite of his open and liberal attitudes, İkmen wasn't comfortable with women's fertility issues. 'I suppose I'd better get out and do my walk soon.'

'It's that or die young.'

As he encouraged Marlboro to get off his lap and stood up, he said, 'You call this young?'

The two men, both red eyed and smoke dried, looked at the footage again. Time-stamped at 10.05 a.m. two days ago, it showed Ateş Böcek entering the tiny Urfa Bakkal on Baghdat Caddesi to buy cigarettes. Twenty Marlboro and a cheap lighter.

Mehmet Süleyman rubbed a hand across his aching forehead. 'Dr Sarkissian places the time of death at around ten.'

The owner of the bakkal, a small old man with arthritic fingers, had not been pleased when the police had turned up to take his CCTV tapes, but they'd proved illuminating.

Kerim Gürsel, whose shirt was stained with cigarette ash, said, 'Maybe this was just before . . .'

'Maybe,' Süleyman said. 'But he doesn't look exactly agitated, does he?'

'He's not exactly normal, though, is he?'

'No . . .' He leaned back in his chair. It had been a terrible night and both men were desperate to sleep, but that wasn't on the horizon any time soon.

Until this footage had emerged, Süleyman at least had hoped that the death of Ceviz the stripper and the attack on Şevket Sesler could be quickly and easily connected. Of course that was still possible, but less likely in light of this.

'We'll need to see whether we can track his movements before and after this,' he said.

'Tech are on it,' Kerim replied. 'There's a lot of footage – which is hopeful – but . . . We mustn't jump to conclusions.'

'I'm not!'

Süleyman was tetchy because he was tired, and also because he didn't like even implied criticism. Kerim, however, was far too tired as well, and so he said, 'Don't take offence, Mehmet Bey!'

'I'm not!'

Fortunately, at that point, Ömer Mungun arrived.

When they had finally arrived back at Gonca's house in Balat, the Spanish Roma had crawled into their tent and fallen asleep. But Gonca herself couldn't. She hadn't wanted her husband to leave after he had driven them all home, but she knew he had to. She tried to make herself relax in the shower, but it hadn't worked. Now, sleepless, she lay in bed wondering what the outcome of the previous night's incidents might be.

Şevket Sesler was both her people's protector and the author of many of their troubles. He dealt drugs to them, he made the girls work as lap dancers and prostitutes and he bullied others, like Gonca, to provide services to him for nothing. Not only did she read his cards, she had also been commissioned by him to create a collage portrait of his disgusting father. It was that or provide him with information about her husband, and she was never going to do that.

Gonca Şekeroğlu had been married twice before Mehmet Süleyman. She'd had twelve children by her Roma husbands, but she'd never loved either of them. Back then, her love for men had been limited to her father, her sons and her brothers. She hadn't loved a man romantically until she met Mehmet. Then she had fallen hard, and it had taken her twenty years to pin down her prince. The younger Mehmet had not been the man he was now. And although he was still arrogant and at times dictatorial, he no longer, it seemed, had a thirst for extramarital affairs. Or did he? She looked up at the place in the wall beside her bed where she had hidden the charms she had made to keep her husband by her side. So far she had resisted the urges to get them out and recharge the spells she had placed in them. She knew it was not necessary, not yet.

Every time he touched her, she could feel his love for her pouring out of his skin. And when they made love, he was completely transported, as was she. He worshipped her; he even sometimes, usually in the heat of passion, called her his goddess. She loved him so much, which was why she now feared what might be about to happen. If Şevket Bey was at war with one or more of his rivals, things were going to get ugly, and the police were bound to be involved. Mehmet never held back in a fight, never just let people go for the price of a bribe, and always put his colleagues first. But then as well as being a true Ottoman gentleman, he had also been trained by Çetin İkmen, whose honour was legendary.

*

131

Dr İlker Koca had spent most of the previous night thinking about Ateş Böcek. And while he'd come to no actual conclusions about the young man, he had decided how he would move forward with him.

'I'd like to speak to the family,' he told Süleyman and Ömer Mungun.

Kerim Gürsel had left to go back to the crime scene in Tarlabaşı and an appointment with Şevket Sesler.

'To what end?' Süleyman asked.

'It's my belief, given his current apparently uncommunicative state, that Ateş Böcek is either genuinely mentally ill in some way, or he's faking,' he said. 'I can't make up my mind which it is. Unless, of course, it's both.'

'According to his family, he is a paragon of virtue with no history of mental illness,' Süleyman said.

'So I understand.'

'And there is a family split,' he continued, 'with regard to his relationship with the girl he may or may not have murdered. Basically, his brother İlhan is aware of what he describes as Ateş's promiscuity. He knew of this girl, knew she was Roma, but claims that his father was not privy to that information. The father and the grandmother speak of Ateş as a good boy. No mention of mental ill health. That said, there is some anecdotal evidence that Ateş often walked around his local area in a disordered fashion. This may be as a result of drug use. As you know, he had cocaine in his system when he was brought in. What's your plan regarding the family?'

'Twofold,' the psychiatrist said. 'Firstly, I am aware that you have a limited amount of time for which you can hold the suspect . . .'

'We are gathering evidence.'

'. . . but as you know, I can in effect extend that period by applying for an involuntary assessment order. Lack of communication makes this case problematic, and so I suspect that any further time spent with Ateş outside a clinical setting will be fruitless. To that end, I would like to speak to the family in order to gain their support in applying to have him admitted to hospital for a period of three weeks.'

Süleyman nodded. 'Perfectly reasonable. Although I believe the family will be difficult. The father Esat and his mother Neşe Hanım live, we believe, in a state of denial regarding Ateş's mental health and resultant behaviour. Also remember that Esat heads up one of the most lethal criminal gangs in İstanbul. Thus far we've never been able to convict either him or his blood relatives of anything bigger than speeding tickets or petty possession. Further, the Böceks claim they are pious Muslims, something about which they make a lot of noise and for which they receive some attention from many of our political and social movers and shakers. I fully support what you propose, Doctor, and to that end I will insist on Esat Böcek meeting here with the two of us as soon as possible.'

'Thank you, Inspector.'

'It is I who should thank you for your honesty,' Süleyman said.

'There is something genuinely amiss here,' the doctor said, 'but I don't know what and there's nothing in the medical records. Of course he wouldn't be the first person in this country to be the victim of his family's shame. Stigma remains an enormous barrier to families getting proper help for their loved ones.'

'Where are you going, Aylın?'

As soon as she'd touched the front door, Aylın Ayhan's father Murad had appeared.

Briefly closing her eyes before she turned and looked at him, she said, 'I'm going to meet Esma.'

'Are you?'

'Yes!'

133

Murad Ayhan was in his late fifties, slim and handsome. Taken at face value, he was a sophisticated middle-class man with liberal values. But those who knew him, like his daughter, were aware that behind the dental veneers and the gym-honed body was a coarse thug from the back streets of the old Roma quarter of Sulukule. And while not Roma himself, Murad had grown up tough as one of the very few Turkish boys in the mahalle. The adult Murad was even tougher and certainly more ruthless.

'Why are you meeting her and where?' he asked. 'Remember, I don't want you consorting with those brothers of hers. They're trash, you can do better.'

Aylın put a hand on her hip. 'Their dad is a surgeon,' she said. 'Their grandad fought in the War of Independence.'

'Faruk Nebatı is a thief!'

'You only say that because he's Roma.'

'I grew up with him!' Murad thundered. 'Little shit would rob the dead!'

'Well then he's mended his ways.' Aylın knew that it did no good to keep shouting at her father. If she did that, he would eventually resort to violence.

'I won't have my children going with gypsies,' he said.

'Esma's mum isn't a gypsy.'

'No, but he is, Faruk. You keep away from those boys if you value your inheritance. You will marry much better than them.' He moved towards her. 'I have my eye on you, Aylın. If either of those gypsy boys touches you, I will know and I will kill him. Make no mistake about that! Now go out, if you must, but know that I am watching you.'

'Really, Daddy?' Aylın said. 'Well I'm watching you too. I may not have been at your party last night, but I heard you.' She lowered her voice. 'And I heard the woman you were fucking in your wife's bedroom.'

Murad Ayhan turned white. He went to hit his daughter,

but the look on her face made him stay his hand. In many ways, Aylın was much more like him than Murad chose to acknowledge.

Aylın left the house and walked down the drive. She could see Esma waiting for her on the street and so she waved. Her father was such a bigot! Supposed to be secular and yet he still saw her as a commodity to be bought and sold by men like some house-bound woman in Saudi Arabia. And he had affairs. He'd fucked some random woman only last night! He had mistresses all over the city and Aylın had no doubt that at least one of his conquests was Roma. He'd grown up amongst them. He'd happily employed their men in his various businesses. If they knew how he really felt about them, they'd cut his throat.

'Kerim Bey!'

The whole area was still stiff with police officers, and the Şekeroğlu meyhane plus the road in front of it was cordoned off. But Rambo Şekeroğlu senior was out and about and so he spotted Kerim Gürsel as soon as he arrived.

The policeman went over to the gypsy and said, 'How are you, Rambo Bey?'

Rambo shrugged. 'Alive.'

Kerim shook his head. 'Any idea what last night was about?'

'None. But what I do know is that we're all very grateful to Mehmet Bey for saving old Rahul Mengüç's life. His daughter went to see him in hospital this morning and he's doing well.'

Kerim had been about to ask how the old man was and was glad that he seemed to be recovering.

'Of course my sister was behind it,' Rambo continued. 'Saw that the old haberdasher was hit and started to run towards him.'

'I know, I was there,' Kerim said.

'Pushed her out the way, he did, and went to him hisself.' Rambo shook his head. 'He's a brave man. But then again, my sister's crazy, so what can you do except stop her for her own good?'

Kerim smiled. 'She's his wife. He loves her.'

'God knows why!' Rambo said. 'But then . . .' He shrugged. 'What you doing down here, Kerim Bey?'

'I'm working with Superintendent Şen on this case. We've an appointment to see Şevket Bey.'

'He's in his club,' Rambo said.

'That's where we're meeting him.'

'Mmm.'

Rambo was an easy-going man in his thirties. And while proud to be a member of the Roma community, he was much less tied to their rules and traditions than his older siblings. He said, 'You know that even if he knows what's going on, he won't tell you, don't you?'

'I'm fully aware of that,' Kerim said.

'So what's the point, Kerim Bey?'

'The point is to be seen to be doing our job,' Kerim said. 'Mehmet Bey talked to Sesler last night, and I've no doubt I won't get any more out of him than he did.'

So far the only intimation that Sesler could be in the midst of a turf war had come from this man's sister, Didim Hanım. But that was only hearsay. Maybe Kerim and Şen could get Sesler to open up, but it was unlikely. In the world of İstanbul organised crime, those involved tended to dispense their own justice without recourse to the police. Besides, Kerim had doubts about Didim's story. If Sesler was feuding with the Böceks over the death of a dancing girl, wasn't that a bit over the top? The level of violence used on the streets of Tarlabaşı had surely been excessive if the disagreement was simply over a girl. Sesler, after all, had lots of girls. What had been so special about this Ceviz Elibol? If indeed the body Mehmet Süleyman had discovered in Kadıköy had been hers.

*

He was a little later than usual, but Çetin İkmen was happy to see that Numan Bey was waiting for him. He'd even placed İkmen's stool on the ground right on the dockside for him.

As soon as İkmen sat down, the old man gave him a glass of pickle juice, which he drank immediately.

'So,' Numan Bey said as he refilled the glass, 'you were in Tarlabaşı last night?'

'I was,' İkmen said.

'I heard about the shooting.'

'As you can see, I managed to avoid confronting my own mortality on this occasion.'

'We always knew that Şevket Bey had enemies, but do you have any idea who may have done it yet, Çetin Bey?'

'No.'

İkmen drank his second glass and Numan Bey went to take it from him but frowned instead. 'There's some detritus at the bottom of your glass, Çetin Bey.'

'I don't care,' İkmen said.

'No, no,' the old man said, 'shake it out over the water.'

İkmen did as he was told, and it was as he was looking down that he saw the sculptures.

Attached to the wood and metal piers used to construct the nineteenth-century dockside were three colourful, extremely well-made sculpted human heads. Three men, they looked out into the mouth of the Bosphorus. Each face, İkmen felt, looked incredibly sad.

While graffiti was common in İstanbul, guerrilla sculpture was relatively rare. İkmen could recall only two examples, both in Kadıköy, called *Requiem for a Tree* and *Rejoice for a Tree*. Both these works involved metal 'stick man' sculptures, one mourning the loss of a local tree, the other celebrating the coming of its eventual replacement.

'What are you looking at?' Numan Bey asked when İkmen didn't immediately return his glass for refilling.

137

'Come and look at this,' İkmen said.

The old man left his cart and walked over to the dockside. 'What is it?'

İkmen pointed. 'There.'

'Oh. Well, you know better than most, Çetin Bey, that strange things are always turning up in this city.'

'I take your point,' İkmen said. 'But who are they?'

'What?'

'The sculptures,' he said. 'I mean, look at them, they're beautifully made. This isn't some kid messing around with a bit of clay.'

'I dunno.'

İkmen took his phone out of his pocket and began to take photographs.

'What you doing that for?' the old man asked.

'Preserving them for posterity,' İkmen said. 'To he honest, I'm tempted to remove them before they get damaged, but that's probably not the point.'

'What do you mean?'

'They've clearly been put here for a reason. The artist – and whoever made these *is* an artist – must've been trying to say something when he or she put them in this location. I mean, it's not exactly an easy place in which to display your work.'

'Hardly anyone will see it.'

'Right.'

He took a lot of photographs and then put his phone back in his pocket. As he did so, he felt a rising sense of excitement in his body and his mind. Tracking down who had made these sculptures and put them in such a strange and unusual place was something he would enjoy. It was certainly something better to do than just wander the streets of the Old City with no agenda.

Esat Böcek was a tall, thin, ascetic-looking man. In his early sixties, he had a neat beard and moustache and wore clothes more befitting a humble minor government official than a powerful gang boss. Not for Esat Ferraris and yachts – he left all that kind of display to his children. Since his wife had died, he had lived with his mother in a chic, if discreet, apartment in Kadıköy, his only vice apparently his custom of praying at his local mosque five times a day. Everyone who attended knew him because he was also landlord to most of them. It paid to keep in with a man who owned your home and occasionally travelled to deposit your rent money in either the Cayman Islands or the Isle of Man.

Amongst the many things Esat Böcek disliked were scientists, secularists and Jews. Ticking all three of those boxes, Dr İlker Koca was not going to be his favourite person. And while Mehmet Süleyman as a scion of an Ottoman family should have been at least in part a sympathetic co-religionist brother, he had made it very clear from the beginning of this interview that he considered Esat way beneath him.

Taking his cue from Dr Koca's early findings, Süleyman said, 'How long has Ateş suffered with mental health issues, Esat Bey?'

Esat bridled immediately. 'He's not mad. Where'd you get the idea he's mad from?' He glared at Dr Koca for a few moments before turning back to look at Süleyman.

'Nobody said your son was mad,' Süleyman said. 'Diagnosing a condition of the mind is a delicate and often lengthy process. The doctor bey is asking you to consider giving him the time and space to hopefully understand and improve Ateş's condition.'

Referring to the psychiatrist as 'doctor bey' was insulting, Esat thought. It was as if Süleyman were speaking to some ignorant peasant!

'My son needs no help and he did not kill that girl,' he said.

'How do you know he didn't kill the girl?' Süleyman asked. 'Were you there?'

'No!'

'We found your son at his home carrying a bloodied yataghan.

There was a dead body, at the time unrecognisable, upstairs on a bed. The blood on the yataghan, we now learn, was identical to that exuded by the body, which is, we think, that of a young Roma woman with whom Ateş was having an affair. Tell me, Esat Bey, given those facts, what would you think about the person who may have killed this woman? And in what state of mind would that individual have to be in order to tear apart another human being?'

Esat Böcek was infuriated. 'Oh, so you've made up your mind that Ateş did it!'

The psychiatrist interjected. 'Esat Bey,' he said, 'what Inspector Süleyman is saying is that he doesn't want to simply follow the forensic evidence, because, like me, he believes that your son's state of mind may well be significant in this case.'

'So you think he's mad *and* a murderer!'

'That is one possibility, yes,' Dr Koca said. 'I will not lie and tell you that it isn't. But there are other possibilities, and although I am not aware of any forensic evidence connecting anybody else to the scene, that doesn't mean that none will be found. The investigation is ongoing . . .'

'Yes,' Süleyman said.

'However, if your son did indeed commit this crime, if he did so while in a delusional or other disordered state, that will impact upon how blame may be attributed. Prison is not a suitable place of disposal for such individuals, and so he would be treated for his condition rather than punished. I know that accepting that one's blood relatives may be mentally unwell is difficult. Stigma about such a diagnosis exists . . .'

'He's not mad!'

'. . . and so what I am proposing,' the doctor continued, 'is that Ateş be detained in my care at Bakırköy psychiatric hospital, under an involuntary assessment order. This will last three weeks and will give me a chance to try to unravel what may or may not be wrong with your son. However, I do need your approval in order to do this.'

'I cannot stress enough,' Süleyman said, 'how important this could be for Ateş. Without this assessment, if no confounding forensics come to light in the meantime, he is looking at being put on trial for a murder that will shock and horrify everyone in this city. I would urge you, Esat Bey, to do this for his sake.'

Chapter 11

Kerim Gürsel had left his phone on. Quickly he switched it off without looking at the identity of the caller. This was because if it was Sinem he'd have to answer, and this really wasn't the moment for that.

From the moment he and Superintendent Cihat Şen had entered the Kızlar club, it had been apparent that its owner, Şevket Sesler, was high on cocaine.

'I told the Roma bridegroom everything I know!' he said. 'I don't know anything else! Why are you here?'

Şen was not the most patient man in the world, and so Kerim had taken the lead.

'Because, Şevket Bey, as I am sure my colleague told you, often when you are in a situation, you notice things you only remember afterwards,' he said.

'I don't!'

'You think you don't, no—'

'I fucking don't!'

Şen was unable to sit on his anger any longer. 'You need to account for your movements yesterday. From the time you got up.'

'The Roma bridegroom didn't ask me that!'

'Inspector Süleyman, like all of us, was dealing with a situation yesterday,' Kerim said. 'This is standard procedure, Şevket Bey.'

'You want me to make a statement?'

'Yes, we do,' Kerim said. 'And for your convenience, not ours, we have come to visit you rather than getting you in to headquarters.' He took a sheaf of papers out of his jacket pocket. 'I'll even write down what you tell me. All you have to do is sign it.'

Not many people were aware that Şevket Sesler's writing skills began and ended with signing his name. Kerim only knew that because Gonca had told him.

Sesler narrowed his eyes. 'You'll write what I tell you?'

'Yes.'

'You won't make stuff up?'

'Şevket Bey, you will of course be obliged to read what I have written before you sign it.'

Gonca had said nothing about Sesler's reading skills – or lack thereof.

The gangster turned to the man who seemed to be almost always by his side now, and said something to him in Romani. Munir Can replied in kind.

Superintendent Şen said, 'What are you talking about? Turkish, please!'

Sesler looked at Şen as if he had a bad smell under his nose. 'I have asked Munir Bey to read it with me,' he said. 'A second pair of eyes is needed with the police.'

Kerim, who was sick of this prevarication, took his pen out. 'All right. Now, Şevket Bey, where did you sleep the night prior to your birthday celebration, and with whom, if anyone?'

The gangster smiled unpleasantly, said something in Romani to Munir Can, who laughed, and then said, 'I was here. I have a bedroom here.'

'Why?'

'Why not?'

'Well, do you sometimes work late, or . . .'

'I am a businessman, this is my business,' Sesler said. 'I sleep here sometimes to keep an eye on those who work for me.'

'Can't your staff be trusted?'

'No one can be trusted. I am Roma, we trust no one. Ask the Witch, she'll tell you.'

Kerim knew that he meant Gonca, but he chose to ignore it. Aggravating Sesler at this point would mean that he'd get even less cooperation than the little he was receiving now.

'So you were here,' he said. 'With whom?'

Sesler smiled again, and so did Munir Can.

When Çetin İkmen arrived home, he found his cousin Samsun rocking Melda Gürsel in her arms.

'Sinem Hanım's having a shower,' Samsun said. 'She tried to ring Kerim Bey, but he switched his phone off. Rude.'

'Not rude; busy, I imagine,' İkmen said. 'When he left his ladies here last night, he told me he was going back to work, because that's how it is when something like this happens.'

'Five deaths!' Samsun said. 'Şevket Bey must have really got underneath someone's skin!'

'Well, you work in Tarlabaşı,' İkmen said. 'Know anything?'

'Nothing beyond the usual.'

'And what's that?'

'Rent arrears. You know how he works. You miss your rent once on a dump with no running water or electricity that he doesn't even legally own, and Sesler sends his boys round to break your nose. Lots of them hate him, but they're destitute, most of them. I've no idea how much a gun costs in this city, but probably more than one of his tenants can afford.'

Sinem Gürsel, freshly showered but still looking tired, came into the living room. 'Oh, Çetin Bey, thank you so much for putting up with us last night.' She took the baby from Samsun. 'I hope Melda's crying didn't keep you awake?'

'No.'

Samsun said, 'Would you like a glass of tea, darling?'

'That would be lovely, thank you.' She sat down.

İkmen sat down opposite. 'Kerim was afraid the shooter might still be in the area. Just happy we could give you both a bed.'

'I tried to ring him, but he switched his phone off. I imagine he was probably with someone.'

'It will be hard for him to get away at this stage.'

'I know.' She looked sad.

'You can stay here as long as you like,' İkmen added. 'It makes a nice change to have a little one in the apartment again.'

She smiled.

He said, 'All my children were born here. My wife was only ever attended by a midwife until Kemal was born. Then we had a doctor. Different times.'

'Yes.'

Then something occurred to him.

'Sinem Hanım, didn't you use to work in an art gallery?'

'A long time ago,' she said. 'It was in Karaköy, on Mumhane Caddesi. A space for women artists. It's not there now. Why?'

He showed her the photographs he'd taken of the sculptured heads he'd seen at Eminönü. Frowning, Sinem said, 'I've never seen anything like that before.'

'Me neither.'

Samsun returned with tea and looked at İkmen's phone.

'They're good,' she said. 'Where are they?'

'Eminönü,' İkmen replied. 'Attached to the piers holding up the dockside.'

'Strange place to exhibit. Mind you, this city has become a bit of a magnet for guerrilla art in the past decade. We're stiff with graffiti in Tarlabaşı.'

İkmen looked at Sinem. 'I'd like to find out who the artist is.'

'No one I'm aware of,' Sinem said. 'And I'm not really in touch with the art world these days. But you could do worse than taking a walk around Karaköy and Beyoğlu. There are a lot of small galleries in those areas and artists do tend to know one another.

145

When I was involved years ago, they were always going to each other's exhibitions, meeting up to talk about their work in meyhanes around İstiklal.'

İkmen nodded. 'Thank you.'

It meant more walking, but what else could he do? He was intrigued now. The heads had piqued his interest. And anything was better than being bored, even sore feet.

'Do you have enough evidence to hold him?'

'I do,' Süleyman said to Dr Koca. 'Given the forensic evidence I have so far, I can charge him. But . . .'

Esat Böcek had refused to allow his son to be detained under an involuntary assessment order, preferring, it seemed, to have Ateş held on remand in prison. However, at the present time, both Süleyman and the doctor were more concerned about the immediate future. The police had to either charge him or let him go.

'We've some CCTV footage of Ateş that you should see, Doctor,' Süleyman continued. 'Filmed on the morning of the murder when, according to Dr Sarkissian, the victim would have already been killed. It features Ateş shopping. I'd appreciate your view.'

'Of course.'

He brought the footage up on his system and the two men watched it in silence. Afterwards the doctor said, 'He appears calm.'

'He does.'

'That said, if he is a psychopath, he may well be calm. Lack of empathy is a feature of those with that diagnosis. In the course of my career, I have worked with men and women for whom killing is simply a rational act – like putting down a sick dog.'

'Would you venture that Ateş Böcek is a psychopath?' Süleyman asked.

Dr Koca sighed. 'Difficult to say given that he has been mostly silent ever since we met. If he is faking, he could very well be a psychopath; it's one of the things they do when apprehended. Go silent, actively play out a "mad" role, or both.'

'This silent act could be . . .'

'Fake or genuine, yes,' he said.

'Anecdotal evidence has Ateş talking and shouting in the street, apparently at nothing, for some years,' Süleyman said.

'That would seem to suggest some form of mental distress.'

'Which is why I wanted that extra time for you to assess him,' Süleyman said. 'I'm trying to help him!'

Dr Koca shook his head. 'I know you are. But my reading of the situation vis-à-vis the father is that he is too proud to admit that his son has a problem. Still a common phenomenon in this country, I fear. And of course, Böcek senior is a gangster. People not, I observe, known for their intellectual prowess.'

'No.'

'And yet, luckily for them, you are heading this investigation,' the doctor said. 'And don't think I'm doing some sort of snivelling "Inspector Bey" grovel. You say yourself that you could charge him now and have done with it. Many of your colleagues would.'

Süleyman smiled. 'Don't run away with the idea that I am some sort of moral crusader,' he said. 'I'm not. I am all for justice, but I am equally aware of the fact that evidence could yet come to light exonerating Ateş Böcek completely. There's more than meets the eye here, Doctor. I just don't know what that is.'

Dr Koca nodded. 'You were mentored by Inspector İkmen, weren't you, Mehmet Bey?'

Süleyman laughed. 'Is it that obvious?'

There was only so much interaction you could have with people with whom you didn't share a language. That had been why Gonca Süleyman had thrown Juan Cortes out of her house all those years ago when they had briefly been lovers. That and the fact that he actively chased other women. Now, sitting in her fog-bound

147

garden, she watched as her son Rambo and Juan's son Tomas spoke English, even sharing jokes.

Juan and Lola had made a fire in front of their tent, around which they all sat eating spicy chorizo sausages the old man roasted in the flames. Now that Sesler's birthday was over, the Spaniards wanted to get back on the road. But that wasn't possible. The police still needed to interview them, for which they required an approved translator. Mehmet had told her that should happen within hours, but she'd not as yet been called.

Rambo bounced over and sat down beside her.

'Tomas said that if I want to, I can travel with them to Spain,' he said.

'Do you want to do that?' Gonca asked.

'I don't know. Not much for me here at the moment.'

If asked what he did for a living, Rambo always said 'this and that' or 'whatever'. Like a lot of the Roma boys, he lived on his wits, doing a bit of street performance, working in bars, running errands for Şevket Sesler.

'What do you want to do?' Gonca asked.

'I don't know,' he said. 'Get out of Tarlabaşı?'

He lived only part of the time with his mother in Balat; the rest of his life was spent working in Tarlabaşı and sleeping on relatives' floors.

'You know everyone there,' Gonca said. 'You have contacts.' She put an arm around him. He was her youngest child, her baby, and she didn't want him to go.

'Yeah, but if Şevket Bey's going to war, I'm not up for it,' he said.

'Just because there was a shooting last night doesn't mean that Sesler's going to war,' Gonca said. 'We don't know why that happened yet. Maybe it had nothing to do with Şevket Bey.'

He smirked. 'You don't believe that, do you?'

'I don't know.'

He held her close, kissed her face and then whispered in her ear, 'Şevket Bey is at war with the Böceks. Their boy killed Ceviz Elibol, and Şevket Bey wants compensation.'

'That what happened last night was . . .'

'Şevket Bey asked for money,' Rambo said, 'but the Böceks paid him in death.'

Şevket Sesler had spent the night with a girl called Ayda Taner. One of his strippers, she was a Turkish girl who did what she had to in order to care for her elderly disabled father.

'I'll have to speak to her,' Kerim told Sesler. 'To confirm your story.'

'I can arrange that,' Sesler said. 'She's of age. I won't have weird stuff going on in my places.'

Kerim looked at Superintendent Şen, who said nothing.

'And once Miss Taner had left you . . .'

'She had to go back to her father,' Sesler said.

'So she didn't stay all night?'

'Why would she?'

Kerim had wondered about that, but he didn't say anything.

'So after she left . . .'

'I went back to sleep,' Sesler said. 'Must've got up about ten.'

Kerim wrote it down. 'What happened next?'

'My wife arrived to cook my breakfast. The kids came to wish me happy birthday. You can talk to them.'

'We will.'

'After that, I was here all day,' Sesler said. Munir Can nodded in agreement. 'Ask anyone.'

'I'd like to ask someone who doesn't work for you,' Kerim said.

'Why?'

'Why? Really? Şevket Bey, I know what you do and you know I know that. Let's not waste time trading in fantasy. You and your men run this part of Tarlabaşı. You both care for and terrorise

149

your own people. Put yourself in my position. Would you take the word of someone who either works for or lives in fear of you?'

The Roma godfather frowned. People rarely dared to be as blunt as this Gürsel man, who he knew lived locally. Not that he would ever threaten a cop, at least not directly. Munir Can whispered something in his ear, and Sesler said, 'I saw the entertainers, jugglers and dancers. Those Spaniards Gonca Hanım engaged, they're nothing to do with me, they're foreign. Ask them. I saw them in Rambo Şekeroğlu's meyhane.'

Which was an idea, but as far as Kerim knew, the department had yet to appoint a Spanish translator. Excusing himself to Sesler and Şen, he walked outside and made a phone call.

There was a lot of denim happening in the menswear shop Çetin İkmen found himself staring at on Mumhane Caddesi. He'd started his art gallery quest here because it was on this street that Sinem Gürsel used to curate a small women's gallery before her marriage. The menswear shop was situated beside a very small gallery that appeared to be exhibiting absolutely nothing – hence İkmen's fixation on denim jeans. Also he was putting off entering the gallery because the woman who appeared to be drifting about aimlessly inside kept looking at him, and not in a good way.

Eventually irritated by his own lack of resolve, he stopped looking at trousers and went into the gallery. The woman, tall, blonde and wearing a skin-tight leather or PVC trouser suit, walked over to him and said, 'Are you interested in the work of Dondurma?'

She had, he felt, that look in her eye that was telling him she knew he wasn't.

İkmen said, 'Are you the artist?'

She pursed her lips. 'Dondurma is male. Do I look like a man to you?'

'No . . .'

'So I take it you're not interested in his work.'

İkmen took his phone out of his pocket and brought up a photograph showing the three heads.

'I'm interested in finding out who made these,' he said.

She first squinted at the image and then put on a large pair of spectacles.

'What are they?' she asked.

'Heads,' he said. 'Sculptures. They're attached to the wooden piers holding up Eminönü docks.'

Her expression told him she thought he might be mad.

İkmen swiped the screen and brought up another photograph, which placed the sculptures in their surroundings.

'Oh . . .'

'Any idea who the artist might be?' he asked.

She took her spectacles off. 'No. Dondurma doesn't work in that medium.'

It wasn't until İkmen got outside the gallery that he realised he still didn't know what Dondurma did do.

Ömer Mungun met Bishop Juan-Maria Montoya at headquarters main entrance and took him up to Süleyman's office. As the cleric walked in, the inspector rose to his feet and extended his hand.

'Your Excellency, I can't thank you enough for coming,' he said.

The Mexican shook his hand and then sat down. 'My pleasure,' he said. 'Although I must say that I thought the police would have translation services of your own.'

'We do,' Süleyman replied. 'In fact, we have two Spanish translators, but one has gone home for Christmas, while the other is sick. We were stuck.' He looked at his sergeant. 'It was only when Sergeant Mungun and Inspector Gürsel spoke on the telephone that between them they came up with your name.'

'There will not be a problem that I am not officially a translator?' the bishop asked.

'Not from my perspective,' Süleyman said. 'And you know the Cortes family, I believe.'

'Oh yes. They came with your wife to Midnight Mass on Christmas Eve.'

'Quite.' He smiled. 'Well, I have sent a car to pick them up and bring them here. In the interim, maybe we can talk about the events of last night in Tarlabaşı. Oh, and Ömer Bey, could you please organise some tea or coffee for our guest?'

'Yes, sir.' Ömer turned to the bishop. 'What would you like, Your Excellency?'

'You know you can call me Bishop, or even Juan – it is my name,' the Mexican said.

'I appreciate that,' Süleyman replied. 'And in a social situation that would be preferable. But in an official scenario I would rather keep things formal.'

'As you wish.' The bishop looked at Ömer. 'Coffee, please, Sergeant. Turkish or espresso, very sweet. Sugar is one of my many vices.'

'Yes, sir.' Ömer left.

The bishop said, 'I heard about what happened in Tarlabaşı. I feared the Cortes family may have been affected.'

'No. Fortunately we were all OK.'

'You were there?'

'With my wife, yes,' Süleyman said. 'Inspector Gürsel is lead officer on this case and was there too. However, as I am sure you will appreciate, at this stage of an investigation there is much to do, and so I am taking on certain tasks in order to free Kerim Bey up for what I suppose you'd call the more intense aspects of the investigation. My aim with regard to the Cortes family is to discover what they saw. People are not always aware of what they may have witnessed during a criminal act. The process of consciously recalling, whilst sometimes traumatic, can clarify certain vague impressions.'

'What about false memory?' the bishop asked.

'That can happen,' Süleyman said. 'As I'm sure you know, your Excellency, sometimes our brains fill gaps in our knowledge with safe alternatives.'

Ömer Mungun returned, put a tiny coffee cup down in front of the bishop and said, 'The Cortes family have arrived, boss. Oh, and Gonca Hanım is with them.'

Esma Nebatı was a short, frankly fat girl. Unlike a lot of young women in their early twenties, however, she entirely owned it. In contrast to her best friend, Aylın Ayhan, she wasn't interested in conforming to passing beauty stereotypes and wore the colourful clothes she liked in spite of her mother's disapproval. She was far too involved in her work as a florist, creating expensive, highly artistic displays for wedding, engagement and sünnet celebrations, to spare a lot of thought for the current vogue for what she called 'skinny'. 'I'm all about the plants,' she was wont to say if questioned about her desire, or not, to marry someone herself any time soon. And while her own clothes shopping preference was for the arty little shops of Karaköy and Cihangir, she did enjoy going to malls like İstinye Park with Aylın from time to time.

Situated in the district of Sarıyer on the European side of the Bosphorus, İstinye Park was a vast glass-roofed temple to shopping that featured many high-end outlets, including local brands Vakko and Beymen as well as Prada, Gucci, Hermès and Chanel. However, on this occasion, Aylın was concentrating on a slightly more outré Russian-owned boutique.

As the girls sorted through racks of tiny rhinestone-encrusted dresses, Esma said, 'Isn't this all a bit, you know, "oligarch"?' Not certain that the very groomed and thin sales assistants weren't Russian themselves, she whispered the last word.

Aylın frowned. 'What do you mean?'

'Well . . . a bit, you know . . .'

'Esma Hanım, you know you can say that my father's a gangster, don't you?' Aylın said. 'We both know it.'

'Er . . .'

She smiled. 'Darling, sometimes people like to conform to type. Let me shock my father by looking like one of his whores.'

'Yes, but if he gets cross . . .'

Aylın picked up three dresses and went to try them on. In truth, Esma didn't have a problem with oligarch chic; what she did have a problem with was Aylın's father. Murad Ayhan was a gangster. Like her own father, he had battled his way out of poverty in Sulukule. Unlike Faruk Nebatı, who had used his brains to advance himself, Murad Ayhan had used his fists, and later guns, to get what he wanted. Esma knew that her friend's father looked down on her family because her dad was Roma. Aylın had told her that Murad didn't want her around Esma's brothers, Alp and Semih, because he feared she might fancy one or other of them. In fact, Esma knew that Aylın fancied them both. Alp and Semih were really handsome, like their father, and Aylın was besotted with them. What she didn't realise, or didn't want to realise, was that both boys were way too serious about their careers to be interested in her. Alp was studying for the law and had a girlfriend with similar ambitions, while Semih, a doctor like his father, just enjoyed being single.

Esma sat down on one of the vast velvet sofas provided for the comfort of customers. One of the assistants asked her whether she wanted something to drink, but she declined. Then a lone man walked into the shop and began to peruse the clothing. Young and slim, he wore well-cut jeans and a thick leather aviator jacket. Esma would have described him as a 'good-looking kid'.

Aylın came out of the changing room in the shortest and most excessive of the three dresses and sashayed past the young man without a glance in his direction. Esma was struck by how intensely, by contrast, he looked at her friend.

Chapter 12

None of the residents of Kerim Gürsel's apartment block had seen or heard anything untoward the previous evening, when five people had died because of a sniper based on their roof. The only exceptions to this were Sinem and Madam Edith, who had definitely heard noises emanating from the roof. However, even Sinem and Edith hadn't heard anything from their neighbour's apartment. And yet the middle-aged man Kerim had dubbed 'the pimp' had died from a gunshot wound the size of a fist.

According to the landlord of the building, he had been a fifty-eight-year-old architect called Mete Bülbül. Single, quiet, always paid his rent on time. Nevertheless, he had possessed neither books about architecture nor architectural drawings. Scene-of-crime officers had, however, found boxes and boxes of condoms.

As Kerim surveyed Bülbül's apartment, Superintendent Cihat Şen said, 'Ballistics have identified the bullet as coming from a Glock 17.'

That was one of the Turkish National Police Force's standard handguns. Kerim raised his eyebrows.

'As far as we know at the moment,' Şen continued, 'all the other victims were shot by a rifle.'

Dr Sarkissian and his team had taken the six dead victims away for post-mortem. Kerim didn't expect that process to begin in earnest until the following day, when he and Eylul Yavaş would be obliged to attend at least one of the investigations. Of course relatives of the dead were already calling for the bodies to be released for burial, with the notable exception of Mete Bülbül.

Şen asked, 'Didn't you know Bülbül at all?'

'No,' Kerim said. 'He was already here when I moved in with my wife. We would see him in the corridors and on the stairs from time to time. Always smartly dressed, always quiet. But I did see him on the street too sometimes, usually with working girls. I'll be honest. I thought he was a pimp.'

'Doesn't Sesler control all the girls round here?' Şen asked.

'A lot of them, but not all. He doesn't touch the trans brothels.'

'Did you see Bülbül with trans girls?'

'No,' Kerim said.

'So he could have been one of Sesler's people?'

'He could. But Sesler's pimps are Roma, and I don't think Bülbül was.'

'Why not?' Şen asked.

'Because Roma have family, and to my knowledge, no one ever visited Bülbül.'

'Mmm, and I suppose you'd know.'

'I live here.'

'And your colleague is married to a Roma woman,' Şen said. Then he frowned. 'How does that work?'

'What?'

'Süleyman and his wife. Strange. Especially for someone like him.'

Some of their colleagues had been less than impressed when Süleyman had married Gonca Şekeroğlu. Not so much with the fact that she was older than he was as the fact that she was Roma.

Eventually Kerim said, 'They love one another.'

Şen sniffed. 'Weird.'

Kerim ignored him. Şen, like a lot of men in his experience, couldn't understand cross-cultural relationships. Same-sex partnerships would probably make his head explode.

*

The next two small galleries İkmen tried were staffed by people who wanted to help but knew nothing. He turned on to Bankalar Caddesi, once the centre of the Turkish financial world, now home to the famous Salt gallery, and it was there that he met an old friend.

Aaron Kamhi was the son of one of İkmen's father's old colleagues, Moses Kamhi, who had also worked at İstanbul University. Like his father, Aaron was an academic; if İkmen remembered correctly, he specialised in late-Ottoman history. Some twenty years younger than İkmen, he was a small, elegant man who looked like a nineteenth-century dandy. In summer he always wore an immaculate dark suit, while now, in winter, he walked the streets of İstanbul in a fedora hat and full-length opera cloak. Moses had always dressed like that too, İkmen recalled as he embraced his friend.

'How are you, Çetin?' Aaron asked. 'It's been such a long time . . .'

İkmen had last seen Aaron in the week following Fatma's funeral, when friends and family had come to the apartment with presents of food and drink. Aaron, he recalled, had arrived with a huge basket of fresh fruit and a bottle of brandy, just for him.

'Too long,' he said. 'Although I imagine you've been busy.'

'Not too busy to go and see a friend,' Aaron said. 'I'm sorry.'

'Think nothing of it.'

'Well, the least I can do is buy you a drink. Have you tried the Salt Café? It's very good.'

They both entered the Salt Galata building. An enormous cross between a nineteenth-century Parisian palace and an orientalist fantasy, it had once housed the premises of the powerful Ottoman Bank. The excessive amount of wood panelling and tile flooring was another clue to its former function.

Aaron led the way to a cool space filled with tables and chairs and scented with coffee. İkmen, looking at the drinks menu, decided he would treat himself to a brandy to go with his Turkish coffee. Aaron opted for just coffee. Once their drinks had arrived, he asked, 'So what have you been doing with yourself lately? I still can't believe you've actually retired.'

İkmen smiled. 'I did nothing for a long time after Fatma's death.' He shook his head. 'Useless to my children.'

'I'm sure—'

'Oh, I *was* useless, Aaron. Wallowing in my own misery. But I do a bit of private investigation now. Keeps me busy.'

'And I'm sure you do it well,' Aaron said. 'You've always been excellent at everything you do. Please, no false modesty, Çetin. Your father was so proud of you and Halil.'

'He never told us that.'

'Of course not,' Aaron laughed. 'No more than my father ever told Esther and myself we were doing well. Anyway, what brings you to this part of the city?'

'I'm looking for an artist,' İkmen said.

'Really? What for?'

He sighed. It was going to sound mad.

Mehmet Süleyman knew that his wife, left to her own devices, would want to know where he was all the time. But he also knew that she fought against this urge, and so he was surprised to see her accompanying the Spaniards at police headquarters.

When she saw him, she said, 'They wanted me to come with them. What could I do?'

People were watching them, and so he was disinclined to touch or kiss her. A lot of his colleagues considered his marriage odd, if not downright offensive. What did he see in a woman so much older than himself? And 'one of them' to boot?

'It's OK,' he said. 'But obviously you can't be with them when I conduct my interview.'

'Do you have a translator?' she asked.

'Not an official one, but Bishop Montoya has stepped into the breach. I think it's best if you wait for them in Kerim Bey's office.'

'I can wait here.'

She could, but Süleyman knew that people would stare at her.

'No. Kerim Bey is out and so I can leave you with Sergeant Yavaş,' he said. 'She'll get you a drink and make you comfortable.'

He led the Spaniards up to his office and then deposited Gonca next door.

'Sergeant Yavaş,' he said, 'I'm just about to go into interview. Could I leave my wife with you until I've finished?'

Eylul looked up and smiled. 'Of course, sir.'

But then Gonca said, 'Oh, and Mehmet, I have something to tell you!'

'Not now. Sorry.'

As he walked past her, she kissed his cheek.

Aylın bought two dresses and a jacket. The latter was covered in rhinestones and, Esma thought, looked much cheaper than its enormous price tag. But it made Aylın happy – for a short while.

As they left the shop, Esma caught sight of the boy who had stared at her friend standing outside. And while he didn't attempt to talk to Aylın, she saw the pair's eyes meet for a second. She wondered whether they knew each other, but it wasn't until the two girls were ensconced with coffee at Caffè Nero that she dared to ask.

'There was a boy in the shop who couldn't stop looking at you,' she said.

Aylın frowned. 'What boy?'

'Good looking,' Esma said, 'wearing an aviator jacket.'

'Oh God, you don't mean İlhan Böcek, do you?' Aylın sounded horrified.

Esma said, 'I don't know, do I?'

'Slouching about on the concourse trying to look cool?'

'Well, I suppose . . .'

'He's a moron,' Aylın said. 'Supposed to be religious.' She shook her head. 'My dad knows his dad and they are not friends.'

'Oh.'

Esma had been around Aylın long enough to know that this probably meant that İlhan Böcek's family were business rivals of Murad Ayhan. Her father, who had grown up with Murad, hadn't been happy when the girls had become friends. He'd told her, 'I know you like Aylın, but I don't want you going to any of her family's parties.' Esma had asked why not, and her father had said, 'Because Murad Bey is a gangster. He has blood on his hands.'

And while Esma had always found Murad Bey very pleasant, she knew that her father was right, because Aylın had told her.

Aylın leaned in and lowered her voice, 'You know the police found a dead body over in a palace off Baghdat Caddesi two nights ago?'

Esma had heard something about a murder on the news, but she didn't know anything about it. She said, 'Sort of . . .'

'Well, that was at İlhan Böcek's brother's house,' Aylın said. 'He's called Ateş and he's been arrested.'

'For murder?'

'Yes. I don't always agree with my dad about people, but I think he's right about that family. Apparently Ateş Böcek is completely mad. Talks to himself and everything!'

'So why was İlhan looking at you?' Esma asked. 'If his brother has been arrested, surely he should be with his family.'

'You'd think so, yes,' Aylın said. 'Anyway, he fancies me.'

'How do you know? I mean, I could see from the way he was looking at you . . .'

'He's the same age as my brother,' Aylın said. 'They went to school together. Yıldırım still sees him sometimes. I've seen them on Istiklal Caddesi, laughing at people and acting like children. I think my brother fancies him.'

'How do you know?' Esma said.

'I can tell by the way he looks at him.'

'*Duende*,' Bishop Montoya said. 'When the shooting started, they were all in a state of *duende*.'

Juan Cortes said something else, and the bishop nodded.

'It is essential to their art.'

Süleyman had heard the word before, but couldn't quite recall what it meant. He said, '*Duende*?'

The bishop shook his head. 'Is not really possible to translate. It is I imagine like a spirit.'

'A spirit?'

'A state of consciousness. And . . .' he frowned, 'a goblin. You know, mischief and sexual and . . .'

Ömer Mungun said, 'Like a sort of a trance?'

The bishop smiled. 'I suppose you could say so. It means, in this context, that the performers were caught in the moment, they were not aware of what was happening around them. Just the dance and the music.'

When the shooting had begun, Süleyman remembered that for a while the dancers had just carried on performing. In fact, as he recalled it now, he and everyone around him had been in some sort of altered state. Only the thud of that body on the ground from the balcony above had woken them, and then he recalled seeing Lola Cortes run to give assistance to a woman who had been shot.

The woman in question, a Roma grandmother, was still in hospital recovering from her wounds. Without Lola's intervention, she would almost certainly have died.

The boy, Tomas, spoke in English. 'There was a fight.'

Süleyman frowned. 'Where?'

'When the shooting start, I look up,' the young man said.

'Up to where?'

'There is apartment building . . .' He pointed over his shoulder.

'Behind you?'

'Yes.'

Süleyman tried to recall where Tomas had been, and then realised that wherever he had been standing, there was only one apartment block on that street, and that was Kerim Gürsel's. Tomas, therefore, had to have been facing Rambo Şekeroğlu's bar, which was directly across the road from Kerim's home.

'What made you turn around?' he asked.

The young man frowned as he tried to recall. 'I do not really know,' he said. 'I think maybe I heard a sound. The fight was in one of the windows.'

The rifle that had been used to kill five people had been silenced. However, according to Kerim Gürsel, the weapon that had been used to murder his neighbour had not.

'Señor Tomas,' Süleyman said, 'if we took you back to the scene, could you point out the window?'

'I think so,' he said. 'It was high. Maybe the top of the building.'

Aaron Kamhi was an open-minded man, but İkmen had been obliged to show him his photographs of the sculpted heads in order to convince him that he wasn't seeing things. When he had looked at them, Aaron said, 'This city is extraordinary, isn't it?'

'You could say that.'

'Çetin, did your father hold with all the magic stuff your mother used to do?'

'No, not really,' İkmen said. 'Rather, I suppose, he ignored it. I think that maybe a lot of people do.'

'Living in İstanbul challenges what one might perceive as reality, I find,' Aaron said. 'Any moment one may be thrown into the past. The remnants of a Roman column holding up the doorway into a tiny neighbourhood bakkal; walking around a corner and coming upon some religious ceremony dating back to the dawn of time. One's mind is constantly challenged by sensations one can only sometimes explain. Maybe other ancient places are like this too. I don't know; I've never lived anywhere else.'

İkmen smiled. 'Me neither. But to go back to the sculptures . . .' He'd forgotten how quickly Aaron could go off on a tangent about the city.

'Ah yes, well . . .' Aaron looked at the photographs again. 'I don't recognise them.'

'The subjects or the artist?'

'The subjects,' he said. 'Do you?'

'No,' İkmen replied. He didn't. A mature man and two young men – their faces meant nothing to him. 'What about the artist?' he enquired.

Aaron sighed. He was and always had been an almost exclusively nineteenth-century art man.

'It's modern,' he said. 'Traditional Western-style representational art.'

'I've been inside more art galleries in the last two hours than I've visited in the previous sixty years,' İkmen said. 'When I take my shoes off, I fully expect blood to pour out.'

Aaron laughed. 'I wish I could help you, but . . .'

İkmen took back his phone. 'Don't worry,' he said. 'It was a long shot.'

'Mmm.'

Aaron finished his coffee and then signalled to the waiter to bring them two more. 'Çetin, just a thought, but have you tried any of the up-and-coming cultural areas? I mean, I know that Karaköy is well-established small gallery territory, but there are other places.'

'I know,' İkmen said. 'Lots happening in Bomonti these days, and Moda, of course, although whether I've got the energy to go across the Bosphorus . . .'

'Balat?' Aaron suggested. 'Don't you know Gonca Şekeroğlu?'

İkmen smiled. 'She's not a sculptress, although she does know people.'

'There you are! Maybe she can help you. I've heard, although I've not been to them myself, that there are some very interesting artists' ateliers in and around Kamış Sokak, near the Armenian church.'

The church, Surp Hreşdagabet, was one of those places where miracles were supposed to happen. İkmen knew it, of course; he knew every place in the city where dusty portals to the unseen were said to arise.

'New takes on traditional forms,' Aaron continued. 'Apparently some marvellous examples of ebru . . .'

Ebru, or paper marbling, was a traditional Turkish craft that in recent years had become popular again.

'Ebru is hardly sculpture,' İkmen said.

'Agreed. But I have also become aware of a little place, a family-run studio, I am told, where the art of yorgancılık is used to dramatic, some would say even subversive, effect.'

Aaron Kamhi was not one of Çetin İkmen's magical friends. Unlike Gonca Süleyman, his magician friend Sami Nasi and the dervish İbrahim Dede, the academic was a man who dealt solely in facts. And yet there was something about his eyes as he spoke about the ancient art of quilting that made Çetin İkmen metaphorically sit up and take notice.

'What are you doing?'

Şevket Sesler turned around and found himself looking into the dark eyes of Inspector Kerim Gürsel.

With Superintendent Cihat Şen at his back, Kerim walked into the apartment once tenanted by the late Mete Bülbül and confronted the Roma crime lord.

'I repeat,' he said, 'what are you doing here, Şevket Bey? I've never seen you in this building before, and I should know, because I live here.'

Sesler had been holding something, which he now dropped on the floor.

'Did you know the man who lived here?' Kerim demanded.

'No.'

'So why are you here?' asked Superintendent Şen.

The godfather pulled himself up straight. 'Why shouldn't I be here?'

Kerim rolled his eyes. 'Because it's a crime scene? Because you don't live here? Do you want me to go on?'

Sesler had been spotted entering the Poisoned Princess apartments by the constable assigned to guarding the fire escape. Leaving his post briefly in order to relieve himself, he'd come back to find the gangster making his way breathlessly to the upper part of the building.

Şen bent down to retrieve what Sesler had dropped on the floor. It appeared to be a letter.

'You were reading this,' he said.

'No.'

'You were, I saw you.'

Sesler remained silent for a moment, then he said, 'I was curious, OK?'

'About what?'

'About this man being found dead here. Some of my people died last night. Word is this man could have been the shooter.'

'Word where?' Kerim asked.

'In the mahalle.'

'Amongst your thugs?'

Sesler didn't dignify that with a reply.

Kerim said, 'Even if he was the shooter, what is it to you? It's not your job to bring whoever committed that offence to justice.'

'Like I said, I'm curious.'

'I'm sure you are, and so am I,' Kerim said. 'But only one of us can and indeed should do anything about it.'

Şen, who had been reading the letter he'd picked up from the floor, handed it to his colleague. Kerim took a few moments to read it, then said to Sesler, 'Why are you interested in this?'

'I'm not,' he replied. 'Like I said, I just wanted to know what sort of man this character was.'

'An invoice from a bookshop will hardly tell you that,' Kerim snapped.

Sesler had moved quickly when the officers had arrived. He had been standing next to a small table on top of which was a pile of correspondence. Now Kerim pushed past him and picked up the pile. 'I suggest you leave now, Mr Sesler.'

'Yeah . . .'

'But be aware that I will make an official record of your presence here. You and I both know that I don't buy your explanation.' He looked up. 'Be assured that I will find the real reason.'

'I'm taking the Cortes family back to Tarlabaşı,' Mehmet said. 'Tomas may have seen something significant.'

Mehmet Süleyman had returned to Kerim Gürsel's office. When he'd arrived, Eylul Yavaş had left to give him some time alone with Gonca.

'I'll arrange for someone to drive you home,' he continued.

Gonca put a hand on his shoulder. 'Mehmet, I've something I need to tell you. Something Rambo told me.'

Although he didn't always believe everything Rambo Şekeroğlu said, there was something in the way Gonca was speaking that made Mehmet think this might be serious.

'What?'

'Word from the mahalle is that Şevket Sesler contacted Esat Böcek when he realised that Ceviz Elibol might have been killed by Ateş.'

'Sesler knew that Ateş was seeing Ceviz?'

She shrugged. 'I don't know the actual sequence of events. But somehow Sesler knew or found out. Then he called Esat Bey. Word is that he asked him for compensation.'

'What?'

'For Ceviz,' she said. 'As one of his strippers, she was his property. People are saying that rather than give Şevket Bey whatever sum of money he'd asked for, Esat Bey sent his troops into Tarlabaşı and paid him in death.'

He drew her towards him, wrapping his arms around her waist. 'God!'

'I know that Rambo exaggerates,' Gonca said, 'but I don't think he's doing that this time. He's also talking about leaving the city.'

'He's left before.'

'Only for short periods of time,' she said. 'Tomas has asked him to return to Spain with them. Rambo thinks he can make a new start there; says he's fed up with wasting his life here. Then he added that if there's going to be a war in Tarlabaşı, he wants no part of it.'

If what Rambo had found out proved to be true, 'war' was not an exaggeration. The Böceks declaring war on the Seslers was serious. But over a girl? Gangsters like Sesler and Böcek could fall out over territory, but not something as trivial as a nightclub stripper.

'Was Sesler in a relationship with Ceviz?' Mehmet asked.

'No! I've no doubt he fucked her,' Gonca said, 'but he fucks all the women who work for him.'

'Except you.'

'Of course except me!' she said. 'No, he likes young girls. The point is, Mehmet, that if Rambo's right, what happened on Şevket Bey's birthday is just the start. You know as well as I do that Sesler will have to respond now or lose face. And also,' she put a hand up to his mouth and he kissed it, 'poor Hüseyin Elibol needs to be told now. I mean, I know that he knows, but he must be able to bury his child. He needs certainty.'

Chapter 13

Çetin İkmen got a taxi from Karaköy to Balat, promising himself that he'd walk back to Sultanahmet from there. But it was getting dark now, and walking the streets of Balat was becoming a slightly unnerving affair. Also, after a whole lifetime, İkmen knew when he was lying to himself.

The Surp Hreşdagabet Armenian church on Kamış Sokak was a forbidding-looking place. Covered in graffiti, it existed in a gloomy spot, seemingly lost to time. Until comparatively recently, it had been known as the Miracle Church, because every year, in September, apparent miracles were experienced during the course of one long, charged night of prayer. People of all faiths would go to the miracle service, and it was purported that many of them were healed of whatever ailed them. İkmen's mother had taken him and his brother Halil when they were children. He remembered the place with affection. But that had all stopped years ago. Now the church just sat empty most of the time, attended by an elderly custodian and used by the tiny, and dwindling, local population of Armenians.

As Balat had become more established on the foreign tourist trail, shops, cafés and ateliers had sprung up, and even dismal Kamış Sokak was no exception. In spite of the chill and rain of winter, plus the lateness of the hour, İkmen could see that there were still a few places open. One was the yorgancılık shop, its small front window crammed with big, heavy, intricately decorated quilts.

169

A young woman was the only person in the shop. In her twenties, İkmen reckoned, she had very long wild hair that hung way past her slim shoulders, touching the belt that secured her jeans. She said, 'Can I help you?'

İkmen said, 'Do you make these quilts?'

'With my father, yes,' she replied.

'Extraordinary.'

'Were you looking for something in particular?' she asked. 'We have lots of colours and sizes, many different designs.'

'Thank you,' he said. 'At this stage, I'm just looking.'

'That's fine. Please feel free.'

There were hundreds, maybe even thousands of yorgans piled up against the walls of the shop, which was old and felt a bit like a cave. Their colours were jewel-like – ruby red, turquoise, midnight blue, emerald green. Made from silk or satin lined with multiple layers of cambric, yorgans were heavy and expensive, and in the past had been owned by only the most affluent Ottomans. After a visit to Mehmet Süleyman's family home, İkmen's wife Fatma had wanted a yorgan; the old Süleyman place was graced by numerous old and probably very valuable quilts. But İkmen himself hadn't really taken much notice. He certainly hadn't bought her one, and now that she was dead, he never would.

The sound of a sewing machine broke through the silence, and he looked around. The young woman, who was sitting down now and sewing something by hand, said, 'That's my father. We've a workshop out back.'

'Ah.'

Aaron Kamhi had intimated, or so İkmen had felt at the time, that there might be some sort of connection between this shop and the sculptures he had photographed at Eminönü. But how did that work? And why had Aaron thought that what was being produced here was in some way subversive?

But when he looked at what the young woman was making, he felt he might know . . .

Mehmet Süleyman had been to Kerim Gürsel's apartment a few times, but only when his wife and daughter had been at home.

By way of explanation, Kerim said, 'Sinem and Melda are staying with Çetin Bey again tonight. I don't want them here with scene of crime in and out next door, not to mention the febrile atmosphere in the mahalle.'

'I don't blame you,' Süleyman said as he sat down on the Gürsels' sofa.

'Do you want coffee?' Kerim asked. 'We've got one of those coffee machines, so you can have almost anything you like. Cappuccino, latte, Americano . . .'

'I'd love an espresso,' Süleyman said. He too had a machine like this, bought as a wedding present by Gonca's son, Erdem.

'Good choice,' Kerim said. 'Think I'll have one too. In fact, I think I'll have a double. Do you fancy joining me, Mehmet Bey?'

'Yes, thank you.'

He disappeared into the kitchen, and returned a few minutes later carrying two small espresso cups. As he put them down on the coffee table in front of the sofa, Süleyman asked, 'Do you mind if I smoke?'

Kerim took his own cigarettes and lighter out of his pocket and threw them down on the table. Then he retrieved an ashtray from the kitchen.

'Help yourself,' he said.

Süleyman relayed to him what Gonca had told him about Sesler and the Böceks. Kerim visibly shuddered.

'If that is the case, then we have problems, to say the least,' he said. 'Do you think it's true?'

'I don't know,' Süleyman replied. 'I am aware that sometimes rumours are spread in order to send us off in the wrong direction, but if indeed my stepson is planning to leave the country because of it, then I am inclined to think it is true. Young Rambo, like his uncle of the same name, is a Tarlabaşı institution. My understanding is that he has the right contacts to get you almost anything you might want there. In part, at least, this is because of his mother, whom many people fear. But for him to just give up on all that and go somewhere entirely alien is worrying – and not just because my wife will miss him. She dotes on the boy.'

'So what do we do?' Kerim asked.

'Well, the way I see it, if this rumour is coming from those close to Sesler – or Sesler himself – then either it's true or it's an attempt at obfuscation.

'The Böceks, in the person of Ateş, are in trouble. A heavily mutilated girl in his bed is not a good look for someone from a pious family. Ateş may well have killed that girl, and so to choose this moment to take on the Seslers looks like an act of madness to me. However, I am not a gangster heavily invested in my honour and how this may be viewed by my people. Also, Sesler, as we know, is a loose cannon. I can well believe that he would have contacted Esat Böcek to ask for compensation for his property.'

Kerim sighed. 'At least we now know the identity of the corpse.'

'No, we don't,' Süleyman said. 'And we mustn't say that we do. I've ordered a DNA test on Ceviz Elibol's father, Hüseyin, but until those results come through, we must remain tight lipped. If we are being fed false information about the Böceks' involvement, we need to know why.'

'Sesler would probably like a slice of what Esat Böcek has over on the Asian side,' Kerim said.

'I'm sure he would,' Süleyman said. 'But he's Roma, a minority. They stick to their own, and only engage with us if they need us. The Asian side of the city is not traditional Roma territory.'

Inwardly, Kerim smiled at the idea that the Roma only

172

consorted with outsiders if they needed them. Did Süleyman know that the gypsies called him the Gaco Bridegroom? he wondered.

'If, however, what Rambo Şekeroğlu attests is correct, we must ask ourselves what Esat Böcek thinks he's doing, and why,' Süleyman continued. 'As far as I am aware, the Roma are no danger to him. The only other organisation that even approaches the size and power of his own is Murad Ayhan's set-up.'

'Maybe they're too big to take down?' Kerim said. 'Maybe, by taking over the gypsies' territory, Böcek could put Ayhan out of business by sheer weight of numbers.'

Süleyman shook his head. 'The Roma would never accept protection from someone not their own,' he said. 'It's a fool's errand, and Esat Böcek is no fool. Something strange is going on here, something we need to find out a lot more about before we do anything.'

Kerim said, 'Mehmet Bey, you and I both know that information leaks out of the department . . .'

He stopped short of saying that there were some police officers who were paid for inside information by organised crime. That was a given in almost every police force in the world. But over the years, the problem had grown.

'That's why I wanted to speak to you alone,' Süleyman said. 'I think we need to keep this information to ourselves.'

'What about Sergeants Mungun and Yavaş?'

'You know I trust Eylul . . .'

'And I . . . Well, Ömer Bey is a trustworthy officer.'

Although Süleyman didn't know it, Kerim was aware of his colleague's disputes with his sergeant over the years.

'And so?'

'And so we proceed with the evidence before us,' Süleyman said. 'I will continue my investigation into Ateş Böcek and wait for DNA results on the corpse. While you . . .'

'Tomas Cortes was very sure he saw something happening in my neighbour's apartment,' Kerim said. 'Identified his window straight away. Oh, and talking of which, when I found Sesler in there, he was looking at a receipt from a bookstore called Beloved in the Sahaflar. It doesn't have Mete Bülbül's name on it, but it would seem that he, or someone else, bought a book from them called *Oriental Spiritualism* back in August. That said, I couldn't find the book in the apartment.'

'Do you know it?'

'No,' Kerim said, 'but I googled it. It's an old book, written in 1868 by an American called John P. Brown. A secretary at the US legation to Constantinople, apparently.'

'In English?'

'Yes. I have to say, I didn't have Mete Bülbül down as an educated man. But if he's reading stuff like that, and if Sesler was interested . . .'

'Maybe, given the religious nature of the book, Mr Bülbül had a connection to Esat Böcek and his organisation?'

'My understanding is that a lot of devout people have problems with some of the dervish orders. Things like embracing dance, the mixing of the sexes, some orders allowing drink. Böcek and his people are straight-up devout Sunnis, close to some in power.'

'And yet the waters of that situation are muddy,' Süleyman said. 'When one talks of those in positions of political power, it is well known that some belong to certain orders.'

'Whatever, I don't buy Bülbül as a dervish,' Kerim said.

Süleyman frowned. 'But I may know someone who might be able to enlighten you . . .'

Dr İlker Koca had spent much of the day with Ateş Böcek. Inspector Süleyman couldn't hold on to him indefinitely, unless he felt able to charge him, and scene-of-crime officers were still not done collecting forensic evidence. However, in spite of being almost non-verbal, Ateş was beginning to make some sort of sense to Dr Koca.

Via a combination of personal experience with the young man and what he could see of his actions and behaviours on the CCTV footage taken on the morning of the girl's murder, the doctor was beginning to form a view about the possible reasons behind his silent persona.

Ateş trusted no one. His dealings with shopkeepers were a case in point. Dr Koca had played the pieces of footage over and over, and what struck him about them most forcefully was the way in which the man refused to believe anything said by these people. When buying cigarettes, one shopkeeper had told him that they didn't stock his brand. Clearly, as a vendor of goods, he would have been disappointed that he could not fulfil Ateş's request. And yet Ateş's response was to accuse him of lying. Screaming with rage, he'd accused the shopkeeper of being 'not what you pretend to be'.

His growling hostility when he didn't get what he wanted reflected what Dr Koca had himself experienced in the past several hours. Not only had Ateş not been prepared to believe he was the same doctor he had seen the previous day; he had also accused Koca of being 'one of them' – whoever 'they' were. His other refrain was 'I see you'.

When Koca telephoned Süleyman, just as the inspector reached his home that evening, he told him that he believed Ateş Böcek 'lives in a world peopled by imposters'.

The young woman was called Bayza Akyılmaz, and like her father, she was a maker of traditional yorgans. She also, when she had time, worked on what she called 'yorgan sculpture'. This involved making models out of quilting material: animals, birds, everyday objects and human heads. She held up what she was currently making for İkmen to see.

175

'I make whatever catches my eye,' she had told him when she'd noticed him looking at what she was doing. 'It's my sister's birthday soon and so I'm making a sculpture of her.'

It looked good. It looked remarkably like the sculptures İkmen had seen at Eminönü. He had thought they had been made of plaster or clay, but maybe he'd been wrong. He showed her his photographs. 'Are these yours?'

She paled. 'No,' she said. Then she frowned. 'Where did you take these pictures?'

He told her.

'Eminönü? Really?' she said.

'You can see why they reminded me of your work,' he said. 'The style is similar.'

'Mmm.'

Was she suddenly being guarded, or was he imagining it?

'Do you know of anyone else who does what you do?'

'No.'

'And these are definitely not yours?'

'No.' Then she said, 'You didn't come here to buy a quilt, did you? You came because of these heads.'

'Someone recommended I visit this shop,' İkmen said.

'Who?'

He shook his head. 'Forgive me,' he said. 'I think you might know something.'

She stood up and closed the door of the workshop behind her, then returned to her seat. She looked İkmen in the eye.

'I'll tell you what I know,' she said. 'I do recognise your heads, because I made the originals. What you have there are copies made from clay, by the look of it.'

'So . . .'

She looked over her shoulder, seemingly to make sure her father didn't leave the workshop.

'I worked from photographs,' she said. 'No idea who they are or were.'

'Who asked you to do this?'

'I don't remember her name.'

'A woman?'

'Yes. Very smart. I think she was a doctor, because she talked about her "patients".'

'When was this?' İkmen asked.

She thought for a moment, and then she said, 'Who are you?'

'My name is Çetin İkmen. Now answer my question, please.'

She paused for a moment, fiddling with her phone. Had she maybe sent something?

'It was some months ago,' she said. 'In fact, it was actually about this time last year. She, the lady, wanted them quickly. I was flat out for three weeks working on them.'

'And when you'd finished, where did you deliver them to?'

'She came here,' she said. 'It all happened really rapidly. She came here the first time and ordered what she wanted. I gave her an estimated cost, which she paid immediately. My father wasn't pleased.'

'Why not?'

'Because I couldn't help him making quilts. He's old and . . . Also, he was suspicious.'

'Why?'

'Well, these sculptures I make, they're not something I advertise. I make them for my own amusement. I don't know how she knew about me.'

'Did you ask?'

'I don't think I did. She was a lot older than me and, if I'm honest, a bit scary.'

'In what way?' İkmen asked.

She shrugged. 'It's difficult for me to put my finger on it. There was a tension about her. To be honest, when she came into the shop the first time, I wondered what had happened to her. She was shaky because of something.'

By the time he left, Çetin İkmen didn't know what to think. But one thing was for sure, and that was that Aaron Kamhi had some questions to answer. He took his phone out of his pocket and was just about to make a call when a hand landed on his shoulder and he froze.

In spite of the fact that Esat Böcek's enormous Baghdat Caddesi apartment had three large sitting rooms – one of which doubled as an atrium – evenings were spent in the small, stuffy room occupied by the matriarch of the family, Neşe.

While the elderly lady reclined on a large cushion on the floor, her son Esat and grandson İlhan lay end to end on a vast brocade sofa. There was a television in the room too, but it was off. This was because Neşe was reading tarot cards for her sister, Banu, in Amasya.

Speaking into a phone jammed against her right ear, she was saying, 'Avoid going out. You've two daughters-in-law, make them do something for a change.' She'd been droning on for at least half an hour. Someone had put 'the eye' on Banu, according to Neşe. Speculation was rife, but she had intimated more than once that it could well be either of Banu's middle-aged daughters-in-law. These were women who waited on her hand and foot, in the old traditional way, so it was quite possible that one or other of them wished her ill. Esat Böcek, for his part, had never liked his Aunt Banu, who in his experience was a fat, greasy and deeply ungrateful woman who had probably never smiled in her life.

He looked at his son staring into space and said, 'What have you been doing today?'

'Nothing.'

İlhan Böcek was a young man of few words when it came to

talking to his father. Unlike his brother Ateş, he didn't just burst out with the first thing that came into his head. He'd observed over many years just how badly uncontrolled venting in front of his father could be received. And although Esat had given Ateş, as his direct heir, everything that his often strange heart might desire, there had been a price, especially when the boys had been children. Unlike İlhan, who was the 'extra' son, Ateş had been pushed to do well at everything he attempted. And when he failed, which he had done consistently, Esat had beaten him. It was, İlhan had reasoned, better to fade into the background than attract attention like that, even if it did get you a palace all to yourself.

After another foray into complete silence, he said, 'How is my brother?'

'They have a psychiatrist talking to him,' his father replied.

'Yeah, well you—'

'I do not approve of such people!' Esat yelled. He saw his mother looking at him with disapproval and calmed down. 'I have enough to worry me,' he added.

'Mmm.'

Ever since Şevket Sesler's Romanies had been attacked, Esat Böcek had increased security around his properties. He'd phoned the Roma godfather. 'It wasn't us,' he'd told him. Sesler had let loose a torrent of abuse. Esat had expected that. When Sesler had demanded compensation for the girl, Esat had told him to rot in hell. There was no love lost between them.

Now he turned to his younger son and said, 'Why didn't you tell me your brother was sleeping with that Romany whore?' It wasn't the first time he'd asked and it probably wouldn't be the last.

'Ateş asked me not to,' İlhan said. Again, he'd said this before.

The old woman, now off the phone, was all ears. 'The gypsies are filth!' She looked at her son. 'I told you to take the boy to Ali Hoca, but you chose to ignore me!'

'Mother, with respect—'

'Ah, here it comes!'

'With respect, while Ali Hoca is a learned man—'

'He's a peasant and so not good enough for you now, eh!'

Hocas, or healers, combined traditional Anatolian folk reme-
dies with knowledge from the Koran. In the past they had been
consulted in lieu of doctors in rural areas of Turkey as well as in
poor quarters of cities. Some people, like Neşe Hanım, still consulted them. Those of a secular bent dismissed them all as frauds,
but then so did a lot of very pious Muslims, viewing them as little
more than sorcerers. Those people with whom Esat Böcek mixed
and identified either consulted a narrow band of hocas close to
those at the top of society or they kept well clear. Semi-literate
octogenarian Ali Hoca from Neşe Hanım 's home mahalle was a
blacksmith by trade, and very far from the Muslim elite.

'Mother, I couldn't have it getting out,' Esat said. 'You know
that!'

'Ali Hoca would have been discreet.'

'No he wouldn't!'

'You have money now. You could have paid him to live with us
here so you could have controlled things.'

Esat leaned towards his mother. 'You think an old peasant
stinking of the farmyard wouldn't cause comment in Kadıköy?'

'This is İstanbul,' Neşe said. 'Peasants walk the streets every
day!'

'Maybe, but they don't come to my home.' Esat stood up. 'I've
quite enough to worry me without listening to your nonsense!' He
left the room.

Her face in profile was mannish. Slim, un-made-up, she had a
long Roman nose and enormous brown eyes that twinkled in the
light from the many votive candles that burned in front of the altar
and in every side chapel and niche.

She it had been who had suggested going into the Surp Hreşdagabet. She'd said, 'You'd never guess from my name, but I am Armenian. This was my church when I was a child.'

After recovering from the shock of being woman-handled when he came out of the quilt shop, İkmen had readily agreed to accompany this eccentrically clad female into the ancient church. With the exception of a lack of top hat, Feride – which was what she had told him her name was – looked remarkably like a nineteenth-century European equestrienne. Tight-fitting black jacket over an ankle-length black skirt, the whole ensemble set off by a pair of high buttoned boots. She carried a black backpack, and as they entered the church, she placed a black veil over her head.

As they sat side by side on one of the pews at the back of the church, İkmen was surprised that the custodian, who was sweeping the floor, didn't given them a second look. But then maybe Feride still came to the Surp Hreşdagabet and he was accustomed to her.

Eventually the woman spoke. 'I imagine you're wondering why all the subterfuge.'

'If I knew what was going on, that probably would be a good question,' İkmen said. 'But considering the fact that I am totally bewildered, perhaps you can help me out by telling me whatever it is you seem to need me to hear, from the beginning.'

She leaned forward, her elbows on her knees like a man, and smiled.

'You're a thrill-seeker, aren't you, Çetin Bey?' she said. 'An adrenaline junkie.'

'Am I?' he countered. 'I always thought I was a people-pleaser.'

'You have a family and many friends whom you love dearly, and so in part you are right. But left to yourself, you'd throw yourself into a world of sensation without a thought.'

'Would I? I'd never go bungee jumping, if that's what you mean,' İkmen said. 'One of my boys did it a few years ago. Just

181

the video made me feel nauseous. I'm not a brave man, Feride Hanım. If you think that's me, then you have me confused with someone else.'

'And yet when you were in the police force, you refused to carry a gun.'

'That was an ethical issue, and not entirely true. I always tried to avoid carrying arms, but sometimes it just wasn't possible. Anyway, look, it's been a long day; can you please get to the point?'

'OK,' she said. 'The point is that I am a psychiatrist by profession. And further to the point still, I am Ateş Böcek's psychiatrist.'

Chapter 14

Gonca Süleyman could and did cook. But not often. Whenever she did, she made a huge production of the event, becoming anxious about what people thought of her food and angling for compliments. So in order not to have to put herself through the ordeal, she was inclined to gather food from bakkals and restaurants during the course of the day and then present a huge rolling meze to her family and guests. This evening was no exception, and when Mehmet Süleyman arrived in her kitchen, he found the table groaning under heaps of loaves, bowls of hummus, olives, sliced fava paste, aubergine salad, long green fasulye beans, yogurty cacık, kısır made from bulgur wheat, and a huge plate of anchovies in olive oil. There was also lentil soup for those who needed warming.

The back door was open, and she soon came through it, followed by her Spanish guests. When she saw her husband, she walked over to him and kissed his lips.

'You must be starving,' she said suggestively.

He smiled. 'Always.'

They all sat down and Gonca filled everyone's water glasses. Mehmet had just reached out for some bread when his phone rang. Under Gonca's now thunderous gaze, he excused himself and went to take the call in the living room.

His mother, Nur Hanım, hadn't made contact with her younger son since his marriage. She'd not attended the wedding. She'd felt he had been making a mistake marrying a 'fortune teller' many

183

years his senior. But he'd done it anyway, because he loved Gonca. This was now, he felt, probably the point at which his mother told him she had disinherited him. He took a deep breath and said, 'Good evening, Mama.'

'I shall get straight to the point, Mehmet Efendi,' she said. 'I need you to come and collect your remaining belongings from your old room.'

'Of course.' He had meant to get round to removing his possessions from his childhood home a long time ago. But being near his mother these days was difficult. Ever since his father had died, she'd been impossible. While her own background involved a dirt-poor village in Anatolia, the fact that her late husband had been a prince obsessed her. According to Nur Hanım, both her sons had married beneath them. Her own humble origins did not feature in her thinking.

'As soon as you can,' she continued. 'I need the room.'

Mehmet Süleyman had got over his mother's coldness towards him a long time ago, and so what he said next was not said in the spirit of criticism. Rather, he was curious.

'Why?' he asked.

He heard her bridle at his bluntness, but she answered anyway. 'My brother is coming to stay,' she said. 'I cannot expect him to put up with all your rubbish. I want him to be comfortable.'

Nur's brother, Kemal, was ten years her senior. A strange, distant man, he had been indulged to such an extent by his mother that he'd never either worked or married. Alone since the death of his other sister, he'd lived in the family's village for the past five years, making a very basic living by renting out his fields to sheep farmers for pasture. The way he had always stared blankly at them had caused Mehmet and his brother Murad to avoid him.

'Is he staying long?' Mehmet asked.

'For ever,' his mother said. 'There's really no point in both of us being lonely.'

'Indeed.'

'So please do make arrangements to remove your belongings,' she said.

'I will.'

'Good.'

She put the phone down on him. He sighed. Something else to do. Not that it was a big problem. Or was it? If his Uncle Kemal was coming to live with his mother in Arnavutköy, there was a possibility that despite being ten years older than her, he would still be there when the old woman died. And if that happened, getting him out so that Mehmet and Murad could sell the house would be problematic. Oh, how clever she was in her spitefulness! She wouldn't disinherit her sons, but she would make it hard for them to realise any profit from her estate. Or was he being paranoid?

Gonca came in. 'Are you going to eat with the rest of us, Mehmet Bey?'

'Yes,' he said.

She was an astute woman, and while she didn't know why he suddenly looked so weary, she walked over and put her arms around him.

She said, 'Whatever it is, baby, we'll get through it together.'

'So why are you talking to me?' İkmen asked. 'Ateş Böcek is the subject of a police investigation. You need to speak to them.'

A combination of lack of nicotine and the sharp smell of incense was making him feel slightly nauseous.

Feride pulled her scarf tightly across her head. 'I can't.'

'Why not?'

She looked behind her and then back at İkmen. 'I was employed by Ateş's father, Esat Bey.'

'And?'

'I can't believe you don't know what Esat Böcek does!'

185

'Of course I do,' he said. 'He's in business.'

They looked at each other, both knowing exactly what that euphemism had been employed to disguise.

'I had to sign a non-disclosure agreement before I was allowed to see that particular patient,' Feride said.

'When?'

'Five years ago. He was sixteen and causing problems for his family.'

'What sort of problems?' İkmen asked.

She thought for a moment. 'I'd rather not say.'

'If you want my help . . .'

'Ateş is very sick,' she said. 'There are rumours that he has killed a girl, and I think, if that is true, I might know why.'

The custodian said something to her in Armenian and she answered in kind.

She said, 'He wants to lock up soon.'

'We can go somewhere else.'

'No!' she said. 'We can only meet here! And when we leave, we must leave separately.'

'You fear the Böceks are watching you?'

'I know they are.' She turned to face him. 'Ateş suffers from a disorder called Capgras syndrome. The main symptom is the patient's belief that everyone around him or her has been replaced by lookalikes. These lookalikes then lie to the patient about who they are and what their intentions might be. Those suffering from this syndrome are therefore deeply paranoid and afraid. This affects their behaviour, which ranges from reclusive to loud and violent. They are trying to protect themselves. I should also add that the lookalikes don't have to actually look like those the patient fears they are impersonating. It's a deep psychosis that allows for many different iterations of the so-called imposters.'

'How did Ateş develop this condition?'

'I think, although I'm not a hundred per cent sure, that early

186

exposure to ketamine was the trigger,' she said. 'A few years ago, a lot of kids, particularly privileged ones, experimented with ketamine, which is used mainly by veterinary surgeons to anaesthetise animals. It induces euphoria and a highly relaxed state. It can, however, also cause psychosis, a rupture between the patient and reality. This is what I told the young man's father had happened here. I prescribed antipsychotic drugs.'

'And?'

'And Ateş didn't take them,' she said. 'He accused me of trying to kill him. He said that the drugs I gave him were poison. I told his father that if he didn't take the medication I had prescribed, there was nothing more I could do for him. For the next three years, however, Ateş would return with his father from time to time, and at one point I admitted him to a psychiatric facility in Switzerland. But that broke down too, by which time Esat Bey had spent a lot of money to no good effect and I was dismissed. I didn't hear anything from the Böceks until Esat Bey rang me in the middle of the night after Ateş's arrest.'

'Rang you to say what?'

'To say that if I ever told anyone about his son's condition, he would kill me,' she said. 'He told me that for the foreseeable future, I would be under surveillance.'

'And are you?'

'I've seen men following . . .' She shrugged. 'I don't know, to be honest with you, but what I am aware of is the fact that I can't afford not to believe that.'

İkmen said, 'So what are you doing telling me?'

'Esat Bey selected me to treat his son because he knew that the fact that I am an ethnic Armenian meant that he could, if necessary, slander me without too much trouble,' she said. 'As you know, we tend to keep our heads down . . .'

İkmen was aware that minorities did this, even if his best friend, Armenian Arto Sarkissian, did not.

She continued. 'The way Esat Bey endows pious charities means that no one would believe me were I in dispute with him.' She sighed. 'I think someone followed me here a few hours ago. But because whoever it was would stick out in such an empty place, I am relatively safe. It's why I orchestrated for you to meet me here.'

'In, if I'm not mistaken, a very convoluted fashion,' İkmen said.

She smiled.

İbrahim Dede the dervish always welcomed anyone who wanted to talk to him about the mystical Islamic path known as Sufism, however uninformed that person might be. And Kerim Gürsel was very ignorant.

Because the younger man wanted to smoke, the elderly dervish had his son bring blankets and a samovar out into his small garden, which backed onto the walls of the great Topkapi Palace. Threaded with multicoloured fairy lights, the area was charming even in the winter months.

Once Kerim had expanded upon what Mehmet Süleyman had already told the dervish about Mete Bülbül – whom the old man didn't know – he said, 'But you do know a bookshop called Beloved in the Sahaflar?'

İbrahim Dede laughed. 'It is three shops away from my own premises,' he said. 'I have known the owner, Serhat Dede, all my life. Why do you want to know?'

Kerim explained about the invoice from the shop found in Mete Bülbül's apartment. The dervish said that he knew of the book in question.

'I'll be honest with you, İbrahim Dede,' Kerim said, 'I know nothing about Sufism. I know little about Islam. But do you think that a book like this is the sort of thing someone who is considering following the Sufi path might buy?'

'You say this man was a Turk?' İbrahim Dede asked.

'Yes,' Kerim replied.

'And yet he purchases a book in English.'

'Yes.'

'Which furthermore is one that has been out of print for many, many years.'

'Really?'

'Available online, but that is all,' the old man said. 'Maybe this explains why you couldn't find the volume in his apartment. Perhaps it exists on the man's computer system.'

'Not that I know of, as yet.'

'But what does it mean? If the book were in Turkish, I would say that the man who ordered it had interests in both Sufism and the Western conception of Sufism. It was written by an American at a time when "the Orient" was viewed as some sort of strange artefact by many Westerners. What do you know about this man? Was he an academic?'

Kerim sighed. 'I don't think so. He was my neighbour, but he kept himself to himself. I saw him around and about the mahalle often in company with working women. He dressed a bit flashily, and so for better or worse, I assumed he was a pimp.'

The old man smiled. 'It's possible for a pimp to be interested in Sufism. What are these artificial distinctions anyway? Rumi said, "Why struggle to open a door between us when the entire wall is an illusion?" You are a good man, Inspector, and I believe that you know how wrong it is for people of power to pit us against each other on the basis of such differences.'

Did the dervish know that Kerim was gay? Did it matter if he did?

'So don't judge this dead man before you know the facts,' İbrahim Dede said. 'If he was truly seeking the Sufi way, then there is no circumstance in which he could bring himself to kill. We are spiritual people; we do not judge. Only God can do that.

189

In the meantime, I will speak to Serhat Dede for you and see if he remembers the book and the man who bought it from him.'

Feride looked at the image on İkmen's phone.

Pointing at the heads, she said, 'That's Ateş, his brother İlhan, and that one is their father. I asked Bayza Akyılmaz to make the originals out of quilting.'

'Why?' İkmen asked. 'I get the impression you don't like these people.'

'And you're right,' she said. 'You know that Bayza Akyılmaz is Armenian too? I've known her family for ever. I've always enjoyed her little quilting sculptures. I had her make those so that I could vent my anger at them. Very cathartic.'

'Miss Akyılmaz told me she didn't know whom she had made those heads for . . .'

'Because I told her not to tell anyone.'

'Did she let you know I was here today?' İkmen asked.

She shrugged.

'Or was that Aaron Kamhi?'

She changed the subject. 'And so when Esat Bey told me about Ateş, I knew I couldn't go to the police. Esat Bey, I should add, ordered me to destroy his son's psychiatric records.'

'But you didn't.'

'No!' she said. 'All I did was call an old friend, who told me about you.'

'Aaron Kamhi.'

Again she ignored him. 'But how did I contact you while I was being watched?' she said. 'My friend told me I would need to catch your attention. Create a mystery and İkmen will come, they said. And so I took casts of Bayza's clever sculptures and put them where I knew you would see them.'

Or rather, İkmen thought, where you knew Numan Bey would direct my gaze. It was the pickle-juice seller who had called his

190

attention to the sculptures. Did anyone in the city not know who he was and what he did? Did anyone not realise that what intrigued him most was the truly odd?

'And so having succeeded in your aim of grabbing my attention, what now?' İkmen asked. 'You won't or can't go to the police. I am no longer a serving officer; what do you want me to do?'

She handed him her backpack. 'Give this to Inspector Süleyman.'

'What is it?' İkmen asked.

'These are Ateş Böcek's psychiatric records,' she said. 'They also contain my observations vis-à-vis possible violence. Ateş has been an accident waiting to happen for years.'

Rambo arrived and sat down at the table next to Tomas Cortes. The two young men smiled at each other.

Süleyman, though making a heroic effort to eat the meal that Gonca had prepared for them, was still thinking about his mother, which he found unsettling. But still his wife heaped yet more food onto his plate.

'Darling, I can't eat all this,' he said. 'I've got to keep my weight down.'

'Baby, you worry too much!' Gonca said. 'You've no fat anywhere, and I should know.' She kissed his cheek. 'Just muscle.'

Rambo, who like all of Gonca's children was accustomed to expressing himself freely, said, 'Get a room!'

His mother was about to reply when the doorbell rang. Because she was on her feet anyway, she went to answer it.

While she was away, Süleyman said to Rambo, 'You know you shouldn't criticise your mother in front of guests.'

Rambo looked at the Spaniards. 'They don't speak Turkish.'

'No, but they're not stupid,' Süleyman replied. 'Don't do it again.'

The young man sighed. 'No wonder I want to leave this dump.'

'Yes, well we need to talk about that . . .'

'No we don't,' Rambo said. 'You're not my father. When Tomas and his family go, I'm leaving with them.'

'At the moment, they're not allowed to go,' Süleyman said. 'We need them—'

'You've taken statements, let them go!'

Süleyman stood. 'Rambo.'

The boy stood too. 'Yeah?' he said. 'You gonna fight me with all your muscles, are you?'

It was at that point that Gonca returned with Çetin İkmen in her wake.

The girl was awake. He could feel the tension in her body all the way over from the other side of the bed. And while she wasn't actively pretending to be asleep, Ömer Mungun felt a distinct coolness coming from her direction. Would this marriage ever be right?

They'd only had sex twice. He couldn't call it 'making love', because he didn't love her. The first time had been on their wedding night back in Mardin. She'd been so frightened! He thought he'd tried to reassure her, but he'd still hurt her. The second time, just after they had arrived in İstanbul, she'd lain beneath him like a stone.

Eventually he spoke her name. 'Yeşili?'

She didn't reply. He looked at her back, turned towards him, and imagined her frightened eyes. She was beautiful, much more so than the older women he'd enjoyed sex with. But then that was the problem. She saw sex as a duty. He had no doubt she would do her part by getting pregnant at some point. His mother was already asking about it on a daily basis. And he wanted a child. He'd seen how much happiness little Melda had brought into Kerim Gürsel's life. But Kerim loved his wife, and she adored him.

He repeated her name. 'Yeşili?'

'Ömer Bey.' She didn't move.

He said, 'May I put my arms around you?'

For a moment she said nothing, and then she whispered, 'You are my husband.'

'Yes, and I'm trying to make sure you are all right,' he said.

What he'd wanted to say was that they should talk about the situation they found themselves in. He should be able to say that he didn't love her but hoped that one day he would. Initially she had aroused him, but her horror of the sex act had made his ardour cool. Frustrated, he began to think about his old loves, and also about Gonca Hanım, his boss's wife. Old she might be, but she was so sexy. The way she moved and spoke, the way she wound herself around Süleyman's like a snake with its prey. It was erotically charged, and just thinking about it made him hard. What those two got up to in bed . . .

He heard Yeşili say, 'Do you want to . . .'

She couldn't even say 'sex'!

'Not unless you do.'

'I want to please you,' she said.

She was a product of her upbringing. A young girl from a dying minority, brought up to believe that her only function in life was to bear children, as many as possible, for her co-religionist husband. Ömer closed his eyes. How did he even begin to tell her that he had no intention of returning to the Tür Abdin any time soon, that he wanted only two children because he couldn't imagine being able to afford any more? How did he take even that away from her?

He said, 'It's all right, go back to sleep.'

Again she said nothing. She just curled herself into a tight ball, drawing her legs up to her chest. Poor kid, he thought; and then he thought, poor me.

'She won't speak to you.'

'So how can I verify her story?' Süleyman said. 'Çetin, you

193

know I would trust you with my life, but look at this from Ozer's point of view.'

Commissioner of Police Selahattin Ozer was Süleyman's superior. A deeply religious man, he was also stern, unforgiving and entirely wedded to the idea that there was only one way of doing things. That way did not involve intervention from people like İkmen.

'I think that for the time being, you must just simply bear in mind what is here,' İkmen said. 'Dr Feride – you'll notice her surname has been redacted – simply wants you to be aware of it at this stage.'

Ateş Böcek's psychiatric notes had turned out to be photocopies of the originals. Great care had been taken to obliterate any identifiers of either the doctor or her clinic.

'Give me a description and I can ask Dr Koca whether he knows her,' Süleyman said.

'You can't put her in danger, Mehmet,' İkmen said. 'I promised her I would give these notes to you provided you told no one at this stage.'

'So when can I tell anyone?' he snapped.

For some hours they'd been going over what Feride had told İkmen, in conjunction with the notes. While they had talked, the Cortes family had returned to their lodgings in the garden, Rambo had gone out somewhere and Gonca had retired to bed.

'She's afraid for her life,' İkmen said. 'You know how these crime families operate.'

Süleyman deflated. 'Yes,' he said. 'Forgive me, I'm sure you can understand my frustration.'

İkmen put a hand on his shoulder.

'So,' Süleyman said, 'this Capgras syndrome . . . If indeed Ateş Böcek is a witness as opposed to the actual murderer, this would seem to imply that he is unreliable.'

'Yes.'

194

'He doesn't know or trust the identity of anyone.'

'It seems not,' İkmen said. 'How is Dr Koca getting on?'

Süleyman sighed. 'He's actually come to a similar conclusion to that outlined in these notes. Although he described it more as Ateş living in a world of his own, he is of the opinion that the young man doesn't believe that people are who they say they are. Whatever the cause, he's hard to reach. And of course, all the evidence so far points to him as the most likely candidate for the girl's murderer.'

İkmen narrowed his eyes. 'But you don't think so?'

'I have doubts. According to Dr Sarkissian, it would have taken some hours to dismember, mutilate and, let's face it, flay the body. Given that time of death was in the morning and we turned up in the evening, Ateş could of course have spent all day doing that. But not only do I doubt he had the skill to perform such a task, we have CCTV footage of him entering a shop that morning. Further, it is footage in which he appears to behave not normally, but not like a man who has just killed someone. Were he in the middle of performing such a difficult and gruesome act, would he have been able to just stop and walk away like that? And were he truly deranged, would he not have been drenched in blood? We found no sign of protective clothing at the site, just Ateş wielding a yataghan, covered in the girl's blood.'

'Do you think someone, knowing about his condition, set him up?'

Süleyman thought for a moment. 'Of course it's possible.'

'His father?' İkmen ventured. 'I know these godfathers can be very forgiving of their progeny's peccadillos, but maybe Ateş has proved too much for Esat Böcek? If it's true that Esat did indeed threaten Dr Feride if she ever made her knowledge of Ateş's condition public, it would seem to me that he is struggling with that situation. Ateş is meant to be his heir. He has enabled and indulged the boy. And didn't his brother İlhan come to see you separately?'

'He saw Kerim Bey,' Süleyman said. 'Told him that in spite of their father's desire to portray Ateş as a saint, he was far from that happy state. It was İlhan Böcek who told us that his brother had been seeing a Roma girl. He claimed his father didn't know about it. Said that Esat, had he known, would have lost his mind, which makes sense. Esat Böcek's unique selling point is his piety, which hardly works well when his son is sleeping with a Roma stripper.'

'So maybe if İlhan wanted to take over from his brother . . .'

'Why go to the bother of killing Ateş's woman when he could just wait and let him metaphorically hang himself?'

İkmen sighed. 'And if it's true that Esat was protective of Ateş, that maybe he ignored many of the strange things he did, it has to be possible that he loves the boy literally beyond reason.'

'Maybe he does.'

'Or maybe, Mehmet, there is something else at play here. Something that no one as yet is seeing.'

Chapter 15

'He was writing a book.'

It was easy to miss Technical Officer Türgüt Zana. Usually sequestered in an office with other technical operatives, Zana was a man of few words and absolutely no social skills. And so when he quietly entered Süleyman's office, nobody actually noticed he was there.

Kerim Gürsel and Eylul Yavaş, both drinking from enormous paper coffee cups, sat in front of Süleyman's desk while the boss held forth about what might or might not be wrong with Ateş Böcek. Pale and dark around the eyes, he'd got very little sleep, because after İkmen had left Balat to go home, Süleyman had discovered his wife in tears. Sara, one of her pet snakes, was ill, and so a midnight trip to a veterinary surgeon had happened. Mercifully the animal wasn't dangerously sick, and they had returned home in the early hours with liquid antibiotics. Gonca, alarmed by this incident, had then insisted upon sleeping with Sara while her husband failed to sleep in one of the spare beds. Ömer Mungun, for his part, interjected his opinion re Ateş Böcek every few seconds. He too had not slept well and was trying to keep himself awake.

'So don't ask me where I received this intelligence,' Süleyman said. 'Because—'

'Yeah, but sir, this is a doctor, right? I mean, this syndrome . . .'

'Capgras, yes.'

'It's a real thing?'

'He was writing a book,' Officer Zana reiterated.

They all turned to look at him.

'Mete Bülbül,' he said. 'He was writing a book.'

This, together with what İbrahim Dede the dervish had told him the previous night about Bülbül's possible interests, made Kerim Gürsel particularly sit up and take notice. He said, 'About what?'

'Sin,' Zana said.

A knock at her bedroom door woke Gonca Süleyman from her doze.

Putting an arm protectively around Sara, she asked, 'Who is it?'

'Rambo.'

'Come in.'

He opened the door, and she could see immediately that her youngest son was suffering from a hangover.

'You look dreadful,' she said.

'Thanks.' He closed the door behind him. 'Blame your husband.'

'What for?'

'Telling me we needed to talk about me going to Spain,' he said. 'I'm going, and that's that.'

Gonca sat up. 'He doesn't want you to make a mistake,' she said. 'Spain is a long way away, you don't speak the language, and you don't have a European Union passport. What are you going to do over there?'

He shrugged and then noticed that his mother was cradling the snake. 'What's Sara doing in here? I thought Mehmet Bey didn't like her?'

'He doesn't, but last night when I went to feed her, I noticed she had sores on her skin. Mehmet Bey took her to the veterinary surgeon, who has given her antibiotics.' She stroked the snake's head. 'Poor baby. I don't give her enough attention these days!'

'Because of *him*,' her son said.

Gonca ignored him, preferring to cuddle the serpent and kiss her snout. Sara had been with her for almost twenty-five years. As a young snake, she had appeared with her mistress in an act Gonca had sometimes performed at her father's old house in Sulukule. The gaco, it seemed, had liked the idea of Romani women dancing with snakes back then. But just as the dancing bears had been outlawed, so the snake dancers had become few and far between, relegating Sara to the status of a pet. And when Mehmet Süleyman had come to live in the house in Balat, she had spent far too much of her time in her terrarium in the basement. Her skin infection, which the veterinary surgeon had told Gonca had been developing for some time, had been a sign of this neglect.

Gonca kissed her again and said, 'From now on, you live up here, my angel.'

'He won't like it,' her son said. 'Especially if you have her in the bed. He won't sleep with her . . .'

'Rambo, what do you want?' Gonca asked.

'Oh.' He sat down on the stool in front of her dressing table. 'Tomas says that Lola wants to speak to your husband.'

'She doesn't speak Turkish.'

Lola Cortes might be hugely pregnant, but she was also a lot younger than Gonca. Because of this, and because she was convinced that every other woman desired her husband, Gonca was suspicious of her motives.

'She saw something in Tarlabaşı on the night of the shootings,' Rambo said.

'But he interviewed her!' Gonca said.

'Yeah, but the bishop was there too and so she felt she couldn't speak freely.'

'Oh that's ridiculous!' Gonca said. 'What's she up to?'

'I don't know,' Rambo said. 'But she told Tomas she saw the devil that night.'

*

199

'Sin?'

'How we all do it, how we can stop doing it,' Türgüt Zana said.

'From what perspective?' Süleyman asked.

Mete Bülbül, the neighbour Kerim Gürsel had once reckoned was a pimp, had at the time of his death been writing a book. The team knew it was possible this man had been interested in Sufi philosophy, but had he been taken with it enough to actually detail his own thoughts on the matter?

'Sufism,' Zana confirmed.

'I would never have had him down as a dervish,' Kerim Gürsel said.

'Yes, but sir, the Sufi path is one that treads lightly,' Eylul Yavaş said. 'It's something that is open to all. Rumi himself was all for inclusivity. I always come back to his most famous quote: "Come, come, whoever you are, come. Infidel, idolator, wanderer, fire worshipper, it doesn't matter, come." The Mevlevi dervishes want only union with God. They don't condemn, they always forgive.'

Unknown to the others, Ömer Mungun had a slightly different view on the Mevlevi order of dervishes. As a worshipper of the Şahmeran snake goddess, he had always been warned about the dangers of consorting with dervishes, who, it was thought, would seek to convert him to Islam.

Kerim Gürsel said, 'Bülbül drank and smoked. I saw him. Did it openly in the street.'

'As I say, dervishes can be very accepting of such things,' Eylul continued. 'Do we know anything about this man's past?'

'Only what is on his kimlik,' Süleyman said. 'He was sixty, native İstanbullu, Muslim.'

'I've put a call out for the landlord,' Kerim told them. 'He's in Dubai. Hopefully he will return my call . . .'

A lot of the big city landlords lived abroad. Their local agents were often less than helpful.

'It seems to me,' Süleyman said, 'that Bülbül may have had some sort of conversion.'

'Which could explain his death,' Eylul added.

'In what way?'

'Some people who consider themselves pious have a problem with dervishes. The inclusivity, the open invitation to infidels, the dancing. But Tarlabaşı doesn't have many people like that.'

'Bülbül's assailant came from elsewhere,' Kerim said. 'Well, that's what I think.'

'And you're probably right.' Süleyman nodded. 'What about prints from the apartment?'

Zana said, 'No matches.'

'Was Bülbül's death even connected to the shootings of the Roma?' Ömer asked.

'We know the sniper was on top of that building,' Süleyman replied.

'So how did he come to be in Bülbül's apartment? If as Kerim Bey says Bülbül rarely went out . . .'

'I don't know.' Süleyman looked at Kerim. 'Do you think that maybe Bülbül tried to stop the sniper?'

'From what I observed, he was a man who kept to himself. Not one to court danger. But maybe I'm wrong,' Kerim said.

'Mmm.' Süleyman steepled his fingers underneath his chin. 'These working girls you sometimes saw him with, do you have any ideas about names?'

Of course Kerim knew some of the working trans girls in the area; his one-time lover, Pembe, had been among their number. But even though he knew that Süleyman and Ömer Mungun were aware of his true proclivities, he couldn't allude to that in front of people who didn't know.

'No,' he said. 'But I'd know them if I saw them, and there are people I can ask.'

'I may be wrong,' Süleyman said, 'but I wonder if Bülbül had a past.'

'What do you mean?'

'We know that in all probability Ateş Böcek murdered one of Şevket Sesler's strippers. It's claimed that Sesler demanded financial reparation from Esat Böcek. The Böcek family is noticeably pious. Now while I accept that nothing in Bülbül's apartment points towards a previous life of crime, what if he *was* a criminal? Kerim Bey, you found Şevket Sesler sorting through Bülbül's papers . . .'

'Bülbül wasn't Roma as far as I know.'

He was right. The victim's name and description had rung no bells with Gonca either.

'So maybe he has some connection to the Böceks.'

Ömer said, 'He was killed by someone who could have been one of their soldiers.'

'Or not,' Süleyman said. 'Until we know more about him, we won't be able to judge. We know that neither Sesler nor Böcek will talk to us in anything like a meaningful way, but I feel that if we can unlock who and what Bülbül was, it will help us to move forward. I may be wrong, but . . .'

Çetin İkmen's dead wife Fatma didn't appear as often as she once had. He was, İkmen owned, coping rather better with her death these days, mainly because he kept busy. When she'd first died, he'd almost lost his mind. For almost the entire year afterwards, he'd stayed inside his apartment talking to her silent ghost out on their balcony. So this morning when he got up to find her waiting for him in the thin winter sunshine, it was like a blessing.

'Hello, my darling,' he said as he sat down opposite her, tea in one hand, cigarette in the other. 'Late home last night, but I think – I hope – I managed to help Mehmet Süleyman. Criminal gangs have always operated in this city, but rarely can I think of another time when they were quite so powerful – and respectable. They have friends in high places not just here but across the world. And the fear they inspire is, in my experience, unprecedented. That psychiatrist went to, well, Byzantine levels of stealth to catch my attention! She had help, of course. I wonder how Aaron Kamhi knows her and why he felt the need to assist? Ditto the pickle-juice man.'

A voice shouted from the kitchen. 'Are you with Fatma Hanım or have you lost your mind?'

'Fatma's here and I lost my mind years ago, Samsun,' İkmen replied.

'So situation normal.'

'Yes,' he said. 'Having a think.'

He turned back to Fatma. 'I am inclined to get back to Aaron Kamhi and Numan Bey. But should I? If what Dr Feride says is true, I could be putting them at risk. However, because I see Numan Bey almost every day, my talking to him would not seem too out of the way, would it? I had some involvement with the Böceks years ago. Nasty people, but no worse than their secular contemporary Murad Ayhan. I'd put them on an equal footing when it comes to excessive violence and horrific disregard for human life. Şevket Sesler, however, he's sort of in his own league on account of being Roma. His fiefdom is much smaller than the others, and as Tarlabaşı becomes more and more respectable, it is shrinking. He's no threat to Böcek. And if Ateş Böcek was having sex with one of Sesler's gypsy strippers, that was no threat to his father. Of course his father would be angry, but it's a big step from anger to murder. If Esat disapproved of the girl, why didn't he just have her beaten up? Unless of course Ateş did murder her whilst in a state of delusion.'

But İkmen shared Mehmet Süleyman's concerns about that. Why would a man engaged in dismembering a dead body and expertly flaying it just leave his house to go and get cigarettes?

Also, why had Esat Böcek attacked Şevket Sesler in his own mahalle? Sesler was nothing to him! He didn't have Böcek's wealth, his influence or his territory. If Sesler had asked for money in compensation for his girl, that was annoying. But all Esat Böcek would have had to say was 'no'. Sesler was no threat to him. Why attack the Romany and risk retaliation?

As he'd told Süleyman, there was more to this situation than met the eye.

Aylın left the lounge. Her brother was talking to Serdar, and seeing the two of them together was making her skin crawl. It was just football talk in the main, but when it drifted into macho discussions about the women they fancied on TV, Aylın found she couldn't bear it.

Serdar İpek, like her father, was in his fifties and had grown up on the mean streets of İstanbul fighting and hustling to claim his place in a dog-eat-dog world. Unlike her father, however, Serdar was just a thug. With no education and very little natural intelligence, he'd always been destined to be someone's hard man. That he performed that function for his friend Murad was fortunate, because just his face was enough to make most people reject him. Covered in scars and old bruises, it was wide, square and uneven and featured small, mean eyes and a huge crooked nose. Add to that a body that was bulky from steroid abuse, and he was like a maltreated old bull, damaged and bitter and given to wild, uncontrollable fury. Some of her father's other men called him ugly behind his back, but they also feared him. Serdar was one of her father's 'soldiers', which meant, Aylın knew, that he would kill for Murad, and probably already had. Her father had after all given him a very stylish apartment in Sarıyer, even if he did laugh at the way his old friend could never persuade a woman to go back there with him.

In part, the Ayhan empire was ideological. Murad, Serdar and several of his other soldiers had been members of the ultra-nationalist Grey Wolves group in their youth. Devoted to Turkish racial superiority, the original Wolves had been mainly secular. However, when it came to women, they would often invoke religion as a way of controlling and shaming them. Aylın's mother, Irmak, had long ago taken the decision to put up with her husband's sexism and infidelity in exchange for material wealth and a quiet life. Hugely overweight, she no longer slept with her husband, and she was just fine about that. She spent most of her time watching TV in company with the real love of her life, Yıldırım, her spoilt, tantrum-inclined son. But none of this was palatable to Aylın, who, while liking the things her father's money could buy, also wanted a man who really loved her and who would offer her freedom. She knew it was a big ask, but she also knew that she was not prepared to settle for less.

She heard her brother snigger and turned around to look at him and Serdar. They were both staring at her, smirking. Aylın had long suspected that Serdar had the hots for her. Just the thought of it made her shudder. She also knew that her brother would find that funny. When Serdar left, Yıldırım pointed two fingers at her, mimicking a gun.

A very large basket was needed, because Sara was a large snake. She was also a creature with sore skin, and so Gonca had to pad the basket out with blankets so that Sara wouldn't damage herself. Once she'd done this, she carried the boa down to her studio, which was where she intended to work for the rest of the day.

Although her collage art was no longer as fashionable as it had once been, Gonca still received commissions from people both at home and abroad, including one from Şevket Sesler. A lot of her customers were fellow Roma who had made successes of their lives and wanted to use her art to impress their friends. One customer, a Bulgarian Roma called Dragomir Hutz, was besotted with her oeuvre. He said it spoke to him about his early life in a poor, semi-rural suburb of Sofia – the horses, the music, the dancing. But as a man of a certain age, Dragomir also, Gonca knew, desired her. And even though he was aware that she was now married, he still wanted her work and the excuse it gave him to visit her from time to time.

She was currently working on a piece for him based around the Tarot. But once in her studio, she took it off her easel and replaced it with a fresh canvas, then reached for the skin Sara had shed several years ago. As they aged, snakes shed their skin less frequently, and so, in recent times, Gonca had taken to saving Sara's skins. She held it up in front of the serpent and said, 'I think it's time I made a portrait of you, my darling. Dragomir can wait.' She smiled. 'I know you're asleep now, my angel, but I also know that every living creature likes to have soothing, familiar voices around when they are ill. We all recover more quickly when we are loved.'

Using a scalpel, she began to separate out individual scales from the skin and placed the glittering fragments in a small earthenware pot. As she worked, she said, 'Don't tell Mehmet Bey, but I'm going to use those tiger-eye stones from that platinum ring he bought me years ago. I'm only taking two tiny ones. He won't notice. And anyway, he owes you, we both do. I've neglected you since I became his wife, and that's wrong. Love is too precious to ignore, and I know you love me as much as I love you.'

Sara, curled up in her padded basket, didn't move. As Gonca knew, it was possible for snakes to sleep for up to twenty hours in winter.

'Mehmet Bey has sacrificed a lot for me,' Gonca continued. 'His mother has all but disowned him, and some of his colleagues laugh at him. But sacrifice is necessary when you love someone. I've given things up too, sometimes too much, like you.' She stroked Sara's back. 'But that ends today. You were here before he was. You will sleep in my bed until you are well again, and then I will have Rambo bring your terrarium up into the living room. If that means my husband and I have to sleep apart for a while, then so be it. Love isn't a tap that can be turned off. And if he sleeps in my bed with both of us, then I will know that his love for me knows no limits. Because love should have no limits if it is true, don't you agree, Sara?'

The snake did not of course reply, but then Gonca remembered something she needed to do and picked up her phone.

Dr Arto Sarkissian rarely ventured into the mean streets of Tarlabaşı. But these were exceptional circumstances.

Wrapped up in a thick Persian lamb coat against the cold, he had his driver set him down outside Hüseyin Elibol's basement apartment, on one of the mahalle's most impoverished and litter-strewn streets.

As was his custom, the old man was sitting outside covered in blankets, smoking a cigarette. When he saw the doctor come down the stairs, he said, 'Can I help you, efendi?'

Only too painfully aware of the mismatch between himself, an educated, wealthy Armenian, and this poor Roma man, Arto bowed to kiss his hand when he reached him.

'Hüseyin Bey,' he said. 'My name is Arto Sarkissian, I am a doctor. I work for the police.'

'Oh . . .' For a moment, Hüseyin Elibol appeared to descend into fugue, but then he called out, 'Beren! We have a visitor! Bring tea and a chair for the doctor efendi!'

A scraping sound came from inside the apartment, and then a thin young girl appeared with a battered wicker chair Arto was afraid wouldn't bear his weight. But he sat down on it when directed, and to his immense relief it held.

'We will wait for our tea before we speak,' Hüseyin Elibol said.

'I know why you're here, efendi, and I want to take just a few more minutes for myself before you shatter my world.'

Arto nodded, and they waited in silence until the girl brought them their tea and then went back inside the apartment.

After dropping two sugar lumps into his tea and stirring until they dissolved, Arto said, 'May I . . .'

'You may,' his host replied. 'And spare me nothing, doctor efendi.'

Arto leaned forward. 'The human remains found in the Şehzade Rafık Palace in Kadıköy I can now confirm are those of your daughter Ceviz Elibol. This has been established via DNA comparison between samples taken from the body and from yourself. I am sorry to have to tell you that the results of the comparison performed are beyond reasonable doubt. You have my deepest sympathies.'

Hüseyin Elibol nodded. 'I knew it,' he said. 'I thank you, doctor efendi, for doing me the honour of telling me personally. You are a man with heavy responsibilities, and I appreciate the time you have taken to be here.'

'It is the least I could do,' Arto said.

'I wish I could offer you more than tea, but we are poor people. That was why my Ceviz sold herself in the way she did. It was not through choice.'

'I know.'

'Poverty makes whores of us all,' Hüseyin Elibol said. He was dry eyed, but Arto could hear gentle sobbing from inside the apartment. 'I understand that you are a friend of Gonca Hanım,' he continued.

'I have that honour.'

'And her husband.'

'Yes, and I can assure you that Inspector Süleyman and his team will do everything they can to bring your daughter's murderer to justice.'

208

Hüseyin Elibol nodded, then he said, 'Justice has always been lacking for our kind.'

'Not in this case,' Arto said.

'I had an idea.'

Mehmet Süleyman had left his office to go outside, firstly to take this call from his wife, and secondly to smoke.

'Oh?' he said. 'What's that?'

'Sara gave it to me.'

He'd already had quite enough of the boa for one day, having been obliged to give his bed up to her. He felt his heart sink.

'What do you think about inviting the Munguns and the Gürsels over for New Year? It's next Tuesday,' she added.

'That sounds good,' he said. 'Now you must check—'

'I've already spoken to Peri Hanım and Sinem Hanım, and I've invited İkmen too. They're all free and have all said yes.'

Which meant that Mehmet, the host, had been the last to know. With either of his previous wives, an oversight like that would have precipitated, at the very least, a bout of cold anger. But this was Gonca; she just did things, and he was infatuated with her.

He smiled. 'And Sara's part in all this?'

'Yeşili Mungun is like Ömer Bey, isn't she? A snake person,' she said.

Mehmet lowered his voice. 'They do worship the Şahmeran, yes.'

'Well, then she will love Sara!' Gonca said. 'My poor darling should be better by then, and the girl can spend as much time as she likes with her. Isn't that marvellous?'

Frankly, Süleyman was speechless, but he made approving noises. Many years ago he had briefly worked in the east and had come across several families who, like the Munguns worshipped the snake goddess. But in his experience, they had far too much respect for serpents to have them in their homes.

'Gonca,' he said, 'Sara is not indigenous. I doubt whether Yeşili Hanım will have seen a boa constrictor before.'

'But she's a snake!' Gonca said. 'They love them! Anyway, there was something else. Lola Cortes wants to see you.'

'What about? I can't give permission for them to leave yet.'

'I know, and believe me, I am grateful that you are holding them up. I don't want Rambo going off with them.'

'Whether Rambo goes to Spain with them is not my concern,' he said. 'As witnesses—'

'Lola Hanım saw the devil or a demon or something on the night of Şevket Bey's birthday celebration,' she said. 'She didn't say anything because Bishop Montoya was translating and she was afraid he might think she was possessed.'

This world was not Süleyman's. This was Çetin İkmen territory. He sighed.

'What?' she said.

'I assume Rambo told you this?'

'Yes.'

'All right,' he said. 'Ask Rambo to bring Lola and Tomas in to see me as soon as possible. Tomas can speak English and so he can translate. Are you sure she said she saw a demon, or just something that looked like one?'

Kurdish Madonna had started life as a shepherd in a village in the eastern province of Van. Back when she was called Mehmet, she had been a tall, very dark, very unhappy boy. Now a tall, platinum-blonde trans woman, she was, if not happy, at least true to herself, and as the madam of a trans brothel in Tarlabaşı, she also had a bit of money.

Fed up with being pickled in cigarette and dope smoke inside her house, she'd come out onto the street to talk to her friend Nikki, a straight prostitute of a certain age. Bewailing the many woes inherent in their profession, neither of them saw Kerim Gür-sel approach.

'Good afternoon, ladies,' he said as he held his badge up for them to see.

Nikki gulped. 'Fuck!'

Madonna put a hand on her arm to stop her bolting and smiled at Kerim. She'd known him for years, even before he'd taken one of her girls, Pembe, as his lover. However, his relationship with Pembe was only common knowledge in the LGBT community, and so Nikki was rightly alarmed to be confronted by 'a copper'.

'It's all right, Nikki dear,' Madonna said. 'Inspector Gürsel is local and he's not a bastard. What can we do for you, Inspector?'

Kerim knew that Madonna, for all her sass, would be discreet. He also recognised Nikki, even if she didn't know him.

'Ladies,' he said, 'I'm trying to find out about a local man, now deceased, called Mete Bülbül. He lived in the Poisoned Princess apartments for over ten years and was sometimes seen speaking to local working women.'

'A customer?'

'We don't think so,' Kerim said.

He took out the only recent photograph they'd been able to find in Bülbül's apartment and showed it to the women. He had hoped to find Madonna alone, but now that her friend was here, that was all to the good. Bülbül had only ever been spotted talking to straight working women.

They both looked at the picture, and then Nikki said, 'Looks like the Condom Man.'

'The Condom Man?'

'He gives out condoms to working women,' she said. 'Says we need to protect ourselves because the men we service won't. He's a nice man. Did you say he's dead?'

'I'm afraid so.'

She shook her head. 'That's sad. He was lovely. Only met him once or twice myself, but saw him about a lot.'

'Handing out condoms?'

'Mainly,' she said. 'Bless him. Religious, but not judgemental, not one of those Muslims who call us all whores. They always shout the loudest. You forget about the others.'

'Do you know anything about him?' Kerim asked.

'Not a lot,' Nikki said. 'Not married, I don't think.'

Madonna spoke up. 'I did hear, if it's the same person, that he was once a police officer . . .'

Chapter 16

'I'm so glad you decided to come and see me,' Çetin İkmen said to Peri Mungun as he poured water into her glass.

They were sitting outside his favourite bar, the Mozaik, waiting for their coffees and borek to arrive. It was a cold day, but if İkmen didn't sit outside, he couldn't smoke, and that was unacceptable. In addition, his cat, the feral ginger and white monster known as Marlboro, was not allowed inside the bar because yet again he was riddled with fleas. That, however, was about to change.

As soon as the cat jumped up onto İkmen's lap and settled down, he took a spot-on pipette out of his pocket and squirted anti-flea liquid into the fur at the back of the animal's neck. Now meowing with rage, Marlboro first hissed and then leapt down and ran away into the gardens that surrounded İkmen's apartment block to try to lick the awful stuff off.

İkmen laughed. 'Sorry about that, but I have to grab him to put his flea stuff on when I can.'

'You're lucky he didn't scratch or bite you!' Peri said.

'Oh, he wouldn't do that. He will never bite the hand that feeds him,' İkmen said. 'Just swears at me, as you heard.'

Peri smiled.

'So,' İkmen said once their coffee and pastries had arrived, 'we've both been invited to a New Year party at the Süleymans' house.'

'Yes,' she said. 'My brother told me that Mehmet Bey had spoken to him about such an event, but Gonca Hanım's phone call came out of the blue. Ömer said that Mehmet Bey wants to introduce my sister-in-law to our friends and colleagues. But I don't think he can know just how very timid Yeşili is. And I'll be honest, I do worry about her meeting Gonca Hanım.'

'Why?'

'There are a lot of travelling Roma down on the Mesopotamian Plain,' she said. 'Settled people like my family and Yeşili's carry a lot of superstitions about them. Roma are feared by many. And knowing how besotted Ömer is with Gonca Hanım, I am afraid that if Yeşili cringes away from her, he may lose his temper.'

'Mmm. And yet on the plus side, it will give me a chance to see how Ömer Bey is with Gonca Hanım and, if he will tolerate it, to speak to him about his behaviour.'

Peri bit into her spinach borek and then wiped flaky pastry crumbs away from her mouth. 'I thought that too,' she said.

İkmen frowned. 'I wonder why Gonca asked me.'

'She likes you.'

'And I like her, but . . .' He paused. 'Ah, however . . .'

'Because I am single too, she may be matchmaking,' Peri said.

İkmen sighed. 'I do hope not.'

'Oh, thank you, Çetin Bey!'

Suddenly appalled at what he'd just blurted out, İkmen said, 'Oh God, that is no criticism of you, Peri Hanım! Absolutely not! No, I'm just appalled that she may have ideas about matching a lovely young woman like you with a broken-down old bastard like me!'

Peri laughed. 'You do yourself a disservice.'

İkmen shook his head. 'Anyway,' he said, 'we have no way of learning what is in Gonca Hanım's mind, and so it's all academic.'

Commissioner of Police Selahattin Ozer was not an easy man to talk to. Tall and thin, with startlingly cold grey eyes, he was devoted not only to his religion – he was well known to pray five times a day – but also to anything to do with figures, money and time. All legitimate concerns for a commissioner of police, unless one worked for him. Then, as Mehmet Süleyman was feeling now, such concerns could be deployed to oppress.

'Sir, while our investigation into the murder of Ceviz Elibol is in its infancy, I believe we've already come a long way in our examination of the crime scene and our principal suspect, Ateş Böcek,' Süleyman said as he sat in front of Ozer's enormous oak desk.

The commissioner nodded, then looked up as if expecting more information.

'Unfortunately for us, while Ateş Böcek is exhibiting signs indicating mental illness, his family deny he is unwell,' Süleyman continued. 'Plus there is no official record of any mental distress.'

'And our psychiatrist? What does he think?' Ozer asked.

'Dr Koca believes that Ateş Böcek is living in a fantasy where no one is who he or she seems. However, he is still assessing him. He may yet be playing at being deranged in order to escape a prison sentence. Dr Koca has watched CCTV footage of Böcek on the morning of the girl's murder and says that his behaviour may be interpreted in several ways, including simply that of a young, privileged man. What his behaviour does not imply, he says, is that of a man who has just killed someone and is now flaying her body. Apart from anything else, Dr Koca doesn't think Böcek has the requisite skill set to do this. In order to try to address some of these issues, he requested that the boy's father, Esat Böcek, grant him leave to assess Ateş's condition further by allowing an involuntary assessment order. In spite of support from me, this was denied.'

'But Ateş Böcek remains in custody?'

'Yes. And now some more information has come to light,' Süleyman said. 'Hence my request for this meeting. It has been brought to our attention by an anonymous source.'

215

'Always questionable.'

'I agree. But in this case, I believe there is a chance it may be valid.'

'What is it?'

'Medical notes.'

'Relating to Ateş Böcek?'

'Yes,' Süleyman said. 'They purport to originate from a psychiatrist who claims to have worked with Ateş over some years.'

'Name?'

'Unknown.'

He put the file İkmen had given him on Ozer's desk. The commissioner picked it up and leafed through it.

'I intend to give it to Dr Koca for perusal,' Süleyman said. 'It states that Böcek is suffering from something called Capgras syndrome, or the delusion of doubles. This means that the patient lives in a psychological world peopled by counterfeits. Hence he doesn't believe that anyone is who they say they are. It's the opinion of this doctor that it was abuse of the drug ketamine that precipitated this problem.'

Ozer sighed. 'Esat Böcek endows many charitable enterprises.'

Süleyman considered his options and then decided to just tell the truth.

'Esat Böcek is known to us as the head of a criminal organisation operating out of Kadıköy,' he said. 'He controls the supply of drugs, women and slum accommodation on the Asian side.'

'If that is the case, why isn't he in prison?' Ozer asked.

'That is a good question, sir. The answer is frustratingly common in the case of organised crime, and simple. Böcek covers his tracks. He pays heavily for the loyalty of those around him and successfully deploys his position as a generous man to cover his activities.'

'Mmm.'

Süleyman knew this was hard for Ozer to accept. Whether

he truly believed that Esat Böcek and his organisation were a force for good was unknown. He had to know that they also had a lot of power over a lot of people. In addition, Süleyman was very aware that the Böceks might well have friends in high places.

Ozer said, 'Do you think Dr Koca may be able to identify this unknown doctor from these notes?'

'I think it's possible, sir.'

'Mmm.'

Possible but not probable, as Süleyman was not going to ask Koca for a name. Not yet.

Eventually Ozer said, 'All right then, Mehmet Bey, present this to Dr Koca and let us see where it leads.'

Süleyman smiled. 'Thank you, sir.'

When he got outside the commissioner's office, he breathed a sigh of relief. He had toyed with the idea of not telling Ozer about the anonymous intel, but he'd realised how risky that was. Now he knew and they could all get on, operating in light of this new information. Provided, of course, Ozer didn't tell anyone close to the Böcek family about it. As Çetin İkmen had told Süleyman many years ago, life was a gamble.

'Ankara,' Kerim Gürsel said as he peered at his computer screen.

Eylul Yavaş was drinking her usual vast cup of Starbucks coffee. 'Sir?'

'Mete Bülbül,' he said. 'Our dead pimp stroke dervish was a police officer in Ankara. He retired in 2005, after which he returned here to İstanbul. No family that I can see.'

Eylul walked over to him and looked at his screen.

'So he'd have been on a reasonable pension.'

'Enough to keep him in the Poisoned Princess without much trouble,' Kerim said. 'I wonder what he did with himself all day when he wasn't handing out condoms to working girls?'

His phone rang and he looked at the screen. It was İbrahim Dede, the dervish. Maybe he had some answers for him.

'İbrahim Dede . . .'

'Inspector,' the old man said. 'I've now had a chance to speak to my colleague Serhat Dede about this man Mete Bülbül.'

'Ah.'

'Yes,' he said. 'A voracious reader, it seems. Bought many publications from Beloved bookshop both analogue and digital.'

'All about Sufism?'

'Yes, and including pieces, like the one you found, by foreigners.'

'Did Serhat Dede know him well?' Kerim asked.

'Not well, but he would go to Beloved from time to time for books and also for discourse with Serhat. My colleague is a very knowledgeable man, and so a lot of those who seek the Sufi path make contact with him. According to Serhat Dede, Mete Bülbül was a troubled soul.'

'Oh?'

'Born in Sulukule to a Roma woman. Apparently his father took him with him to Ankara when Mete was a child. Any questions pertaining to Bülbül's mother were deflected. We are dervishes, not therapists.'

'I understand,' Kerim said.

'He returned to İstanbul, or so he told Serhat Dede, to busy himself with good works. Giving out food to the poor and suchlike.'

Did İbrahim Dede know about the condoms? He didn't say.

'That he performed his good deeds in the place his mother's people had migrated to was it seems important to him,' the dervish continued. 'And here is where I think his story may become interesting to you, Inspector . . .'

Her father was furious. Roaring at that bastard Serdar as the thug cowered in front of his desk.

'You work for me, not that fucking stupid little moron!' he yelled.

'I'm sorry, Murad Bey,' the ugly man responded. 'He's your son, your heir. I give him respect only because of you, efendi!'

'Respect? You don't show me respect when you're not here when I need you! I don't give a shit what Yıldırım Bey wants! Whatever it is, let him do it himself! Fat pig could do with some exercise!'

Aylın had seen her brother and Serdar İpek sharing a joke together earlier. Now apparently the thug had been out doing her brother's bidding in some capacity. Her father was right, Yıldırım was a fat pig. Not that she could ever say that to his face. Their mother idolised him, which meant that not even their father would openly oppose him even when the kid commandeered one of his men. The employee had to pay.

'I've given you everything,' Murad continued. 'You know what you are without me? You're cheap muscle in a strip club is what you are! That's where I found you and that's where I'll send you back to if you ever do this to me again!'

'Yes, efendi.'

Murad Ayhan put his fingers on his wrist, feeling his own pulse.

'And now my fucking blood pressure's up!' He sat down in his chair. 'Fucking Dr Sezar's off!' He shook his head. 'If I have a stroke because of you, Serdar Bey, I will make sure your life is hell!'

'Efendi—'

'Oh, get out of my sight!' he yelled. 'And before you decide to put my needs last again, think about how easy it would be for me to get hold of another brutal psychopath. The streets are heaving with them!'

Serdar ran out of Mehmet's office, passing Aylın as he did so. She noticed he was smiling.

*

219

'It came to Serhat Dede's attention that Mete Bülbül was spending a lot of time with the working girls of Tarlabaşı,' said İbrahim Dede to Kerim Gürsel. 'I don't know how he found this out, but he did. Anyway after some gentle probing, Mr Bülbül finally admitted what he was doing.'

Kerim thought about the condoms Bülbül had handed out. 'Which was?'

'Looking for his mother, apparently,' the dervish said. 'He told Serhat Dede that she was a Roma woman who, he thought, worked as a prostitute in the area. It seems he had been told little about her by his father, who is now dead. He was curious and wanted to make contact if possible. It also, it seemed, gave him much sympathy for women who walked the streets for a living.'

'He handed out free condoms,' Kerim said. 'Spoke to the girls about keeping themselves safe.'

'Most laudable,' İbrahim Dede said. 'Who on earth would want to kill someone like that?'

Kerim's mind turned back to the time he'd found Şevket Sesler sorting through Mete Bülbül's correspondence in his apartment.

According to Lola Cortes, the devil himself had come out of the Poisoned Princess apartments via the fire escape. This had been in the brief period after the shooting stopped, before the police arrived. When Süleyman had been trying to save the life of haberdasher Rahul Bey. It had been chaos.

Her stepson had translated for her, from Spanish into English. It was the only language Mehmet Süleyman had in common with him.

Tomas described the 'entity' Lola had seen as 'a figure completely black apart from the face'. In all probability a white person dressed in black clothing, with a hood. The face Lola described as 'hideous', by which she seemed to mean it was inordinately hairy and had a long nose. Then there were the horns.

'The head is completely black and there are horns,' Tomas had told him.

'Horns? Where?' Süleyman had asked.

'On the head. She say they flash with red light,' Tomas had elaborated.

Headphones maybe? Music? Or was 'the devil' in contact with someone, possibly someone involved in the shooting, someone very human?

Now Lola Cortes was looking at mug shots. So far she'd seen nothing that jogged her memory. However, she was also still firmly wedded to the idea that the creature she had seen that night was not human. So even if she were to be presented with an image of the man she'd seen, would she recognise it?

Süleyman, leaving Ömer Mungun in charge, left to return to his office, where Dr Koca was waiting to speak to him. After his meeting with the commissioner, Süleyman had given Koca access to the file İkmen had obtained from the young man's psychiatrist.

When he entered his office, he saw that the doctor was taking notes.

'Interesting reading?' he asked, sitting down behind his desk.

'Indeed.' Dr Koca looked up. 'You know, Inspector, I think I know who this practitioner is. She has a reputation for working with difficult people.'

Süleyman held up a hand. 'The identity of the doctor isn't some-thing I want to know, İlhan Bey. This was given to me on the understanding that their identity be obscured. According to them, Ateş Böcek's condition was to be kept secret. They signed a non-disclosure agreement, and believe me, when you sign such a thing given to you by Esat Böcek, you'd better keep your side of the bargain if you want to live. Now, in lieu of Ateş Böcek himself requesting legal representation, due to his apparent fugue state, his family have appointed counsel. So tomorrow morning, I will attempt to formally interview him in the presence of his lawyer, Eyüp Çelik.'

The doctor rolled his eyes.

'You've heard of him?'

'Who hasn't?' Dr Koca said. 'Advocate to the stars. My daughter is addicted to those celebrity gossip magazines people half her age stare at on their phones. Eyüp Bey it seems spends much of his time defending the "honour" of some awful creature accused of horrifically abusive acts. The Böcek family must have deep pockets.'

'They do. But to return to Ateş, I am still awaiting some scene-of-crime forensic information. I expect that tomorrow morning. However, this interview may well be the last chance I have to either charge him formally with murder or let him go. And as you know, Doctor, I am still conflicted about that. You spent some time with him today. Is there anything you can tell me about that which may help me?'

'Not much,' Dr Koca said. 'I really do think that he's shut down completely now.'

'You don't think he could be faking?'

'Let's put it this way. As so often happens in cell blocks, an inebriated offender was brought on site by a couple of officers. Shouting, swearing and general scuffling noises could be heard in the corridor outside Ateş Böcek's cell. One could hardly hear oneself think. From Ateş, however, I discerned not a flicker. Not one tiny tell that might make me think he was faking his condition. No.'

'You're late today, Çetin Bey,' Numan Bey said.

Although İkmen had been very attentive to his daughter's insistence that he go for his daily walk first thing every morning, on this occasion he had given it a miss. When he'd woken up that day, he'd needed to think about the implications of what Dr Feride had told him. And then of course he'd had lunch with Peri Mun-gun. Now he had caught up with the pickle-juice seller in his usual spot beside the docks, catching the mid-afternoon ferry trade. Fewer hung-over men and more traditional families drinking his brew for the sake of their health.

'I was busy last night,' he replied.

'Ah.'

'Mmm.' İkmen looked over the side of the dock and saw that the three sculpted heads had gone. 'No sculpture today.'

'Seems not,' Numan Bey said. 'Would you like a glass of—'

'Did you take them down or did she?' İkmen cut in, his eyes boring into Numan Bey's with something like ferocity.

But the old man remained calm.

'Take what down, Çetin Bey?'

'Those representations of the Böcek family,' İkmen said. 'Surely our Armenian friend told you who they were.'

Numan Bey passed İkmen a glass of pickle juice. 'Take, for your health.'

Realising that he was unlikely to make Numan Bey say anything he didn't want to, İkmen took the juice and changed tack.

'This falcı you go to, here in Eminönü,' he said, 'the one you claim told you that nothing is real here in the city, was it her? Did she help you set me up for this convoluted little trail that led me to Balat? Or did you make her up? And what of my old friend Aaron Kamhi?'

Numan Bey sighed. 'When fear takes hold of a place or a per-son, it spreads out and affects us all,' he said. 'I genuinely and sincerely know of no one called Aaron Kamhi, but I can tell you that my falcı is real. As for her credentials? She is related by blood to Gonca Şekeroğlu.'

'Is she—'

'And I have already spoken too many names.'

'You know that this city will explode if there's full-scale gang warfare,' İkmen said.

'If it is written—'

'Oh, don't give me that fatalistic bullshit! You know I have a British daughter-in-law, and you know what they say over there? God helps them who help themselves. And you know that even I, an atheist, believe that to be true. If we don't do something to prevent what could become, what already has caused, considerable bloodshed, we do not deserve God's help. And so for the sake of *your* God, Numan Bey, tell me what you know.'

The old man slumped a little, clearly wrestling with his conscience. 'And if I do that . . .'

'If you do that, you may help to save lives,' İkmen said.

Moments passed, during which the sky blurred and the ferries' foghorns began to sound.

Numan Bey sighed. 'It's about desire, Çetin Bey. Sexual lust. No more, no less.'

'How unoriginal,' İkmen said. 'Who are we talking about, Numan Bey?'

But the old man shook his head. 'That's it. That is all I will say.'

And İkmen knew that he was telling the truth. But he had also given him a clue whereby he might find out more. As he walked back up towards Sultanahmet, he took his phone out and called Gonca.

Ömer Mungun closed and locked Süleyman's office door so that his boss and Kerim Bey could smoke. He and Eylul Yavaş were used to it by this time, even though they didn't like it. Their superiors both claimed they could think more effectively if they lit up. It was nonsense, but it was foolish to think their minds could be changed about it, especially Süleyman's.

'Do we have anything more on the CCTV analysis from

Kadıköy?' Süleyman asked. 'I have what could be my last inter-view with Ateş Böcek, with Eyüp Çelik in tow, tomorrow morning at nine.'

'Still working on it, boss,' Ömer said. 'Nothing so far.'

'DNA from the scene?'

'Tomorrow morning if we're lucky,' Eylul said. 'Sir, are you still uncertain about Ateş Böcek's guilt?'

'I am. While all the evidence so far points towards him, his behaviour, both now and on the day of the murder, tells me he didn't do it.'

'There's enough evidence for the prosecutor to convict,' Kerim said.

'There is, but should we convict just because we can? Anec-dotal evidence points towards Şevket Sesler pursuing compensation for Ceviz Elibol from Esat Böcek. Then we had the shooting in Tarlabaşı, to which we have not as yet been able to connect any operative or member of the Böcek family.'

'It now seems possible that the Poisoned Princess victim, Mete Bülbül, may have been shot with his own gun,' Kerim said. 'He was in the job in Ankara for many years and it's possible the Glock we found in his apartment was his old service weapon. I've messaged Ankara and am waiting to hear back. Further to that, I've been told by someone who knew him that Bülbül was in the process of investigating Sufi philosophy. A native of Tarlabaşı, he moved back to the district after he retired from the force in Ankara. His aim in returning seems to have been to locate his mother, who had been a Roma working girl. Whether he found her or not, we don't know, but I would say he probably didn't. But in order to get other working girls who might know her to speak to him, he was friendly towards them and well known for his habit of giving them condoms, which he urged them to use.'

'He wasn't a customer?'

'Seems not.'

225

'You found Şevket Sesler going through his things,' Eylul said. 'Do you think he knew about Bülbül's mother?'

'He may have done. It's something I need to look into. Maybe as a start, Eylul, you could get out amongst the Roma girls.'

'Yes, sir.'

Süleyman said, 'Ömer Bey, what of Lola Cortes and our gallery of rogues?'

'Nothing from the mug shots so far, boss,' Ömer replied. 'According to her stepson, she's convinced that what she saw was some kind of demon. I don't know how we manage to convince her otherwise.'

'We don't,' Süleyman said. 'What I do suggest is that we review our CCTV footage of Sesler's birthday celebration and see whether we can identify anyone who might fit Lola Hanım's description.'

'Yeah, but—'

'Remember, there were a lot of circus and street performers present,' Süleyman said. 'We've got a list of the acts who were employed for the evening. Get a team set up to hit the phones. I've spoken to Ozer, and while he's keen for us to tread carefully around the Seslers and the Böceks, he wants any possibility of gang warfare averted at all costs. Now, I've briefed you all about the medical records purporting to be those of Ateş Böcek that I came into possession of last night, and while our psychiatrist, Dr Koca, concurs with the diagnosis of this unnamed doctor, he cannot properly assess Böcek when he has clearly shut down. I cannot stress the importance of finding evidence that will unconditionally convict or exonerate Böcek as quickly as we can. To that end, I suggest we review everything we've done so far and pursue whatever new information we may have tonight. Both Inspector Gürsel and myself realise this is a sacrifice, but if it is possible, we will make sure you get overtime payment.'

Ömer Mungun looked positively exultant. 'Can always do with a few more lira,' he said.

Eylul nodded. 'Of course.'

'Thank you.' Süleyman smiled. 'As far as we know, Sesler and his people have not retaliated.'

'They know we're watching them, boss.'

'They do, but if we're right about these being the opening shots of a territorial war, they won't hold back for ever. We have to either tie Ateş Böcek to this or not, and we have to do it now.'

Chapter 17

'The only relative I know of in Eminönü is my cousin Şeftali,' Gonca said as she put on her coat. 'I'll take you to her.'

İkmen, who had diverted home to get his car and driven up to Balat, said, 'Now? Don't you have food to prepare?'

'Mehmet Bey called to say he won't be home tonight because he's working, Rambo is who knows where, and the Spaniards are cooking for themselves. Why should I bother just for me?'

It was a fair point and one with which İkmen had some sympathy.

'But how do you know your cousin will be in?' he asked.

She smiled. 'Şeftali is always in. She's got bad legs. She's worked from home for years.'

'And she's definitely a falcı?'

'She was last time I heard.'

'Which was when?'

She thought for a moment. 'She definitely made it to my father's funeral. That was five years ago. She used one of those walking frame things. She may have come to my wedding.'

'You don't know?'

Gonca hustled him out of the door.

'You know how big my family is,' she said. 'And I had other things on my mind. My cousin the scryer was not one of them.'

'She uses . . .'

'A bowl of oil,' Gonca said. 'And a demon. But she's always been very accurate.'

*

Esat Böcek was always lecturing those who worked for him about something. Often it was the evils of alcohol, frequently the sin trap posed by women. But cigarettes were also on his hit list, and so whenever Hakki Bürkev wanted to smoke, he had to hide from Esat Bey. On this occasion, he was actually guarding the Böcek apartment and its environs, which meant that he had to slip away down an alleyway beside a designer footwear shop and smoke by the dustbins, which he leaned on now. He'd done it before. Not that he was often on guard outside the Böcek place. Security had been beefed up since the problems with the gypsies. That filthy old bastard Şevket Sesler had accused Esat Bey of trying to provoke a war. But he hadn't. No one knew who had attacked Sesler and his people on the gang boss's birthday, but it certainly wasn't the Böceks. Hakki had worked for the family since he was fourteen, and he knew that Esat Bey would never do such a thing. Besides, what did Sesler have that he might want? His territory in Tarlabaşı was gradually eroding due to property development, and his people were generally poor and unpopular. Of course he controlled a considerable drug supply operation over there, but it was nothing like the scale of Esat Bey's business.

Hakki lit one cigarette from the smoking butt of the other. He might as well get in as many as he could. His partner for the evening, old Bilal Bey, had allowed him to leave his post only on condition that he didn't stay away too long. Bilal had become nervous in his old age, and the thought that he might be alone with hordes of angry gypsies made him anxious.

Hakki, with the arrogance of youth, was not that bothered. No gypsy would get the better of him! Even if the threat had come from Murad Ayhan's infidel warriors, he wouldn't be that worried. Esat Bey had God on his side, and although Hakki knew that he was sinning by smoking as well as lusting after all the beautiful rich girls on Baghdat Caddesi, he also knew that because he worked for Esat Bey, God would forgive him. Also he planned to go on the Hajj next year, and so that would more than make up for his nicotine addiction and his unclean thoughts.

Relaxed and really quite pleased with himself, he leaned on the dustbins again – for the very last time.

'Gonca?'

Strictly speaking, Şeftali Şekeroğlu didn't live in Eminönü but in Tahtakale, in a small apartment above a ceramics shop on Fındıkçılar Sokak. In order to get to her apartment, Gonca had pulled Çetin İkmen behind her up a flight of crumbling Byzantine stairs, which led to an extremely rickety wooden platform on the other side of which was a scarred open door.

'Yes,' Gonca called back. She glanced at İkmen. 'That will be her demon telling her we're here.'

Or maybe, İkmen thought, Şeftali had simply seen them from the street. But whatever the case, he had to admit that this small corner of İstanbul esoterica had been previously unknown to him – and he knew most of the places where the magic was thick and reality thin.

Şeftali was seated at a round table covered by an elaborately embroidered cloth. In front of her was a large copper bowl into which she stared fixedly. Although strong, her face was not beautiful like Gonca's. However, when she looked up, İkmen could see that she was strikingly handsome – heavily lined and thin, she looked like one of the old Roma musicians he remembered playing their violins and drums in the streets of Sulukule, their previous home. She was also filthy.

She said something to Gonca in the Romani language, and Gonca replied, 'Turkish. He only speaks Turkish.'

There was a smell, indescribable and unpleasant.

Şeftali looked him up and down without smiling, then said to Gonca, 'He's not your husband.'

'No, this is Çetin İkmen. His mother was the Albanian witch, Ayşe.'

'Ah.' Şeftali nodded and then shifted uncomfortably in her chair. 'What do you want?'

'He believes you know Numan Bey, the pickle-juice man.'

'What if I do?'

'Numan Bey told him that things are not as they seem in the city. He said that came from you.'

'Did he?' She tilted her head.

Silence rolled in. The room, which was small, was lit by a freestanding tree of candles. If the long black smoke trails on the wall behind it were anything to go by, it had stood in the same place for many years.

'Does he know he'll have to pay?' Şeftali said.

The women were talking about him as if he wasn't there.

'He knows,' Gonca said.

Şeftali motioned for İkmen to take the chair opposite her.

'Sit.'

The streets of Tarlabaşı were subdued. There were a lot of people moving around – drag queens, working girls, drug dealers – but more quietly than usual, probably nervous in light of the recent shooting incident on Sesler's birthday. However, in spite of the cold, the mahalle was open for business, and so Eylul Yavaş was not lacking women with whom to talk. And while she didn't know the local working women as well as her boss did, she knew who the Tarlabaşı madams were, knew some of their girls, and was easy with the way some of them tried to shock her. She'd put her hijab away in favour of a hat. For those women who knew her, this was cause for a few raised eyebrows, while amongst those who didn't, she was just a 'woman copper'.

In pursuit of information about the late Mete Bülbül, Eylul went to a small bar on Tavla Sokak known to be a front for a brothel run by a Roma madame called Sibel. Short and fat, her tiny black eyes almost disappearing into the doughy fat of her face, Sibel had a stable of twelve Roma women and girls whom she protected like a tigress. Did she know anything about Mete Bülbül, the Condom Man?

'I saw the fucking moron a few times,' she told Eylul. 'Giving out condoms! Who did he think was gonna use those?'

Nearer the bottom than the top of Tarlabaşı's prostitute society, Sibel and her girls catered for the many men who came to the quarter specifically to 'ride bareback', as some of them put it. Working without a condom was the only way some of her older girls could even get punters.

A girl on a street corner, high on heroin, mumbled something about how the condom Man was a sweetheart, and then Eylul met Fındık Hanım.

In her fifties, with at least forty years on the streets behind her, Fındık Ayavefe was one of the Romani population's dirtiest secrets. Once the child mistress of Şevket Sesler's father, Harun, she had borne him three stillborn babies before he threw her out of his house. Because her family refused to have her back, she lived on the streets making her money from what some said were the most depraved men in the city. Stories about her passed around the quarter like bad smells. Fındık Ayavefe, it was said, would fulfil all and any fantasies a man might have, and a few he might never have dreamed about.

Now here she was, standing in front of Eylul Yavaş, drunk and high and stinking.

'Grubbing around in the filth, Sergeant Yavaş?' she said.

Instinctively Eylul pulled her coat tight around her body. 'Fındık Hanım?'

'Asking about the Condom Man?' the woman continued.

'Mete Bülbül, yes,' Eylul said. 'Did you know him?'

Fındık laughed. 'Everyone knew him!' she said. 'Interfering old twat.'

'I gather his products weren't welcome?'

She laughed again. '*He* wasn't welcome.'

'You know his mother was Roma?'

The laughter stopped.

'Well, do you?'

'Know nothing about him except he peddled free sheaths,' she said. 'He was on his own here, that one. You'd be wise to remember that.'

'In what sense?' Eylul asked.

Fındık moved in closer, so close that Eylul could smell her foul breath.

'Fuck off,' she said. 'And I say that for your own good.'

Lola Cortes had not identified anyone from the department's mugshot files. She and Tomas had now returned to Balat, while their hostess, Gonca, was either out and about or she'd switched her phone off. Mehmet Süleyman called Rambo junior, who said he didn't have a clue where his mother might be.

He said, 'She won't be screwing around, she's way too into you for that.'

Maybe she was on Romani business of some sort? They kept so much to themselves, it was almost impossible to break into their *omertà*. It irritated him, but that was what he had taken on and that was what he now had to live with.

A team of uniforms had been assembled to make contact with all the entertainers engaged to perform at Sesler's birthday party, and already three jugglers and a fire-eater had been contacted and ruled out of the investigation. At the head of the team, Kerim Gürsel was speaking to a Romani woman who claimed she'd been at the celebration with her pet dog, who, she said, was magical and possessed three heads. As far as she knew, he hadn't managed to slip his lead during the festivities.

Süleyman and Ömer Mungun were reviewing CCTV footage from that evening. They could slow down the footage from one of the cameras outside Rambo senior's meyhane so that they could see the shots emanating from the roof of the Poisoned Princess apartments. Closer to the ground, images were blurred.

Türgüt Zana, lead technical officer, arrived just as Ömer was giving himself a break from the screen.

'You won't see anything with your eyes closed,' he said as he perched himself on the end of the desk. Although universally acknowledged as an excellent officer, Zana did neither irony nor humour. Some of his colleagues described him as autistic, although Süleyman, who by virtue of having been married to a psychiatrist knew rather more than most about atypical mental states, found that explanation rather too simplistic. Zana was different.

'I was giving them a rest,' Ömer explained.

'Oh.'

Süleyman said, 'Officer Zana, we are reviewing footage from the night of the Tarlabaşı shooting. I'd value your input provided you're not going off duty.'

Zana, who probably was going off duty, pulled up a spare chair and sat down with them.

'Do you want to see my legs?' Şeftali Şekeroğlu said. 'You want to see for yourself why I don't go out?' Then she spoke in Romani to something or someone that appeared to be underneath her table.

As the night outside deepened, the candles in the room guttered and the smell of cannabis from the scryer's pipe made İkmen cough. Şeftali laughed.

'You don't like dope, Çetin Bey?' she asked.

'I am indifferent to it, Hanım.'

'So, you want to see my ugly legs or not?' she said.

234

İkmen looked at Gonca, who nodded. 'You may as well. She wants to prove to you she isn't a charlatan.'

İkmen said, 'All right, and thank you, hanım.'

Şeftali struggled to stand. Then she lifted her skirts to reveal legs widely bowed by what İkmen imagined was the effects of rickets.

'That's . . .'

'Been like it since I was a child,' she said. 'Why I never married. Who'd marry them legs, eh? Anyway, I'm happier with my own company, and her.' She lowered her skirts and sat back down. 'Gonca Hanım tell you about her, did she?'

Gonca whispered, 'Her demon.'

'Oh . . . yes.'

'She's everywhere, my honey,' Şeftali said. 'My dear, my pet.' She spoke in Romani again, smiling.

Was it the cannabis that was making İkmen feel a little dizzy?

'Know what she is?' Şeftali continued, then went on without waiting for an answer. 'Poreskoro. Brings plague, smallpox and cholera. She's a very busy girl. She knows what goes on in this city and every city. I expect you with your education regard something like her, with her cat and dog heads, her snake-head tail, as something mythical, don't you?' She lifted her tablecloth a little. 'But if you come down here . . .'

Gonca put a hand on İkmen's arm. 'Don't,' she said. 'It's truly revolting. It's clever, but it's vile.'

Caught between wanting to see Şeftali's demon and his own fear, İkmen said, 'I wish only to know what you meant when you told Numan Bey that what is happening in this city isn't real. I want to know about the real driver behind all this chaos, which he said you told him was sexual lust.'

'*She* told him,' Şeftali corrected. 'She goes out, she is everywhere.'

'As some sort of embodied plague?'

'As my honey, my love.'

İkmen turned to Gonca. 'I'm sorry, I've been dealing with these unseen things all my life, but . . .'

Şeftali lifted up the tablecloth. For a moment, he saw nothing.

'Disease and sex live a happy life together,' she said.

As he peered into the blackness, did he see something resolve? Pinpoints of light? Eyes? He pulled the tablecloth back down again, shaken.

'And if you add in greed, well,' Şeftali continued, 'that is very attractive to my honey. Open your eyes and follow the lust, my friend. Whose, I don't know. I don't go out. But you will know. My honey purrs her admiration for the next generation of filth.'

'I don't know,' Türgüt Zana said.

Ömer Mungun was infuriated. 'So if you don't know who he is, why point him out?'

'Because I *should* know,' Zana said.

'Fucking—'

Süleyman put a hand on Ömer's arm. 'I think what Officer Zana is trying to say is that he should recognise this person, but at present he can't recall who he is.'

The figure, whose features were indistinct, appeared to be an overweight man wearing some sort of animal costume.

Ömer Mungun was now a little calmer than he had been. 'Is that a dog or a bear? A rabbit?'

They all shook their heads. Whatever it was appeared to be something grey and furry, with ears and a small opening for the face. Something that could have been a furry jaw hung beneath the man's chin.

And then Süleyman said something he would afterwards come to see as significant.

'Is it,' he asked, 'a wolf?'

*

Still shaken by Fındık Ayavefe's words, which she had taken very much as a warning, Eylul Yavaş headed off back to where Inspector Gürsel had told her to park her car, behind his apartment building. Police tape still hung close to what remained a crime scene.

She'd spent five hours in Tarlabaşı and learned not much beyond the fact that nobody was going to tell her much about the victim. But why? From what she could gather, he'd been harmless. Also, he was, through his mother, Roma. So what was the problem?

It was nearly two o'clock in the morning, and while some of the clubs, like the Sailor's Bar, were still open, everybody was too drunk or high or both to make a whole lot of sense. Just before she reached her car, Eylul called Inspector Gürsel to let him know she was on her way back to headquarters. He was of course disappointed that she'd not been able to find out very much, but he was grateful that she'd been so keen to carry on working. It didn't sound as if anyone else had had a breakthrough of any kind either.

She used her remote key to unlock the car. As she was lowering herself into the driving seat, arms wrapped themselves around her waist and pulled her onto the frozen ground.

Eylul screamed. She had her gun on her hip but she couldn't get to it. And then a large figure covered in darkness was sitting on her chest. Eylul gasped for air.

'What did you see underneath Şeftali's table?' Gonca asked.

Holding tight to İkmen's arm, she was walking with him through the slush back to his car.

'I don't know,' he said. 'Eyes? Your cousin, she exists towards the black.'

Gonca laughed. 'Oh İkmen, I thought you understood better than that. You know there's no black, no white, only shades of grey.'

'Yes, so let me put it like this then. Şeftali Hanım is at the darker end of the magical spectrum. I thought that was what I said, but . . .'

'When your mother used to produce kittens out of thin air to entertain the children all those decades ago, she made a pact with something,' Gonca said. 'Şeftali sends her Poreskoro out to find the bad things. As a creature of plague, it is attracted to filth. All the dirty deals, the old men foisting themselves upon children, the peddlers of disorder and death. This is where she goes, and then she comes back and tells Şeftali. Make no mistake, you were meant to know these things.'

'Know what? What do I know?' he said. 'Follow the lust! Whose lust?'

'I don't know.'

'And that is my problem with magic. It's an avenue of communication that deliberately makes itself obscure.'

She laughed. 'If magic doesn't retain its mystery, it dies. You know that.'

İkmen shook his head. 'And what on earth was that smell in her apartment?'

'Filth,' Gonca said. 'Şeftali neither cleans nor washes. If she did, the Poreskoro would leave her, and then how would she make a living?'

'I thought I knew every esoteric location in this city,' he said. 'But that was a new one on me.'

'You are not the only one busying him- or herself with the city's protection, İkmen. İstanbul is older than Turks, Greeks, Roma, even the Jews. She has found ways of protecting herself none of us can even dream about.'

'The Wolves aren't known for dressing up, are they?' Süleyman asked. 'I thought they were too serious for such stunts.'

He was referring to the far-right political organisation known as the Grey Wolves. Started in the late 1960s, it had been the face of extreme Turkish nationalism for decades. Ostensibly secular, some members had drifted close to Islamist ideology in recent years in line with their political wing, the MHP. Now in an alliance with the ruling party, the MHP was mainstream even if the Wolves were still considered outliers.

'Anything's possible,' Ömer Mungun said. As a member of a minority from eastern Turkey, he had grown up being afraid of the Grey Wolves.

Kerim Gürsel pointed at the image on the screen, 'Well, if this man is a Grey Wolf, he is seriously out of shape. Don't they pride themselves on being the best specimens of Turkish masculinity?'

Süleyman snorted. Then he said, 'But if this man does have a connection to the Wolves, that should be a red flag to us. On the night of Sesler's birthday, the Roma – not fans of the Wolves – were out in force, and we think they could have been attacked by Esat Böcek's pious gang of thugs from Kadıköy. Now, we know that the Grey Wolves hate the Roma. They consider them to be subhuman. And although some of them have claimed in recent years to be born-again Muslims, we also know that their main focus is not religion but nationalism. So if a Wolf or Wolves were in Tarlabaşı for Sesler's birthday party . . .'

'Maybe the Wolves shot at the Roma?' Kerim said. 'Why? To cause trouble between Sesler and the Böceks?'

'Maybe. And why not? Maybe the death of Ceviz Elibol was irrelevant to what happened that night. Or perhaps we have been deliberately misdirected.'

'Or maybe the man in the wolf costume is just a man in a wolf costume,' Türgüt Zana said.

They all looked at him.

'I thought you said you might recognise him, Türgüt Bey,' Ömer Mungun said.

'Yes, but I wasn't the one who attributed Grey Wolf membership to this person. That was Mehmet Bey.'

239

He was right, even if he had been the one who had started the conversation.

Süleyman sighed. 'For the moment, then, we carry on making contact with the acts that were booked for that night. Ask about costumes. Do we still have some left to speak to?'

Ömer Mungun consulted a list. 'Three, boss. A Karagöz puppet show, a sword dance troupe and a snake dancer.'

'Right, I'm going back to talk to Sesler—'

They all heard the door into the squad room open and then close with a bang. They all saw Eylul Yavaş lean against it. And then they all watched her slide down it and land on the floor.

Chapter 18

All of them, except Türgüt Zana, who just stood to one side look-ing awkward, came to her assistance. Süleyman got her a chair, Ömer Mungun a glass of water, and Kerim Gürsel held her hand, which, he noticed, was covered in mud.

'What happened?' he asked her. 'Are you hurt?'

'No. I was getting into my car,' Eylul said. 'I parked behind your building, sir. He jumped me.'

'Definitely a man?'

'Oh yes, the voice . . . Oh God,' she said, 'my hat! I lost my hat!'

Her hair, which had come loose from the bun she'd created underneath her hat, was hanging loose and limp around her shoulders.

Kerim said, 'Ömer Bey, Sergeant Yavaş has a headscarf on her chair back in my office. Can you please go and get it for her?'

'Yes, Kerim Bey.' Ömer left.

Kerim said, 'Did you see his face, Eylul?'

She shook her head. 'No, sir. He was wearing a balaclava. I smelt rakı.'

Süleyman pulled up a chair and sat down beside her.

'Sergeant Yavaş,' he said, 'you mentioned his voice. What did he say to you?'

She took a deep breath. 'He said I was not to pursue informa-tion about the Condom Man. As you know, I'd been talking to working women, particularly Roma.'

'You think he was Roma?'

241

'I don't know. We know the Condom Man was half Roma. He, this man, told me that if I carried on asking questions, it would go badly for me.'

'In what way?'

'He didn't say. He was sitting on my chest, sir. I was trying to get hold of my gun. I was distracted . . .'

Süleyman put a hand on her shoulder and stood up. Ömer Mungun returned with her headscarf and gave it to her.

Kerim said, 'I think you should see a doctor, Eylul.'

'No . . .'

'You must,' Süleyman said. 'And you'll need to make a statement. I want to do this officially. I want to catch this man.' He looked over at Kerim. 'If you can organise that, Ömer Bey and I will take a couple of uniforms and go over to Tarlabaşı. Let's see what Şevket Sesler has to say about this – and other things.'

'OK.'

'And in the meantime,' he picked his coat up and put it on, 'keep digging. Look for performers – and wolves.'

'Ateş?'

The young man looked up. He'd asked to see 'that man who says he's my doctor', and so Dr İlker Koca had attended.

Although clean, the cell still smelt of the faeces that had so recently littered the floor. And if Dr Koca was not mistaken, his patient had rather more bruises than last time he'd seen him.

'My mother used to say that I had to trust someone,' Ateş said. 'I trusted her.'

The doctor sat down. 'You loved your mother.'

'Of course. My mother always told me the truth. She's dead now.'

'I know. Do other people not tell you the truth, Ateş?'

The young man narrowed his eyes.

'Or is it that you don't believe that people are who they say they are?'

He said nothing.

The doctor sighed. 'All right, let us try this honesty business, shall we? You trusted your mother, and now I think you are saying you might be able to trust me. So let me tell you about myself. My name is İlker Koca and I am a doctor of psychiatry. I was born in Izmir seventy years ago to an ethnic Jewish family, and I obtained my medical degree from Hacettepe University in Ankara. I was married for many happy years to my wife Gulse, who sadly died in 2010. I have two children and four grandchildren, whom I love very much.'

'But that could be a lie . . .'

'It could, but it isn't.'

The guard who watched over these proceedings shuffled his feet slightly.

'Why don't you tell me about yourself?' the doctor said. 'I know your name is—'

'What is wrong with me?' Ateş cut in.

'Well . . .'

Was the young man deflecting the doctor's invitation to introduce himself, or did he actually want to know what his diagnosis might be? And did this demonstrate a level of insight?

Dr Koca said, 'What did your other doctor say? The one your father used to take you to see?'

'You mean the snake woman?' Ateş said. 'She said she was a doctor, but I could see through her disguise.'

'And are you seeing through *my* disguise now? Do I have a disguise? What's it like?'

Şevket Sesler was pissed off.

As he lowered himself down into the huge leather seat behind his desk, he said, 'I had a killer hand . . . What do you want, Mehmet Bey?'

A poker addict, Sesler held regular schools in the basement of his Kızlar club. However, as a desperately bad player, when he talked about his hand, he was actually talking about the hand that was being played for him by his henchman, Munir Can.

Süleyman, who sat on the other side of Sesler's massive oak desk, with Ömer and two uniformed constables at his back, surveyed the godfather's office. Faux-oak-lined walls occasionally interrupted by false bookcases, the seating enveloping black leather . . . it was like a location from a 1970s porn movie.

'One of my officers was attacked outside the Poisoned Princess apartments an hour ago,' he said.

'And you thought of me?' Sesler shook his head and cleared his throat.

'Not exactly. But I thought of your organisation.'

'Do I have to ask why?'

'Only if you want to. But when I tell you that my officer was given a message by whoever attacked her, I hope it will pique your interest.'

'What message?'

'He – and it was a man – told her to stop asking questions about the late Mete Bülbül.'

'Who?'

'The man who was killed in his own apartment on the night of your birthday party,' Süleyman said. 'You must remember, Şevket Bey. My colleague Inspector Gürsel found you in said apartment the day after Bülbül's death, sorting through his paperwork.'

There was a heavy silence. Flanked only by Munir Can, who, like his boss, stank of rakı, Şevket Sesler steepled his fingers underneath his chin. Eventually he said, 'Your officer, was she hurt?'

'She has not yet seen our doctor, so I don't know. I do not believe any injuries she may have are life-threatening.' Süleyman looked pointedly at Munir Can. 'But you know, Şevket Bey, that the penalty for assaulting a police officer is punitive.'

Can did not so much as flicker an eyelid. But given that the man was Sesler's heaviest as well as one of his most alcohol-dependent thugs, Süleyman felt that his hunch about the identity of the offender was pretty safe.

Sesler took a deep breath. 'You and me, alone, Mehmet Bey.'

'If you wish.' Süleyman motioned for Ömer Mungun and the constables to leave him.

His sergeant said, 'Boss . . .'

'I'll be fine, Ömer. Şevket Bey will, I am sure, treat me with respect.'

Sesler, for his part, turned to Munir Can. 'You can go too.'

'But Şevket Bey—'

'Fuck off!' he roared.

All the men left. Now it was just Şevket Sesler and Süleyman, alone.

'I'm so sorry we're still here,' Sinem Gürsel said to Çetin İkmen as he walked into his living room.

'I'm not,' he said.

Çiçek was sitting next to Sinem on one of the family's huge, battered sofas. 'It's lovely having you here, Sinem.'

'Yes, but Melda cries . . .'

'It's what babies do,' İkmen said as he sat down and lit a cigarette. 'My wife and I had nine of them. Believe me, Sinem Hanım, little Melda has not woken me up once since you've been here.'

'I did phone Kerim,' Sinem continued, 'but he's working tonight.'

'With Mehmet Bey, yes,' İkmen said.

'He was adamant I stay here.'

'Quite right. You're family. Kerim was my deputy for many years and, like Mehmet Bey, I have always considered him to be a brother.'

'Yes, but you're feeding us . . .'

'It's only money,' İkmen said. 'It's not important.'

Çiçek patted Sinem's hand. 'You know how Dad is,' she said. 'Please, Sinem, stop feeling guilty.'

Sinem managed a half-smile. 'You're all so kind.' Then she stood up. 'But I think I'll go to bed now. Melda's been down for two hours, and I should be with her in case she wakes.'

İkmen said, 'Do whatever makes you feel comfortable, Sinem. Goodnight.'

When she had gone, he looked at Çiçek. 'Wasn't expecting to see you this evening. Thought you were supposed to be out with your young man.'

Çiçek had been watching a dizi with Sinem. Now she switched the TV off and said, 'You mean my young bigot?'

'Ah. Want to talk about it?'

'Not really, but I will. I phoned Sedat Bey this afternoon to ask whether he was still on for our date tonight. He said he was, and then told me this "hilarious" story about how he'd needed to catch a taxi over to Maltepe for work this morning.'

'Oh?'

'Beat a couple of trans girls to the taxi, apparently. Very pleased with himself, he went on to tell me how "ugly" and "disgusting" they were, how they smelt of rakı and would bring down society if we didn't do something about it. I cancelled our date. I also told him to fuck off.'

'I see.'

Çiçek frowned. 'Is that all you've got to say, Dad?'

'Your date.'

'Oh yes, and how do you think he'd fit in with us in this family, eh?' Çiçek said. 'I couldn't bring someone like that here! God, he'd probably punch Auntie Samsun in the face!'

'And live to regret it,' İkmen said. 'Samsun fights dirty, always has.'

'Yes, but . . .'

246

She was upset. At forty-eight, Çiçek was beginning to feel as if she'd never meet a man with whom she could have a meaningful relationship. İkmen put his hand out to her and she walked over to him. As she had done when she'd been a little girl, she sat beside him in his rancid old chair and put her head on his chest. He stroked her hair.

'I know you're hurting, my beautiful daughter,' he said. 'But if someone isn't right for you, then what is the point?'

'I know, but . . .'

'I'm aware how much men have hurt you in the past. I also know how strong your need is to be special to someone. You deserve to be loved, Çiçek, but only by someone who is worthy of you.'

'I thought that was Mehmet Süleyman,' she said. 'We agreed about politics, religion, social responsibility . . .'

'Ah, but he was already in love with Gonca.' He hugged her. 'If I could make it better for you, you know that I would.'

'But you can't,' she said.

'No,' he conceded. 'All I can do is love you and be proud of you.'

Ateş Böcek had admitted that he couldn't see beyond Dr İlker Koca's disguise.

'Maybe I don't know you well enough yet,' he said. 'That other doctor, I went to her for years. But I only knew her as the snake she was after about a year, I think.'

'And who was that doctor, Ateş? Do you know?' Koca asked.

'No.' The young man leaned forward in his seat and the guard at his back straightened. The doctor signalled to him that all was well. 'Dr Koca, what is wrong with me? Do I have a disease?'

Whenever a patient asked for a diagnosis, Koca was always faced with the choice of telling the unvarnished truth or a truncated, almost infantilised version thereof. In his soul, he knew that anything but complete honesty was both confusing and insulting to the patient.

'Like your previous psychiatrist, I believe that you are suffering from something called "delusion of doubles",' he said. 'This is a condition where someone believes that people are not who they say they are.'

'That's because they're all lying,' Ateş said. Then, as if that information had unsettled or overwhelmed him, he changed the subject. 'Do you want me to tell you who I am?' he asked. 'You told me who you are, now it's my turn.'

'Of course,' Dr Koca said. 'Tell me about yourself, Ateş.'

The young man nodded for a few seconds, then said, 'My name is Ateş Böcek. I am twenty-one years old and I was born in İstanbul. I try to be a good Muslim.' He looked down at the floor.

Dr Koca said, 'And what else? What about your family? I told you I had a wife and children . . .'

'My father . . .'

'And is he—'

'Oh, he's a real person,' Ateş said. 'He's a good person. They haven't got inside him.'

'Who?'

He looked up. 'You know!' he said.

'Rakı?'

Şevket Sesler took a bottle out of his desk drawer with a couple of glasses.

'No thank you,' Süleyman said.

Sesler poured himself a large measure, which he didn't top up with water. A lot of men drank the powerful anise spirit neat.

'Your loss,' he said.

'What do you want to talk about, Şevket Bey?' Süleyman asked.

Sesler sighed. 'You know now that you're practically family.'

'My wife,' Süleyman said, 'is not to my knowledge related to you. Let's get straight to the point, shall we? Why are we on our own, Şevket Bey? Something you want to tell me, maybe?'

The gypsy drank. Then he said, 'I don't know who attacked your officer tonight.'

'Why don't I believe you?'

'I don't know, Mehmet Bey. Maybe you resent me because I employ your wife.'

'My wife does as she pleases,' Süleyman said. 'Her Romani culture is very dear to her. She practises her various arts in order to promote and remain in touch with it. What I may or may not think of you has nothing to do with Gonca Hanım.'

'Well, maybe it should.'

'Stick to the point, Sesler,' Süleyman said. 'Mete Bülbül. You know something about him. What is it? The man is dead, murdered . . .'

'I never knew him.'

'So what was your interest in him? Why did Kerim Bey find you in Bülbül's apartment going through his correspondence? Tell me now, or I'll go down and take a look at your poker school.'

Everyone knew that Şevket Sesler liked to snort cocaine, especially when Munir Can was playing poker on his behalf. It enhanced his enjoyment of the game.

Sesler sighed. 'I'm not lying when I say I never knew Mete Bülbül. I knew of him, however.'

'Now maybe we're getting somewhere.'

'I'm going to tell you something,' he went on, 'something personal. It's on condition you don't do anything about it.'

'I can't agree to that, Şevket Bey. I don't make deals.'

'No one has died,' Sesler continued. 'On the life of my mother, I swear to you that no one connected or known to me killed Mete Bülbül.'

'Or attacked my colleague?' Süleyman asked.

Sesler remained silent.

'I see,' Süleyman said.

249

'No,' the godfather said, 'you don't. I don't either, to be honest, though I know what I suspect.'

'Tell me about this personal business.'

'Bülbül's mother was my aunt,' Sesler said. 'My father's sister. She used to dance for the gaco when we lived back in Sulukule. She got pregnant by one of them. This was before my time, but it was a great scandal back then. The gaco took the child.'

'Mete Bülbül.'

'Yes.'

'How did you find out about this?'

'My sister Kumru told me – she's fifteen years older than I am.'

'When?'

'Years ago,' he said. 'I didn't know Mete Bülbül from a hole in the road when he came here. Then people started saying that this man in the Poisoned Princess apartments was looking for his mother, who was Roma. Kumru remembered the name Bülbül. She warned my father, and me, that it was possible this man wanted money.'

'So I take it your family didn't make contact?'

'No,' he said. 'His mother died a long time ago; what was the point?'

'To find a long-lost relative?'

'His father was a gaco. He dishonoured my aunt,' Sesler said.

'And he might potentially want money,' Süleyman added.

'Yes, well . . .'

'So you broke into Bülbül's apartment after his murder to—'

'I didn't break in, the door was open,' Sesler said. 'Your people had been all over it. I wanted to see whether Bülbül had known.'

'About his mother?'

'Yeah.'

'And what did you find?' Süleyman asked.

The godfather shrugged. 'Nothing. Some receipts for books

he'd bought from the Sahaflar. He was some sort of religious nut. Then Gürsel turned up.'

'So why didn't you tell Inspector Gürsel what you were doing at the time?'

Sesler leaned across his desk, whispering now. 'I don't want people to know, of course! The only reason I'm telling you is because . . .'

'. . . I'm a gaco married to one of your women. Pity your father, or whoever ran Bülbül's father and his child out of town all those years ago, didn't take a similar view, eh?'

Sesler was quiet for a few moments, then he said, 'What if Mete Bülbül has children? What if they were to come with their hands outstretched? Our family is one that many would like to join, Mehmet Bey.'

Süleyman wanted to say *you're a crime family, you're scum*, but he didn't. Instead he said, 'And you, I imagine, want me to keep this to myself. You know I can't do that.'

'How about I deal with Munir Can in my own way?' Sesler said.

Süleyman sat back in his chair. 'So are you saying he did attack Sergeant Yavaş?'

'No.'

'Does Munir know about Mete Bülbül's connection to you?'

'Yes.'

'Who else?'

'My sister. My dad took the knowledge to the grave.'

'I will require you to take a DNA test for comparison to Mete Bülbül,' Süleyman said. 'This is to verify your story. As for Munir Can . . . As you know, Mr Sesler, I do not make deals. However, should Can insult or upset you in any way and thereafter receive some sort of minor reprimand from you, that is not my business.'

And then his phone rang.

Chapter 19

'Everyone knows that gypsies are masters of blades,' Bilal Aksu told Constable Birol Türgüt, the first police officer to attend the scene in an alleyway off Baghdat Caddesi. Aksu had also told Türgüt that the victim was called Hakki Bürkev and, like Aksu himself, he worked for Esat Böcek. Not that Türgüt was paying much attention to the old man. He was too busy calling the incident in and securing the scene.

By the time Inspector Kerim Gürsel and his team arrived, Bilal Aksu had been joined by his boss. Esat Böcek's first words to Kerim reflected those of his employee.

'When are you going to take the threat from these filthy gypsies seriously?' he demanded. 'Do we all have to die?'

Kerim held up a hand to silence him. Pathologist Dr Arto Sarkissian had just arrived, and he didn't have time for an anti-Roma tirade.

Clearly separated from his bed to attend the scene, the Armenian was still wearing slippers. Placing a foot down on the slush-covered ground as he got out of his car, he said, 'Oh God!'

Kerim walked over to him. 'Would you like me to find you a pair of shoes, Doctor?'

'No thanks.' Dr Sarkissian sat back down in his car and pulled plastic over-shoes over his slippers. Then he stood again. Kerim assisted him over to the tent that his team had erected over the corpse.

'Male, mid twenties, name of Hakki Bürkev. Looks like he's been stabbed.'

'Mmm.'

Without any further comment, the doctor entered the tent, and Kerim returned to speak to Esat Böcek and the old man.

'What was Hakki Bürkev to you, Esat Bey?' he asked Böcek.

'He worked for me.'

'In what capacity?'

Esat Böcek fixed Kerim with one of his signature hard gazes. Not a large man, he used his rather frightening eyes as vehicles for his iron will.

'He came to me as a boy,' he said. 'I put him to work guarding my properties.'

'Was he guarding your apartment tonight?' Kerim asked.

'He was. Ever since this business with Sesler's gypsies, I have increased security around my home.'

'But until tonight, if indeed we can count tonight, you have not experienced any sort of attack on your business or property, have you, Esat Bey?'

'You think the gypsies framing my son for the death of one of their strippers isn't an attack?' Böcek said.

'Esat Bey, that is pure speculation on your part,' Kerim countered.

'Is it?' Böcek stepped towards him, chin jutting. 'Is it really?'

'As far as I'm aware, it is Sesler's people who have been attacked.'

'Not by me!'

'No one is saying that, Esat Bey.'

'I am just as invested in finding out who killed those gypsies,' Böcek continued. 'Because until we find out who it was, I cannot rest easy in my bed.'

'Has Şevket Sesler threatened you?' Kerim asked.

'No! The fuck wouldn't dare! But even if he did, do you think I'd tell you?'

'Oh, I'm sure you wouldn't tell us. But if you haven't done so already, I would open up channels of communication with Sesler if I were you.'

'Would you?'

'Yes. Because if someone other than you or Sesler is starting a war, you need to know who that is, and so do we.'

'İlhan is dead.'

For a moment Dr Koca thought that Ateş Böcek was talking about him. After a long period of silence between them, it was a strange way to begin a conversation.

'İlhan?' he asked.

'My little brother,' Ateş said. 'He died.'

İlker Koca looked down at his notes. Unless it had happened within the last twenty-four hours, İlhan Böcek wasn't dead. But how did that fit into Ateş's wider delusional profile? This was new. Should he run with it, collude, challenge . . .

'Nobody knows except me,' the young man said.

So it was part of the over-arching delusion, and yet how did Ateş perceive it in the case of his brother?

'Behind the eyes there's nothing,' he continued. 'He walks and talks and he tells me he loves me, but he's lying. And anyway, I don't want him loving me. He's dead and I can smell his rot.'

'So your brother has been replaced by . . . What? A corpse?'

Ateş leaned forward and hissed, 'He seeks to enter my body.'

'He's called Hakki Bürkev, he was one of Esat Böcek's men,' Kerim told Süleyman as they stood on the corner of the alleyway off Baghdat Caddesi, waiting for Dr Sarkissian to give them his preliminary findings.

'Any leads?'

'Esat Bey reckons it was the gypsies.'

'He would.'

'How did you get on with Sesler?'

Süleyman told him about Sesler's apparent connection to Mete Bülbül.

'So Sesler could've had him killed,' Kerim said.

'He could've done.' Süleyman nodded. 'He's agreed to take a DNA test to establish his familial claim. He wanted me to keep quiet about it – as an honorary Roma.'

Kerim laughed. 'No chance.'

'Of course not.'

'Did you manage to quiz him about the Wolves?'

'No. You rang before I could do that,' Süleyman said.

'I spoke to Esat Böcek about the possibility of a third party being involved,' Kerim said. 'But he's convinced that the gypsies have it in for him.'

'Do you think he wants a war?'

'He'd beat Sesler, so maybe. Somehow we need to shut this down.'

'Tell me about it!'

Süleyman's phone rang. Too late, he noticed that the caller was his mother. He rolled his eyes and answered. 'Mama?'

'I was hoping you would have visited to collect your possessions,' his mother said.

Of course, his uncle was coming and he needed to make space for him in his old bedroom. He turned away from Kerim, signalling that he wouldn't be long.

'I'm sorry, Mama, I meant to,' he said. 'But I've hardly had a second to myself.'

'That's not my problem. Come tomorrow, Mehmet Bey.'

'Mother, I—'

'Or I will have the servants put it all out for the rubbish collectors.' She hung up.

The things she was alluding to included his great-grandfather's Ottoman military uniform, including his sword. As an avowed royalist, she would hardly leave those out for the bin men, would she? Or was it just his old university textbooks, his toy soldiers and foreign-language novels that would be sacrificed?

Kerim was obviously still thinking about their previous discussion. 'And why now?'

Süleyman put his phone back in his pocket. 'Why now what?'

'Sesler and Böcek, why go to war now? They both have their territory, their sphere of influence, they both make a good living. I mean, I know that gangsters always want more . . .' Kerim paused before continuing. 'Wasn't Murad Ayhan in the Grey Wolves, years ago?'

'He was,' Süleyman confirmed.

'He is arguably the most powerful of the big three godfathers.'

'So why take on Böcek, or a nothing like Sesler?' Süleyman asked. 'Ayhan is largely legitimate these days. The only whisper I've picked up about him is the opinion in some quarters that he may be courting the religious elite. I don't know. He still gave a lavish Christmas party for his Christian customers this year. Nothing connects him to this.'

'Except that he was once a Grey Wolf . . .'

Süleyman frowned. Then Dr Sarkissian arrived.

As he approached his colleagues, he said, 'Hakki Bürkev was stabbed. One blow to the abdomen. Looks to me as if the blade was twisted as it was pulled out. Death by exsanguination.'

Although he knew that his friend Mehmet Süleyman respected and loved him, Çetin İkmen had nevertheless long inferred that the younger man also regarded him as slightly out of his mind. He was probably right, even though he hid it well most of the time. That said, İkmen's dealings with things and people occult over the years had always enhanced and sometimes assisted him in

256

his criminal investigations. However, that had all happened pre-Şeftali.

It was two o'clock in the morning and he was sitting bundled up in his overcoat and numerous blankets, talking to the ghost of his dead wife on the balcony of his apartment.

'I could enlist Gonca's help, I suppose,' he said as he lit one cigarette off the end of his last. 'Şeftali Hanım is her cousin. But I know Mehmet doesn't like to get her involved. This is difficult for him anyway, because Sesler is involved – a man his wife works for. But I am compelled to tell him what Şeftali told me.'

Fatma, as she always did, just smiled.

'The woman's completely deranged,' İkmen continued. 'Living in filth, never washing. I can just imagine how you would have responded to her. You would have dragged her out of there, pushed her under a shower and then scrubbed that place until it shone.' He smiled. 'She would have gone even more mad, of course. And you know, much as I have spent a lot of my time in strange places with strange people, her demon, the Poreskoro, is entirely new to me. The embodiment of plague! Who knew? And yet, Fatma, you know I would never lie to you, but I saw something underneath that table, and it was malevolent. I can see those eyes peering into the dark corners of people's black souls.' He sighed. 'And Mehmet Süleyman needs to know that. All I have to do is find the right words . . .'

'It's all part of the same syndrome,' Dr Koca told Süleyman.

Now back at headquarters, the inspector had responded to a call from the elderly psychiatrist by inviting him to his office. It was just past 2 a.m., but both men were aware that time for Ateş Böcek was ticking. If no new evidence raising doubts about his guilt had been discovered by midday, he would be charged with murder.

'So do you think it is significant that Ateş believes his brother to be dead?' Süleyman asked.

'I'm interested in any deviation from what appears to be an established delusional norm,' the doctor said. 'Everyone else in his life is a living being, albeit one he believes is impersonating a friend, relative or acquaintance. Why is his brother "dead"? I did try to probe, in the gentlest possible way, but he retreated into silence.'

'Do you have any theories?'

He sighed. 'Ateş was very clear about the notion that his brother stank of rot.'

'Well, if he's dead . . .' Süleyman began.

'Yes, but what does that observation mean in this context? In Ateş's world, everyone is seeking to trick or betray him in some way, but only his brother is doing that from beyond the grave – not that İlhan Böcek *is* dead. And only İlhan smells. He's rotting and he smells.'

Süleyman shook his head. 'Do you think that Ateş is more afraid of İlhan than of other people?' he asked.

Dr Koca frowned. 'Yes, I do.'

'And so if I said that I intended to interview İlhan Böcek again with that in mind . . .'

'I don't think that would be a waste of your time, Inspector.'

The girls giggled quietly. Although they were both in their early twenties, Aylın Ayhan and Esma Nebatı still sometimes liked to behave like schoolgirls. On this occasion it had manifested as an unauthorised and impromptu sleepover at Aylın's house.

At midnight, when apparently the whole Ayhan family had gone to bed, Aylın had let Esma in via one of the back doors. Then, ensconced in Aylın's bedroom, they'd made a picnic from the food and drink Aylın had stolen from her parents' kitchen. Leftover imam bayıldı, köfte and cacık, followed by passion fruit cake from her father's last party.

As they made inroads into the food, Esma said, 'I'm surprised your brother left any cake for anyone else.'

'So am I!' Aylın said. 'Fat pig usually stuffs his face. And if it's not him, it's Mum.'

They laughed. Then Aylın reached underneath her bed and produced two bottles – one of vodka, the other peach schnapps – and two cartons of juice.

'Esma dear,' she said, 'Tonight I am going to teach you how to make sex on the beach.'

'Sex on the Beach! What's that?'

'It's a cocktail,' Aylın said. 'Vodka, peach schnapps, orange juice and grenadine. It's supposed to be cranberry juice, but I couldn't find any.'

'Oh wow!'

Aylın produced a jug and was about to demonstrate her mixologist skills when from outside her door she heard a voice. Alarmed, she put a finger to her lips. 'I think it's my dad!' she whispered.

Esma pulled a face and hid behind a chair. Aylın switched her light off and flopped back onto her bed. By the sound of it, her father was on his phone, and he wasn't best pleased.

She heard him hiss, 'That's between you and Sesler, Esat Bey! Don't you dare bring me into it! I have nothing to do with your shabby little war! And don't call me again, do you hear? Not ever!'

Aylın waited a long time after her father had moved away. Eventually it was Esma who said, 'Can we put the light back on now?'

After pausing for yet another moment, Aylın turned her bedside lamp on and sat up. Esma was shocked to see how pale her friend's face was and how much she was shaking. She knew that Murad Ayhan was a harsh man and that Aylın was sometimes afraid of him, but now she looked terrified.

'God, Aylın!' she said. 'I know your dad's a bit fierce . . .'

'But Esma,' Aylın said, 'don't you see? He was talking to Esat Böcek, that awful İlhan's father.'

'So?'

'So you've seen İlhan stalking me! And now there's something going on between my father and Esat Böcek and Şevket Sesler.'

'So?' Esma reiterated. 'I didn't hear him talking about you.'

'He doesn't need to,' Aylın said. 'Esma, your father's a decent man, you don't have to consort with gangsters like I do. God, I'm even related to them! So you have to believe me when I say that even if my father isn't directly at odds with Esat Böcek, if they're calling each other, it's serious. A war between these people can throw up all sorts of horrors, and when they make peace, well, then there are more casualties.'

'What do you mean?' Esma asked.

'I mean that last time there was trouble between my father, Şevket Sesler's father and Esat Böcek, my cousin Senay was sent over the Bosphorus to the Böceks, who married her off to some crazy relative of theirs who drooled when he talked, and pissed himself.'

Şevket Sesler looked at the clock on his office wall and knew that it was pointless trying to get back to sleep now that 3 a.m. had come and gone. It was hardly surprising after the night he'd had. First a visit from the police in the person of Süleyman, the Bewitched Bridegroom, and then a very unsatisfactory attempt at sex with a new stripper he'd just taken on. His body just didn't want to comply, not even when she went down on him. Only drink remained to him now, and so he poured himself a large glass of rakı and gulped down half of it in one go. Maybe booze would take away the bad taste of Mete Bülbül's name in his mouth. God knew why the fucking bastard had persisted in his search for his mother for so long.

Şevket's sister Kumru had told him all about their Auntie Fulya. Apparently there had been two things she'd loved in life – gaco men and ether. The latter, an anaesthetic gas, had indirectly caused her death, which according to Kumru had happened when she'd fallen down a flight of stairs in Balat. Also according to Kumru, Mete Bülbül had looked just like Fulya. And yet Şevket would still do the DNA test Süleyman wanted him to take. Now that Bülbül was dead, any chance of him wanting anything from the Sesler family had died with him. He had to admit to himself that someone had done him a big favour by killing the poor sod.

As he took another swig from his glass, his phone rang. Fuck!

'Sesler,' he slurred into the machine. 'Whaddya want?'

'Şevket Bey, it's Inspector Süleyman.'

That posh fucking voice of his! Made Sesler want to spit.

Disinhibited by drink, he said, 'I told you everything I fucking know!'

'I'm not calling you about Mete Bülbül,' Süleyman said. 'I've a question to ask you about the night of your birthday party.'

'I've told you about that too!'

'Well, I've got another question,' Süleyman said. 'Put down the rakı bottle and listen.'

'How did you know I was drinking rakı?' Sesler asked. 'You got your wife with you, looking through walls?'

'I'm alone in my office. I just know you.'

There was a silence, then Süleyman said, 'Now look, we've been reviewing CCTV footage from the area and we've come up with someone we can't identify. I'm hoping you can help. Do you remember someone who came in a costume?'

'There were a lot of people in costume! Belly dancers, jugglers . . .'

'Someone in an animal costume of some sort,' Süleyman said. 'A bear or a wolf, perhaps.'

And then Şevket Sesler began to laugh.

Chapter 20

Gonca got out of bed. What was the point of being there if her husband wasn't with her? Mehmet had told her he would possibly have to work all night, and that appeared to have come to pass. She looked out of the window into the garden. Her guests were still asleep in their tent.

Lola Cortes was now so large she could give birth any day, and as Tomas had apparently explained to Mehmet, if she didn't have her baby in the EU, there could be administrative problems. Gonca didn't know about that, but she did know that they could be in either Bulgaria or Greece within twenty-four hours – provided their old van didn't break down. Not that she wanted them to go, because when they left, they were taking Rambo with them. Her baby.

After peeping in the basket to make sure that Sara was all right, she sat down on the chaise longue underneath the window and lit a cigarette. Rambo, although often infuriating, was her youngest child, and in spite of frequently losing her temper with him, she doted on the boy. Though she loved the freedom his absence gave her when he decided to sleep elsewhere, she missed him if he stayed away for more than one night. She also wanted the best for him and knew that he wasn't making the most of himself in İstanbul. Bright as the sun, Rambo was also lazy and easily distracted, especially by women. They found him irresistible, especially older, sophisticated Turkish ladies who appreciated his lithe body, sweet face and that feeling of transgression she imagined they experienced at going to bed with a Roma. In Spain, where he'd have to work to learn the language, maybe he would pull himself together and find out what he wanted to do with his life. Then again, maybe he'd just go to bed with a lot of Spanish ladies.

Çetin İkmen had been a little spooked by Şeftali, Gonca felt. That was strange for him, but then she could sort of understand it. Her cousin had always been odd. Choosing the company of a demon was something few people did, because demons were not entities one could control. But then maybe having such a thing involved in what was happening in the city was the only way to . . . To do what?

Just prior to Şevket Sesler's birthday, she'd read the godfather's cards. A simple three-card layout in which his past had been represented by Death, his present by the Devil and his future by the gift of the Wheel of Fortune. That Death was now behind him was a good sign, and in spite of the need to act quickly in order to prevent something negative from happening, indicated by the Devil, the Wheel of Fortune, right way up, did point to a favourable outcome. But then was Sesler acting quickly to prevent disaster?

So far, although she couldn't be sure, he hadn't retaliated against the Böceks because of Ceviz's death. Mehmet was unsure about whether Ateş had killed Ceviz Elibol. Was Sesler unsure about that too? And yet the cards had said he had to be decisive.

Gonca knew that sometimes one had to wait for the universe to catch up with the cards. She also knew that she would have to find out more from Mehmet and maybe meditate upon that. He, of course, would protest that he couldn't tell her anything. But he would, because this situation involved her people, her world. He'd tell her what he knew in the way he walked and talked, how and what he ate, and when he made love to her.

*

263

Yeşili was crying again. Peri Mungun looked at the clock beside her bed: 5.30. She had to be out of the apartment to get the 8 a.m. bus. It wasn't worth going back to sleep. She switched on her bed-side light and sat up. It was still going to be dark outside, and so she'd have to put the light on in the kitchen if she wanted to make tea, which would signal to Yeşili, whose bedroom was opposite, that she was up. Well, the girl either talked to her or she didn't. All Peri could do was offer her a glass of tea and, if she wanted it, a shoulder to cry on.

As she put the kettle on in the kitchen, she thought about the fact that her brother hadn't come home at all. Admittedly he'd told the two women that it was unlikely he would be back because of something he had to do at work, but Peri wondered.

Nothing had improved in recent days, and although she knew that Ömer's boss had been assigned to a brutal murder, she didn't know any details and could not therefore judge just how involved her brother had to be in the case.

'Peri?'

She looked round and saw the girl standing in the doorway.

'Yeşili, what are you doing up?'

'I don't feel well,' she said.

'In what way?'

'My body hurts.'

As a nurse, Peri was accustomed to patients making somewhat vague statements about their bodies.

She took the girl's hand. 'Where do you hurt?'

Yeşili's face reddened.

'What is it?'

She swallowed. 'My hips.'

'Your hips?'

'Yes.'

Peri said, 'Have you injured yourself? Do you want me to take a look?'

'No!'

She began to feel cold. Had Ömer done something to hurt his unwanted bride? She couldn't believe it. For all his faults, her brother wasn't a violent man. Or rather, he hadn't been. She led the girl over to the kitchen table and sat her down. 'Yeşili, please let me look. I'm a nurse, I won't be shocked. I've seen just about everything.'

Yeşili's eyes filled with tears. 'I don't know where they came from, Peri, honestly.'

'They?'

The girl stood and lifted her nightdress. Her hip bones were covered in dark purple bruises and her lower abdomen was slightly swollen. Peri reached out to touch her, but Yeşili pulled away.

'I just—'

'It's sore,' the girl said. She let her nightdress fall again.

The two women looked at each other, Peri not daring to think what her brother may have done to his wife.

Then she carried on making tea.

Mehmet Süleyman had grown up in a house that had staff. A maid, a gardener and his Armenian nanny. His parents had been barely able to pay the bills, much less the servants, and the family's retainers had worked for them for not much more than board and lodging. Now his mother was left with a young girl who acted as her maid and about whom she complained continually. The Ayhan family, however, had a butler and, Süleyman surmised, probably a whole fleet of retainers behind the huge front door of their mansion.

The Ayhans' house was situated in the Bosphorus village of Bebek. High in the hills above the more graceful waterfront Ottoman yalıs, it was a modern building that had been created to look older than it was. Categorised as 'faux Ottoman' by people who didn't like the style, it was nevertheless expensive, and, even the little Süleyman could see of the interior was enough to convince him that it was opulent. He imagined that in the master bedroom the bed was raised from the floor on a dais.

'Police,' he announced.

The butler, a rough-looking man in a tail coat who spoke with a smooth, cultured voice responded with, 'What do you want?'

After his call to Şevket Sesler, Süleyman had taken Ömer Mungun with him to hopefully get to the bottom of what the Roma godfather had told him.

'I want to speak to Yıldırım Bey,' he said.

'He's in bed,' the butler replied.

'Then get him up,' Ömer Mungun said.

The butler blinked. 'Wait here.' He closed the door on them.

The two men looked at each other. Then Ömer said, 'Couple of the surgeons Peri works with live out this way.'

'I've no doubt. All doctors, lawyers and gangsters in Bebek. Dr Sarkissian lives here.'

Ömer moved closer to Süleyman. 'Boss, if what Sesler told you is true . . .'

'On its own, it doesn't mean much,' Süleyman said. 'But—'

The butler opened the door again. 'Murad Bey will see you now. Shoes off, if you please.'

As one of İstanbul's premier shopping streets, Baghdat Caddesi and its environs was bristling with CCTV cameras. Eylul Yavaş, with a twinkle in her eye, told her boss, Kerim Gürsel, 'The rich can afford to protect themselves.'

And coming as she did from a wealthy family who lived in upscale Şişli, both Eylul and Kerim knew she was speaking from experience.

As the shops adjacent to the alleyway where Hakki Bürkev had died opened for business, police officers began questioning the owners and requesting CCTV footage from the previous evening.

Kerim and Eylul, however, were in Esat Böcek's apartment, standing underneath his vast atrium while the man himself raged.

'What I've done to deserve all this horror brought to my door, I don't know,' he said as he paced up and down in front of enormous palm trees and leathery cheese plants. His younger son İlhan sat on a huge brown sofa and said nothing. Still in his pyjamas, the boy was good looking in a sulky sort of way.

Esat Böcek walked up to Kerim and pushed his face into his. 'So is Süleyman going to release my son today or charge him?'

'You'd have to ask him that question,' Kerim said. 'Esat Bey, can you tell me what your relationship was to Hakki Bürkev?'

'I was his employer, I told you! He'd worked for me since he was a boy.'

'As his employer, you must have a record of his next of kin,' Eylul said.

'I imagine I do.'

'May we see that, please? We'll need to let his family know what has happened,' Eylul continued.

It was at this point that İlhan Böcek spoke. 'Was he the one whose dad died in Moda?'

Esat Böcek looked at him with fury and disbelief in his eyes.

Kerim said, 'What's this?'

Tearing his gaze away from his son's face, Esat Böcek said, 'What İlhan Bey here is referring to is the fact that Hakki Bürkev's father died some years ago.'

Eylul looked at İlhan. 'You mentioned Moda . . .'

'Hakki's father, Burhan, was working for me at a development in Moda when he had a heart attack and died,' Esat Böcek cut in before his son could reply. 'I gave the boy a job. I do what I can for my people. But Hakki had been alone ever since. I suppose you could say that I am his next of kin.'

A look passed between father and son that Eylul couldn't fathom. Esat Böcek was angry, while his son . . . Was İlhan smirking?

267

'Where did Hakki live?' Kerim asked.

'I have a small apartment block I rent out to my employees in Üsküdar,' Esat Böcek said. 'He lived there.'

'We'll need access,' Kerim told him.

'Why?'

'We need to find out why Hakki was murdered, so we need to see where he lived.'

Esat Böcek approached the officers, his face taut, his eyes blazing.

'We know why he was murdered! And by whom! The dirty gypsies!' He pointed out of the huge plate-glass window looking over Baghdat Caddesi. 'Do your duty and go after them! They were coming here to kill me!'

'You don't know that, Esat Bey,' Kerim said.

Esat Böcek moved even closer and hissed, 'Don't tell me what I do and do not know, Kerim Bey! I am one of this city's most successful entrepreneurs, while you are a policeman. Know your place!'

Murad Ayhan was a good-looking man. It was said that he'd bedded most of the eligible single women in İstanbul – and some of the married ones. However, Süleyman doubted whether any of his conquests ever saw him like this – wearing only pyjama bottoms, manically taking his own blood pressure with the aid of a monitor on his huge walnut desk, occasionally screaming out figures.

'One-eighty over one-twenty! Seriously!' he yelled. Then, looking up at the butler who had shown the officers into his office, 'Where's Sezer, for God's sake? Get him here! Now!'

The butler, who the officers later learned was called Efrim Bey, said, 'Murad Efendi, Dr Sezer is I believe still on vacation.'

'Bloody Christian bastards!'

Murad Ayhan pressed the button on his blood pressure monitor again and then pointed at Süleyman and Ömer Mungun.

'Who are these?'

'The police officers I told you about, Murad Efendi,' the butler replied. 'They wish to speak to Yıldırım Bey.'

But Murad Ayhan was watching the cuff around his left bicep deflate. 'One-eighty again, over one-ten this time! A bit better, I suppose.' He pressed the start button again and then looked at Süleyman, 'So you're police.'

'I am Inspector Süleyman and this is Sergeant Mungun,' Süleyman said. 'We are investigating multiple homicides in the city. We'd like to speak to your son Yıldırım.'

'What?' Ripping the blood pressure cuff off his arm, Murad Ayhan got to his feet. 'Is this some kind of sick joke? You suspect my son of murder?'

'I didn't say that, Murad Bey. We would just like to—'

'Because if you knew my son, you'd know he wasn't capable of taking a shit without his mother holding his hand, much less killing a man!'

'Murad Bey, we want to speak to your son because we have reason to believe he may have been in the vicinity of one of these offences when it was committed on the night of the twenty-sixth of December.'

There was a moment when they all looked at each other, and then Murad Ayhan began to laugh.

Irritated by this, Süleyman said coldly, 'I fail to see the humour in this situation, Murad Bey. Perhaps you would kindly let us know why you do.'

Murad Ayhan sat down again and replaced the cuff on his arm. He smiled.

'Because my son was here. And if you don't believe me, you can ask at least seventy other people who will verify that.'

'Oh?'

'Every year on the twenty-sixth of December, I have a party here at the house for my employees,' he said. 'Keeps them on side if I ask them to work on New Year's Eve. That's a ridiculous holiday anyway, we're Muslims . . .'

'So everyone who can verify Yıldırım Bey's presence here at your house on the twenty-sixth works for you?'

Murad Ayhan looked at the monitor as the cuff deflated. 'One-forty over ninety. That's much better.' He smiled. 'Yes.'

'Mr Ayhan, I need to speak to your son,' Süleyman reiterated. 'Now.'

Murad Ayhan frowned, and his face flushed with anger.

'I would not,' Süleyman added, 'take your blood pressure at the moment.'

Çetin İkmen didn't like texting. His fingers were, he felt, too big for the keypad and he always ended up making mistakes. He'd just sent *I need to takk to you* to Süleyman. God alone knew what he'd think! But he couldn't be bothered to correct it.

Tired, but not sleepy, he'd come out onto the balcony to see dawn break. Even in the winter it was worth doing, staring over towards Asia, watching the light rise in the east. Often when he did this, the ghost of his wife would be with him, but not today. He wondered what it meant that Fatma was not appearing as often as she once did. The other magical entity that haunted the apartment, the djinn in the kitchen, was still very much in evidence.

Thinking back to his encounter with Şeftali, İkmen yet again wondered why encounters with magical practitioners like her often raised more questions than they answered. For many years he had wrestled with the abilities he had inherited from his mother, which he had frequently shrugged off as coincidence or 'taking a punt'. But he knew to the bottom of his soul that they were real. However, if that was the case, why was what they revealed often so oblique? It was maddening. Perhaps what Şeftali had told him would resonate with Süleyman. After all, İkmen didn't know everything about his latest case.

His phone rang. Who could that be at this hour?

'Çetin Bey?'

It was Peri Mungun.

'I'm sorry to call you so early,' she said. 'But I don't know what to do.'

'No problem, Peri Hanım, I was up. What's the matter?'

She told him about Yeşili and the bruises on her hips. She also told him about her fears. 'Unless she's hitting herself, I can't see how else she could have got those bruises other than Ömer hitting her. She never goes out!'

'Mmm.' This wasn't good.

'The poor girl is so unhappy,' Peri said. 'She cries all the time, although not in front of my brother. This is wrong, Çetin Bey, but what can be done? If my parents weren't so old, I'd tell them and suggest Yeşili return home to her family.'

'How is Ömer Bey?' İkmen asked.

'How should I know? He's never in. Didn't come home at all last night. Supposedly working.'

'Well, he must have been, because I know for a fact that Mehmet Bey was, and I think still is,' İkmen said. 'Peri Hanım, I'm sorry, but I think you will have to speak to Ömer about this. He would, probably rightly, resent any intervention from an outsider like me. But really, knowing him as I do, I can't see that he would hurt his wife. He's not in my experience a violent man.'

'But as I've told you, he is unhappy,' Peri said. 'I saw him on his wedding day and it was as if he was going to a funeral. He married Yeşili to please our parents, and now I think that sacrifice is eating away at him. To be clear, I'm not afraid of him. If or when I confront him, I have no worries about what he might to do me. I just don't want to get it wrong.'

İkmen said, 'I agree. He loves you, that's very clear for anyone to see.'

'But what if I bring the subject up and then he takes his anger out on Yeşili?'

'Then you must be honest and tell him that is what you fear. He will take that from you.'

'Will he?'

'I feel you have to trust that he will. You are his older sister and I know he respects you. And anyway, if he became violent with you, I imagine your parents would be furious and ashamed of him.'

'They would!'

'So speak to him, alone, when you can,' İkmen advised. 'And maybe try to find out what Yeşili does when you are both out.'

'She does the housework,' Peri said.

'Are you sure she doesn't go out?'

'Not completely sure, no. But her Turkish is minimal, and she's so timid!'

'Have you ever asked her whether she's been out?' he said.

'Well, no . . .'

'So do so. You may find that she's been exploring her new environment. I mean, I wouldn't blame her. Maybe she fell over in the street or something.'

He didn't believe that for a second. But when he ended the call, İkmen had to admit to himself that he couldn't believe that Ömer Mungun had brutalised his wife either. That said, he was uneasy.

As dawn broke over the Asian side of the city, he pondered yet again upon how lucky he had been with Fatma. Lots of rows, yes, their relationship had been fiery, but never any violence, and certainly no lack of love. He phoned Peri Mungun back.

'Are you all right?' Kerim Gürsel asked Eylul Yavaş.

It was only a few hours since she'd been attacked in Tarlabaşı, but she showed no sign of distress and was, indeed, rather more awake than he was. Also Eylul didn't have a family to go home to, other than her parents. And while Kerim's wife and child were not yet back home in Tarlabaşı, he longed to see them. As soon as he could, he would call Çetin İkmen to ask whether he could visit. He imagined İkmen rolling his eyes and saying, 'You come whenever you like, you know that!'

Eylul smiled. 'Fine, sir.'

The 'apartment block' owned by Esat Böcek and rented out to his employees came as a bit of a surprise. Firstly it was in an upscale part of Üsküdar, Kuzguncuk, on a pleasant tree-lined street called İcadiye Caddesi. It was also not an apartment block, but three storeys of bedsits above a neighbourhood bakkal. That too was owned by the Böcek family, and so the shopkeeper was waiting for the police when they arrived and, together with his son, let them in via a back door.

Since leaving Kadıköy, Kerim and Eylul had been joined by a four-man squad of uniforms, who were to be tasked with speaking to the other residents. The shopkeeper gave Kerim a duplicate key he kept to Hakki Bürkev's bedsit and then left. Unlike the street outside, the apartment block was grim. The overriding smells were those of toilets, onions and cigarette smoke. Bürkev's bedsit was sparse and shabby, consisting of one room with a sink in the corner.

The two officers put on gloves and began to look around. Kerim went straight over to the unmade single bed and peered underneath. Eylul picked up a book from a table otherwise occupied by one dirty plate and a fork.

'Well-thumbed copy of the Koran, sir.'

'Böcek likes his people to be pious,' Kerim said.

She looked up. 'One thing I don't get.'

'What?'

'Pious gangs. Don't care which religion we're talking about.

What are religious people doing involving themselves in organised crime? How do they justify that?'

Kerim was tired and wanted to say, *because some of them are just as venal as the rest of us*, but he didn't. Instead he said, 'I don't know.' Then he added, 'Look for anything that might indicate Bürkev was in debt. That's a really popular motive for murder.'

'Don't you think, as Mr Böcek says, that it might be Sesler's people?' Eylul asked.

'I'm not ruling it out. But I also don't want to slip into easy options or lazy thinking. Yes, Böcek and Sesler appear to be at odds, but that doesn't mean we can't have an open mind on the subject.'

'No, sir.'

There was a knock on the door and Kerim went to answer it. Outside was the shopkeeper's teenage son.

'Yes?'

The boy looked around nervously. 'Can I come in and talk to you, Inspector Bey?'

'What about?'

He shook his head. 'Please can I come inside?' he said. 'I can't talk out here.'

Voices from other bedsits drifted up the stairwell.

Kerim stood to one side. 'All right, come in.' After closing the door behind him, he went and stood beside Eylul. 'What do you want, er . . .'

'Kasım,' the boy said. 'I want to say something about Hakki Bürkev, but I don't want anyone to hear and I don't want you to tell anyone, especially not my dad.'

Kerim crossed his arms over his chest. 'Well now, Kasım, that all depends on what you want to tell us, doesn't it?'

'Yeah, but if my dad finds out I've told you, he'll kill me. He loves Esat Bey and won't hear a word against him. I mean, I like him too, but . . .'

'But what?' Eylul asked. 'Has Esat Bey done something wrong, Kasım? Because if he has, you have a duty to tell us. I'm sure your dad as a good Muslim will understand that.'

The boy seemed conflicted. Spotty and a little sweaty, he had to be sixteen at the most.

'Well, er . . .'

Eylul said, 'Kasım, as you can see, I'm an observant woman. I take my faith very seriously. I am aware of the fact that Esat Bey is also a religious person, but remember, no one is perfect except Allah, and if Esat Bey has done something wrong, we need to know about it.'

The boy shuffled his feet. 'I expect people have already told you that Hakki's dad died from a heart attack.'

'Yes . . .'

'But that's not true,' he said. 'Not really.'

'So how did he die?' Eylul asked.

'Esat Bey killed him.'

Chapter 21

Yıldırım Ayhan was one of those young men who appeared to be engaged in a permanent sulk. Overweight and, so far, monosyllabic, he wore a pair of adult Star Wars pyjamas and pulled away every time his doting mother tried to stroke his hair. Süleyman's hands itched as he wrestled with a desire to hit the kid.

His mother, Irmak Ayhan, a hugely fat woman enrobed in a frilly pink nightdress, said, 'My son's just told you he was here all night. He never misses one of Murad Bey's parties. He never lies. Anyway, I was here too, and I can vouch for him.'

The room Süleyman and Ömer Mungun found themselves in was the Ayhan family's salon. A ghastly faux-Ottoman space filled with vast gilded sofas, an enormous television, and poorly executed paintings of Murad Ayhan in various Ottoman military uniforms. Süleyman could just imagine how someone like his late father would have viewed such an abomination. He could almost hear him laughing from beyond the grave.

'Madam,' he said, 'we have good reason to believe that your son left your husband's party.'

'Who says so?' she yelled.

'That is not something I'm at liberty to divulge.' He looked at the boy again. 'What did you wear to your father's party, Yıldırım?'

Yıldırım didn't so much as look up. 'Why?'

'Just answer the question.'

He shrugged. 'Dunno.'

The officers still hadn't been invited to sit down. Now

276

Süleyman picked a chair, sat, and motioned for Ömer to do the same. Irmak Ayhan looked on in horror, but said nothing.

Once settled, Süleyman turned to her. 'Can you tell me, madam, whether your husband's party was themed?'

'Themed?'

'People like yourselves, community leaders, large employers, those with money, sometimes like to have a theme when they throw a party. It may be that the decoration and what people choose to wear may be Ottoman . . .'

'Oh, you mean fancy dress?' she said. 'No. No, Murad Bey's party for his staff is a chance for them all to dress up smart. Black tie and evening gown. It's very sophisticated.'

Unlike, Süleyman thought, Mrs Ayhan herself.

'Why?' she asked.

He didn't answer her. If, as Şevket Sesler had told him, it had been Yıldırım Ayhan in the wolf costume the night of the shooting, either she was lying or the boy had got changed somewhere. But he didn't want to give too much away, not yet.

'If you like, you can ask my husband to show you the video he took of the party,' Irmak said. 'He always videos our parties.'

It was hard to miss the furious look Yıldırım shot his mother, but Süleyman opted to do so.

'I'd like that,' he said.

'I'll go and ask him,' the woman said as she levered herself up onto her feet and waddled across the room. Murad Ayhan had finally agreed to let them see his son and had returned his attention to his blood pressure. His wife would probably find him still doing it now.

As they all sat waiting for her to return, Yıldırım turned his head away from the officers. Ömer Mungun raised his eyebrows. Then Süleyman's phone pinged to let him know he had a text message. It was from İkmen, and it was misspelled.

*

277

'That's quite an accusation,' Kerim Gürsel said to Kasım, the grocer's son.

The boy looked down at the floor.

Eylul said, 'Do you mean that Esat Bey actually killed him, or that he caused his death in some way?'

'Burhan Bey, Hakki's dad, worked with my brother Sınan,' he said.

'For Esat Bey?'

'Yeah. It was five years ago or something. Over in Moda. They were re-plastering the side of a building near the All Saints Church. They were using scaffolding, but my brother said it was faulty.'

'In what way?' Kerim asked.

'Wasn't properly fitted together. Sınan was too young to face up to Esat Bey, and so Burhan Bey did it.'

'What happened?'

'It had taken a long time for the scaffolding crew to put it all up,' the boy said, 'and so Esat Bey was already angry. He told Burhan Bey to get the men on the job anyway. You don't argue with him, and so they all went up. But Burhan Bey fell . . .'

'And?'

'He was all right for a bit, but when Esat Bey made him go back up, that was when he had his heart attack.'

'What happened then?' Kerim asked.

'They called an ambulance but Sınan said he was already dead. Esat Bey told them all not to tell the doctors that he'd had a fall first.'

'Mum!'

'I'm in my bedroom,' Gonca called out.

Rambo opened the door and walked straight in.

Looking around he said, 'Where is he?'

'Mehmet? Working.'

278

'Where?'

'How should I know? Could be on the moon for all I know. I've sent him some texts but he doesn't reply. Why do you want to know?'

Rambo sat down on the bed.

'Toprak told me that Şevket Bey beat up his dad,' he said.

Seventeen-year-old Toprak was one of Munir Can's sons.

'Why?'

'Dunno. But apparently Mehmet Bey was over at the club last night talking to Şevket Bey, and then later, Şevket Bey called Munir in and broke his nose.' He looked down at the snake in the basket. 'She all right?'

'She's getting better,' Gonca said. 'So why do I need to know about Munir Can? He's a cunt.'

'You don't need to know, but your husband might,' Rambo said. 'If the cops don't shift their arses to find out who killed those people on Şevket Bey's birthday, there'll be trouble. The whole Sesler family is up in arms, and people like Munir Can are gagging to have a go at the Böceks. They'd better do something soon, or it'll be war.'

Murad Ayhan's video of his party was poor in both quality and artistic endeavour. Jerky and unfocused, it was like the footage small children took of themselves. But in spite of that, and although it proved nothing with regard to the whole duration of the party, there was footage of Yıldırım Ayhan looking very uncomfortable in a tuxedo.

The question the two officers had to ask themselves now was had Şevket Sesler lied to Süleyman? If he had, the inspector was not shy about how he might respond.

'I'll eviscerate the bastard!' he told Ömer Mungun as they got into his car. He'd given the keys to his deputy so that he could drive while Süleyman himself read his messages.

Ömer fired up the engine and they left the Ayhan property.

Süleyman decided to deal with İkmen's message first, before he got to the seven texts from his wife and two from Kerim Gürsel. As Ömer turned onto the coast road, he called the older man.

'Not like you to misspell a word, Çetin. What's the matter?'

'What, you mean apart from the fact that my old fingers resemble sucuk these days?'

Sucuk, thick spicy beef sausages, were, Süleyman felt, a good description of İkmen's hard-worked digits.

'These iPhone keyboards are a tiny nightmare,' he continued.

Süleyman smiled. 'I feel your pain.'

'What with your long, slim fingers? Anyway,' İkmen said, 'I need to talk to you.'

'What about?'

'I had an interesting encounter with one of Gonca's relatives last night. A cousin called Şeftali. She lives with a demon in Tahtakale.'

'New one on me,' Süleyman said.

'She came to your wedding, apparently.'

'Did she?' He shrugged. 'But then the whole world came, so why not some woman who lives with a demon.'

He saw Ömer looking at him, but ignored it.

'So why do I need to know about this?' he asked.

'Because Şeftali gave me a message for you. I don't know whether it'll make any sense in light of your investigation so far, but for what it's worth . . .'

'Yes?'

'You need to look at lust,' İkmen said.

Süleyman laughed.

'No, no, not your own! There's something in this, in your investigation, that has to do with unrequited love or lust, wanting someone you shouldn't. Maybe adultery? I don't know, I'm just the messenger. Do you see that, or . . .'

'Not really. Unless it's lust for power.'

'No, no, it's definitely sexual,' İkmen said. 'And it's hugely destructive.'

'And this is what her demon told her?'

'Yes.'

'Mmm.' Süleyman paused for a moment. Anyone else who talked about demons would have got short shrift. Even so, when he asked his next question, he did cringe.

'And did you see it, this, er . . .'

'Just its eyes,' İkmen said. 'That was enough, believe me. And while not impugning the honour of your wife's family, I am aware it could have been a trick. Sometimes I think the Roma believe that the only way they can get our attention is via parlour games. They're probably right. But Şeftali's intent was genuine.'

'Then I will take it seriously,' Süleyman said.

Next he called Kerim Gürsel, who opened with 'Mehmet Bey, how do you like the idea of bringing Esat Böcek down?'

'Sounds interesting,' Süleyman said. 'What have you found out?'

'The father of our stabbing victim, Hakki Bürkev, was killed in what amounts to an industrial accident.'

'Says?'

'Says the very frightened son of one of Böcek's employees. Bürkev senior died from a heart attack, but only after he'd fallen off scaffolding that he'd told Böcek was unsafe. According to the boy, Böcek told his men to keep quiet about it. The witness to all this was the kid's older brother. I'm going to see him now.'

'Gets us no further with Ateş, but could be interesting,' Süleyman said. 'You know that the American gangster Al Capone was finally brought down on charges of tax fraud? Nothing to do with being a murderous crime lord. Wonder if we can get Böcek on worker safety legislation?'

Kerim laughed.

Then Ömer Mungun said, 'Boss, we're being followed.'

Süleyman ended his call. 'Sure?'

'Yeah.'

He looked over his shoulder. 'Red Mini?'

'That's the one. Subtle as an earthquake.'

Süleyman said, 'Turn right at the Greek church. Let's see if it follows.'

Ateş Böcek had asked for him. According to the custody sergeant, he'd become unsettled and aggressive about an hour ago. In the meantime, Inspector Süleyman had been called away and so could the doctor come anyway?

Now in Interview Room 5, a uniformed officer at his back, İlker Koca watched as Ateş Böcek walked around and around the space in front of the nailed-down table at which the doctor sat. He made noises rather than talking; either that or he was speaking in a language only he understood. The doctor, much to the consternation of the police officer, let him do this until eventually Ateş seemed to reach a sort of ending and then sat down.

Once the young man was seated, the doctor looked at him and smiled. 'Ateş, I am told you wanted to speak to me. Is that right?'

Ateş stared. Then he put his fist in his mouth.

'Is there something you're afraid to tell me?'

As if in response to pressure inside his body, the young man's eyes began to water. He wasn't crying so much as exuding moisture.

'Ateş, this is very important,' the doctor said. 'Unless the police can find evidence to the contrary, they are going to charge you with the murder of Ceviz Elibol. Now, whatever you tell me, you must know that I will believe you. If you tell me that you didn't kill that girl—'

'I loved her!'

'Yes, I think you did. But I also think you are confused, because it's my belief that you feel someone has betrayed you. Is that the case?'

Ateş shook his head from side to side. A creature in pain.

'Ateş . . .'

'He isn't my brother!' he screamed. 'He isn't my brother!'

It was one of those tiny roads that had started life as a donkey track. They were all over the city but were particularly prevalent in Bosphorus villages like this one, Yeniköy. Lined with huge stone walls, a Greek church at one end, a derelict Ottoman mansion at the other, it was so narrow it was impossible for vehicles to pass. Halfway along, Süleyman told Ömer to stop the car and got out. The red Mini jerked to a halt centimetres from the BMW's boot.

The driver, a woman, rolled down her window when Süleyman approached. Holding his badge up for her to see, he said, 'Why are you following us, hanım?'

She got out. Young, plump and dressed in a fur jacket and full-length black lace dress, she looked like one of the goth girls who hung around some of the tattoo parlours in Beyoğlu.

'I need to talk to you,' she said.

Süleyman frowned. 'Me in particular, or the police?'

'You,' she said. 'You were at Murad Ayhan's house just now, weren't you?'

'Yes.'

'I need to speak to you about his daughter. My name's Esma Nebatı, I'm Aylın Ayhan's oldest friend.'

'And you're worried about her?'

'Yes,' she said.

Another car had pulled up behind the Mini and the driver was sounding his horn. Süleyman walked towards it and held up his badge. The driver took his hand off the horn immediately.

Walking back to the girl, Süleyman said, 'We can't talk here, we're blocking the road. Look, you follow us and we'll take you somewhere quiet.'

'OK,' she said and got back into her car.

Süleyman instructed Ömer to drive to the tea garden at the junction between Tatil Caddesi and Talaat Paşa Caddesi. Once the car was moving, he called Gonca.

'Hi, darling. Sorry I've not got back to you. Busy.'

'I know,' she said. 'You had no sleep last night, baby, and I'm worried.'

He smiled. 'I'll be fine. Just about to top up my caffeine levels, as it happens. Was there anything else?'

'Yes,' she said. 'Rambo told me that Şevket Bey beat up Munir Can last night, broke his nose. It's all over the mahalle. No one knows why.'

'Really.' Süleyman smiled again. So Şevket Sesler had made good on his promise to discipline Can for his treatment of Eylul Yavaş. Good.

'What else is all over the mahalle is that the Roma are getting restless with regard to Esat Böcek,' she continued.

'In what way?'

'Sesler's men are anxious to take revenge for the killings on his birthday.'

'I'm sure they are, but they need to be patient.'

'Patient!'

'Gonca, things are happening,' he said. 'I can't tell you what. But if you get the chance, tell Şevket Bey that if he moves against anyone, he'll have me to deal with, and he won't like that.'

'Mehmet—'

'How is Sara?' He changed the subject because he didn't want to tell her anything else. She had a way of wheedling too much information out of him sometimes. And he knew that enquiring about the snake would please her.

284

'Much better,' she said. 'You are a sweetheart for asking. I do love you so much, Mehmet.'

'Tell me about İlhan,' Dr Koça said to Ateş Böcek. 'How did he die?'

There was a pause. Colluding with a delusion was always a risk, but the doctor felt that in this case he needed to do it. Was Ateş trying to work out whether he was attempting to trick him?

Eventually he said, 'I don't know.'

'Do you remember his funeral?' Dr Koca continued.

'No.'

Was this a dead end? Was he trying to say that his brother had killed Ceviz Elibol?

'Dad kept it from me,' he said.

'Your brother's death?'

He nodded.

'So how did you find out about it?'

Another pause, and then the young man said, 'He started to smell.'

'İlhan?'

'Yes.'

'When?'

'I don't know. A few months ago.'

'So his death is recent?'

'Yes.'

And then the young man said something that made İlhan Koca wince.

'He would never have allowed those things to happen to Ceviz if he'd been alive. The dead are evil, Doctor. When they walk the earth when they should be under it, they are evil.'

Chapter 22

Mehmet Süleyman had lived in Cihangir for a few years before he married Gonca and went to live with her in Balat. It was an artsy, liberal, café-society sort of place, which Kerim Gürsel had always liked. Not far from his home in Tarlabaşı, Cihangir was somewhere he liked to take Sinem and Melda when he had a free Sunday. They'd find a small café, have breakfast and coffee, and read the newspapers while Melda giggled at all the young people who came to admire her.

Sınan Babacan lived on Türkgücü Caddesi, at the top of a nineteenth-century Parisian-style apartment building. The views across the Bosphorus from the living-room window were spectacular.

Sınan, with whom Kerim had spoken earlier, said, 'Would you like a cup of coffee, Inspector? I was just about to have one myself.'

'That would be nice,' Kerim replied.

'Please, sit down.'

While Sınan went into his kitchen, Kerim flopped down into a chair. Although exhausted himself after a full night of no sleep, he'd sent Eylul Yavaş home to get some rest. She, after all, had also been attacked by one of Şevket Sesler's thugs. He just hoped he had managed to do it without appearing patronising or sexist.

Sınan Babacan returned from the kitchen with two tiny cups.

'I hope you like espresso, Inspector,' he said. 'It's all I have in at the moment.'

Kerim took the cup from him. 'Perfect. I've a lot on at the moment, and caffeine is just what I need.'

Sınan sat down opposite. 'I'm glad my brother spoke to you. His actions have galvanised me to face this thing.'

'About Esat Böcek?'

'Yes. My father, as you may have gathered, is a religious man. He's sincere, too, which is why I resent people like Böcek. Like his father before him, Dad used to own that bakkal, but he now works for Böcek. Admittedly, we were just subsisting back then, which was why Böcek was able to buy him out so cheaply. Now he thinks he owns him. In a way he does, but it turns my stomach. I used to work for him, as you know. I was there when Burhan Bürkev died and it was entirely down to faulty scaffolding. I wish I'd said something at the time, but I too was beholden to Böcek back then – and I was young and a coward.'

'Not a coward, I'm sure . . .' Kerim began.

'Oh yes, Inspector, I fully own that!' Sınan said.

'So what has changed your mind now?'

He sipped his coffee. 'When my brother called me and put you on the phone, I knew I had to do something. I work in modelling. I am very privileged and I make good money. I can easily support my elderly father and young brother and I will do so gladly. Böcek exploits people like them. When I heard that Burhan Bey's son had died protecting him, it made up my mind.'

'So you'd be prepared to make a formal statement?'

'Absolutely.' He leaned towards Kerim. 'The other reason I want to make him pay is because, as I expect you know, a lot of people who work in my industry live alternative lifestyles. Not me, I should add, but many of those I work with and consider my friends are people who for one reason or another cannot be themselves in the public arena. People like Böcek persecute such folk, and I hate it.'

Kerim nodded, whilst screaming inside.

*

'I didn't know what else to do,' Esma Nebatı said. 'When I saw you leave Aylın's house, I ran over to our place and jumped into my car.'

'So you were going to follow us for how long?' Ömer Mungun asked.

In spite of the cold, the two officers and the girl sat at a table in the sparsely populated tea garden, waiting for their drinks.

She shrugged. 'Until you got to where you were going. I've not been driving very long and couldn't even begin to think about going to police headquarters.'

Their tea arrived, and when the waiter had gone, Süleyman said, 'So tell us about Aylın Ayhan, hanım.'

She took a sip from her glass. 'Aylın and I are best friends, even though our parents don't talk.'

'Why not?'

Esma looked down. 'My dad is a surgeon, but he's also Roma. Murad Bey, who isn't Roma, grew up with him. According to Dad, Murad Bey thinks he's a loser for not going into business like him. My dad says that Murad Bey is a gangster.' She looked up, 'And so does Aylın.'

Neither of the men spoke.

'Anyway,' she continued, 'I was at Aylın's last night. Silly, I know, but we've been having sleepovers like kids for years. My parents are fine with her staying over, but her parents would . . . her dad would . . . Look, he hits her . . .'

'Murad Ayhan?'

'Yes.' She shook her head. 'I'm sorry, forget that, I told Aylın I'd stick to the point.'

This was pure gold, but Süleyman knew he couldn't get excited. People like Ayhan and Böcek had friends in high places.

Esma went on. 'Last night, Aylın and me heard her dad on the phone. He was on the landing outside his bedroom. Aylın reckons he was talking to one of his rivals about another rival. Anyway, that's not important . . .'

288

'Who?' Süleyman asked. 'Do you remember names?'

'I know he talked about Şevket Sesler. He wasn't speaking to him, but . . .'

'Do you know Şevket Sesler?' Ömer asked.

'Not really. My dad does, though. When his family lived in Sulukule, my dad knew everyone.'

'OK.'

'So,' she said, 'Aylın and I talked about her dad once he'd gone.'

'He didn't know you were listening?' Süleyman asked.

'No. We were hiding in Aylın's bedroom. Anyway, the point is that Aylın said she was scared that her dad and these other gangsters might be having a war.'

'Why?'

'I don't know. But from what we heard of Murad Bey's conversation, it sounded serious. Not that it bothered me too much. But then Aylın told me about her cousin Senay.'

'What about her?' Ömer asked.

'Years ago, apparently, Murad Bey was at war with Şevket Sesler's father and also this Esat Böcek. He's the father of İlhan Böcek, who . . .' She blushed. 'Sorry, getting ahead of myself.'

Süleyman said, 'Take your time, hanım.'

Esma swallowed. 'İlhan Böcek has been following Aylın around.'

Süleyman felt a cold tingle run up his spine.

'He wants to have a relationship with her,' Esma went on. 'Aylın isn't interested. But she's worried that if there's a war between their two families, she might be used as some sort of bargaining chip. That was what happened to her cousin Senay. Her dad and his family married her off to one of Böcek's people as a way of ending their dispute. That man was a drooling idiot, and according to Aylın, this İlhan isn't much better. Not that he dribbles or anything, but he is unpleasant and she doesn't want him. And there's something else . . .'

*

289

Süleyman's phone was off, so Dr Koca left him a message. Not exactly ideal, as the doctor was now, if not entirely convinced that Ateş Böcek had not murdered Ceviz, erring on the side of believing what the young man had told him.

According to Ateş, his brother had arrived at the Şehzade Rafık Palace early in the morning on the day of the girl's death. He hadn't been alone. Another man had been with him, and it had been this man who had eviscerated and partially flayed Ceviz. How did Ateş know that? Because İlhan had told him. So who had killed Ceviz? All Ateş would or maybe could say was that it was 'one of them' – İlhan, his dead brother, or this unnamed man.

Dr Koca had determined that in the absence of Süleyman, he would speak to the public prosecutor, a man called Kemal Gurkan. However, Gurkan was in a meeting and so the psychiatrist sat alone in his car with his thoughts. Watching police officers come out into the car park to smoke and chat wasn't the worst thing he could be doing, even if it achieved nothing except to give him more time to think.

It wasn't unknown for an offender to make up a story exonerating them of responsibility for a crime. You didn't need to be mad to do such a thing. Even sane offenders made things up. But Ateş wasn't what could reasonably be called sane. He'd suffered from illusions, delusions and mental distress for a long time. So why would he make up such a story? Possibly to protect himself from the truth: that he had killed and mutilated Ceviz, who, the doctor was sure, he had loved. That was not unusual in scenarios like this. But although the police forensic team had found some unknown DNA in Ateş's home, there had been very little, and none on the body. How would one prove that someone as unreliable as Ateş could be trusted in this instance? His brother might have been to his home multiple times since Ateş had lived there and so could reasonably explain the presence of his DNA. No, the way forward was via the other DNA from the site, now in the possession of the forensic services. But then none of that DNA had belonged to anyone with a criminal record.

The doctor leaned back in the driver's seat of his car and closed his eyes. He had a headache.

If Ateş had loved Ceviz so much, why had he allowed his brother and this other man to kill her? He'd shown no sign of any defensive wounds . . .

The Surp Pirgic Armenian Hospital, where Peri Mungun worked, was in Yedikule, in the Old City. Though not that far from the apartment she shared with her brother and his wife in Gümüşsuyu, via public transport it could be exhausting. In the scheme of things, Peri hadn't left İkmen waiting outside her small basement apartment for long, but she was still full of apologies when she arrived. Brushing these aside, he followed her into a small, cluttered hall, at the end of which stood a young girl with long black hair wearing a loose blouse and şalvar trousers. When she saw him, she scuttled away into the kitchen.

'She's very shy,' Peri said by way of explanation. She pointed to her left. 'Go into the living room, Çetin Bey, and I'll bring her to you. Sorry about the mess.'

In İkmen's experience, women often apologised for having messy homes when in fact, to him, said homes were perfect. But Peri hadn't been lying, and he had to move a pile of books and a pair of trousers off the sofa in order to sit down. Both Peri and Ömer were busy people, but what, he wondered, did Yeşili Mungun do with herself all day?

He'd called Peri back after she had phoned him, to suggest that he meet her sister-in-law before the Süleymans' New Year's Eve party. Something about the girl's bruises had been rattling away at the back of his head, and when he'd worked out what that was, he'd asked to speak to her.

Peri came in and said, 'I've told Yeşili you're an old family

friend and that we met on the street. Not exactly the truth, but . . .'
She moved some clothes from a chair onto the floor and sat down.
'She's making tea and will be in soon.'

'Good.'

'Are you sure you'll know as soon as you see her, Çetin Bey?'

'Not immediately,' he said. 'But after a few minutes, I hope. My
system, if you can call it that, isn't foolproof.'

She smiled. 'I don't know whether to hope or not.'

'All I can tell you is that Fatma had—'

Yeşili walked in with a tray upon which were glasses of tea and
a small bowl of rose jam with a set of spoons. Rather than serving
biscuits, olives or lokum to guests, some people offered jam,
which would be eaten in spoonfuls. She set the tray down and Peri
said something to her in Aramaic.

With a shy smile, Yeşili brought tea to İkmen and then offered
him the bowl of jam and a spoon. As she bent to give him these
things, he watched her closely.

When the two officers walked into his office, Murad Ayhan, who
was on the phone, roared, 'You? Again?' Going back to his call,
he said, 'Well tell me when you do find him, I need him!' Then he
threw the phone down on his desk and stared at them.

Süleyman said, 'Murad Bey, we need to speak to you about
your son, Yıldırım.'

'Again?' he said. 'Why?'

'Information has come to light regarding his attendance at your
party.'

'That again? I told you he was here!'

Esma Nebatı, however, had had a different tale to tell. According to her, Aylın had spied upon her father and the officers earlier.
What Murad had told them about Yıldırım being at the party all
night was, she'd told Esma, wrong. Yıldırım Ayhan had been at
Şevket Sesler's birthday party, and he'd been dressed as a wolf.

292

'He thinks I don't know who he is,' Sesler had told Süleyman. 'But I always recognise him. If he doesn't come as a wolf, he dresses in some imperial Ottoman get-up. Old Murad Bey grew up in our mahalle, but he's ashamed of that now that he's a big businessman. Roma are just scumbags he used to play with as a kid. But his son is curious, and much as he comes over as a soft mummy's boy, Yıldırım Ayhan is a rebellious, dark little bastard. Trust me.'

'He was here for part of the time,' Süleyman said now. 'But for probably up to an hour he was at Şevket Sesler's birthday party in Tarlabaşı.'

'No . . .' Murad Ayhan went white. He was truly shocked. Then he exploded. 'Why would he do that? I've given him everything! Why would he betray his own father?'

Süleyman was tempted to say that the boy's transgressive behaviour was very likely to be connected to the fact that his father had spoilt him, but he didn't. Instead he said, 'We will need to take him to headquarters.'

'Why? I'm furious that he went to Sesler's party, but what's that got to do with you?'

'Yıldırım was seen in company with someone we wish to speak to in connection with the murder of a man called Mete Bülbül,' Süleyman said.

Murad Ayhan sat down. 'God!' he said. 'Can this day get any worse?'

'You can't charge him,' Dr Koca said.

Public prosecutor Kemal Gurkan looked at him over the top of his half-moon glasses. 'Why not?'

'Because I don't believe he murdered that girl. He claims that she was killed by his brother, İlhan Böcek, and another unnamed man.'

'Ateş Böcek is delusional,' the prosecutor said. 'How can you rely on anything he says?'

'Because it has taken him such a long time to say it. If you had seen how he struggled to get that out against all his familial conditioning, against all the love he has for his relatives, you would know why I've come to you now, Kemal Bey.'

'Mmm.' Gurkan looked down at the notes in front of him. 'And what does Mehmet Bey think?'

İlker Koca knew that Süleyman had been holding off charging Ateş Böcek because he too was unsure about his guilt. If only the doctor had been able to speak to him about his latest encounter with the boy! And then there were those medical records given to Süleyman by someone who was allegedly Ateş's psychiatrist. What of them? They painted a picture of a young man unable to marshal his own thoughts much less commit an intricate murder.

'Mehmet Bey has been unsure of Ateş's guilt right from the beginning,' he said. 'Such a gross crime! Some may say indicative of a disturbed mind. But that girl's body was carefully taken apart, with skill and precision. It is my belief that Ateş is incapable of such an act.'

Gurkan looked up. 'So what do you propose, Dr Koca? I can see from your notes that the family have not given permission for further assessment and treatment.'

'I believe Ateş Böcek is a danger to himself.'

'As in suicide?'

'I believe he loved that girl and I now fear that her death, followed by his arrest, and the guilt he will be feeling at having, as he might see it, betrayed his brother, may be too much for him. In short, I should like to admit him to Bakırköy psychiatric hospital, for his own protection and for further investigation of his condition.'

The prosecutor sighed. 'It is unusual to admit a patient to an institution without familial consent.'

'Then imagine he doesn't have a family,' Dr Koca said. 'If that was the case, we'd have no option.'

'Unless we charge him.'

'He didn't do it!' the doctor said. 'I'd stake my career on it!'

The two men looked at each other for a moment, and then Gurkan said, 'I will speak to Commissioner Ozer about this.'

The doctor breathed a sigh of relief. 'That is all I can ask.'

'Don't get your hopes up,' Gurkan said. 'Commissioner Ozer is very much a results-driven man. He will always do what is best for the department.'

'You're sure?'

Peri had walked outside her apartment with İkmen when he left, and they were now in the tiny space where she had a few pots containing plants.

'As I can be,' he said. 'It was the bruises that clinched it for me, though.'

'More than the smell?'

'That I learned from my mother. The way a woman's odour may change after conception. Gonca Hanım knows about that too. Whenever one of her daughters was pregnant, she could always tell by just standing next to her. But the bruises . . . Fatma had a lot of pain in her hips when she was pregnant with Sınan, our first. Then she developed bruises around her hip bones. I was terrified our doctor might think I was hitting her, but he didn't. He said that sometimes, albeit rarely, when a woman's pelvis widens to accommodate her baby, that can happen.'

Peri shook her head. 'As far as I can work out, the only time they've, you know . . . was on their wedding night . . .'

'Sometimes once is all it takes,' İkmen said.

She shrugged. 'What to do?'

'I'd get her to a doctor for confirmation.'

'Oh, that's the easy part! Both my brother and Yeşili are unhappy – and now they're having a baby. It's not good, Çetin Bey. It's not the way to start a marriage or a life.'

'Plenty of people do,' he said. 'Admittedly, I have no experience of that. My wife and I loved each other immediately and stayed in love.'

'You were very lucky.'

He took his cigarettes out of his pocket, offered Peri one and they both lit up.

'I know,' he said. 'That woman put up with me for over forty years. We had nine children together – her idea, not mine. But I could deny her nothing, and in return she gave me endless support and a love I . . . Well, she was very special.'

Peri nodded.

İkmen smiled. 'But that is in the past. What we must do now is think about how we might help Ömer and Yeşili and, of course, their baby. I was thinking that apart from you, Yeşili is isolated with regard to female friends.'

'That's why Mehmet Bey has invited us to his house, so that she can at least meet Gonca Hanım and Sinem Gürsel.'

'And Sinem Hanım has a baby herself. But then there's the language barrier . . .'

'I am tutoring her when I can,' Peri said. 'But I have to work too, and so I'm aware it's not enough.'

'Could one of her female relatives maybe come and be with her while she's pregnant?' İkmen asked.

'She doesn't have any. Her mother died when she was a toddler, and she has no siblings. There's only her ancient father.'

'Well then, maybe you should think about just the first step,' he said. 'Get her to a doctor.'

'I can do a pregnancy test for her myself,' Peri suggested. 'But she might not believe me. So yes.'

'Has Ömer spoken about her health to you at all?' İkmen asked.

'No. He barely notices her. He's certainly said nothing to me. I'll tell him she should see a doctor, but I won't tell him why, otherwise he'll just let me get on with it. If he tells her she has to go, she'll do as he says.'

Murad Ayhan's question about whether this day could get any worse for him was answered by his wife Irmak.

When he asked her where their son had gone, she said, 'Don't know.'

'Do you know when he left?' Süleyman asked.

She looked him up and down as if she had a bad smell under her nose. 'No.'

'Do you know where he's gone?' Ömer Mungun said.

'No,' she replied, 'and even if I did, I wouldn't tell you.'

'Irmak!'

She looked up at her husband from the vast golden sofa on which she was reclining. 'I heard you, Murad. Bad-mouthing our son to these two.'

He bent down and put a hand on her shoulder. Süleyman noticed that he winced as he did so.

'Irmak, it's important,' he said. 'On the night of my party, it would seem that Yıldırım took some time out to go to Şevket Sesler's birthday celebrations.'

'Did he?' She seemed unmoved. Had she known?

'The police have footage of him with a man they want to talk to about a murder,' he continued.

'Yıldırım had nothing to do with that,' she said.

'No one is saying he did,' Süleyman interjected.

'Anyway, why was he with the gypsies?' she asked. 'We've always taught the children to avoid them.'

'Which may have made your son curious about them,' Süleyman said. 'Şevket Bey has told us that Yıldırım's visit on his birthday was not the first time the boy had been seen in Tarlabaşı. And you, Murad Bey, grew up around Roma when you lived in Sulukule, did you not?'

'Yes. Which is why I avoid them now,' he said. 'Irmak, where has Yıldırım gone?'

'I don't know!'

A young woman walked into the room. She was pretty rather than beautiful, and she looked nervous.

'I think I might know where he's gone,' Aylın Ayhan said.

Chapter 23

'How would you know where he's gone?' Murad Ayhan yelled. 'You hardly speak!'

'I've got eyes, Daddy,' Aylın said. 'I've seen him with İlhan Böcek walking around İstiklal, laughing at people and behaving like kids.'

Irmak Ayhan looked up at her daughter. 'Your brother went to school with İlhan Böcek. Why would he see him now?'

The girl spent a moment apparently wrestling with herself.

'See? She can't answer,' her mother said. 'She knows nothing.'

Süleyman said, 'Aylın Hanım?'

She looked him in the eyes. 'Inspector Bey, what neither of my so-called liberal parents will tell you is that my brother Yıldırım is gay. They try—'

'Absolute rubbish!' Irmak cried. She looked at her husband. 'Tell them it's all nonsense, Murad Bey!'

Before her husband could speak, Aylın said, 'Yıldırım is in love with İlhan Böcek.'

Murad Ayhan sat down. 'I need to see my doctor! Not even his wife knows when the bastard will be back!'

Irmak pulled herself up into a sitting position and then stood up.

'My son is not a pervert!' she hissed at her daughter. 'If anyone is a pervert, it's the Böcek boy! See how his older brother kills people! Your brother would never consort—'

'My brother is a selfish, arrogant shit!'

Irmak made to hit her daughter, but Ömer Mungun put himself between them.

'We'll have no fighting, ladies,' he said.

The two women, eyes locked, stayed where they were.

Süleyman said, 'Do you, Miss Ayhan, have any reason to believe that your brother has gone to see İlhan Böcek?'

'He may have,' she said. 'He ran out of here about an hour ago. I saw him get into a taxi. But if he did go and see him, he wouldn't have gone to his place. As I'm sure you know, Inspector, our fathers do not get on.'

'Aylın—'

'Be quiet, Murad Bey!' Süleyman said. 'Miss Ayhan . . .'

'Like I said, I saw them on İstiklal,' she said. 'They were going into a café called the MorKedi on Imam Adnan Sokak.'

Süleyman knew it. By day it was a café, but by night it turned into a bar, frequented by a lot of the LGBT crowd.

'And does İlhan Böcek reciprocate your brother's affections, Miss Ayhan?'

'No,' she said. 'He's heterosexual. Sometimes he follows me around.'

This was what Esma Nebatı had told them.

Süleyman turned to Murad Ayhan. He was holding his own wrist, taking his pulse.

'Did you know anything about this?'

'No,' he said, 'I did not. Had I known, I would have put a stop to it.' He looked at his daughter. 'Why didn't you tell me?'

Aylın glanced at her mother, and Süleyman said to Irmak, '*You* knew, though, didn't you, hanım? You knew because your daughter told you.'

'I . . .'

'Yes, she did,' Aylın said. 'She told me I was lying.'

Süleyman's phone rang. He'd forgotten he'd switched it

back on. He looked at the screen and saw that the caller was Dr Koca. He said, 'Excuse me, I have a call I must take. I will be back.'

He walked out into the corridor outside the Ayhans' lounge and pulled the door shut behind him.

'İlker Bey?'

'Mehmet Bey, I've been trying to call you,' the doctor said. 'The prosecutor has charged Ateş Böcek with the murder of Ceviz Elibol. I tried to stop him, but now that it's done, I don't know what to do.'

Süleyman sighed.

'I take it you've not yet been able to find anyone else, Inspector.'

'No, we've been following leads all night. I'll be honest with you, İlker Bey, this investigation is unravelling in ways I never imagined. On some level it now appears that the Ayhan family are involved with the Böceks.'

'Ah, yes, and of course while you were about your business, Ateş Böcek told me that his brother plus another unnamed man killed the girl.'

'And you believe him?'

'As I told the public prosecutor, if you'd seen the way he wrestled with himself to get those words out, you would have believed him too,' the doctor said. 'Of course, I couldn't tell Kemal Bey, but if you put that together with the notes from the boy's psychiatrist, to my mind reasonable doubt about his guilt is the only conclusion you can come to.'

'OK,' Süleyman said. 'Thank you, Doctor. I need to speak to İlhan Böcek anyway, and I've a message from Kerim Bey that someone has raised a charge against his father.' Then, more to himself than to the doctor, he added, 'All we need now is for Şevket Sesler to appear . . .'

*

301

He just walked straight into her studio without knocking. Like her family and friends, Şevket Sesler knew there was a back way into the Şekeroğlu property via the garden.

When she saw him, Gonca stood up.

'What do you want?' she asked.

He looked at her work, which lined the walls, and at her latest collage on her easel, of Sara the snake.

'Don't like that,' he said, pointing to the picture. 'Don't like snakes. Where's your husband?'

Gonca glanced down to where Sara lay curled up in her basket. 'He's working.'

Sesler gave a short laugh like a bark in his throat. 'I thought he might be. I gave him some good-quality information last night.'

'Did you?'

'He seemed to think so.'

Gonca could smell the rakı on him, the stench of anise pouring out of his skin. Just like her son had told her, Sesler was smarting from the attack on his people in their own mahalle. Maybe that was why he had lost his temper with Munir Can. Perhaps that fat yes-man had finally irritated his boss one time too many. Whatever, she could see that Sesler was drunk, angry and aggressive. Apart from her Spanish guests out in the garden, she was alone. And she didn't want to get Juan and his family into any sort of fight with Sesler. And yet . . . He was dangerous when he was angry, and when he was drunk as well, he was entirely unpredictable.

Sesler said, 'You and me, we've unfinished business, witch.'

'Şevket Bey, if you want me to read your cards on a more regular basis, rather than the current ad hoc one, I'm sure we can come to an arrangement.'

He took a step towards her. 'I'm not talking about the fucking Tarot!'

'Then—'

'I'm talking about how you laughed at me all those years ago when I offered you my love,' he growled.

Gonca began to feel cold. Drunk, angry and probably dissatisfied with Mehmet's almost inevitable lack of outward gratitude, Sesler now intended to take all of that out on her. And she knew how he meant to do it too.

'Şevket Bey,' she said, 'when you came to me all those years ago, I was a married woman. I am married now, you must understand.'

'You humiliated me! And now that you're an old woman, I intend to humiliate *you*. You think I desire your wrinkled old flesh? You think I actually want someone who looks like you? The only reason Mehmet Bey married you was because you bewitched him.'

'I didn't.' It was difficult to keep calm amid this onslaught.

He reached out and grabbed her by the throat. His hand closed her windpipe and all she could do was gag.

'I know you won't tell him,' he said. 'Because you're scared that if he comes for me, I'll kill him. And I will. Now . . .' Suddenly his eyes widened and he let her go, scuttling backwards as he yelled, 'Get it away from me!'

Gonca, her heart hammering in her chest, looked in the direction Şevket Sesler was staring, and then she smiled. Gently she picked the snake up and put it around her shoulders. Stroking Sara's head, she said, 'Oh baby girl, you came to help Mama. I love you so much.'

Sesler, sweating, took a knife out of his waistband. 'I'll cut the bastard's head off!'

Gonca stepped forward. 'You touch her and I will end you!' she roared.

Sesler moved back even further. 'Fuck! The thing's looking at me!'

'And if you don't get out of here, she'll bite you!'

He didn't know Sara was a constrictor, he was too stupid.

'Now fuck off, Şevket Bey,' Gonca said. 'And don't ever cross my threshold again. If you do, Sara will be waiting for you!'

Was that Çetin İkmen?

A man in late middle age, bundled up in an over-large coat and smoking a cigarette, was swinging along İmam Adnan Sokak, apparently talking to himself. If it *was* İkmen, he was probably having a conversation with a dead relative. But then who else could it be?

'Çetin?'

The man looked up. Recognising Süleyman, he puffed his way up the hill and embraced him, then shook Ömer Mungun's hand.

'What are you doing here?' Süleyman asked.

İkmen had just come from his meeting with Peri and Yeşili Mungun, but he didn't want to say that, and so instead he said, 'Why shouldn't I be here?' Then, looking at the small squad of uniforms behind his friend, 'What's going on?'

Süleyman knew he shouldn't answer, but he did.

'We need to talk to İlhan Böcek and Yıldırım Ayhan.'

'Ah, the spawn of the godfathers.'

'There's an alert out for them. We think they may be together.'

'Odd.' İkmen waved to a couple of the older uniforms, who waved back. 'So where are you going?' he asked.

'The MorKedi.'

'You think they're, what, having a coffee in there?'

'Yes.'

'And you're going in with this lot?'

'No. Ömer and myself are going in. These men will cover the exits.'

İkmen crossed his arms over his chest. 'You're going in,' he said. 'And have they seen you before? I'm assuming they have.'

'It's not ideal, but this is urgent. I'm sorry, Çetin, but I've a job to do.'

As Süleyman began to move away, İkmen said, 'Neither of those boys know me. You got photographs?'

Esma could hear screaming from inside the Ayhan house. It sounded like Aylın. She ran around to the kitchen door, which was often unlocked, and went inside. A maid who was rolling out pastry on one of the steel worktops said, 'Hey!'

But Esma just ran past her and headed up the stairs to the ground-floor landing. The door to the salon was open, and as she got closer, she could hear that the screams were coming from there. Without any thought for her own safety, she ran in.

Murad Bey, one fist aloft, was standing over Aylın, who was crouched on the floor, bleeding from what looked like a broken nose. Irmak, her mother, was lying on a couch, crying. As Esma entered, they all turned to look at her.

Eventually Murad Ayhan said, 'What the fuck are you doing here?'

Aylın staggered to her feet and ran to her friend. Esma put her arms around her.

Irmak, incensed, yelled at her husband, 'If anyone's unnatural around here, it's those two! Look at them! Like lovers!'

'That's not true!' Aylın yelled.

Esma looked at her friend's bloodied nose and said, 'Put your head forward.'

Murad Ayhan began to advance towards the girls. Esma started walking backwards, taking Aylın with her.

'Don't you touch us, Murad Bey!' she said. 'Aylın needs a doctor. I'm going to take her to my dad now, and don't you try to stop me!'

'What right do you think you have to take my daughter away!' Murad Ayhan roared. 'You're going nowhere; you're especially not taking her to Faruk Bey!'

'Don't say anything about my father, Murad Bey!' Esma shouted.

'Your father was born a thieving Romani and he'll die a thieving Romani!'

'My dad's a doctor, and Aylın needs one of those because of what you've done to her!' Pulling Aylın with her, Esma left the room and made for the kitchen.

Murad Aylın began to stride after them, but his wife stopped him.

'Let them go,' she said.

'And have Faruk Nebatı call the police on me?'

She walked up to him and tried to put a hand to his face, but Murad Ayhan flinched away.

'He won't call the police,' she said as she retreated from him. 'As you said yourself, Murad, he's a Romani, they don't do police.'

'Oh, and so—'

'The time is long past when you and I needed to talk about Yıldırım,' she went on. 'But now we have to.'

She sat down again, then reached over to a cigarette box on the small table beside her and took out a black Sobranie. She lit up. Her husband, unaccustomed to his wife being quite so frank with him, sat down too.

'Aylın was right,' she said. 'Yıldırım is attracted to men. I've seen him lust over actors like Alp Navruz in the dizis we watch together. He thinks I don't notice, but I do.'

'So why didn't you tell me?' Murad asked.

She smiled. 'And risk you cutting off my allowance? Because I've no doubt you'll use Yıldırım's sexuality as a stick with which to beat me. It being my fault, of course. And if you ditch me, that will give you even more time with all your mistresses.'

'Irmak!'

'Hear me out!' she said. 'I don't give a fuck if you screw your whores all day and all night. I don't care if you divorce me. But

306

you'll have to pay me to go, Murad. I've put up with your whoring, your business, the scum you surround yourself with, like that murderer Serdar, and I've said nothing for decades. But what you've done to Yıldırım is unconscionable.'

'Done to him? I've done nothing to the little bastard!'

'Exactly,' she said. 'You've ignored him. I've had to do everything, and while that should mean that Yıldırım loves me, unfortunately for him, he can't love either of us.'

Murad Ayhan got to his feet and began pacing the room. 'What are you talking about?'

'I'm saying the boy's not right,' she said. 'I've known it for years. Remember when Aylın asked us to buy her a guinea pig? No, I don't suppose you do. Well, I bought it, Aylın loved it. Then one day she went to the animal's cage only to find that someone had cut off its head. Yıldırım.'

'Nonsense!'

'Not nonsense! Fact.'

'Then why didn't I know about it?' he yelled.

'Because what was the point of telling you? You had no interest in the children – not now, not ever! I've been trying to prevent him from acting on his baser urges for years. And yes, I knew about the Böcek boy. Yıldırım used to cry himself to sleep because he was in love with him. All İlhan Böcek wanted from him was to get close to Aylın. And yes, I knew he'd sneaked out of your party to go to Sesler's birthday. He does things he knows will upset you. He's trying to get your attention!'

'I didn't know.'

'No, Murad, you didn't, because you take no notice of him. And now the police are looking for him because he was there when someone shot at the gypsies. God knows what he's done. I dread to think. But he ran away from this house for a reason, and I fear that reason is because he at the very least knew who shot Sesler's people!' She began to cry. 'All I know now is that I am done. I am done with protecting him and I'm done with putting you first. If the police come back, I am telling them the truth.'

Gonca Süleyman was crying when Rambo and Tomas walked into the kitchen. With Sara still draped around her shoulders, she was drinking coffee at the table and smoking a cigarette.

'Mum?'

Rambo sat down beside her, while Tomas stood awkwardly by the back door, unable to understand what they were saying.

'What's the matter?'

Gonca wiped her eyes. 'Oh, it's nothing, just silly-old-woman stuff.'

Although she hated and was in no way attracted to Şevket Sesler, his words had hit her hard. Yes, of course she had bewitched her husband. His flesh was bound to hers by numerous spells and magical workings. But when he had first come to her, he'd done so of his own accord. Love and passion were what had kept him coming back. That she had created a glamour to ensure his continued intoxication was not grounded in nothing. And yet . . .

'Tomas said he saw Şevket Bey here,' Rambo said. 'Did he hurt you, Mum?'

'No, of course not! He wouldn't dare!'

She could tell no one what had happened between herself and Sesler, especially not Mehmet. If he knew that Sesler had threatened to rape her, he'd kill him. His pride would allow no other course of action. And her children wouldn't be far behind.

As if to underline this point, Rambo said, 'Because if he did, I'd have him, Mum. Me and the boys'd have him. Don't give a shit what it costs.'

'The boys' were her seven sons – Rambo, Erol, Haluk, Alp, Selahattin, Deniz and even Erdem, her eldest boy, who had married a gaco and worked in IT.

Gonca took his hand. 'Everything's fine.'

The boy looked at the snake. 'Sara's back to her old self,' he said.

'Yes, she is,' Gonca agreed. 'My baby girl will be a great comfort to me when you go off on your travels, Rambo.'

He sighed. 'You don't want me to go, do you, Mum?'

'No,' she said simply. 'But I also know that as a Romani man, you have a right to roam.'

'You know it won't be for ever, don't you? I'll always come back to you.'

'I know,' she said. 'But don't leave it too long, eh?'

The four flights of stairs up to the MorKedi Café were challenging. And so when İkmen finally arrived, he was out of breath. Why did he do these things to himself? Why did he always offer to help? It was insanity. He looked at Ömer Mungun and Süleyman at his back and then gasped, 'I'll phone you,' before he opened the door to the café and went inside.

He didn't know the MorKedi well. When it converted to a bar in the evening, it was somewhere Samsun would sometimes go. But trans people were a minority here, and so he wasn't surprised to find that most of his fellow customers were gay men.

As soon as he sat down and surveyed the premises, he saw Yıldırım Ayhan. The kid was so fat, it was difficult to miss him. However, rather than being in company with one young man, who may or may not have been İlhan Böcek, he and his friend had been joined by a smart middle-aged character.

A waiter approached and İkmen ordered a double espresso. It was the nearest thing one could get in trendy places like the MorKedi to his favourite Turkish coffee. There was a decent background hubbub of conversation to cover his words, and so he took his phone out of his pocket and called Süleyman.

'The Ayhan boy's here.'

'Is he alone?' Süleyman asked.

'No. There's a lad who could be the Böcek boy with him, but he's got his back to me, and there's also a middle-aged man I don't recognise. They're all talking rather intensely.'

Süleyman said, 'OK. See you in a minute.'

İkmen ended the call and waited.

Chapter 24

Yıldırım Ayhan recognised Süleyman immediately. As soon as the inspector placed a hand on İlhan Böcek's shoulder, he blurted, 'Cops!'

İlhan looked confused. 'Where?' Then he looked up at Süleyman, brushed his hand off his shoulder and said, 'Don't touch me, man! I'm not like these guys.'

Yıldırım tried to get to his feet, but Ömer Mungun pushed him down in his seat. The middle-aged man with the boys went white and his eyes bulged.

Süleyman said, 'Now I'm sure you don't want to make a scene, gentlemen. If you'd quietly come with us . . .'

'Why?' The middle-aged man was sweating now. 'What for?'

'I wish to speak to İlhan Bey and Yıldırım Bey,' Süleyman said. 'And you are?'

The man said nothing. İkmen positioned himself a little way behind him and watched as the other patrons of the café began to realise that something was going on.

'We just want to talk,' Süleyman said. 'Clear a few things up about a recent party.'

'What party?'

'All will be explained when we get to headquarters. Now . . .'

The middle-aged man pushed his chair back so hard and fast into İkmen's legs that it knocked him to the floor. Süleyman attempted to catch the man as he ran towards the door, but missed. Ömer Mungun let go of Yıldırım Ayhan and gave chase, pushing

311

his way through packed tables and elbowing a customer out of the way.

Knowing that Süleyman had stationed uniforms at the front and back entrances to the building, Ömer was not too worried about whether he could catch the man. He just needed to block his escape once he'd got to the ground floor and seen the officers. As he began to descend the stairs, he called after him, 'We've officers at the bottom! You might as well come with me.'

The man stopped and looked up at him.

'I don't know why you're running,' Ömer said. 'But if you stop and talk, we can sort this out.'

The man was one floor down. About fifty, he was well dressed, his hair, though grey, thick and stylish. What had he been doing with the teenage sons of gangsters?

'Sir . . .'

The man glanced down and saw one of the uniformed officers walking towards the bottom of the stairs.

Then something happened that Ömer could hardly believe. After looking first up and then down again one more time, the man climbed over the banister and, without the slightest hesitation whatsoever, threw himself down into the stairwell.

Çetin İkmen was still in pain, but in spite of this, he managed to get a hand on Yıldırım Ayhan's arm and clamp his fingers around it tightly. Süleyman meanwhile held İlhan Böcek's arm up his back with one hand while he pulled out his badge and showed it to the waiter with the other. Then, looking at the Ayhan boy, he said, 'We just want to talk to you. Why the resistance?'

Yıldırım's face flushed with fury. 'Everyone knows what you lot are like!' he said. 'You make up stories about people like us.'

'People like who?'

He looked around the café for support, but found only people looking away from him.

'This has nothing to do with your sexuality,' Süleyman said. 'This is to do with your family.'

'Oh?' The boy wriggled in İkmen's grasp.

'But if you hurt my colleague in any way, you'll also be looking at a charge of assault.'

It was then that a wild piercing scream was heard out on the landing, followed by a heavy thumping noise.

After that, Süleyman heard Ömer Mungun yell, 'God!'

Dr Faruk Nebatı had faced most things during the course of his sixty years on earth. As a Romani child in the old gypsy quarter of Sulukule, he'd experienced the overwhelming love of his family and friends, along with hunger; as a medical student, he had suffered prejudice and sometimes violence; and as a highly regarded orthopaedic surgeon, he had been obliged to deal with jealousy and derision. Romani people didn't become doctors, apparently. A man who had once been his best friend, Murad Ayhan, had told him that. Now here he was gently packing the nose of Ayhan's daughter, whom he strongly suspected had been assaulted by her father. Murad had always solved his problems with his fists – and anything else that came to hand.

However, it wasn't for Faruk to either judge or accuse, and so he did what he always did and offered practical help.

As he cleaned the blood away from Aylın's cheeks, he said, 'You should rest now, Aylın. I'm sure that Esma would be delighted if you stayed here with us.'

'Thank you, Faruk Bey,' Aylın said.

Esma put an arm around her shoulders. 'Come on, let's go and sit in the conservatory. I'll put some music on and get you some tea.'

Faruk watched the girls go, and then sat down to consider his options. If Murad had hit Aylın, he shouldn't be allowed to get away with it. The girl would never betray her father, but . . . For

313

decades Murad had treated his former best friend like a piece of dirt, and Faruk had ignored it. And although he had long suspected that Murad terrorised not just his employees but his own family, he had stayed away. Or rather, he had supported Esma's friendship with Aylın. That in itself, he knew, had annoyed the man. But now maybe it was time to put a stop to Murad's reign of terror. Maybe now was the time to tell Murad Bey what he'd seen in his garden on the night of his famous family and employees party. But first he'd have to speak to an old friend . . .

Süleyman locked down not just the café, but the whole building. He called for backup, and scene-of-crime officers arrived hot on the heels of Arto Sarkissian. Screens were erected around the body, which the pathologist described to Süleyman as a 'fearful mess'.

As he suited up to accompany SOCO officers already attending the body, the Armenian spotted Çetin İkmen.

'Good God, what are you doing here?'

İkmen lit a cigarette and shrugged. 'I was passing.'

The doctor scowled. 'Is that right?'

'Yes.'

He shook his head. 'Çetin, we both know that you're very rarely just passing—'

'Mehmet Bey wants an ID on that body as soon as you can,' İkmen interrupted.

'And he will have it!' the doctor said as he disappeared behind the screens.

Hearing footsteps on the stairs, İkmen watched as Süleyman and four uniforms escorted the two young men, cuffed, out of the building. When the inspector returned, he said, 'I take it you'll be off to question those two.'

Süleyman dragged a hand down his face. 'Provided I can stay awake. I think I slept the night before last, but it's open to question. But Ömer is in the same position – and Kerim Bey and Sergeant Yavaş.'

'Amphetamines,' İkmen said. 'Always worked for me.'

Süleyman snorted. 'You were and are an adrenaline junkie, Çetin. You don't do speed.'

'True.' İkmen offered Süleyman a cigarette, which he took. 'But I do partake in excessive amounts of coffee and nicotine. And seeing as you appear to be turning into a more good-looking version of me, I'd suggest you invest in a coffee machine for your office.'

Süleyman smiled.

'I never achieved such dizzying heights of privilege myself,' İkmen continued. 'But you have a machine at home. Why not another one at work?'

Süleyman leaned down to whisper, 'Maybe I can't afford one.'

'Then I'll buy you one. It's only money. Anyway, what's the thing with the two kids?'

'Not sure yet,' Süleyman said. 'All a little hearsay at the moment.'

There was a grunt from behind the screens and Arto Sarkissian emerged holding a card, which he gave to Süleyman.

'Kimlik. Sixty-one years old. Name of Gibrail Sezer. He's a Christian.'

Süleyman looked at the identity card. 'Don't know him.'

'Me neither,' the doctor said. 'But whoever he is, he's broken his neck. Dead as Latin. I spoke to a haunted-looking Sergeant Mungun, who seems to think he committed suicide.'

'Yes.'

'Excessive,' the Armenian said. 'Reminds me of a body I worked on years ago. Silly boy whose girlfriend cheated on him and so he threw himself off the Galata Tower. Appalling state.'

He went back behind the screens, leaving Süleyman looking at the card.

315

İkmen said, 'You remember what Şeftali Şekeroğlu told me about this all being about lust?'

Süleyman looked up at him.

'Şevket Bey.'

There was a silence at the other end of the line, and then Şevket Sesler said, 'Who's this? Nobody calls me on my landline.'

Faruk Nebatı smiled. The young Şevket Sesler he remembered from Sulukule had always been a rude kid. Now he was a gruff, rude man.

'Faruk Nebatı,' he said. 'Remember me?'

Again a silence, and then Sesler said, 'You were that kid who always had his nose in a book. Your brother went to prison for fraud. Sınan Nebatı.'

'Yes,' Faruk said. 'But he's out now. Lives in Edirne.'

'What do you want?'

'You may or may not know, Şevket Bey, that I live near an old mutual friend of ours. When I left the mahalle to go to medical school, I lost touch with everyone except my closest family members.'

'So?'

'So, quite unwittingly, I found myself buying a house behind that of Murad Ayhan. I'm sure you know him, you being in a similar line of work . . .'

'Murad Ayhan's a bastard,' Sesler said. 'His family were so shit they had to live with us. We treated them like brothers . . .'

'Yes, well . . .'

'. . . and yet Murad treats me like dirt. I hate the bastard. What of him?'

'Şevket Bey, indulge me,' said Faruk. 'Did Murad Ayhan's son make an appearance at your birthday party?'

'Why?'

'Did he?'

'Police asked me the same question. Answer's yes. He often comes over here. Murad's ashamed that he was brought up in Sulukule, but I think the kid's curious about us.'

'So he was there?' Faruk asked.

'Yeah. What of it? He's fat and useless but I don't mind him. Amuses me that his dad would go mad if he found out. Not that I talk to the boy. There were thousands came out to see me that night. The only reason I noticed him was that he was in some sort of costume. Like an animal. Didn't cover his face, daft kid. You know, you're being really annoying, Faruk, like you were when you were a kid. Get to the point!'

'The point is, Şevket, that I saw Yıldırım Ayhan in my garden on the night of your party. He and another man I couldn't identify were using it as somewhere to change their clothes.'

'So why didn't you tell them to fuck off?'

'Because I don't get involved with gangsters, as you know. You mentioned the police . . .'

'Yeah, picked him up on CCTV. Couldn't identify him themselves, so they asked me. No bother to me to tell them the truth. Anything that'll piss Murad off. Do you remember Gonca Şekeroğlu?'

'Of course,' Faruk said. 'We were all both scared of and besotted by her. Why?'

'She married the man investigating the shootings at my party. Inspector Mehmet Süleyman. It was him I told about Yıldırım Ayhan.'

As usual, Esat Böcek was ahead of the game. That, or maybe he'd been at headquarters when Ateş was charged. Either way, there he was with a woman Süleyman recognised as Havva Sarı, another well-known celebrity lawyer.

İlhan Böcek and Yıldırım Ayhan had been brought through the back of the building and so Esat Böcek and his lawyer hadn't yet seen them. Süleyman walked over to speak to them.

317

'Mehmet Bey,' Sarı said as she held her hand out to him.

He shook it. 'Havva Hanım.'

'Why have you brought my son here?' Esat Böcek cut in. 'You've charged Ateş with murder! Now İlhan. What is this? Some sort of witch-hunt? Why have you detained my boy?'

'Information has come to our attention—'

'What information?' Böcek cried. 'From where? About what?'

'Mr Böcek, I simply want to ask your son some questions,' Süleyman said. 'Havva Hanım, I have yet to ascertain whether İlhan Bey requires your services.'

Böcek began, 'Well, of course—'

The lawyer put a hand on his arm. 'Mehmet Bey will give İlhan the chance to choose.'

'Will he?' Böcek said. 'Will he really? Because it looks to me as if the police mean to bring my family down.'

Süleyman left and joined Ömer Mungun outside Interview Room 4. As he approached, he put a hand on the younger man's shoulder. 'Holding up?'

'I'm mostly coffee now, boss,' Ömer said.

'Right. Have you spoken to Kerim Bey?'

'Yes, sir. Filled him in on what we want.'

'Good.'

'Sergeant Yavaş is here too,' Ömer said. 'Kerim Bey made a bit of a performance about telling her she should have stayed home, but you can tell he's glad she's back. Oh, and our dead man is a doctor, apparently.'

The two officers walked into the room and sat down opposite İlhan Böcek.

Süleyman said, 'Mr Böcek, you have a right to legal representation.'

'I haven't done anything wrong, so why would I need a lawyer?'

'Your father has brought along a very expensive advocate.'

'I'm sure he has, but I don't need him.'

'Her.'

'I don't need her. I'm not my brother, I can speak for myself. After unceremoniously dragging me out of that café, what do you want?'

Süleyman smiled. 'All in good time.'

'What does that mean?' İlhan asked.

'Mr Böcek, can you tell me why you were in the MorKedi Café, and with whom?'

He shrugged. 'I go where I please. I was with my friend Yıldırım Ayhan. We went to school together.'

'Are you homosexual?'

'No, but Yıldırım is.'

'He is also the son of one of your father's business rivals.'

He shrugged again. 'Why we don't meet at each other's houses,' he said.

'So who was the other man with you?' Süleyman asked.

'A friend of Yıldırım's.'

'His lover?'

İlhan laughed. 'No. Ask him.'

'Who?'

'Yıldırım's friend.'

Süleyman looked at Ömer, who said, 'We can't.'

'Why not?'

'You heard the commotion just after the man in question ran out of the café,' Süleyman said. 'He threw himself down the stair-well to his death. Didn't you notice that the ground floor was screened off?'

İlhan Böcek, whose face had now drained of all colour, said nothing.

'Clearly not,' Süleyman said. 'Well, I can tell you that his name was Dr Gibrail Sezer. Familiar to you?'

'No.'

Süleyman looked down at his notes. 'What were you doing on the morning and afternoon of the twenty-fourth of December?'

'This again?' İlhan sighed. 'I told you, I was collecting rent for my father.'

'In Kadıköy?'

'Yeah. Ask my dad's tenants. Anyway, you've got my brother for the murder of the whore, haven't you? What are you trying to do? Tie me in to all the mad shit he's done?'

'No, Mr Böcek, we're trying to find the truth,' Süleyman said.

Irmak Ayhan put the telephone receiver back on its cradle. 'That was the police. An Inspector Gürsel. They've found Yıldırım.'

Murad Ayhan looked up from his blood pressure monitor and then took the cuff off his arm.

'I don't know whether to be relieved or furious,' he said.

'With your blood pressure?'

'No, with that stupid boy! Why did he run away like that, Irmak?'

'He's homosexual.'

'No he isn't!' her husband roared. 'He's attention-seeking!'

'He's in love with the Böcek boy, who in turn follows Aylın about like a stalker,' Irmak said.

'So why the fuck didn't you tell me? I would've put a stop to all of it. I'd've told Esat Böcek that if he couldn't control his son, he'd find himself at war with me. The other boy, Ateş, is a murderer! I mean, what kind of family are they?'

His wife folded her arms across her chest. 'You want to know what kind of family they are, Murad?' she said. 'Just look at us. Spoilt, out-of-control children . . .'

'You spoil that boy, not me!'

'. . . men – you and Esat Bey – who cheat on their wives and go all holy-holy while fucking prostitutes. And then there's the fact that we're surrounded by people like Serdar,' she added. 'An animal!'

320

'Serdar is loyal.' Murad stood. 'We need men like him to keep us safe.'

'Because you and Esat Böcek extort money from people!' she said. 'Because you kill—'

He punched her in the face. Irmak fell on the floor, her nose, like her daughter's had been, pouring with blood.

'Enough!' her husband hissed at her. 'Enough from the woman content to take my money while I work myself into an early grave! While I pay good money to keep her and our useless children alive!' He bent down and slapped her cheek. 'Keep your opinions to yourself, Irmak. Unless you want to join the ranks of my enemies and either fend for yourself or go and sleep with the fish in the Bosphorus!' He straightened up. 'Now I am going to police headquarters to bring that stupid boy home. I suggest you retrieve our daughter from the Nebatıs' house. In the meantime, I will leave Serdar in charge of things here.' He called out, 'Serdar Bey!'

The thug was in the room in under two seconds. He looked down at Irmak and then at his boss.

'Murad Bey?'

'I want you to take care of things while I'm out,' Murad said.

He couldn't decide whether the excessive crying Yıldırım Ayhan was doing was genuine or an act of defence. The boy had certainly caught a glimpse at least of what had been behind the screens on the ground floor of the MorKedi building – Süleyman had seen him look. But whether he had recognised what it was, Kerim didn't know.

Also, while as a gay man he empathised with this boy, alone and frightened in police headquarters, the fact that he was also a gangster's son made him less sympathetic.

Eventually, when it seemed the boy wasn't going to stop crying of his own accord, Kerim opted for shock tactics.

'Yıldırım,' he said, 'can you please tell me what you know about

Dr Gibrail Sezer? And yes, we do know the name of the man who threw himself down that stairwell. He was carrying his kimlik. You and your friend İlhan Böcek were talking to him just before he died.'

Although by this time Yıldırım had stopped crying, he was still making sobbing noises in this throat.

'Take your time,' Kerim said. 'What is Dr Sezer to you?'

In the silence that followed, Eylul's phone rang. She answered with her name, which was followed by a 'yes', an 'are you sure?' and then another 'yes'. Then she put the phone down and whispered into Kerim's ear.

Scrutinising them the whole time, Yıldırım Ayhan's eyes were wide and full of fear. What did the boy think was coming next?

Kerim leaned forward. 'Yıldırım, what were you doing in a gay bar?'

Yıldırım raised his eyebrows.

'Don't try to pretend you didn't know. The location of your meeting doesn't actually have any relevance. Neither does the fact that you were there with the son of one of your father's rivals. You were, after all, friends at school. No, what interests me is why you and your friend were talking to your father's physician.'

The boy stared glassily at him.

'Further,' Kerim continued, 'I would like to know why, when Inspector Süleyman and his team approached you and your companions, Dr Sezer first attempted to escape, and then, when he realised he couldn't get away, killed himself by throwing himself down a stairwell. Correct me if I'm wrong, but to me that seems like a very final way of avoiding the attention of the police. It strikes me that Dr Sezer wanted to take something very secret or shameful to his grave.'

Chapter 25

'I'd like you to scan through every piece of footage we have of Ateş Böcek from local CCTV cameras on the twenty-fourth of December,' Süleyman said.

Eylul Yavaş, who had volunteered to review the footage alongside technical officer Türgüt Zana, Blu-Tacked photographs of İlhan Böcek and Dr Gibrail Sezer to her desk – much to the chagrin of Zana, who had taken screenshots of them.

'We're looking for evidence that either İlhan or this Dr Sezer, or both, were in the vicinity of Ateş's house when Ceviz Elibol was killed,' he continued. 'Sergeant Yavaş, you will recall that Dr Sarkissian was of the opinion that someone with medical knowledge was probably involved in the girl's dismemberment. This is urgent. I don't want to have to release İlhan Böcek until we can be sure he wasn't at his brother's place or nearby on that day.'

'Yes, sir.'

'In the meantime, Sergeant Mungun and myself are going out to Sarıyer to see Gibrail Sezer's wife.'

'Murad Bey!'

Faruk Nebatı had seen his neighbour walk over to his block of garages. Murad Ayhan rarely looked beyond the fence that divided his property from that of his former friend, but now he did.

'What do you want, Faruk?' he said. 'I'm on my way out.'

'A moment of your time is all I require,' Faruk replied. 'It's about Yıldırım.'

Did his old friend's face momentarily flush at the mention of his son? Murad looked exhausted. According to Esma whenever she visited, he was always talking about his health, getting his doctor over all times of the day and night.

Now he walked up to the fence and demanded, 'What's he done?'

'To me? Nothing,' Faruk said. 'I just think you ought to know that on the night of your party, when Şevket Sesler had his birthday celebration in Tarlabaşı, your son and another man changed their clothes in my garden. Sesler has told the police.'

Murad growled, 'I know.'

'However, what only I know so far is that your son and his friend were also armed.'

Disbelieving and infuriated, Murad said, 'Fuck off, Faruk! That boy wouldn't know a firearm from a hole in the road.'

'I don't know much, Murad Bey. I'm a doctor, I don't do guns. But like you, I did my military service, and so I know a sniper rifle when I see one.'

Murad went white.

'Now, I don't know what they were doing with it. But in light of what happened at Şevket's birthday party, and knowing that your son was there . . .' Faruk paused. 'I haven't told Şevket. I haven't told the police. But I'm going to.'

'No! No . . .'

'Murad, I don't know what you do. I don't care. I want nothing to do with that life. But I do know it isn't good, and I've seen that directly with my own eyes today.'

'What . . .'

'I've just set a nose,' he said. 'Broken by you. My daughter told me about your attack on Aylın. So you know I'm going to call the police. There's nothing you can do to me. And you know what else? The lead officer on the Sesler investigation is married to Gonca Hanım. Remember her? We all lusted after her when we

324

were kids. So I know this Inspector Süleyman will listen to me even though I'm a Romani because he is married to her.'

He turned his back and began to walk towards his house. And even though Murad had a gun in his pocket, he didn't attempt to stop him.

'He went to Midyat. His family come from there,' she said. 'He always goes to see his mother around Christmas time.'

Yasemin Sezer, on hearing of her husband's death, had turned to stone, with not a tear in her eye. Her emotions appeared to settle into a deep, quiet pain that made her whisper.

Ömer Mungun, who came from nearby Mardin, said, 'Didn't you go with him, Yasemin Hanım?'

'I am a Muslim, Sergeant,' she said. 'My husband's family are Suriani Christians. Christmas is a time for them, not me.'

A young maid brought tea for them all and then left.

Stirring sugar into his tea, Süleyman said, 'So when did Dr Sezer leave for Midyat, hanım? I'm so sorry we have to question you in this way . . .'

'Of course you do,' she said. 'It's fine. That Gibrail would kill himself . . .' She shook her head. 'He was a committed Christian, you know. Suicide is anathema to them.' She sighed. 'He left home on the twenty-third. We don't have children and so I went to stay with my sister in Yalova for a few days. I returned home on the twenty-seventh.'

'And did your husband call you during that time?'

'Yes,' she said. 'We're close, we called each other. Oh, and of course his employer badgered me. When Gibrail is away for any reason, Murad Bey is always chasing. He's a hypochondriac.'

Süleyman said, 'Your husband is a family doctor.'

'He trained as a surgeon,' she said. 'But yes, he's a family doctor now. He's retained exclusively by a rich family these days.'

'This Murad Bey?'

'Yes. Murad Ayhan. I expect you've heard of him, Inspector.'

'Oh yes,' Süleyman said.

'When he first came to Gibrail, my husband managed to get his headaches under control for him, and Murad Bey became obsessed with the idea that he was some kind of super-doctor. He made Gibrail an offer he couldn't refuse – to become his private physician.'

'When was this, hanım?'

'Ten years ago,' she said. 'It's because of Murad Bey and his family that we can afford to live in this house. But it's come at a price.'

'Which is?'

'Gibrail being on call 24/7, having to put up with abuse, sometimes physical, from that family. He only really got on with the daughter, Aylın. She always treated him with respect. But the rest of them . . . He wanted to leave. It was making him ill. I told him to just give notice, but he was more concerned about how he'd be able to make enough money to keep us in the style to which we had become accustomed. I told him I didn't care . . .'

Then, finally, she began to cry. Süleyman looked at Ömer Mungun, who he knew was thinking the same thing he was: Gibrail Sezer had been a surgeon, and Dr Sarkissian had said that whoever had dismembered Ceviz Elibol had possessed surgical skills.

Süleyman's phone rang. It was headquarters. Apparently a man called Faruk Nebatı needed to speak to him urgently.

Nobody but İkmen would have recognised Şeftali Şekeroğlu. Swinging through the narrow, muddy streets of Tahtakale wearing a black tailored trouser suit and designer sunglasses, her hair twisted into a stylish chignon, this was obviously the falcı of Eminönü on her day off.

Smiling, he walked over to her and took her arm. This caught her unawares and she gasped.

'I've been trying to work out why I'd never heard of you until a

326

few days ago, Şeftali Hanım,' he said. 'And now I think I've found the answer. You're only part-time, aren't you?'

Outraged, she said, 'Who are you? Don't you dare touch me . . .'

Narrowly missing bumping into sacks of dried apricots and figs outside a bakkal at a crossroads, he said, 'Oh, please don't insult my intelligence, Şeftali Hanım. I know who you are and you know who I am. If magical people try to glamour each other, then we are truly lost.' He increased the pressure on her arm. 'Come on. I know a place round here where we can talk. Nice trick with the legs, by the way.'

They walked up Tahtakale Caddesi until they came to the hairdressing supply emporium, the Zaza Han. The tiny unnamed café was down the side of this shop, in an alleyway so narrow it was impossible to traverse without turning sideways at least once. Called the Peri Kale – the Fairy Castle – it consisted of one room containing two tables and a stove, plus a table outside for smokers. İkmen gestured to Şeftali to sit on one of the chairs outside and then called out, 'Rabia Hanım!'

An elderly woman in broken slippers, hot-pink şalvar trousers and a black cardigan, a wrinkled green scarf on her head, came outside. 'İkmen! God, what do you want?'

'Two coffees, please,' he said. 'Mine very sweet. Şeftali Hanım?'

'Oh, er, medium,' Şeftali said. When the woman had gone she continued, 'I've never been here before. What is this place?'

İkmen smiled. 'Somewhere we won't be overheard. Because I'm sure that what you're going to tell me will be for my ears only.'

'And how did you know it was me?' Şeftali asked. 'Nobody has ever seen through my disguise.'

He pointed underneath the table.

'Taking your honey out for a walk in the hours of daylight is probably not a good idea,' he said.

*

This was going to be interesting, especially in light of Mehmet Süleyman's recent phone call.

Kerim Gürsel settled himself behind his desk and said to the white-faced man in front of him, 'So what can I do for you, Mr Ayhan?'

'Where's Süleyman?' Murad Ayhan asked.

'Out.'

'Where?'

Kerim shrugged.

'You must know!' Ayhan said.

'Why do you want to speak to him?'

'He's got my son here.'

'No.'

'No?'

'No, *I* have Yıldırım, Murad Bey,' Kerim said. 'I need to ask him some questions about what he did on the night of the party at your house.'

'I've already told Süleyman about that!' Ayhan snapped.

'Yes, I believe you have. However, further evidence has now come to light that challenges your account.'

'You don't mean from that lying gypsy Nebatı, do you?'

Süleyman had enjoyed telling Kerim about Faruk Nebatı's call. Here, possibly, was further evidence for regarding Yıldırım Ayhan as a viable suspect in the Sesler shooting. But who had been the other man with him? Lola Cortes's 'devil' . . .

In lieu of an answer from Kerim, Ayhan said, 'So, can I see my son? Has he got himself a lawyer?'

'No,' Kerim said. 'Just like his friend İlhan Böcek, he refused legal representation.'

Murad Ayhan flinched.

'So come on,' Çetin İkmen said, 'it'll get dark soon and then it'll be too cold to sit out here. Tell me what all the demonology was about.'

Şeftali was unfazed. 'What are you doing here, İkmen?'

'You're the third person to ask me that today. Why shouldn't I be here?'

'Fair,' she said.

'So come on, what was all that theatre with the old crone act and the malevolent eyes under the table? And how did you get Gonca to set me up?'

She laughed. 'Oh, Gonca knows no more about me than anyone exposed only to my public persona. Come on, İkmen, I'm a woman of a certain age, but I'm not dead. How on earth do you think Şeftali the falcı would ever get laid, eh? I'm not my cousin, I don't have access to all the spells she uses on her gorgeous husband.'

'My question remains,' İkmen said, 'why the theatre? Why the whole "lust is behind what is going on in the city"?'

Their coffee arrived and they both sipped.

Şeftali said, 'Excellent! Why don't I know about this place?'

'Best coffee in İstanbul.' İkmen put his cup down. 'Now, the truth, please, Şeftali Hanım. If you know anything about me, you will realise that I won't stop until I get it.'

She sighed. 'Organised crime is a scourge today like never before. In the old days a local godfather usually contented himself with extorting money from his own mahalle. He might have the local bakkal owner pay a fee to stop his thugs from destroying his business, take a cut from the local car-cleaning cartel. But such people now have bigger ideas. People have been coming to see me and my honey, my Poreskoro, for decades. I've always operated as a sole trader – ask Numan Bey.'

İkmen nodded. He would ask the pickle-juice man next time he saw him.

'But then about ten years ago, everything changed,' Şeftali went on. 'The made men moved in on anyone they thought they could make a lira from. That included me and Numan Bey. I am

Roma, and so you will know whom I pay my dues to. Numan Bey pays that shit Murad Ayhan . . .'

'So?'

'. . . as does your friend Aaron Kamhi. And before you ask, if you think academics are exempt from the attentions of the gangs, think again. Godfathers have children who sometimes manage to get to university. Ateş Böcek managed one term and sometimes his psychiatrist used to attend lectures with him – at his father's request. I know this because Feride Hanım is one of my friends. As a psychiatrist, she finds what I do fascinating. Numan Bey is a customer and Aaron Kamhi knows Feride Hanım. So yes, İkmen, we all know each other. We all also share a . . . what can you say, a gang-related problem. To wit, we don't want to pay up or be in thrall to them any more. I'm sure you've noticed how prices have risen in this country in recent years. The economy is tanking and godfathers, just like legitimate companies, are squeezing dry those they protect while they still can.'

'I repeat,' he said, 'why the theatre?'

She continued as if he hadn't spoken. 'But not paying up is not an option if you don't have something over your enemy, as it were. So that was when I sent my honey out to find out more.'

'OK,' İkmen said, 'up until now we've done it all without demonic intervention . . .'

'Feride knew that İlhan Böcek was in love with his friend Yıldırım Ayhan's sister. Forbidden love across the gangland barricades, Romeo and Juliet – except not, because the girl can't stand him. This I admit we knew, but when my Poreskoro began telling me tales of chaos in those quarters . . .'

'Why didn't you call the police?'

'And have Mehmet Bey look at me the way you're looking at me now? No, İkmen. We had to get to you to get to him. We had to make you aware that lust is behind this.'

'İlhan Böcek's lust?'

'Amongst others,' she said.

'I don't suppose you'll tell me . . .'

'No. Why should I make your life easy?'

He shrugged.

'The other thing we needed to make sure you and the police knew was that Ateş Böcek was too sick to kill that girl. Ateş is as much a victim of gangland warfare as poor Ceviz Elibol. But I'm sure I don't have to tell you what they do to people they think might have betrayed them, do I? We played this very cautiously, İkmen, but as I'm sure you'll understand, when poor Ceviz died, we had to escalate things. Why is it always the Romani girl who dies, eh?'

'I heard Esat Böcek had arrived,' Eylul Yavaş said to Kerim Gürsel.

'Yes,' he replied. 'But when you called, it sounded urgent.'

'May or may not be.'

'Show me.'

She sat down and pulled a chair up in front of her computer for her boss. Türgüt Zana, who had also been reviewing CCTV tapes, looked on.

Eylul said, 'This footage comes from a pharmacy two doors down from the bakkal where Ateş Böcek bought his cigarettes on the twenty-fourth of December. As you watch Ateş walking past the pharmacy, you'll see that a man is walking alongside him. This man is obscured from the camera by Ateş. It may or may not be his brother, I don't know. But look at the man who appears to be following the pair.'

Eylul unfroze the screen, and although the image was blurry, the face of the man behind Ateş was familiar. It was Dr Gibrail Sezer.

Chapter 26

The interview room, though not hot, was stuffy. It also contained, as well as his son, a constable who was listening in to their conversation.

Murad Ayhan, infuriated, got to his feet and paced.

'What did Gürsel ask you about?' he said to Yıldırım.

'Your party,' the boy replied.

Murad put a hand up to his head. 'That? Again? I told him you were at home all night. You were, weren't you?'

'Yeah.'

'So why . . . Anyway, why did you run off like that? And what's this about some bar and a man killing himself?'

Kerim Gürsel had told Murad only the bare bones of the story of Yıldırım's capture.

'A man threw himself down the stairs,' the boy said.

'And you were with İlhan Böcek, I understand,' his father said. 'Why?'

'We're friends.'

'Mmm.' In light of what Aylın had told him, Murad now wondered whether that was indeed all the boys were to each other. 'So who killed himself? Did you know him?'

Yıldırım said nothing.

'Well?'

After first looking at the constable, he said, 'The police say it was Dr Sezer.'

'What? Gibrail Sezer? Our doctor?'

Yıldırım nodded. 'So they say. I don't know. I wasn't with him, Dad.'

When Mehmet Süleyman had finished outlining the progress of the investigation to Commissioner Ozer and prosecutor Kemal Gurkan, the latter said, 'So what does all this have to do with the death of the gypsy girl? I've charged Ateş Böcek with murder. He's the only one—'

'Sir, as I told you,' Süleyman said, 'Ateş was seen in company with another, as yet unidentified man, possibly his brother, and this suicide, Dr Gibrail Sezer, on the day of the girl's death.'

'Where's your forensic evidence?' Ozer asked.

'I have instructed Dr Sarkissian to compare unknown blood samples from the scene to that of Dr Sezer. It's his opinion that whoever killed Ceviz Elibol had some surgical knowledge.'

'But you said that Sezer was Murad Ayhan's personal physician,' the prosecutor said. 'Ayhan and Böcek are rivals, are they not?'

'They are. However, as you know, sir, relationships between crime families are often complicated.'

'Böcek performs many charitable works,' Ozer cut in. 'We should be wary, Mehmet Bey, of putting labels on people.'

This wasn't unexpected, given that Ozer, like Esat Böcek, was a very performative man of faith.

Süleyman nodded. 'Yes sir.'

'Anyway, Ateş Böcek is on remand in Silivri,' the prosecutor said. 'Very unfortunate for a family to have a person who is insane in their midst. This leaves you, Mehmet Bey, and Inspector Gürsel with outstanding work to do with regard to the attack on Şevket Sesler and his people and the death of Esat Böcek's man, Hakki Bürkev. Whilst not casting aspersions on anyone, we need to make sure that businessmen like Esat Bey and, to some extent, Murad Bey do not, shall we say, fall foul of involvement with gangsters like Sesler.'

Süleyman took a deep breath. What he was about to say would not play well. Ozer, he knew, had sometimes socialised with Esat Böcek. They moved in the same circles. The prosecutor was less well known to him, but there was a high chance that he too knew Böcek on some level. He was, after all, outwardly a very conservative man.

'It is my belief and Inspector Gürsel's that all these incidents are connected.'

'How?'

'Beyond simple rivalry, we don't yet know, but we are pursuing several lines of enquiry.'

'Like?'

'Like a possible romantic connection between the Böceks and the Ayhans.'

'So where does Sesler come into all this?' Ozer particularly wanted to make this all about the Roma godfather.

'I don't know that he really does,' Süleyman said. 'Remember, two of the people killed by an unknown assailant on Sesler's birthday were his cousin Alaadin and a man called Mete Bülbül who was a distant relative of Sesler's father. As yet, we have no reason to believe that Sesler himself has killed anyone.'

The other two men looked at each other. Süleyman knew they were both thinking about his wife and whether she was behind his apparent support for the Romani godfather.

Eventually the prosecutor said, 'What about the death of Esat Böcek's bodyguard Hakki Bürkev?'

'The only thing we know about him so far is that he was the son of a man Esat Böcek allegedly involved in an industrial accident,' Süleyman replied. 'Inspector Gürsel has a statement from a previous employee of the Böcek organisation to that effect.'

'Meaning?'

'Meaning that maybe Hakki Bürkev had issues with his employer.'

The room went silent, then Ozer said, 'So what do you want from us, Mehmet Bey?'

'I want permission to follow emerging leads and evidence trails that may exonerate Ateş Böcek. Inspector Gürsel and myself believe that there's something about this, specifically involving the Böcek and Ayhan children, that we are just not seeing right now. The team are willing to work through the night and do whatever it takes.'

'All right,' Ozer said, waving a hand limply as if in submission. 'Just don't get the department into hot water with these families, Mehmet Bey. They have money as well as, in the case of the Böceks, solid moral capital. Do not mess this up.'

'You can go home,' Havva Sarı said to her client, İlhan Böcek. 'They can't hold on to you simply because you witnessed a suicide.'

'That Inspector Süleyman said they still have questions,' İlhan said.

'What about?'

'I don't know.'

She smiled. 'They can't hold you like this for no reason. To me this is harassment. They have your brother in custody, and now you.'

'I dunno . . .'

'Well I can get you out,' she said. 'I've your father outside.'

'No!'

İlhan hadn't wanted to see his father when he'd been offered the chance. Now just the mere mention of him made the young man turn away.

The lawyer moved in close so that the police constable couldn't hear her. 'İlhan, what's the matter? What have they done to you? Have they told you not to speak to Esat Bey?'

But İlhan Böcek didn't answer her.

*

Mehmet Süleyman was outside his office in the corridor talking to his wife when he saw İkmen walking towards him.

'Çetin . . .'

'Oh, İkmen's arrived, good,' Gonca said over the phone.

'What?'

'Şeftali called and told me that she'd just left him and that he was coming to see you. Or rather, she called you my "gorgeous man". Why you'd be concerned about what the poor old thing might think . . .'

Süleyman embraced İkmen. 'What are you doing here? Go into my office.'

İkmen did as he was told and Süleyman closed the door behind him.

'Are you coming home to sleep tonight, baby?' Gonca asked.

'I hope so,' Süleyman said.

'You hope so? You must! Forty-eight hours you've been awake now! It's not normal! You'll get sick! And if you get sick, I will die!'

When he finally managed to placate his wife enough to get her off the phone, Süleyman joined Ömer Mungun, Kerim Gürsel, Eylul Yavaş and İkmen in his office. It was easy to see who had managed to get any sleep the previous night. The two inspectors and Ömer Mungun looked ghastly. But it was Ömer who left to get İkmen a chair.

'Oh, and bring one for Dr Koca too,' Süleyman said. 'He will be joining us presently.'

'Yes, boss.'

While they all waited for Ömer's return, Kerim gave İkmen his chair, which he placed next to Süleyman. As Kerim and Eylul talked quietly to each other, Süleyman said, 'Why *are* you here?'

'Does it matter?'

'No. How did you get here?'

'Get here? I drove,' İkmen said. 'Then I walked through the front entrance and got in the lift.'

336

'Çetin, you don't have a pass.'

'No,' he agreed.

Ömer returned carrying two chairs and accompanied by Dr Koca. Before sitting down, the psychiatrist peered at İkmen. 'Forgive me, you are . . .'

İkmen rose from his seat and shook the doctor's hand. 'Çetin İkmen,' he said. 'I used to work here.'

'Ah yes,' Dr Koca said. 'I've heard some good and also some very strange things about you.'

'Yes, well . . .' Süleyman said. 'Colleagues, I've asked you all here so that we can discuss how we might go forward with our investigation into the deaths of Ceviz Elibol, five other Roma victims in Tarlabaşı, Mete Bülbül, also in Tarlabaşı, and Hakki Bürkev in Kadıköy.'

'Not forgetting the suicide of Dr Gibrail Sezer,' Ömer said.

'Indeed. So where are we? Perhaps it might be a good idea for each of us to go over what we know. I should add that at present we have İlhan Böcek and Yıldırım Ayhan in the building for questioning. Böcek senior has brought a lawyer; Murad Ayhan hasn't as far as I know. We can't hold them for long, so time is of the essence. Oh, and Dr Sarkissian is going to try to expedite DNA analysis on unknown samples taken from the Ceviz Elibol scene and match them to those of our suicide.' He turned to İkmen. 'This is because Dr Sarkissian thinks that the skills used to kill the girl were surgical, and we have CCTV of Dr Sezer in the vicinity of Ateş Böcek's home on the twenty-fourth of December.' Then he looked at Kerim. 'Kerim Bey?'

'OK. Hakki Bürkev, employee of Esat Böcek, was murdered with a knife. CCTV in the vicinity of Baghdat Caddesi has thrown up a couple of known faces but no one with any sort of connection to Böcek. Also, the alleyway where Bürkev died is a blind spot. Esat Bey and his people believe that Sesler was behind the murder, which is a possibility given the attack on Sesler on the

337

twenty-sixth. We know that Sesler has pointed the finger at Böcek right from the start. However, during the course of our investigation, Sergeant Yavaş and myself came across an ex-employee of Esat Böcek who told us that the father of this Hakki Bürkev, another employee of the Böceks, died in an industrial accident directly related to employer neglect.'

'If you're implying that Böcek killed Hakki Bürkev, why?' Ömer Mungun asked.

'I'm not necessarily saying that,' Kerim said. 'Sesler's people could have killed him. But I've a statement from this ex-employee that raises questions about Böcek. Perhaps he used the current febrile atmosphere to get rid of someone who may well have hated him?'

'Şevket Sesler is, I believe, staying his hand,' Süleyman said. 'And to address what some of you may be thinking, no, I do not believe every word he says. I trust him no more or less than any other purveyor of organised crime.'

The office fell silent for a moment. While everyone believed in Süleyman's professionalism, the fact that he was now married to Gonca Şekeroğlu weighed somewhat.

'We know that the man who was killed in his apartment on the night of the Tarlabaşı shootings was called Mete Bülbül. Sesler claims he was a relative and was happy to undergo DNA testing to prove it. We are still awaiting those results. And while Sesler was not keen to be related to this man, I don't think he murdered him. On that killing we have a statement from a Mrs Lola Cortes, a Spanish national, identifying a masked figure who was picked up on CCTV cameras outside the Poisoned Princess apartments. Significantly, this unidentified figure was standing next to someone we now know was Yıldırım Ayhan. According to Ayhan's sister Aylın, Yıldırım was curious about the Roma community and would sometimes go and spy on them.'

'Murad Ayhan was brought up with the Roma,' Ömer said. 'Won't acknowledge it, though. Doesn't like them.'

'Which brings me to Murad Bey's neighbour,' Süleyman said. 'Dr Faruk Nebatı, one of the Roma he grew up with. Now an orthopaedic surgeon, his daughter and Aylın Ayhan are good friends in spite of Murad's disapproval. Just today, Faruk Bey told me that on the night of Sesler's party, he saw Yıldırım Ayhan and another, unknown man changing into what he described as animal costumes in his back garden.'

'Mrs Cortes described the man she saw as a devil,' Eylul put in.

At which point, İkmen said, 'If I may interject . . .'

Irmak Ayhan hadn't seen Faruk Nebatı for years. This was firstly because her husband didn't like him and secondly because unless she was going shopping or to the beauty parlour, Irmak didn't go out.

Now, sweating from the climb up to the Nebatı house, as well as nursing her painful face, Irmak was surprised to see that the eminent doctor opened his own front door. She couldn't believe he didn't have servants.

'Ah . . .' she said as he looked down at her.

'Irmak Hanım.' He smiled. 'What can I do for you?' Then, noticing the bruise on her face, he added, 'You're hurt. What has happened to you? Did your husband . . .'

Irmak cleared her throat. 'I believe you have my daughter here,' she said. 'I've come to get her.'

He nodded. 'Well, Irmak Hanım, she is currently sleeping in a chair in my conservatory. As you may know, Aylın has recently had a shock of some magnitude.'

She gave a nervous little laugh.

'I don't think this is funny, hanım. As you know, bones are my specialty, and I can tell you that Aylın's nose was broken when she arrived here. And from what my daughter has told me, it would

339

appear that the break was occasioned by contact with Murad Bey's fist.'

'That's a lie!'

'No it isn't. And just like I told your husband when he asked about her, I am not prepared to allow her to go home until I can get an assurance from both of you that this will not happen again.'

Irmak Ayhan, like her husband, came originally from a family of urban poor folk. Her early life had been characterised by hard work, little education and some hunger. When she'd married Murad, her hard work had stopped and she'd made up for lost time with regard to hunger. Education, however, was not something she'd craved. And so thirty years on from her marriage, Irmak Ayhan, now apparently thwarted, regressed into the foul-mouthed, streetwise girl Murad had fallen in love with.

'Fuck you, you gypsy bastard!' she said. 'That's my daughter you've kidnapped.'

'Kidnapped? I'm protecting her. And don't you dare insult my people, Irmak Hanım. Your husband, let me tell you, wasn't too proud to eat at my parents' apartment when his own father was too drunk to care for him.'

Murad Ayhan's father had died before they'd met, and so Irmak had no idea what kind of a man he'd been. Murad had never complained about him to her.

After a moment's confusion about what to say next, she began to move backwards.

'Well?' Faruk Nebatı said. 'Aylın will come back to you if and when she feels she can. In the meantime, I suggest you consider leaving your violent husband for the good of your own health.'

'Fuck you! Irmak yelled again, and then, almost slipping on a patch of mud on the driveway, 'And fuck your fucking family too!'

Faruk Nebatı closed the door. He still hadn't phoned the police. Murad Ayhan was a bastard, but at one time he'd been a brother.

He turned and saw Aylın standing behind him. She said, 'I need to go home to my mum now, Faruk Bey. I think she needs me.'

When Çetin İkmen came to the end of his story about Şeftali, he said, 'But whether you believe in demons or not, people like Şeftali, the pickle-juice man and even academics and doctors are finding themselves unable to pay the inflated protection money demanded by the godfathers.'

'But doesn't the fact that Ateş Böcek's psychiatrist appears to be mitigating against his guilt . . .'

'She's been put in an ethical bind,' İkmen said. 'She can't say anything publicly about her patient if she wants to live, she can't treat him consistently, but she still doesn't believe in his guilt. He's damaged.'

'Çetin, we need proof,' Süleyman said. 'The way things stand, Ateş is still firmly in the frame for Ceviz Elibol's death. He was there, he has a serious mental health condition . . .'

'He loved her.'

The office became quiet again. Then Süleyman looked at İkmen. 'Follow the lust, the falcı said.'

'She did.'

'Well, we have anecdotal evidence that İlhan Böcek has the hots for Aylın Ayhan. She in turn is of the opinion that her brother Yıldırım is in love with İlhan. If true, I can clearly see the lust. What I can't do is connect those alleged feelings to multiple murders. For example, Yıldırım Ayhan went to Sesler's birthday party with a man in disguise. Just for a moment let us assume that one or both of them shot into the crowd outside the Şekeroğlu meyhane. Let us also assume they killed Mete Bülbül. Why?'

Kerim said, 'Bülbül very likely interrupted whoever was taking shots and was killed with his own firearm. He considered himself Roma. He was trying to protect his own.'

'So who killed Sesler's people, and why?' Süleyman said. 'We

341

know that once Şevket Bey found out about the death of his strip-per, Ceviz, he wanted compensation. Böcek would, we know, have told him to fuck off. But why would Böcek then go to war?'

'That's what I came to tell you, Mehmet Bey,' İkmen said. 'My source, whatever you may think about her, is obliged to hand money over to these people for protection. Given the state of the economy, this has increased in recent years.'

'So maybe you think some of these protected people . . .'

'I'm saying it's possible. Kill Ceviz Elibol, pin it on the spawn of a godfather, discredit him.'

'But then,' Eylul said, 'won't another one just rise up to take his place?' She looked at Süleyman. 'Remember, sir, that on the day of the girl's death, Murad Ayhan's doctor was seen with Ateş and another man. Could Ayhan have been setting out to destroy Böcek?'

'And what of the two kids?' Ömer asked. 'Yıldırım Ayhan could have been involved in killing Sesler's people – he was there, we know he was. And we know he was with İlhan Böcek and Dr Sezer at the MorKedi. When we found him, Sezer killed himself, and he must have done that for a reason.'

The maid gave her a funny look, but Irmak ignored her. It wasn't the first time Murad had hit her. The girl was lucky she hadn't known them when they were newlyweds. Back then, Murad had used his wife as a punchbag on a daily basis.

Irmak took a bag of ice out of the freezer and held it to her cheek. Then she walked upstairs and back into her lounge. Had the door to Murad's office not been left open, she wouldn't have gone through it. He usually locked the place up when he was out. But he'd been in a state of anxiety when he'd left and so he'd for-gotten. If she could go in there, maybe steal a few items, or at the very least rearrange stuff so he couldn't find things, that would give her some grim pleasure.

But when she walked through the door, she saw that she wasn't alone. Furthermore, Murad's safe was open.

'What are you doing?' she said.

'Murad Bey said he wanted some money taken out,' Serdar replied.

'Oh.'

She walked over to him and watched as he removed something she knew wasn't cash from the safe.

'Those are my Ottoman diamonds,' she said. 'Bought from an actual princess, they were. Murad gave them to me when Yıldırım was born. What's he want with those?'

'I don't know, hanım.'

'Well put them back,' she said. 'They're mine. If he wants to sell them, he can think again.'

But Serdar didn't move.

'Put them back!' she shouted. 'Do as you're told!'

Still he did nothing; just looked at her.

'Put them back!' she reiterated. 'Ugly fucking thug, do as you're damn well told!'

And it was then that Serdar took a knife out of his belt and stabbed Irmak Hanım in the throat.

Murad Ayhan and Esat Böcek had much in common at the present time. They were both sitting on hard benches in police headquarters, both had a son undergoing police questioning, and both of their said sons had rejected legal representation.

For a while, they pointedly looked away from each other; then there was a period of ill-tempered eye contact. Eventually it was Murad Ayhan who broke the silence.

'I have been told that your İlhan has been following my Aylın about,' he said. 'Did you know about this?'

'I did not,' Esat Böcek replied. 'Had I known, don't you think I would have put a stop to it?'

'I don't know. Maybe you were after some sort of partnership.'

'Ha! With you?' He shook his head. 'I have a very nice girl lined up for my son.'

'And my girl isn't nice?'

Böcek shrugged. 'I don't know her. All I am aware of is that she doesn't cover, and that isn't acceptable to my family.'

'If I wanted Aylın to cover, she'd cover,' Murad said. 'But she finds your son creepy. Whatever happens here today, İlhan is looking at stalking charges.'

'Says the man with a pervert for a son,' Böcek countered.

Murad Ayhan narrowed his eyes. 'My son isn't a pervert.'

'So why does he follow my İlhan around like a little dog, eh? Two can play at the stalking game, Murad Bey.'

'Oh yeah?' Murad shook his head. 'You know that I admire you, Esat Bey, I really do.'

Esat Böcek frowned.

'The way you do that holy act all the time.'

'It's not an act! I am a sincere—'

Murad leaned towards him and whispered, 'Anyone who can carve a man's face up the way you did my man Serdar's cannot also be on the side of the angels.'

The elderly man who was sharing the space with the two gang bosses dribbled in his sleep and then started to snore.

Aylın had insisted on going home.

'Don't misunderstand me, Faruk Bey,' she said to Faruk Nebatı. 'I don't get on with my mum. But if Dad's hitting her again, I need to at least try to put a stop to it.'

'But your father has gone out,' Faruk Nebatı said as he followed Aylın into his garden.

'So maybe I can get her to leave. We can go to her sister's place in Fatih. My Aunt Selin would understand. She's always been wary of my dad.'

'Well, let me come with you,' Faruk said.

She put a hand on his arm. 'It's really kind of you, Faruk Bey, but you know what my parents are like. I think it might make things worse. I'm sorry.'

Faruk Nebatı shrugged. 'As you wish.'

Aylın set off down the hill to her house, and after a moment's reflection, Faruk Nebatı followed her. He had a bad feeling about her going back in there on her own.

Chapter 27

'Dr Gibrail Sezer was your father's personal physician,' Süleyman said.

'Yeah.'

Süleyman and Kerim Gürsel had swapped interviewees. Sometimes it was all about keeping those you wished to expose the truth off centre.

'Why did your father employ a personal physician?' he asked. 'Most of us make do with our family doctor.'

'My dad's got health issues,' Yıldırım Ayhan said.

'Like?'

He shrugged.

'Do you think your father's issues had anything to do with Dr Sezer's suicide?' Süleyman asked.

'Don't know. Ask my dad.'

'I will.

'You were seen talking to Dr Sezer and İlhan Böcek just before the former died. What were you talking about?'

'I dunno. This and that.'

'And yet shortly after we arrived and interrupted your conversation, Dr Sezer took his own life.'

'I've only your word to say that he did.'

'And why would I lie?' Süleyman said.

Yıldırım shrugged.

'OK, let's go back a little. We have CCTV evidence that places Dr Sezer and İlhan's brother Ateş together on the day that Ateş allegedly killed the Romani woman Ceviz Elibol. We also know that in all probability Elibol was dismembered by someone with medical knowledge.'

'I don't know nothing about that.'

'Was your best friend İlhan also present when Miss Elibol died?'

'No! Ateş did it, he's mad!'

'Is he? How do you know that?'

'İlhan told me.'

'İlhan.' Süleyman leaned back in his chair. 'Must be inconvenient you and İlhan being friends. Given that your fathers are rivals. But then of course love will always find a way, won't it?'

'What do you mean?'

'You're in love with İlhan Böcek, aren't you?' Ömer Mungun said.

The boy's skin flared. 'No! You ask İlhan! We're friends! You ask him and he'll tell you it isn't like that!'

'Maybe not from his point of view, no,' Süleyman said. 'But you'd like it to be, wouldn't you, Yıldırım?'

Aylın had her back to him. She was staring at something on the floor. Because he'd seen Serdar İpek in Murad's office, Faruk Nebatı had hidden behind a faux-rococo pillar in the lounge.

The girl said, 'Mum? Mummy!'

The body of a woman lay on the floor in front of her. Faruk couldn't see the face, but he assumed it was that of Irmak Ayhan. He heard ragged breathing and then a man's voice. Serdar.

'Aylın,' he said, 'it wasn't meant to be like this . . .'

'Like what?' the girl said. 'You are supposed to protect our family . . .'

'I do protect you,' Serdar replied. 'I hate the way Murad Bey hits you. It ends now. Come with me.'

Faruk took his phone out of his pocket. Murad's safe was open and bundles of cash and jewels were strewn across his desk.

347

'But this is my dad's money!' Aylın said.

'And now it's mine, or rather ours. Look, I'll tell you all about it later.'

Serdar lunged towards her, but Aylın pulled away. 'No!'

Faruk dialled 155, hoping and praying that he was far enough away from the action in the office to avoid being overheard.

A voice said, 'Police.'

'I don't know him!' İlhan Böcek said. 'He's Yıldırım's dad's doctor. I can't go round Yıldırım's house, just like he can't come to mine. How would I know his dad's doctor?'

'You were talking to him in the MorKedi,' Kerim Gürsel said.

'Yıldırım was talking to him.'

'What about?'

'I don't know!' İlhan was almost crying now.

Eylul Yavaş said, 'What were you doing in a café for homosexuals?'

Kerim felt his heart squeeze, even though he knew that in this context the question was legitimate.

'Yıldırım wanted to go there,' İlhan said. 'He likes those sorts of places. I don't.'

'So why go with him?'

'He's my friend. I can't help it if he's like . . .'

'Like what?' Kerim asked.

'Like . . . You know . . .'

'I don't,' Eylul put in. 'Tell us.'

'He's like . . . well, he likes men.'

'And you?' Kerim asked. 'Do you "like" men? Did Dr Sezer like them too?'

'I'm not a . . . I'm not unnatural!' İlhan said.

'And yet you have a friend who is?'

'Yıldırım does what he wants. It doesn't affect me!'

'What about Dr Sezer?'

'I don't know anything about him.'

'And yet your brother Ateş was seen with him on the day Ceviz Elibol was murdered at his house,' Kerim said. 'Now, given that your two families do not speak, it seems strange to me that your brother apparently knew Dr Sezer.'

İlhan stopped speaking.

Eylul said, 'Do you want legal representation, İlhan?'

'No!'

'Why not?'

'Because my father . . .'

There was a knock at the door. Eylul stood up and answered it. The voice Kerim could just about hear outside was Süleyman's. But he continued.

'Because your father what?'

İlhan shook his head.

Eylul turned around but didn't return to her chair. Instead she spoke into the recording device. 'Interview with İlhan Böcek suspended.'

He was in love with her! Serdar İpek, her father's most brutal thug! Oh God, why did horrible men always like her? First that creepy İlhan Böcek, and now Serdar. And although he hadn't admitted that he'd killed her mother, Aylın knew it had to be him. Her brother had told her, his eyes shining with the thrill of it all, about the things Serdar had done. Like chopping a man's fingers off one by one; like raping a woman in front of her husband, who had refused to pay his debt to her father. He enjoyed doing such things. And now, by apparently stealing from her father, he had also lost his mind.

Cringing away from him, Aylın said, 'Put everything back and . . .'

She had been going to add *we'll say no more about it*. But that was hardly possible with her mother lying dead on the floor. Serdar might be delusional, but he wasn't stupid.

She said, 'You know that Murad Bey will kill you, Serdar. He trusts you, and now you're betraying him.'

'I've no choice.'

He loaded cash and then the first of the jewellery bags into a huge holdall.

'You do,' Aylın said. 'You can just leave.'

'Not without you. The money's only a small part of the dream. You've always been the rest of it.'

Aylın had to concentrate so that she didn't visibly shudder. Serdar had been with her father since before she was born. She'd sat on his knee as a toddler; he'd taken her and her brother to school. She wanted to be sick.

'Serdar . . .'

'I won't hurt you, Aylın,' he said. 'I promise you that.'

Aylın looked at her mother's body. Serdar followed her gaze. 'That was an accident. I'm sorry.'

A movement at the periphery of her vision made her want to look around, but she didn't. It was probably one of the servants. But if she called attention to it, would Serdar kill someone else? There it was again. She felt her heart begin to hammer.

Why didn't posh people ever have net curtains? Or proper blinds? And why was it that when people wondered what might be going through a marksman's head when he lined up a shot, they always got it wrong? Curtains and blinds were significant, particularly when you were shooting through glass. Taking a shot was an art, and attaining the perfect shot relied upon minute calculations and adjustments, things often mitigated by curtains and blinds.

Until he'd been invalided out of the armed forces, Constable İsmail Toksoy had been one of the elite OKK Special Forces unit's most accomplished marksmen. He could take shots other people deemed impossible. He'd even taken part in the OKK's trust shot exercise, where two members of a three man-team stood beside paper targets while the third member walked forward, shooting continuously with a handgun. Anyone who so much as flinched was out; it was a demonstration of both courage and trust in one's fellow officers. However, Toksoy had broken his leg on a routine exercise, which was why he was now standing beside a tree in a gangster's garden being observed by Inspector Mehmet Süleyman.

Keeping his voice low, Süleyman said, 'From the little information we have, it would seem that the assailant, Serdar İpek, is unlikely to hurt the girl.'

'Yes, sir.'

They could both see what looked like the body of a woman on the floor of Murad Ayhan's office. Their contact inside the building, a Dr Faruk Nebatı, was not visible but was thought to be somewhere in the lounge, which was behind the office.

'You only take the shot on my signal.'

'Yes, sir.'

'I will touch my left eyelid.'

'Left.'

'Left. You go on my signal, and this will be when I have deemed that the only way forward,' Süleyman said. 'Whatever he does, you take your cue from me, understand?'

'Yes, sir.'

'And avoid lethal force. I want to take him alive if I can. I know that if anyone can do that, you can, Toksoy.'

'Understood.'

Süleyman put on the Kevlar vest Ömer Mungun was holding out to him, then checked his pistol and returned it to its holster. Kerim Gürsel fitted his colleague with recording equipment, then said, 'Strategy?'

'Once the front door's in, he'll know he's not alone and will, I think, make a grab for the girl,' Süleyman said. 'So with that in mind, I think I will be using the İkmen gambit.'

'Which is?'

'Friendly and jocular. Not my strong suit, but what can you do?'

'I'm here to see Inspector Süleyman.'

'Are you drunk?' Esat Böcek asked the old man propped up on the corner of the bench.

'Might be,' the man said. 'What about you?'

'I'm not drunk. I don't drink!' Esat Böcek said.

'What are you here for then?'

'They have my son in custody,' he said. 'Boy's done nothing wrong.'

'And you?' the old man asked Murad Ayhan.

'My son is in custody too,' Ayhan said. 'Ridiculous.'

'Oh, police, police!' the old man said. 'What can you do, eh?'

'Mmm.'

Çetin İkmen had been sitting with the men for over an hour. He'd only left them once, when he went to the toilet. There he had relayed what he'd heard to Mehmet Süleyman, who was now on his way out to the Ayhan house in Bebek. Neither Böcek nor Ayhan knew this. What they also didn't know was that İkmen had told Süleyman about that whisper he'd heard between the two men, the one about how Serdar İpek had got his terrible facial injuries. The man who was currently holding Aylın Ayhan hostage had issues with Esat Böcek.

İkmen fell easily into drunk old man guise these days. When he'd been younger, it had been drunk young man. But time had passed, time during which his body had started to round on him by making his heart hammer, as it was doing now. Süleyman, he knew, would want to negotiate before he took Serdar İpek down. He wanted to know what İkmen was now beginning to believe he already knew.

As he walked through the Ayhans' lounge and into Murad's office, Süleyman noticed a man hiding behind one of the large couches.

This was probably Dr Faruk Nebatı, who had called the incident in. But he didn't acknowledge him. Instead his eyes were fixed on the man with his arms around Aylın Ayhan, a gun at her head.

'Police.'

'Stop there!' Serdar barked.

'Can't do that,' Süleyman said. 'We need to talk, you see.' He kept moving. 'Can't shout from one room to the next when a couple of metres more will save both our throats.'

He stepped into the office. Bundles of cash and a large holdall sat on Murad Ayhan's desk.

'Stop there!' Serdar repeated.

Süleyman said, 'Here's fine. Don't have to shout. I am Inspector Süleyman. What's going on, Mr İpek? Going away somewhere?'

'Me and Aylın, yes,' he said.

Aylın made a gurgling sound in her throat.

'Are you sure about that?' Süleyman asked. 'Looks to me as if Miss Ayhan is not keen on the idea.'

The casual, jocular approach was a strain, and Süleyman began to sweat. Serdar İpek was a brutal man, and although he had a record only for petty crime, it was well known that he'd killed, and not just for his master. Serdar İpek was one of those mobsters who, people said, killed because he liked it.

His dead eyes bored into Süleyman's. 'The best place for Aylın is with me.'

'Why is that?'' Süleyman asked.

'Because I love her. I'm the only one who does.' Serdar kicked Irmak Ayhan's corpse. 'She didn't love her. None of this family love Aylın as she should be loved.'

'And how is that, Serdar?'

The thug thought for a moment, and then said, 'How I'd love her.' Süleyman waited for him to expand, which he did.

'I'll give her everything. Or I would if her brother and that stupid Böcek kid hadn't fucked everything up.'

'What do you mean?' Süleyman was aware that his voice was becoming dictatorial again. He took a breath.

'Do you know what it's like to work for someone who treats you like a cunt, Inspector?' Serdar said. 'Like a stupid cunt, too thick to know when you're being abused. Decades of it.'

Süleyman had no doubt that Murad Ayhan had treated probably everyone who worked for him badly. He was a gangster, it was what they did. If Murad hadn't inspired fear in those who worked for him, he would have ceased to be years ago. Serdar knew that. But . . .

'Tell me about Yıldırım Ayhan and İlhan Böcek,' Süleyman said. 'How did they fuck up?'

'The Böcek boy's a nutter, like his brother. There was no need to cut the girl up like that!'

'What girl?' He knew, but in case they did have to take Serdar down and he didn't survive, Süleyman had to get as much out of him as he could now.

'The gypsy his brother was seeing,' Serdar said. 'I told them just to kill her, but they'd got the doctor on board by that time. What can you do?'

Sara's portrait glowed, now sealed underneath a glaze Gonca had made from egg whites. She showed it to the snake when she briefly raised her head from her basket.

'There! You see? What a beautiful girl!'

Someone knocked at her studio door.

'Who is it?' she said, making ready to hide Sara away in case it was Mehmet.

'Rambo,' her son said. 'Got someone you need to meet.'

Gonca wandered over to the door and opened it. 'Well?'

The boy wasn't alone. With him was a smiling Lola Cortes holding a tiny baby.

'Oh!'

'Called Carmen, she is,' Rambo said.

Gonca put her hands out to take the baby, which Lola put into her arms. Still smeared with blood, the little girl looked as if she'd just been born.

'She's beautiful!' Gonca said. 'When?'

'Just now,' her son said. 'In the tent.'

'Oh God, why didn't you call me? I could've helped! What about the afterbirth?'

'Juan buried it underneath the olive tree,' Rambo said.

Gonca looked around. 'Where is he now?'

'Him and Tomas are drinking brandy.'

'Men!' She shook her head. 'Well, go and get Tomas and have him dig it up!'

'Why?'

'Why? Because it may not have all come away,' Gonca said. 'And if it hasn't, it can be dangerous.' She reached out to Lola. 'And you, girly, you come with me. I know you don't understand what I'm saying, but come here anyway.'

The young woman made as if to pull away from her. But Gonca was adamant.

'I need to look at you, make sure you're all right,' she said. Then she pushed her son back out into the garden. 'Fetch Tomas, and get that afterbirth to me, now!'

'So why kill Ceviz Elibol?' Süleyman asked.

'I know what you're doing,' Serdar said. 'You're trying to keep me talking. But I've done with that. Now we have to go, me and Aylın.'

Tears fell from the girl's eyes.

'Go where?' Süleyman asked.

'Somewhere.'

'Serdar, as soon as you leave this building, you will be a legitimate target. You are armed and dangerous and every force in the country will be notified about who you are. By tomorrow, if you survive that long, the whole of Europe will know your face. Give Aylın to me.'

'No!' Serdar pulled her closer. 'You get me out of here, you bastard. Me, her and the money. That's it. No negotiation.'

'The deal is this,' Süleyman said. 'You give me Aylın, along with Murad Bey's money and jewellery, and we will talk. I think your plan was to bring your employer down, and possibly Esat Böcek too. Esat Bey cut your face up, didn't he?'

'They're all cunts!' Serdar said. 'Esat cut me and Murad Bey did nothing, just laughed. Said it was an occupational hazard, said if I'd been lighter on my feet it would never have happened. Blamed me!'

'Maybe Murad Bey didn't want to start a war with the Böceks.'

'Well, he should've done! I was his number one. He used me to frighten money out of people. Wouldn't do it himself. Ponce! Good enough to get cut up, not good enough for his daughter!'

'Serdar,' Süleyman said, 'did you think that Murad Bey would give you Aylın?'

'I bled for that bastard!'

'Yes, but it doesn't work like that, does it?'

'It fucking ought to!' Serdar began to cry.

'Serdar, give Aylın to me,' Süleyman said. 'You and I both know that you're going to prison, but if you do this, your sentence will be reduced. Also, if you give me as much information as you can about who else was involved and, in particular, who killed Ceviz Elibol . . .'

Serdar threw his head back and screamed, 'Fuck off, cunt!'

Süleyman touched his left eyelid.

Chapter 28

'Not my finest hour,' Süleyman said to Kerim Gürsel as he handed a weeping Aylın Ayhan over to him.

'You had no choice,' Kerim said. 'He was becoming hysterical; anything could have happened.'

'Is he dead?' the girl asked. Süleyman could see that she was avoiding looking back where she'd come from.

As soon as Süleyman had given the signal, Constable Toksoy had taken the shot. While Serdar had held Aylın with his left arm, the constable had shot him in the right shoulder, causing him to let go of her and fall to the floor, screaming.

'No,' Süleyman told the girl. 'Constable Toksoy is a brilliant marksman.'

'I've called for an ambulance,' Kerim said. 'He'll live.'

Aylın shook her head. 'Shame. He killed my mum.'

Süleyman said, 'Aylın, he will go to prison for a very long time.'

'I mean, my mum and I, we didn't get on, but . . .' She began to cry.

'Come on,' Kerim said as he moved her out of the lounge and into the hall. 'My sergeant, Eylul, will take care of you.'

Eylul Yavaş put an arm around Aylın and led her to some chairs underneath the stairs. Kerim joined Süleyman and other officers in Murad Ayhan's office. Down on the ground with the body of Irmak Ayhan, Serdar İpek groaned in pain as Ömer Mungun applied pressure to his shoulder wound.

Süleyman said, 'You'll need to thank our marksman that you're not dead, Serdar.'

The man gasped, foaming at the mouth. 'Wish I was.'

'Well, I'm glad you're not, because we have a lot to talk about, you and me.'

Serdar said, 'Cunt!"

'Yes,' Süleyman observed. 'You like that word.'

'His status is basically voluntary,' the lawyer said.

Esat Böcek shrugged. 'So why can't I just take him?'

Havva Sarı had worked for the Böcek family a few times before. She knew who and what they were.

'My understanding is he won't leave,' she said. 'Now whether that is because he wants to wait for the return of Inspectors Süleyman and Gürsel, because he wishes to clear this matter up—'

'The matter of a suicide?' Esat Böcek said. 'İlhan didn't even know the man.'

'No, but the police did wish to speak to both your son and Yıldırım Ayhan, who were together with Dr Sezer at the MorKedi café.'

'So where are Süleyman and Gürsel now?' Böcek asked.

'My understanding is they are attending an incident in Bebek.'

'Bebek!' He laughed, then turned round to make sure that his rival wasn't in the room with them. 'That's where Ayhan lives.'

'I don't know . . .'

'Oh no, that would be too much to hope for,' Esat Böcek said. Then his face fell. 'You said İlhan wouldn't come?'

'No,' the lawyer said. 'And there's nothing I can do to change his mind.'

'So then maybe I—'

'Oh no, Esat Bey,' she said. 'I'm afraid he won't see you. I've no idea why. But he was very specific about it.'

Esat Böcek, for the first time, began to feel chilled.

*

Serdar İpek was taken to the Maltepe Emergency Hospital, where his shoulder would be operated on to remove the bullet. Under police guard, he was not expected to be able to undergo questioning until the following morning.

'Which leaves us with the Ayhan and Böcek boys,' Süleyman said to Kerim Gürsel when they entered the latter's office.

Kerim sat down behind his desk. 'Who Serdar named as co-conspirators.'

'As well as Dr Sezer. And conspirators in what, exactly?'

'Implication from Serdar was that he and the kids were trying to bring the old godfathers down,' Kerim said. 'But then . . .'

'But then was he lying? Was he just trying to get away with Murad's cash and his daughter? And are the old godfathers aware of what their offspring were doing?'

Kerim shook his head.

'Once Aylın Ayhan has been checked out at the hospital, I want to talk to her,' Süleyman said. 'See what she knows.'

'I agree.'

'Apparently neither of the boys is keen to return home. I wonder why. But if that's the status quo, let's leave them to sweat until we can talk to Aylın.'

'And the fathers?'

'Ömer Bey is with Murad Ayhan now,' Süleyman said. 'Breaking the news about his wife. Maybe he'll want to take his boy home with him – if Yıldırım will go. Watch and wait.' He put a hand up to his head. 'God, I want to go home and sleep!'

'Me too.'

'Sorry. Anyway, depending upon what Aylın tells us, I'm wondering whether I can charge the two boys with conspiracy. I mean that's what Serdar was implying.'

'Absolutely.'

The two men sat in silence for a moment, and then there was a knock at the door.

Kerim said, 'Come in.'

Çetin İkmen slumped into the empty chair beside Mehmet Süleyman. 'So?'

'So,' Süleyman said, 'I followed the lust, just like you and your demon said.'

'Oh, and what did you find, dear boy?'

Süleyman smiled. 'Serdar İpek,' he said. 'Standing in front of Murad Ayhan's open safe taking his money, Murad's daughter Aylın by his side.'

'She was robbing her father?'

'No. She was Serdar's hostage. In love with her, apparently. The story, in short, appears to be some sort of power grab by Serdar, Murad Bey's doctor, Sezer, and his son, Yıldırım, who was in some sort of unholy alliance with İlhan Böcek.'

İkmen put a hand up to his head.

'We had to shoot Serdar to bring him down,' Süleyman said. 'Our Constable Toksoy shattered his shoulder, but he'll live.'

'In surgery?'

'Yes. In the meantime, we've got Yıldırım Ayhan and his sister plus İlhan Böcek to interview.'

'I know I'm talking to myself,' İkmen said, 'but neither of you boys has slept for . . . how long is it?'

'Don't know,' Kerim replied. 'Çetin Bey, are you going home soon?'

'I was, unless you need me.'

'We always need you, Çetin,' Süleyman said. 'But Ozer will lose his mind if he finds you here.'

'I know.'

'If you are going home,' Kerim continued, 'could you reassure Sinem that I'm all right? I'm so sorry my family are still cluttering up your apartment.'

İkmen smiled. 'We love having them there. Çiçek is delighted to have another woman her own age to talk to, and Samsun has started knitting. Apparently it's a coat for Melda, although I have to say that to me it looks like a costume for an octopus. I'll tell them you're fine.'

Süleyman's phone rang.

It was the hospital. Aylın Ayhan was being released.

Kerim Gürsel had to walk past the waiting rooms on his way to interview Yıldırım Ayhan. The boy's father Murad had been taken away from Esat Böcek and his lawyer and was now sitting alone. Looking through the window at him, Kerim saw that he appeared more stunned than distressed. He opened the door and said, 'Murad Bey, I am sorry for your loss.'

The man didn't even look up. When he did speak, he said, 'Does Yıldırım know?'

'I am told he does.'

'Does he want to see me?'

Ömer Mungun, who had informed both the father and the son about Irmak's death, had told Kerim that the boy wanted no one.

Diplomatically Kerim said, 'Not at this time. I'll let you know when he does.' And he left to join Eylul Yavaş, who was now with Yıldırım.

When Kerim arrived, the boy stood up, shaking. 'Is it true Serdar killed my mum? Why would he do that? Mum was nothing to do with it! I love my mum! You're lying!'

Kerim sat down. 'Firstly, I'm not lying,' he said. 'I wish I was. And secondly, your mother was nothing to do with what?'

The boy sank into his chair and turned his face away.

'What I now have to tell you, Yıldırım, is that while earlier you were free to go if you wanted to, now I have applied for you to be detained under suspicion of conspiracy to murder. Ditto your friend İlhan Böcek.'

'I didn't kill my mum! I didn't kill anyone!'

'We are working on what Serdar İpek said to us when we

arrested him,' Kerim continued. 'Now, you are entitled to a lawyer . . .'

'I don't want one!'

'You need one.'

'What? One of my father's tame advocates? No!'

'You can have a different lawyer.'

'No!' Yıldırım shook his head. 'No, you just ask your questions and I'll see whether I can answer them.'

Aylın Ayhan was the sort of pretty young girl Süleyman knew his wife would probably put a curse on if she saw him talking to her. In spite of telling her many, many times that he was really over girls now, Gonca refused to believe him, but it was true.

In order to make things easier for her, he met Aylın at the Nebatıs' house in Bebek. Faruk Nebatı was still recovering from his ordeal and had given a statement to an officer some hours ago. Esma Nebatı sat beside Aylın and held her hand. Süleyman asked her about Serdar.

'He's always been my dad's right-hand man,' Aylın said. 'When my brother and I were little, he used to play with us. Then he got his face cut up and . . .'

'Do you know who did that to him?' Süleyman asked.

'No. It must have been about ten years ago,' she said. 'Around the time I was beginning to realise who my dad really was.'

Esma looked at her and frowned.

'It's OK,' Aylın said. 'Inspector Süleyman is police, he knows about my dad.' She returned her attention to Süleyman. 'Dad's a gangster. He likes us to call him a businessman, but he extorts money from people and so he's a gangster. Serdar was his man, body and soul, or so I thought. But what do I know? I didn't know he was in love with me. I had no clue! The only man I thought was in love with me was that stupid İlhan Böcek, who kept on following me around.'

'For how long?' Süleyman asked.

'About a year. My brother and İlhan have got really close in that time. Yıldırım hoped that İlhan was in love with him.'

'Your brother is homosexual?'

She shrugged. 'I think so. I think he's in love with İlhan. But he was out of luck there, because the way İlhan looked at me was . . . well, it was sexual.'

'And you didn't tell your father or mother about this?'

'My mother wouldn't have cared,' Aylın said. 'Do not misunderstand me, I'm devastated that my mum is dead, but I learned a long time ago that she only cared for my brother. We're not a nice family, Inspector Süleyman. My parents hadn't loved each other for years, Dad has got mistresses, Mum had Yıldırım for company. The only time anyone noticed me was when I got drunk or embarrassed my dad in some way. I told Yıldırım to get his friend to back off, but he just laughed and said that İlhan had better taste than to be attracted to me.'

Esma squeezed her hand.

'Aylın,' Süleyman said, 'who will inherit your father's businesses in the event of his death? Do you know?'

'Yıldırım,' she replied.

'Not you.'

'Not as far as I know.'

'Do you think your brother might want your father out of the way?'

'Challenge Dad?' she laughed. 'Yıldırım is an idiot! He spends his time . . . spent his time watching dizis on TV with Mum. He couldn't run a business! Not unless he had help.' And then she said, 'Oh . . .'

'Yıldırım,' Eylul Yavaş said, 'what was Serdar İpek to you?'

'He's my dad's man,' he said.

'Yes, but what was he to you?'

363

'Nothing. I don't know why he killed my mum! Maybe he wanted to take over my dad's business.'

'You do know that Serdar will survive?' Kerim said. 'He will talk to us, so anything you feel you want to tell us before that happens . . .'

'No!'

'Did you, with Serdar and your friend İlhan Böcek, plan to take over your father's businesses?'

'No! He'd kill me!'

'Because Serdar has already told us that you and İlhan planned to do just that,' Kerim said. 'In addition, there was Dr Sezer . . .'

'He's dead.'

'. . . who we now think may have murdered İlhan's brother's girl-friend, Ceviz Elibol. Now, it's well known that Ateş Böcek, for better or worse, is Esat Böcek's heir, which means he is due to come into a lot of money when his father dies. Did İlhan, together with your father's doctor, kill Ceviz in order to discredit Ateş and get him out of the way? We have CCTV footage of Ateş Böcek with a man we think may be İlhan and Dr Sezer in Kadıköy on the day Ceviz was murdered. Were you the link between Dr Sezer and İlhan?'

The boy said nothing, but his face reddened.

'Because,' Kerim continued, 'we know that Dr Sezer wasn't happy working for your father. He wanted to leave. Did you and İlhan and Serdar offer him a way out in return for making Ceviz's death as gruesome as possible? And why are you so set against seeing your father in your time of need? Are you afraid that if the truth about what you have done comes out, he will punish you, maybe even kill you?'

Faruk Nebatı walked into the room and said, 'My apologies, Inspector Süleyman, I have been meaning to give you some information.'

'Oh?'

He sat down opposite Süleyman and then looked at his daughter and Aylın Ayhan.

'I'm sorry, girls,' he said. 'I should've done this before. On the night Şevket Sesler's people were attacked, I saw Yıldırım Ayhan and another man I didn't recognise changing into party costumes in my garden. They obviously didn't want Murad to see them. I thought at the time they might be getting ready to surprise him at his party. But they also had a gun – what looked like a sniper rifle. I assumed it was a fake, or an air rifle, but when I heard about the shooting in Tarlabaşı . . .'

'Do you know Şevket Sesler, Dr Nebatı?' Süleyman asked.

'Oh yes. I am Roma, Inspector. I grew up in Sulukule with Şevket. Murad Ayhan grew up there too, and of course, your wife, Gonca Hanım. Last time I spoke to Şevket, he told me she was marrying you. Not that I speak to him often. My wife is a gaco, and so I am very much on the periphery of Roma life now.'

Aylın said, 'Dad has always been rude to Dr Nebatı because he is Roma and because he remembers Dad when he was poor.'

Faruk Nebatı sighed. 'For what it's worth, I don't think Murad would ever start a war with Şevket Sesler, or vice versa. Esat Böcek, I don't know.'

Süleyman nodded and then looked at Aylın. 'Do you think that Serdar and your brother were planning to either rob your father or kill him?'

She thought about the question, her eyes now filled with tears.

'Did Yıldırım and Serdar have a relationship?' he asked. 'I don't mean a romantic one. I mean, were they close?'

She cleared her throat. 'We were all close when we were children. But as we grew up . . . No. Although in the last year, I would say, Serdar has done more for my brother than before. Running errands and that sort of thing. Made my dad angry. And yes, they talk, whisper. I don't know what about. They don't let me hear them.'

*

Kerim Gürsel left Yıldırım Ayhan to think about what they had discussed and took a call from Süleyman, who told him about the gun Yıldırım and another man may have taken with them to Şevket Sesler's birthday party.

'Do you think Yıldırım wanted to start a war with the Roma?' Kerim asked.

'Maybe he felt his father's ambitions were too small,' Süleyman replied. 'But looking at him, you'd never know it. Got anything more out of him?'

'Shows no sign of cracking yet. I've left him to sweat.'

'Is Murad Ayhan still there?'

'Yes, and Esat Böcek and his lawyer. Neither of the boys wants to see their father. I put it to Yıldırım that perhaps he was afraid of what Murad might do if he discovered he'd been plotting against him.'

'Mmm.'

'I'm just about to go in to İlhan,' Kerim said.

'OK. Speak later.'

Kerim put his phone in his pocket and followed Eylul into the room where İlhan Böcek was being held.

As he sat down, he said, 'Want to see your father yet?'

'No!'

'Why not?'

'I don't have to tell you why. I just don't.'

İlhan Böcek was being much more confrontational than his friend Yıldırım. But then Yıldırım had just had a shock. His mother had died at the hands of a man he may have been in partnership with. With İlhan, Kerim decided to attack.

'You and Yıldırım,' he said, 'were you fucking?'

'No! He's my friend! That's all. How dare—'

'He wanted to,' Kerim said. 'Do you find Yıldırım's sister Aylın attractive?'

'She's, well, she's—'

'She says you stalked her.'

'I didn't!'

'You sure about that?' Kerim asked.

He could feel Eylul's eyes on him. Her boss was going for it and she knew it.

'So did you kill Ceviz Elibol, or did you get Dr Sezer to do it? We know he carved her up. Only a surgeon could have done it with such skill. You're not skilled, are you, İlhan?'

The boy looked down at his hands, which were shaking very slightly.

'Can't even be out of your mind like Ateş, can you? At least he's interesting. You're just the dull son of a dull ultra-religious gangster, aren't you? I mean, what does your dad do, eh? I bet he prays when he gets one of his thugs to kill someone who maybe is the child of a man his negligence helped to kill.'

'The gypsies killed Hakki,' İlhan mumbled.

'Hakki Bürkev, is that?' Kerim said. 'Good knowledge about how your dad's neglect killed Hakki's old man. The Roma have nothing to do with this, İlhan. They never did.'

'They—'

'No, no,' Kerim said. '*You* killed Ceviz Elibol, you and Dr Sezer, although I think that poor doctor was only drafted in because he wanted to get away from your friend Yıldırım's father so badly. What was the aim, İlhan? From your perspective? Trying to get your brother put away so your father's business empire would come to you? Admittedly, Ateş is a very sick man. But we have it on good authority that he is in fact way too sick to have done what was done to Ceviz.'

The boy stared at him glassy eyed.

'We've got Serdar İpek in custody now,' Kerim continued. 'Although that's not strictly true; he's in the hospital. We shot him while he was trying to raid Murad Ayhan's safe. Oh, and he killed Murad's wife. Yıldırım's mother. He loved his mum, so I'm sure that wasn't the plan, was it?'

367

İlhan said nothing.

'So let me be honest with you,' Kerim said. 'And basically, this is what everything comes down to. During our investigation of the Şehzade Rafık Palace, your brother Ateş's home, we found a number of blood and other samples not belonging to the victim, Ceviz Böcek. One set belonged to your brother, and there was also another sample we are currently having compared with blood obtained from Dr Gibrail Sezer. We expect it to match. I'm going to ask you, İlhan, to give me a saliva sample for comparison to DNA we found at the site. Now I grant you that you and your brother will share similar DNA profiles, and it is my opinion that maybe our forensic team have mistaken your DNA for his. These things happen. So I am going to ask for a retest of all the samples attributed to Ateş. The question you have to ask yourself, İlhan, is can you be sure that none of your bodily fluids – blood, sweat, saliva, urine – remained behind when you and Dr Sezer left Ateş's bedroom? If you can be one hundred per cent sure, or if indeed you were not there, then you have nothing to worry about. In the meantime, however,' he turned to Eylul Yavaş, 'could you please go and get me a saliva kit, Sergeant?'

Süleyman already had a warrant to search Murad Ayhan's house. He knew his scene-of-crime team would find firearms for which Murad Ayhan would almost certainly have licences. If Murad had grown up in Sulukule, he'd have learned a lot of things about how to avoid conflict with the law. But if this sniper rifle Faruk Nebatı had seen did exist, it did so without Murad's knowledge.

'I've no idea what make it is,' Süleyman said when he called the officer leading the scene-of-crime team. 'All I've been told is it's a sniper rifle, probably with a stand. It won't be anywhere obvious and it won't be licensed. Dig up the garden if you have to. Drain the pool.'

He finished the call and went back to Aylın and the Nebatıs. This time, Esma spoke.

'I saw İlhan Böcek stalking Aylın, Inspector,' she said. 'We were at İstinye Park. She was trying on clothes. He was lurking outside, looking at her.'

'Mmm.' Süleyman paused. 'Aylın, did you ever think your father might be considering an alliance between your family and the Böceks?'

'Marrying me to İlhan?'

'Yes.'

'No,' she said. 'For a while I'd realised he wanted to marry me to someone he deemed suitable. I told him I wasn't doing it. But that wasn't İlhan.'

'Then who . . .'

'I don't know. No, Inspector, what I feared was our families going to war and me being used as part of some peace treaty. That happened to my cousin. It was a long time ago, but I was worried that my dad might marry me to İlhan under those circumstances.'

The children of gangsters, crime lords, godfathers were often dismissed by the press, and the police, as spoilt dilettantes whose development had been arrested by overindulgence. But they could also be used and abused in ways that would almost certainly ruin their lives. That said, could Aylın possibly have been in league with her brother? No detective worth his salt should ever just assume . . .

Süleyman's phone rang.

Rambo Şekeroğlu watched his mother lying on the couch in her salon, stroking her boa constrictor, Sara. She was watching some daft dizi on TV while popping an endless stream of lokum into her mouth. Her husband was still out there somewhere, stalking the streets or interviewing people. And yet Gonca, his besotted bride, appeared to be content.

Rambo sat down in a chair beside her. 'Mehmet Bey's been gone almost two days now, Mum. Aren't you worried?'

In the past, Gonca had almost lost her mind if Mehmet was away from her for more than a day.

'He's safe,' she said. She shuffled blocks of lokum around in the box in front of her. 'I thought there were more rose pieces . . .'

'Mum!'

She looked up. 'Listen, baby boy, if Mehmet was in trouble or with another woman, I would know. Now we are married, we're connected.'

'You never knew where my dad was,' Rambo said.

'That was because I didn't love him. And don't pull faces at me. You knew that. I've never kept it from you. Doesn't affect how I feel about you, though. You are my baby boy and I love you a ridiculous amount.'

Rambo said, 'Mum, Lola Hanım wants to get baby Carmen baptised.'

'She can do that when she gets home.'

'Tomas says she wants to do it now.'

'Now?'

'Before they travel back to Spain. They've got to drive all the way across Europe once Mehmet Bey lets them go. They're afraid the baby might die during the journey.'

'Oh.'

Gonca didn't know much about religion. She was nominally a Muslim and had been surprised how religious her Spanish Catholic guests had been. But she recalled that there was something in Christianity about not dying unbaptised . . .

'So what are we gonna do?' Rambo asked. 'Even if Mehmet Bey lets them go tomorrow, they won't hit the road until the baby's baptised.'

'Mmm. I'll have to think on it,' Gonca said.

Chapter 29

İlhan Böcek wasn't impressed by the fact that he had two inspectors of police and one sergeant sitting opposite him, hanging on his every word. He was too busy being terrified. Where would those words lead?

Süleyman had jumped into his car and driven back to headquarters as soon as Kerim Gürsel had called him. The word 'confession' had been used, and that was enough for him.

'So, İlhan,' he said, 'shall we begin?'

The boy took a deep breath. 'I don't know everything. I only know what I know.'

'We understand that.'

'We went to the Lisesi together,' he said. 'Galatasaray.'

The school where Süleyman had gone. He bit down on an urge to say that it had obviously lowered its standards since he was there.

'I knew who his dad was,' İlhan said. 'My dad had told me to stay away from him. But sometimes his sister would come to pick him up, and she was so beautiful. I made friends with him. The other boys in our year didn't like him, used to call him a homo.'

'You didn't?' Süleyman asked.

'I fancied Aylın,' he said. 'I wanted to get close to Yıldırım so I could get close to her.'

'Did you stalk Miss Ayhan?' Eylul asked.

'Later. That came later. But that was the start of it.'

Kerim said, 'The start of what?'

371

İlhan swallowed hard. 'My dad wouldn't hear a word against my brother. He gave him that palace to live in. As Ateş's behaviour got worse—'

'Back up a bit,' Süleyman said. 'Tell us about Ateş.'

'I don't remember him as anything other than weird. He said he heard voices telling him to do stuff.'

'What stuff?'

'Going out with no clothes on, shouting at people in the street. Dad engaged a psychiatrist, a woman, but according to him, all she did was tell him that Ateş was mad and needed treatment in hospital. He couldn't bear the idea that his eldest son was like that. Then Ateş began to say that none of us were who we said we were. He thought we were other people in disguise. But Dad just let it go. He even said that if he died, Ateş would take over his business. I thought Dad had gone mad too. How could he do that? Ateş would destroy the business! But he was so stuck on this thing about his eldest son succeeding him . . . It began there.'

'What did, and when?'

'Last year,' İlhan said. 'I told Yıldırım about it. He said what if we could get Ateş out of the way? He said that perhaps we could kill him. Yıldırım doesn't have a lot of feeling for other people. I think he's bitter. I've always managed to blend in, but he never has. I said no, because I love my brother, in spite of everything. I just wanted him out of the way. Nothing happened for a bit. I thought he'd forgotten about it.'

'Yıldırım?'

'Yes. Then my brother started seeing this Roma girl. My dad didn't know or he would've stopped it. Ateş was really into her, and although he lived like a pig, she kept on coming back. Maybe he paid her or something? I don't know. At first I thought I should maybe tell Dad, but then Yıldırım said that Ceviz, the girl, gave us an opportunity to discredit Ateş and make him go away for good. He said he knew people who would help us.'

372

'Who?'

'His dad's doctor and Serdar İpek, his dad's right-hand man. He claimed that Dr Sezer wanted to leave his dad's employment because of some things Murad Bey made him do.'

'Like what?'

'Get drugs for him. Apparently his dad couldn't sleep much and so he had Dr Sezer give him anaesthesia sometimes. And heroin. He got that for him too. He was always in fear of being found out.'

'And Serdar İpek?'

'Murad Bey treated him like shit. A long time ago, Serdar Bey and my dad had a fight over some drugs. This dealer who was supposed to be working for my dad was also working for Murad Bey. Murad Bey found out and sent Serdar to have a word with Dad. But they fought and Dad cut Serdar's face up. Later, my dad and Murad Bey briefly made peace. But Serdar was left with a scarred face. Murad Bey didn't even try to help him. So he hated Murad Bey and my dad from then on. And he was in love with Aylın.'

'Serdar İpek?'

'Yes. Yıldırım said he always had been. But Aylın didn't know. Yıldırım told me he had a plan . . .'

Peri Mungun had waited until she'd made dinner and was sitting down with Yeşili in front of the television before she showed her the home pregnancy kit.

At first the girl had seemed bewildered by it. 'But it only happened once,' she'd said. 'On our wedding night.'

Mirroring Çetin İkmen, Peri had replied, 'Once is sometimes all it takes.'

Now the two of them were sitting opposite each other, watching the little screen on the top of the device to see whether it changed colour.

'If I am pregnant, Ömer Bey will be pleased, won't he?' Yeşili asked.

Peri didn't know, if she was honest. Her brother had never mentioned having children to her. Then again, the only reason he'd married this girl was so that he could carry forward his family's ancient religion into the next generation. But she said, 'Of course he will be.'

Yeşili smiled.

'We would kill Ceviz,' İlhan said.

The whole room lapsed into silence.

'I didn't want to,' the boy continued. 'And I didn't. I was there. But Dr Sezer killed her. She was fast asleep and she felt nothing. The doctor reckoned she was drugged. '

'So why pull her corpse apart?' Süleyman asked.

İlhan looked down. 'Ateş wasn't there until it was over,' he said. 'When he saw her, he rolled around in her blood, crying. That was all. I put the yataghan the doctor had used to kill her in his hand, and he just laughed. You can't imagine how mad my brother is, Inspector. Like Yıldırım said, it was just a matter of time before he did that to her himself.'

'When I saw him, he was screaming in mental anguish,' Süleyman said.

'I had to discredit him. While my father was constantly protecting him, it would never get any better. Only a truly horrific crime would get him put away for ever. Then I could take his place.'

'And kill your father?'

'No! No. Just . . .'

'Just what?'

İlhan shook his head.

'So what was in all this for Dr Sezer and Serdar İpek?' Kerim asked.

'It was Serdar and Yıldırım who had the idea to attack the gypsies. I had no part in it.'

'By attack the gypsies . . .'

'That girl, Ceviz, was Roma,' İlhan said. 'She worked for Şevket Sesler. Everyone knew that. Serdar said that if someone damaged Şevket Bey's property, it was well known that he would seek reparation. And he did. Because Ateş appeared to be guilty, he asked my dad for money to make up for the girl's lost earnings. Dad told him to go to hell.'

'And it was at that point, on Sesler's birthday, that Yıldırım and Serdar İpek shot at Sesler's people in Tarlabaşı,' Süleyman said.

'Yıldırım told Serdar that if he helped him start a war, the gypsies would think my father had done it and would come for him. They did! They murdered Hakki Bürkev!'

'Did they?' Kerim asked. 'Because as yet, we have no evidence to support that contention. All we know is that whoever killed Hakki knew the area around your father's apartment very well, because we've nothing on CCTV. And as I know you know, Hakki had issues with your father. I think your dad saw an opportunity to pin the death of a possible weak link in his team onto Sesler's Roma and he took it.'

İlhan fell silent.

'But a war,' Süleyman said. 'What was that supposed to achieve?'

'Serdar said my dad would easily defeat Sesler. He's only got Tarlabaşı even if there's a lot of drug trade there. It would make my father even more powerful. It would mean he'd have to bring me in to help him.'

Süleyman looked at Kerim Gürsel and Eylul Yavaş and shook his head. 'That's insane! Think of the risk. Think of the collateral damage. And where do the Ayhans fit into this, eh? What apart from some sort of spectator sport was this supposed to be for your friend Yıldırım and his associates?'

'Yıldırım was going to kill his dad and I was going to have

Aylın,' İlhan said. 'Then we'd run the city and it'd be much better because there'd be no more conflict.'

Kerim said, 'So you and Yıldırım would control everything and you would marry Aylın. What about Serdar, wasn't he in love with her too?'

'Yes,' İlhan replied. 'Long term, he'd have to go.'

'Go where?'

The boy shrugged.

Süleyman said, 'You know, İlhan, sometimes when people call other people mad, they are really describing themselves.'

'Is she asleep?' Çetin İkmen asked Sinem Gürsel when she came out of the bedroom she temporarily shared with her daughter.

'Yes.' She sat down on the sofa and sighed. Then she looked at her phone.

'Still nothing from Kerim?' he asked.

'No.'

'He's OK,' İkmen said. 'I know I shouldn't say anything, but I think he and Mehmet are getting close to the end of this investigation. But it's been tough. Organised crime is a closed world.'

'The godfathers are so brutal! Living in Tarlabaşı, you hear things that make you feel sick.'

'I think Kerim wants you to move,' İkmen said as he lit a cigarette.

They exchanged a look. İkmen had known for a long time that Kerim was gay, and Sinem knew this. Tarlabaşı, for all its faults, was an understanding location for LGBT people.

'We'll see,' she said eventually.

İkmen's phone rang and he looked at the screen.

'Sorry,' he said to Sinem, 'got to take this. Gonca Hanım.'

Sinem smiled.

'Gonca,' he said, 'what can I do for you?'

'I need a baptism.'

'As in a Christian baptism?'

'Is there any other kind?'

'I don't know. For whom? For you?'

She laughed. 'No, with regard to religion, I am a lost soul. For the Cortes baby, born this morning.'

'Oh, Maşallah!' İkmen said. 'Were you there?'

'No. The girl did it all on her own in the tent like a good Roma woman. She's fine. But she and Juan are now keen to have the baby baptised before they head back to Spain. Something about the child dying en route. God doesn't give a shit about the unbaptised, apparently. I have no idea when my beloved husband will allow them to leave the country, but I feel we must try to help with this. Do you agree?'

'Of course.' He smiled. Süleyman always said that Gonca was impossible to deny, and he was right.

'So I was thinking that maybe Bishop Montoya might do it,' she said.

'Gonca, he is head of the Catholic church in this country.'

'Yes . . .'

'So he's busy.'

'Yes, but he's also so kind and charming and handsome, I'm sure he'd love to do this if you asked him.'

'Well, I can try . . .'

'So that's settled,' she said, and put down the phone.

Yıldırım Ayhan didn't deny what İlhan Böcek had confessed to. He just said nothing. Now detained on suspicion of murder, both boys were transferred to the cells together with Esat Böcek, who was to be questioned in the morning about the death of Hakki Bürkev. A dazed Murad Ayhan left headquarters in the early hours.

Kerim Gürsel let himself into the İkmen apartment and groped his way along the hall until he came to the bedroom his wife and daughter were using. As soon as he closed the door behind him,

Sinem sat up in bed and put a finger to her lips, 'She's asleep,' she whispered.

In her Moses basket on the floor beside her mother, Melda Gürsel made small snuffling noises in her sleep. Kerim bent down and very gently kissed her cheek. The little girl briefly opened her eyes and then went back to sleep again.

Once her husband had got into bed with her, Sinem said, 'That was risky.'

'Sorry, just had to kiss her.'

'You OK?' she asked.

'Exhausted.'

She put her arms around him and pulled him down under the covers.

'Kerim, is everything going to be all right?'

'Yes,' he said. 'I think so.'

'Can we go home soon?'

'You want to go back to Tarlabaşı?'

She smiled. 'It's our home.'

Across the Golden Horn in Balat, Mehmet Süleyman took his clothes off and uncharacteristically let them fall on the floor. It was the first time he'd got into his bed for forty-eight hours. As his muscles finally began to relax, he sighed with pleasure, which woke Gonca.

'Baby, you're home,' she said as she curled into his outstretched arm.

'Yes . . .'

His eyes were closed and it was clear he was about to collapse into sleep, but Gonca kissed his lips. 'Missed you.'

'Missed you too,' he said. 'Gonca . . .'

'Yes, yes, I know you want to go to sleep. Don't worry, my darling, I'll be quiet now.'

She saw him smile with his eyes closed.

*

The morphine helped with the pain, but it did make him see things that weren't there. Serdar İpek knew there was a cop sitting on a chair in the corner of his room. But he was fairly certain the fox was simply an effect of the drug. The fox would go, eventually, but the cop wouldn't.

Soon the police would come to ask him questions. Drugged, he wasn't anxious about that. Anyway, he knew what he was going to tell them, which was nothing. What were they going to do? Smash him into the ground in a hospital room? And even if they did, he still wouldn't talk. He was only going in one direction now, and that was to prison. And in prison there were a lot of people who remained loyal to Murad Bey.

Serdar had killed before he shot those gypsies in Tarlabaşı. He'd killed for Murad Bey. In many cases people feared his boss because of him. Murad didn't have the stomach for war these days. All he wanted to do was get off his face and have sex with hookers. And Yıldırım? That soft kid and his friend İlhan would quickly disappear once their daddies were out of the picture. Only a man of ruthless courage could control a city like İstanbul.

When he'd first started working for Murad Ayhan, they'd both been on the same page. He'd respected his boss then, and so, when Aylın was sixteen and he'd asked Murad Bey for his daughter's hand in marriage, he'd fully expected him to say yes. After all, Serdar had a job, a nice apartment, he was part of the family . . . But Murad Bey had laughed at him, and then, when he'd had his face destroyed by Esat Böcek, he'd laughed at him again. He'd told him, 'Now you've as much chance with my daughter as you would have with a star of those dizis my wife likes to watch!' Serdar had hated him more than Esat Böcek then.

Those spoilt kids, Yıldırım and İlhan, hadn't worked out that they'd never run their daddies' companies. Too stupid, the pair of them. Had things gone to plan, he would have sunk them both in the Bosphorus, along with the doctor. Nothing against the man, of course, but he'd been too frightened, too horrified by what he'd done. He'd be a perpetual weak link. It was a mercy he'd killed himself.

Sesler's gypsies were nothing to him. Thieving scumbags, the lot of them. Although that man he'd met coming down from the roof of the Poisoned Princess apartments had been an unfortunate death. An ex-cop, by the look of his gun. It had been a pity Serdar hadn't been able to keep that after he'd shot him with it. He'd just wiped his prints off and chucked it down. Maybe the police would think the man had killed himself.

What had it been about Aylın Ayhan that had grabbed him so violently all those years ago? She'd been a kid when he'd first wanted her. Thirteen. He'd fantasised about her. But even as she grew, he'd still wanted her. By that time, probably as a way of getting at her father. But if he'd managed to get away with her, he would still have taken pleasure with her. The thought of her trying to stop him made him feel aroused. Oh Murad Bey, he thought, when you laughed at me, you did a bad thing!

He wondered vaguely whether the two boys had spoken to the police. He wondered whether they'd go to prison if they had. He didn't care. His only task now was to keep his own mouth firmly shut, so that Murad Bey's people didn't come after him.

Chapter 30

New Year's Eve

A quiet dinner party for Mehmet Süleyman's colleagues and their wives had turned into an enormous event involving Gonca's family, Mehmet's brother and his daughter, various İkmens, the Spaniards, and Bishop Montoya. The reason for this change of plan had been the baptism of the Cortes baby, Carmen. As a favour to İkmen, and as the bishop had said, 'with joy in my heart at bringing another soul to Christ', Montoya had performed the ceremony at the church of Saint-Antoine earlier that afternoon. Many, many members of the Şekeroğlu family had attended, none of them Christian, but a lot of people cooed at and handled the new baby and went back to Gonca's house happy.

Now it was night-time, and because it was dry outside, Gonca had lit the lamps in the garden while her sons ignited a huge fire to warm everyone and under which cooked kumpir, for which Gonca and her daughters had made numerous fillings. Inside the house, the kitchen table groaned under the weight of bulgur, rice, chicken, sis kebab, preserved fruit, kaymak, yogurt and baklava, while Gonca's salon was now a bar.

Kerim Gürsel held his daughter up so that she could see all the brightly coloured lamps and watch the Roma girls dance around the fire. Gonca, barefoot, was with them, the now recovered Sara the snake coiled across her shoulders.

Bishop Montoya approached Süleyman, who had his arm around his niece, Edibe.

'Inspector,' he said, 'I trust your troubles are fewer than they were?'

Süleyman introduced the bishop to Edibe and then said, 'Somewhat, yes.'

'Organised crime is a scourge,' the bishop said. 'I am Mexican. I know.'

'Well, it looks as if we're going to be able to put one godfather in prison.'

Esat Böcek had been arrested for the murder of Hakki Bürkev, his inconvenient employee. No one seemed to know whether Bürkev had been blackmailing his boss over the death of his father, but Esat Bey had clearly wanted him out of the way.

'What of the others?' the bishop asked. 'I understand three cartels were involved.'

Süleyman smiled at the Mexican's choice of words. 'No, we were led to believe that Şevket Sesler's Romani syndicate were also implicated, but they weren't.'

'A power play?' the bishop asked.

'Very much so.'

Although Serdar İpek hadn't spoken since his arrest, there was enough evidence to charge him, together with Yıldırım Ayhan, with the murder of the Roma at Sesler's birthday party, as well as the death of Sesler's relative Mete Bülbül and that of Irmak Ayhan. There were also further charges of kidnap, conspiracy and theft to be taken into consideration. İlhan Böcek had told them everything he knew, and so his sentence for conspiracy to murder Ceviz Elibol was going to be lighter than the others'. Maybe, eventually, he would indeed inherit his father's empire – if there was even an empire left when Esat Böcek got out of jail.

Someone who would not inherit his father's empire was Yıldırım Ayhan. Murad, though still operating from his mansion in Bebek, would now have to repair his reputation with those who depended upon him and those who opposed him. Perhaps he would enlist the help of his daughter Aylın, although that seemed unlikely. She had gone to stay with her friend Esma and her family while she tried to decide what to do next. Her family was irrevocably broken, and what she needed now was time to explore her options.

The bishop said, 'And what of the young man who killed that Romani girl in such a ghastly fashion? Do you know what is happening with him?'

Süleyman sighed. 'Well, to begin with, Ateş Böcek didn't kill Ceviz Elibol. The poor young man was so disordered, he didn't know what was going on. Basically he was set up by his brother. We believe that it was a man who is now dead who actually killed her. As for Ateş, the only family he has outside jail now is his grandmother. A fierce, determined woman thought to be behind some of the Böceks' worst crimes in the past. You would not want to meet her in a dark alley.'

The bishop smiled.

'However,' Süleyman continued, 'she's got money and she's already had Ateş moved to a private clinic for treatment. I doubt the poor lad will ever leave, but . . .'

'But while there is life, there is hope,' the bishop said.

Across the other side of the garden, Peri Mungun stood in front of the old cistern with a glass of rakı in her hand. Wearing a stylish short coat and knee-length boots, she looked handsome rather than glamorous. She also had a sparkle in her eye. When she saw Çetin İkmen, rakı glass in one hand, cigarette in the other, she called him over.

He smiled and walked across to join her. 'Peri Hanım.'

'Gonca tells me this cistern is Byzantine,' she said, looking at the brightly lit cave-like structure behind her.

'Oh yes,' İkmen said. 'Do you want to see inside?'

'Yes.'

383

He helped her down the stone steps and onto the dirt floor of the structure. Looking up, he said, 'You can see it's Byzantine because of the herringbone pattern of bricks. The Byzantines were famous for it.'

'Mmm.'

But she was gazing down at the floor, at earth tinted red and blue and green by Gonca's fairy lights.

'Peri?'

She looked up. 'You were right about Yeşili. She is pregnant.'

He nodded his head.

'I know you probably never doubted it,' she said.

'Well . . .'

'Anyway, Ömer knows now.'

She looked grave, so İkmen said, 'And how is he with it?'

She sighed. 'Accepting. I know that sounds bad, but it isn't. All his life he has known that his purpose is to father children with a virgin of our religion. It's not unexpected.'

İkmen smoked. 'When you came to me, you were worried about Ömer obsessing over other women. Gonca Hanım . . .'

'Oh, I think that's probably passed,' she said. 'He's very quiet. If you look, you'll see he's not been near any other women apart from his wife all evening. I think he's depressed.'

'That's not good.'

'But he's told Yeşili he's happy, and that's all that matters. Anyway, I thought you should know, and thank you."

'I did nothing,' İkmen said.

'You helped me cope, and you reassured me. You know, Çetin Bey, you are way too hard on yourself. Gonca Hanım agrees with me.'

'Oh does she?'

She smiled. 'She told me that if she hadn't married Mehmet Bey, she had her sights set on you.'

'Nonsense!'

But he knew that he and Gonca had had one very long-ago romantic moment.

'Gonca doesn't do ugly old bastards,' he said. 'The handsome Prince Mehmet and the Queen of the Gypsies were made for each other. Dangerous as hell, both of them!'

Peri laughed, then put her glass down on a ledge and moved towards him. And because İkmen was the son of a witch, he knew what was about to happen, and felt the raw fear of it grab him tightly. 'Ah no, Peri Hanım. I think this would be a mistake . . .'

'I don't,' she said. And then she kissed him.

Far away, in a distant corner of Gonca's garden, a very glamorous woman, whom only one person at the party would recognise, knelt down to speak to what only the keenest eyes would perceive as a creature.

As fireworks burst above İstanbul to signal a new year, she said, 'So let us welcome in 2020, my honey!'

The thing lifted its snouts into the air and ran off into the city. Şeftali smiled. It was going to be a busy year for sin.